THE HANGMAN'S DAUGHTER

MARIA BARRETT

For David

1

RESENT DAY – *London*
       Friday p.m.

ON THE STEPS of St Martins in the Fields, Lydia dug her hands deep into her pockets and Matt bent down to kiss her on the cheek.

"You sure you don't want me to come home with you?"

She shrugged. "No, it's tradition; a drink in the Harp. You shouldn't miss it."

"You won't come?"

She shook her head. She had the beginnings of a headache in the corner of her right eye, and she was tired. Holding her case, she rubbed her thumb across the worn handle; an old nervous habit that she had. Matt reached out and tucked a loose strand of hair behind her ears.

"I'd better go; catch the others up."

"Yes." Lydia stood on tip toes and kissed his mouth. She was five foot three and in her long skirt and high heeled

Mary Jane's, with a heavy duffle coat on top, Matt thought she looked like an eccentric child. "I'll see you later," she said, "Don't drink too much."

"I won't!" He smiled as she turned, strode down the steps towards Leicester Square tube and disappeared into the crowd.

THE TRAIN STOPPED and Lydia's head rolled forward. She jerked awake. Blinking rapidly, she took several breaths, momentarily disorientated. She glanced around and saw empty seats next to her, the man opposite reading a Metro. There was a small crowd of girls further down the carriage, all laughing and chatting loudly. She reached down and pulled her case onto her lap as the train pulled into the next stop and rubbed the handle with her thumb. She was at Kennington; there was one more stop to go.

At Stockwell Lydia made her way up the escalator, through the barriers and turned left into Clapham Road. It had started to spit rain, so she pulled her scarf up over her head to prevent frizz and picked up her pace. She turned right again into Jeffry's Road and made her way down towards Larkhall Park. She liked this bit of green space in the middle of London, the pavement bordered with trees, the quiet road; it felt like a breath of fresh air on the way home. The rain had increased to a steady pelt and just past the park she crossed the road and stopped under a street-lamp for a moment to find the small pack-away umbrella she kept in her bag. She found it and put it up, glancing briefly behind her as she did so. Out of the corner of her eye she thought she caught sight of someone by the park move into the shadow of the trees and out of sight. She stopped and turned. Scanning the road and the trees she searched for a figure but there was no-one; nothing there. She felt a nudge of anxiety in the pit of her stomach but pushed it down and quickened her pace, her heels slightly slippery on the wet pavement.

At the end of Larkhall Lane, she turned into Union Road and began to relax a little. Her building was halfway down the street, and she'd be home and in the warm in a few minutes. Kenvil House was an old council building that housed one hundred and fifty flats. It was a 1950's façade, with some modernisation inside that didn't extend to the damp stairwell or gloomy lift. As Lydia walked across the patch of grass at the front and turned the corner of the building towards the side entrance, the streetlight behind her flickered and for a moment she thought she saw something again... a figure, a shadow; someone or something. Afraid now, that old familiar thud and sickness in the pit of her stomach, she felt in the front pocket of her bag for her key and took it out ready. She was almost home. She pulled the heavy fire door open and stepped into the darkness...

WHEN THEY FOUND her several hours later, she was dead by asphyxiation; her head had been severed from her body; her scarf had caught in the lift doors.

MONDAY A.M.

Kate woke with a start and lay in the dark listening to the piercing wail of a police siren in the distance, her heart thumping. It was a painful noise. Reaching for her phone, she glanced at the time; one a.m. – someone, somewhere was in trouble she thought. Kate believed that you always pay for what you do, at some time, in some way and now, closing her eyes, making conscious effort to focus on her breathing, she couldn't escape that thought. Sleep eluded her as she listened in the darkness, for what exactly, she didn't know. She heard a footfall outside her door, sat up and called out.

"Annie?"

There was no response.

"Annie, is that you?"

Annie, her daughter, was fourteen; she normally slept the sleep of the dead. There were a few more moments of silence and Kate dropped her legs over the side of the bed, still listening hard, her heart thumping again. There was another creak, then the flushing of the toilet in the bathroom. That was Annie, a night-time pee.

'You are being foolish,' she told herself, 'Imagining things.' She relaxed back against the pillows, but her old fears had begun to niggle in the back of her mind, and she couldn't rest. So, she dropped her legs onto the floor and stood. Pulling on her dressing gown, she crept out of her bedroom and along the short corridor to her daughter's room. She cracked open the door and peered in. Annie was in bed, curled on her side, asleep and breathing deeply. Safe.

Kate went back to bed and lay in the dark, eyes wide open. Staring up at the ceiling as the streetlight outside filtered through the blinds, she had the oddest sensation that someone had been in the flat. And try as she might to dismiss it, it skirted the edges of her consciousness until she fell into a fitful and troubled sleep.

$\sim$

THE FOLLOWING MORNING, at half past seven, after their usual twenty-minute walk from the flat, Kate opened the door to her office – an old shop that used to sell electrical goods - and went in, turning on the lights and then the storage heater.

"Mum its freezing in here!" Annie followed her though the reception area to a small back office and stood by the door, waiting as Kate unlocked it, "Not to mention weirdly tidy."

The waiting area was floored with carpet tiles and had chairs placed against the wall, a vertical blind covered the shop window, and all were in the same shade of mizzling grey.

"Well, it won't be by the time fifty or so people have come through here, with their worries and their problems and their children, with nowhere to live. It'll be a complete mess."

"Which you'll hate,"

"Which I'll hate."

"And which you'll clear up before you leave."

Annie thumped her hands together in their woollen gloves and made a dull thudding sound, but despite the cold, she unwound her scarf and dropped it onto the desk along with her hat. She waited for a few moments and as expected, Kate picked them up and handed them back to her in one swift, involuntary movement.

"Very amusing," Kate said when she saw Annie smiling. Tidiness was something Kate had learned early in the wreckage of her life. When everything else is out of control, fastidious cleaning and tidying was a small way of harnessing the chaos.

"Give the OCD a rest, will you Mum? Seriously."

"Seriously what? You can't end a sentence on 'seriously', it doesn't make sense." Kate squeezed past Annie into the back office.

"Mum?"

She turned.

"You could lighten up a bit you know?"

"Oh really, could I?" The wisdom of a teenager, Kate thought wryly. What did Annie know about how tough life could be? Kate looked at her daughter, at the clumsy, aspiring style, at her self-conscious beauty. Nothing of course, and that had been Kate's driving force; to look after Annie in the way that she had never been looked after herself. She smiled, stepped forward and kissed the top of Annie's head which smelled of hair shampoo.

"Well yeah, you could, like, a bit, you know?" Annie said.

"Okay, well, I'll try. Now, come on; let's leave the office to warm up. It'll be less like a fridge once I've got you onto the bus."

THEY WENT BACK out onto the street where it had begun to rain. It was still dark, and the sheeting rain was lit orange and pink in places by neon signs. As they made their way down Lower Marsh towards Westminster Bridge Road and the bus stop, Kate said,

"It's too wet; we'll have to wait in the café for the bus."

"Suits me," Annie replied.

"Of course it suits you." Kate raised an eyebrow and smiled. "Never one to turn down a caramel soya latte." She hooked her arm through her laughed, hooking her arm through Kate's. They had been going to the café for five years, the length of time Kate had had her office, and Annie had charmed the staff like a Svengali.

"I think I'll have a soya milk mocha," she said, "If Kerrie's on the early shift."

"Will you now?" Kate looked sidelong at her. "I don't approve of freebies Annie, you know that."

"Yes, I do, but Kerrie's new and she loves me. She says I crack her up, and if she offers, which she usually does, it would be rude to refuse. Right?"

"You have an answer for everything."

"No, not everything. I can't explain dark matter...-"

"You and Stephen Hawking that is."

"Yes, me and Mr H, but I also can't fathom why you still puree vegetables into Quorn bolognaise. It's like, ok mum, I eat veg now, you know? You don't need to disguise it."

"Ha." That seemed to be Kate's go-to response for Annie's precociousness. She opened the door to the café and let Annie go in first. Kerrie, the new Australian waitress, *was* on the early shift and waved to Annie as she was wiping the tables.

"D'you wanna drink guys? On the house?"

Kate shook her head, "Not for me thanks," but Annie said quickly; "Yes please, a soya milk mocha please, to go. I mean, if that's OK?"

Kerrie glanced at Kate. "She's super-polite, your girl. Of course, it's OK, gotta be some perks of the job, making the odd coffee for mates."

Kate smiled politely. Were Annie and Kerrie mates? Had she missed that? Kerrie was in her late twenties by the look of it, so it was an odd friendship - if that's what it was. She felt herself bristling and glanced at her watch. Kate was self-contained, reticent to get involved; her trust wasn't easily gained, but Annie was a people magnet; she had a crowd of girls that followed her at school, she chatted freely to anyone she met, and she trusted effortlessly. Why wouldn't she at fourteen, Kate often reasoned with herself, but it was difficult to let go. Sometimes, she thought, without knowing quite what to do about it, she blurred the line between protection and control.

Annie took her coffee and chatted with Kerrie while Kate sat by the window and kept her eye on the bus stop across the road. A few minutes later, she called,

"BUS! Come on!" She stood and headed for the door. "Annie?! Sorry to rush Kerrie, but thanks for the coffee."

"Hey, no worries. Just nice to see you guys." Kerrie was easy going – perhaps that was the attraction for Annie. "You're welcome any time," she finished.

Annie sipped the last of her drink as Kate opened the door and they hurried out into the sleet.

Pulling her hat down and her collar up, Kate said; "What were you chatting to Kerrie about?"

Annie was barely visible under her hat and scarf. "She was telling me about her engineering degree."

Kate pulled a face. "Really? She's got an engineering degree? What's she doing...?"

Annie cut her off mid-sentence. "Travelling and paying for it with odd jobs. She decided to take a break after her PhD." She grinned. "Don't look like that mum, it's like totes normal."

"Really? Totes normal, is it?" Grudgingly Kate smiled. It was a big sister thing then, not a friendship as such; Kerrie was very probably at least twenty-eight. Kate led the way to the bus stop and as the bus pulled up, she turned to Annie.

"OK, you've definitely got everything? Sports kit, home-work, clean...-"

"Yes! It's a sleepover mum, not the DOE. Anything I've forgotten I'll borrow, and I'll make sure I do my homework at lunch time, we'll get to bed early, and I won't be on my phone all night... Okay?!" Annie leant forward and kissed Kate on the cheek. "Mum, I meant what I said earlier, you need to lighten up a bit, you know? You need to have more fun. You're like, really serious, all the time."

"Oh, right, thanks for that vote of confidence."

"No, I mean it Mum! You should try and have a good time at the party tonight! Go for it."

Kate shook her head then smiled and Annie stepped close for a hug. There was something so comforting about the smell of a child, Kate thought, and, despite the Doc Martin shoes and the mascara, Annie was still a child, her child. Kate squeezed extra tight. The bus pulled up and the door opened. Kate released her daughter.

"See you tomorrow. I'll meet you off the bus."

As Annie climbed onto the bus Kate turned and made her way back to her office. She had quite a bit to get through and she would have to work fast if she was going to get to the parliamentary debate on homelessness on time.

DC Nella Walsh was tired. It was eight a.m., and they should have finished over an hour ago, officially at six thirty a.m. Here she was though, waiting on the new DS just back from maternity leave who'd taken on one last call to prove that she was still up for it. It had been a crappy shift too; new job, new faces - new shit. And she'd thought her big promotion to CID – fast-tracked through the exams and out of uniform - was going to be all murder and under cover ops. Ha. As she filed her paper-work for the shift, she reckoned it was practically the same, bar the badge. Same levels of teeth-grinding work, same lack of resources, same five jobs at once - paid for one; the only thing that differed was the banter - less of it. She didn't like to call the racist card, but being new, young, black and female, add in ambitious (zealous Mo said), nerd, subscriber to electronics weekly and computer boffin and she wasn't ever going to be one of the lads.

There was a rumble of laughter in the corner as several of the CID officers stood round drinking coffee. It was now light out, her stomach was telling her it was breakfast time, and she was obsessing about the sausage roll and *Boost* bar she was going to buy on the way home. She would have liked a coffee, but she hadn't been asked. Glancing round at the bloke's huddle, she saw the office door open, and DS Sallie Dennis came out, pulling on her raincoat, customary scowl chiselled into her features. She crossed to Nella and said,

"Come on, I committed to this call. I know its afterhours - great fucking timing – but I said we'd do it so let's go." She turned with an afterthought; "You're OK with this aren't you?"

Like I'm gonna say no, Nella thought. "Of course," she said. She stood, grabbed her coat and bag and followed DS Dennis out into the corridor and towards the lifts. She wasn't sure what was worse, isolation or an enquiry with the new boss operating at full throttle.

Ten minutes later, Nella drove, and DS Dennis looked at her phone. As they made their way towards the call, DS Dennis said; "Let's make this as quick as we can, shall we? Don't ask too many questions, keep it neat and we'll leave most of it to the next shift to sort out, OK?"

"Sure."

Nella kept her eyes on the road. "How's your baby?" she asked. "Does your husband look after it when you're at work?" As soon as she said it, she realised it was wrong; the boss didn't do chit-chat.

DS Dennis glanced up from her phone. "She's fine and yes she does look after Rosie when I'm at work."

"Ah, you're..." Shit, Nella thought - leaving the sentence hanging in the air - think before you speak.

"Married to a woman; gay, lesbo, rug muncher, drinking from the furry cup. Yes, I'm one of those, always *so* nicely referred to in our job." DS Dennis waved her arm. "Pull in here, will you? Let's have a quick chat about the call out before we go in, OK?"

Nella swung the car into a space by the curb and pulled up to park outside Kenvil House. She cut the engine and DS Dennis turned to her. "I don't do personal chit chat and, contrary to what you might think, I don't like having to take a call out an hour after I should have knocked off but needs must. The upside is that if we work well together, we tick all the right boxes, black, gay, female. OK?"

Nella nodded; she hadn't really thought boxes before and the OK, she realised, was a verbal tick that was going to irritate her.

"So, listen to what I say, do what I tell you to, and we'll make a good team. Don't think too much until you're more experienced, leave that to me. OK?"

Nella blinked. This was clearly meant to be encouraging. "Yes, of course," she said. She took the keys out of the ignition and held them in her hand while DS Dennis read the call out sheet.

"It's an odd one," she said, "boyfriend of the sudden death last week. Young woman, asphyxiated, scarf got caught in the lift?"

Nella nodded. It had been all round the nick.

"Says he's got something in her diary that suggests it

wasn't an accident, but murder." DS Dennis made a couple
of notes. "Unlikely though, it wasn't my shout, but I'm pretty
sure that DS Patterson signed it over to uniform at the time
and they cleared it." She closed the file. "A case of reassur-
ance I'd say – we should get the FLO over here though.
Come on; let's put this one to bed."

Nella climbed out of the car and glanced up at Kenvil
House. She caught sight of a young man staring out of a
first-floor window, the curtain parted, watching her. She
turned to look directly up at him, but he had gone and, a
few minutes later, the same figure came round the side of
the building.

"Hi, are you looking for Matt Brennan?"

"Yes, we are. Is that you sir?"

Matt crossed the mottled grassy patch in front of the
building and shook Nella's hand. "Yup, that's me." He turned
as DS Dennis climbed out of the car.

"Mr Brennan?" She extended a hand. "Detective
Sergeant Sallie Dennis. Pleased to meet you. Are you OK? Is
there somewhere we can talk?"

"Oh yes, sorry... in the flat," he said, "It's this way." He led
the police officers round the side of the building and into
the gloomy stairwell.

"That's the..." He nodded towards the lift at the end of
the stairwell, sealed off with yellow and black tape. "That's
where she died, Lydia, my girlfriend."

"Right." DS Dennis glanced back at Nella and raised an
eyebrow.

"We're up here, first floor, right by the stairs." He led the
way up, taking his key out as he did so. He opened the door
for the officers to go in, but Nella stood by the door and had
a good look down the stairwell then along the corridor to
the lift several doors down.

"Nice and close to the stairs," she said.

"Yeah, yeah it is..." Matt fidgeted with his keys. "Come in, please."

Glancing a second time at Nella, DS Dennis went into the flat. In the small lounge, she stood looking around and then she said; "So, you said that you found something in Lydia's diary that indicates this might not have been an accident. Can you show that to us?"

Matt stood awkwardly and chewed the inside of his lip. He shook his head.

"OK. Can you tell us what makes you think her death was suspicious?"

"Do you want a cup of tea or coffee?" He hovered, nervous and uncomfortable.

"No, we're fine thanks Matt - is it OK if I call you Matt? The call out? Lydia's diary?"

"Yes... the diary..." Matt hurriedly shoved the mess that littered the sofa to one side, piling all the sheets of music and dropping them on the coffee table.

"Do you want to sit down? I need to explain something."

DS Dennis sat and Matt sat down opposite her on the edge of one of the armchairs. Nella remained standing and wondered if he could sense DS Dennis's irritation; she was covering it quite well.

"So," DS Dennis said, "What's this all about Matt? You said on the phone that you have some information to share?"

Matt nodded and they waited, but nothing was forthcoming. Nella glanced at DS Dennis who sat looking at Matt. They waited for a minute or so longer, then DS Dennis got to her feet and audibly sighed.

"No, wait," Matt said suddenly. "My girlfriend, Lydia, it wasn't an accident like you say. I need to make you understand that it wasn't an accident..." He looked at DS Dennis. "She was murdered."

DS Dennis sat down again. "OK. You think there was something suspicious about her death." She paused. "Can you tell us why you think that? What did you find in her diary?"

"Well..." He stood up, thought better of it and sat down again. "It's not really about the diary... it's more about Lydia. You see, Lydia never took the lift," he said, "Ever."

"Okay." DS Dennis looked at him. "Is that the only thing that concerns you?"

This time Matt stood and paced the floor for a few moments. He turned but couldn't seem to find the right words. DS Dennis said, "Matt, I'm sorry to remind you of this, but were you the one who found Lydia?"

He nodded then abruptly walked out of the room. Nella glanced across at DS Dennis then looked round. There were a few photos, Matt with his arm round Lydia, a pretty, small girl, smiling broadly. A graduation mug shot, Lydia in robes with a heavy gold and blue fur trimmed hood at the Royal College of Music. Matt came back in and sat down again.

"Matt," DS Dennis said, "Have you got any close family near-by or a friend who could come over? You've had a terrible shock; you could do with some support."

He stared down at the ground and shrugged.

"We can ask one of our family liaison officers to call in. They're very good and it might help to talk to someone..."

"Lydia's parents are coming, today. They've got to arrange the funeral, they're staying here."

"OK, that's good."

Matt looked up. "She suffered from claustrophobia, Lydia did. That's why we chose this flat because it was right by the stairs." His face was drawn and ashen, but his eyes were bright with anger. "I told the police when they came but no-one listened to me. I told them, I told them that she always took the stairs."

Nella took a breath. Gently, she said; "Is there a chance, perhaps, that Lydia might have taken the lift when you weren't with her? That it was something she did when she was on her own?"

"No!" He was agitated now, and he wrung his hands. "That's what I keep saying. No! Why would she do that?! It made her nervous, anxious..." He stood again. "Someone forced her into the lift." He shook his head. "But no-one is listening to me..." He stood by the window for a few minutes, his back to them, trying to compose himself.

"Matt?" DS Dennis said quietly, "Matt?"

He turned.

"We're listening." She let him digest this for a few minutes. "Matt, you said that the lift made Lydia anxious. Did she suffer from other anxieties, from depression?"

He shook his head. Then he said, "At least, I...I don't think so. She didn't take any pills or anything and at home, with me she was fine. Why?"

"I was just wondering if there was something bothering her. Something she was anxious about perhaps that might have made her change her habits?"

"No."

"You said that you think she was forced into the lift. Do you know of anyone who might have forced her? Was she in trouble of any kind? Did she take drugs, or owe any money?"

Suddenly Matt put his hands up. "Stop, please!" He shook his head. "Look, I know you have to ask, but you've no idea... Lydia was like... like a young girl even though she was twenty-five, she was kind and funny and... innocent. We worked together; we were going to get married. She was a lovely person... she...she didn't have any enemies... everyone liked her..." he broke off again and hung his head, turning away from them.

DS Dennis stood up and went across to him. She patted his shoulder.

"Matt, when you rang 999, a murder team attended the scene, do you remember? DS Patterson, a colleague of mine? The team spoke to you and interviewed neighbours and then, when they'd had a good look at all the evidence, they handed it over to uniform as an accidental death. There was no reason to believe that there was anything suspicious about Lydia's death and there still isn't Matt. The CCTV footage for the area has been looked at and Lydia was quite alone when she came home. The case has been closed Matt."

He nodded and moved away.

She looked at Nella and motioned with a nod of the head towards the door.

"Is there anything else you'd like to add before we leave?" DS Dennis asked. Matt shook his head. He was staring at the ground, pushing a bit of paper with the tip of his shoe. He had switched off; he didn't seem to be aware that they were still there.

"Right, we'll get on then," she said. She moved towards the door and Nella followed her. She looked back at the tall young man by the window for a moment then they left the flat and clicked the door shut after them.

"Shot away," DS Dennis said as they made their way along the corridor to the lift. "Poor lad. She'd been decapitated –

you knew that anyway, didn't you? No-one's talked about anything else all week."

Nella nodded.

"Finding her must have been gruesome. I really think he needs help."

"But you have to admit, it is pretty odd that she took the lift." Nella said, following DS Dennis down the stairs. "I mean, if she'd never taken it before."

DS Dennis shrugged. "Not really. Was she claustrophobic or did she like the attention? The case was thoroughly looked at and handed over to uniform. There was nothing untoward at the scene, nothing at all, so it was filed as sudden death."

DS Dennis stopped and looked at Nella. "I mean, does the fact that she didn't usually take the lift sound like a valid enough reason to put more resources on a case that's been closed?"

"No, but..."

"People do all sorts of unexpected things..." she went on, "Lydia took the lift on a whim and had an accident. She got her scarf caught in the lift doors, the sensors didn't go off to release them and even though it's tragic, it seems cut and dry to me."

She walked to the passenger side of the car and waited for Nella to unlock it.

"I really do think we've got better things to do with our time." She climbed into the car. "Like get home for breakfast with my little one. Put your foot down DC Walsh."

She took out her phone and began to text. Nella glanced up at the flats and saw Matt's figure in the window.

"Don't let it bother you," Dennis said, not looking up. "People talk a lot of shit in this job..." She pressed call and held the phone up to her ear. "You'll get used to it."

It was mid-morning as Nick hurried through the Central Lobby, the click of his shoes echoing on the polished tiles. Fragments of light fell in kaleidoscope slants from the high stained-glass windows, the buttoned leather sofas gleamed and the aging oak panelling melted into the sand coloured limestone. Nick nodded at a couple of other members he knew before he made his way to join the throng queuing in the Member's Lobby, waiting to enter the Chamber. There was the usual bustle, orderly, but in male boarding school fashion.

"All trying to please our esteemed leader," his colleague, Haroldson said, sotto voce, "Must be a shadow cabinet reshuffle in the offing."

Nick shrugged casually; there was a rumour that he was in the running for a shadow minister post, but he didn't believe it: Westminster was rife with rumours and gossip - whole governments fell on a Chinese whisper. Besides, his source wasn't that reliable, and he wasn't here for the new leader; he was here because homelessness was an issue in his constituency. Unusual, he knew, to be in politics to make a difference and not just an impression; it didn't make him popular.

He took his seat on the back benches and opened his notebook. He always made notes; it helped with the voting, and it meant that he could follow the argument, make an informed decision. Nick liked to follow arguments, but they were the only thing he liked to follow. He was not a man for the chief whip, which was another thing that didn't make him popular.

Later into the afternoon however, Nick abandoned the idea of making any sense of this argument, sat back, his arms folded - his notebook discarded - and yawned. This was a dull debate, and he was bored. He scanned the press gallery behind the Speaker's chair for something to do and saw the same old pallid faces, withered hacks as bored as he was; one snoozing at the back. He saw the door of the gallery open and watched to see who was entering. There was a bit of shuffling, several people turned, and a woman made her way to the front. She sat down, took out a MacBook and, tuning into the debate, she began to type.

Nick stared. He saw the slant of hair that fell over the side of her face, the way that she habitually tucked it back behind her ear only for it to fall over her face again and suddenly he thought; that hair, it has a life of its own. He looked down at his hands and a memory of her hair, of the small crease between her eyes as she concentrated, of her long fingers, made him catch his breath. He looked at her again. No, it couldn't be. It was like her, very like her - or his memory of her at least - but this woman was older, less... he searched for the right word in his head, less expansive, more constrained. She seemed completely absorbed in what she was typing and only glanced up every now and then. Nick watched her for some time, oblivious to the debate and then she looked straight ahead, put her forefinger to her lip and screwed the right side of her face up as she processed a thought. Instantly he knew, he knew with absolute certainty, that it was her.

He watched her for a while, mesmerised and he could hear the memory of the music. What was it? Some pop hit he'd never heard before but played incessantly afterwards - Craig David – that was it. The words popped into his head and suddenly he was back there, fifteen years ago, at LSE and that terrible, wonderful party. He remembered the sense of isolation, of feeling spare, stupid, nodding along to the beat, trying to mouth words that he didn't know; too tall and too uncool to even be at the party, let alone be interesting enough for anyone to talk to.

He was a friend of a friend of a friend, abandoned on entry, a Billy-no-mates in the corner, repeatedly telling himself he'd give it another five minutes before he left. And then, as if out of nowhere, she had appeared; unsteady on her heels, smoking a cigarette, her hair unruly, falling across her face and she had sat down beside him, leaning towards him, her smoky breath full of wine and promise.

"Put your arm round me and look as if we're almost kissing," she murmured. She moved her face close to his and he smelled something woody and floral and exotic. "Quick!"

He didn't think, he simply moved his lips towards hers and kissed her. She tasted sweet and exciting, and the rush of desire was so sudden and so complete that when she pulled away, he had no idea where he was. He blinked rapidly and stared at her. She was still holding the cigarette and looking past him at the crowd.

"He's gone."

Nick watched as she took a long drag of the cigarette and tucked her hair behind her ear. It fell forward again.

"Who's gone?"

"Oh, some Che Guevara reading politics. We slept together at the beginning of term, but he was a bit too left of centre, if you know what I mean?"

Nick didn't, but he nodded. She stood up, held out her hand and he took it mindlessly, still reeling from the kiss. Her fingers were long and cool.

"Thanks," she said. "You saved me from the revolution."

"Oh, it's fine... no problem." His mind was whirring; he needed to say something to keep her there; something smart, witty, erudite.

"You know, most revolutions, historically speaking, begin by usurping the status quo and end up reinforcing it. Take Russia for example." As soon as he said it, he wished he hadn't. Witty? Smart?

"Is that right?" She smiled. "Historically speaking?" She looked at him, still smiling and he felt as if she was making her mind up about something.

She sat down beside him again and said, "Fuck it. You're a good kisser, you know that?"

He smiled back at her. "Yes, actually I do." A total lie. "Want another go?"

She shrugged. "Why not?"

And he was lost. For the next twelve hours, time stood still. When they had finally fallen asleep in the middle of the next afternoon, their limbs wrapped round each other in that thin, hard, hall-of-residence bed, Nick had breathed in the smell of her and realised that he had never felt so happy.

When he woke up, she had gone.

Now, in the chamber, on the hard, leather bench, Nick tuned back into the voice of the honourable Member of Parliament for Southeast Wales and tore his gaze away from the gallery. Some people, some experiences, he thought, you never forget. He'd looked for her of course, relentlessly, and for weeks. He'd a hung round the faculty she'd mentioned, hoping to catch sight of her, the student union, the library, but he never saw her again. By the time Christmas came and term ended he had given up any hope of meeting her again and then, well, then his life had changed anyway, and she became a memory that he held onto tightly for a while, until it became too painful to revisit. At eighteen, she had been his first, his most intense lover; he had been – in all probability – for her, just another fuck.

Nick looked up at the press gallery again and caught sight of her leaving. Suddenly and without thinking, he stood and began to move down along the line of MPs, whispering his apologies, brushing past knees and stepping over bags as he made his way hurriedly along the back benches to the exit. He left the chamber and headed back down the Members Corridor to the Central Lobby where he was sure he'd catch up with her. What he was going to say he had absolutely no idea.

The Central Lobby however was empty. Nick hurried on. He rushed through St Stephen's Hall, watched blankly by the solemn statues of Pitt and Walpole, down the steps into Westminster Hall, standing at the staircase scanning the vast echoing space. There was no sign of her. For the second time in his life, she had completely vanished.

2

P RESENT DAY – *London*
  Monday – p.m.

IT HAD BEEN A FRANTIC DAY, but a good one, Kate thought, and that wasn't something she could say every day. She'd finally secured rehousing for two families, which was no mean feat in the current climate, and Luke, the other lawyer she worked with, had gone out and brought them all Crispy Cream Doughnuts. She could hear him whistling in the office now as she pulled on a clean, unladdered pair of tights in the staff toilet. She put her boots back on, stood straight, glanced in the mirror, and said aloud, "Fricking parties..." She hated them. She eased a little piece of doughnut from between her bottom front teeth with her fingernail and opened the door.

"Nice," Luke said as she walked back into the office. "Love the whole, I don't give a fuck look."

"Thanks, it took me some time." She glanced at her watch. "You OK to lock up?"

"Of course." He looked at her. "You don't have to go you know?"

"I do." She sighed. "Much as I hate it, I know that if we want to get things changed, we have keep being visible." Kate picked up her bag. "So, I've got my notes from the homeless debate this morning and I am off to do some serious lobbying."

"Is that like dogging but in a reception area?"

Kate suddenly laughed. "Ha Ha. Such a wit Luke!" She headed for the door. 'See ya, wouldn't wanna be..."

"...- Oh, I think you would," Luke called back, "I'm off home for a Chicken Katsu and Call the Midwife."

"Ouch. That hurts." Kate left the office and still smiling, hurried down towards the bus.

FORTY MINUTES LATER, she stood in line at the Cromwell Green entrance to the House of Commons, her small pocket brolly barely shielding her from the misery of a sudden downpour and a sharp wind. Once through security, she handed her sodden coat to the girl in the cloakroom, clipped on her pass and ran her hands over the damp mess of her hair. She had a wet stain all along the hem of her dress because the velvet coat that Annie had insisted that she wear was not long enough and her tights were soaked. She smoothed her dress. She would have to do – not that she cared that much - and with very little enthusiasm, she made her way into the party.

·   ·   ·

THE STRANGERS DINING Room was packed with balding pates and shoulder to shoulder suits in fifty shades of grey. Kate wondered if politics and hair loss were synonymous and took a glass of wine that she wouldn't drink off the tray, searching the heads for any sign of any one she vaguely knew. She saw a female MP she'd chatted to once before, and so she waved, and the woman smiled back. Kate began making her way, carefully inching through the crush, across the rooms towards her.

NICK WORKED THE ROOM. The rumour had been right, he was in line for a shadow minister role, he'd been told that afternoon, and he was patted on the back and clasped by the hand more times than he could ever remember. This was an insidious place, he thought – you were either in or out - and at this moment, Nick was clearly in. He represented a 'safer side' of the party, the fairer face of capitalism, nothing too severe or left wing, community focused, with a close eye on where the money came from. He was new old new labour, and he genuinely believed in what he did, and in what he said. He was naive, almost certainly, and foolish, possibly, but he honestly didn't see any point in power unless you used it for the good. As he smiled and shook, and made inane comments, he wanted to enjoy being in demand, to feel the glow of success; he willed himself to enjoy the moment. But he couldn't. His mood had been dampened - no, more than that - his mood had been swamped by old memories, by a terrible feeling of loss. It happened, every now and then, and he was used to it, or as used to it as you can ever be. And to be fair, it happened less and less now. But loss it was, deep and impenetrable, and he knew that he had to get out of there.

He made his way through the crowd towards the door, placing his warm, untouched glass of wine back on a passing drinks tray and keeping his eyes focussed on the exit to avoid being caught in any more chit chat. The heavy flock wallpaper and the patterned carpet that mirrored the patterned ceiling seemed to press down on him, making him hunch his shoulders as he shifted his body to the right and left in order to squeeze through gaps in the crowd. He wasn't watching his footing and he was almost at the door when he tripped on the toe of someone's large shoe and stumbled forward. He was caught, or at least his fall was stopped, by the woman from the gallery in the chamber earlier, the woman with the hair; by Kate.

"Whoa!" Kate held both arms out and just managed to stop a full body blow. She yelped as her toe was crushed and, still holding the man by both arms, she righted him and then glared at him. "That was my toe!"

"Oh God, I'm so sorry, I...YOU?!" Nick stammered, rebalanced, stared at her and then, taking a deep breath, said; "I think we know each other. I think we met at LSE, in the first year, 2008?"

Kate glanced briefly at him then looked away. "Sorry, I don't think that was me," she said quickly. She turned away and instinctively spun in the direction of the exit. She nudged her way through the throng, not looking behind her, determined to leave. She made it out of the room and hurried out towards the coat check. There she realised she was still holding her drink.

"Bugger," she said. She plonked it down and handed over her ticket.

"Sorry love?"

"Nothing, erm..."

The lady came back with her coat. Kate pulled it on and

dug in her pockets. She found a twenty pence coin and placed it awkwardly into the saucer on the counter. "Sorry..." she said, glancing down at it, "Thanks..."

She was heading along the corridor towards the security exit by the time Nick caught up with her.

"Hey, wait!" Nick fell into step beside her. "I'm sorry, I don't want to pester you, but are you sure you weren't at LSE? I'm sure I recognise you, I..."

Kate kept walking but increased her pace. "I was at LSE," she said, not looking at him, "but I'm sorry, I don't remember you." Years of therapy had taught her to be authentic – to tell it as it was. "I'm sorry, it was a terrible time for me back then and I don't really remember much. I left after the first term."

Nick stopped for a moment; that made perfect sense! Kate carried on walking and so he doubled his step to catch up with her. She reached security and checked her pass back in. Nick did the same and followed her out. He kept pace with her along the corridor towards the exit, not speaking, just looking at the side of her face and, as she left the building, he did so as well. It was only when he stepped into the sleeting rain that he realised that he'd left his coat and umbrella back inside.

"Bollocks!" He could feel the rain pelting down on his head; his hair was already plastered to his forehead and his suit would be soaked in minutes. "Fucking bollocks!" he said again.

Kate stopped and turned. She looked out from under her umbrella at the man in front of her; six foot four, attractive in a boyish, clean-cut way, but not her type, or at least not what *used* to be her type. She stared at him as the rain ran down his face and she thought; he looks okay, nice. He looks familiar. She stared a bit harder. She knew her mind had done a clean sweep of that time, but maybe she had known him, shared a tutorial with him, had coffee? Maybe she'd even slept with him when she'd been off her face. There'd been a few like that and she honestly couldn't remember any of them. No, she was sure it was coffee, a lecture, shared notes, something like that. There was a reassuring air about him – although she couldn't put her finger on what made her feel that - and she thought, I don't want to go home at eight pm, alone, and miserable. So, impulsively – unusual for Kate - she said; "Here, come under my umbrella. You're getting soaked."

Nick smiled and it was the smile that did it for her. She'd always thought you can tell a lot from a smile. He stepped forward, closer, under the umbrella, and he smelled lovely. Woody and citrusy and clean. "You know, we could always go for a drink if you like? You might be able to jog my memory?" she said.

Nick's smile widened; he was genuinely chuffed, and it showed. He strode forward into Abingdon Street, whistled with two fingers in his mouth for a taxi and stood in the pouring rain to wave one down. Yes, he's Okay, Kate thought, as one drew up and he opened the door for her, climbing in after her. Yup, definitely Okay, she decided and, as the cab pulled off, despite being damp and cold, she found that she was smiling too.

KATE LEFT Nick paying for the cab and went up to the flat. He had insisted on paying for their second taxi from the bar to hers and for all their drinks, despite her protests. She felt a coffee was the least she could offer in return. Once in the flat, she left the front door open for him and hurried into the sitting room, gathering up the few framed photos she had and stuffing them into a drawer. It wasn't that she was secretive, more that she was private. When she heard Nick in the corridor, she slipped off her coat and boots and met him at the door.

"Come in."

He stepped into the hall and bent to untie his shoes. "Sorry," he said, "My feet are soaked." It was still hammering it down and ten minutes earlier he had stood in the rain again for some time trying to hail a taxi when they left the bar. He was insistently gallant and it both amused and impressed her. He removed his shoes, shrugged off his suit jacket and stood in his wet socks and shirt sleeves.

"Let me take your jacket and I'll stick it over the radiator. At least it might dry a bit."

He handed it to her and looked around the flat as she hung it up. He felt awkward, nervous, not sure why she had invited him back. For him it was a no brainer, once in her company he couldn't bear to leave it, but Kate was difficult to read. It felt as if she were continually evaluating him, as if she couldn't make up her mind.

"Come on into to the kitchen," she said, "I'll make some tea."

Nick followed her through the sitting room, to the small galley kitchen at the end of it.

"Nice flat," he said, "Do you rent it?"

Kate turned as she filled the kettle and said, "No, it's mine."

She finished making the tea, handed him a mug and, holding her own, she leant back against the cabinets and looked at him. His feet had made a small wet patch on the floor.

"Would you like some dry socks?"

"Do you have any that will fit? I've got a giant's feet."

Kate suddenly laughed. She had a fleeting recollection of having heard that phrase before, but she couldn't remember where or how. "I'll have a look." She left her tea and found the storage box that she kept in the hall cupboard. She heard him behind her and said, "I've got socks, but they're all odd."

Nick looked over her shoulder at a plastic box full of gloves, hats, ties and shoes, all men's.

"Someone was very forgetful," he said.

Kate handed him one grey sock and a blue one. "It all belonged to my father."

"Thank you," he said, "These probably mean quite a lot to you then; I appreciate the loan."

"They don't and it's not a loan; you can have them." She stood, closed the hall cupboard and made her way back to the kitchen. There, she took up her mug and Nick came back having changed his socks. She looked at him and he got the sense that she had decided on something.

"The flat was my mother's," Kate said. "I inherited it when she died. She died quite young; she had a break down when my father left her, and she never really recovered. The stuff in the box? That's all the stuff she kept stealing from my father's house when she was ill. Every time she came to visit me - I had to go and live with him for a short while - she'd take something of his." Kate shrugged. "He never knew, thought he kept losing things. I found it all when I moved back in, after she got really sick." She took a gulp of her tea. "And shortly after that she died." Kate raised her chin, defiantly, as if she was bracing herself for his response. He felt the challenge to get it right.

"That must have been hard," he said, "For you and your mum. How old were you when she died?"

"Seventeen."

"My mother died when I was twenty. Breast cancer. I gave up university for a year to look after her." He stopped. That feeling of loss surfaced again, and he acknowledged, as he always did, that it would never go away. He glanced down at his feet. He had absolutely no idea why he'd just told her that about his mother; he never mentioned it to anyone.

"That's surprising," Kate said.

Nick frowned. "Sorry?"

"You said when we had a drink that you'd never done anything surprising, that you'd had a textbook life; university, accountancy, politics blah, blah, blah." She smiled. "I think that's unusual, surprising, to give up university to look after your mum."

"Well..." he was momentarily taken aback by her response, then embarrassed. That's why he never told anyone; he hated to be viewed in that light – with pity – like a special case. "It was a long time ago. I was young." He shrugged. Being here with Kate, close to her, and revealing things about himself made him suddenly uncomfortable. It was intense, difficult but exciting and he knew he had to get out of there. He drank down half his tea in several gulps. He said, "I should get going."

"OK. Where do you live?"

"Wandsworth; on the common."

"Nice."

"Yeah." He put his tea down on the counter and suddenly felt her hand on his arm. He stared down at her long fingers, ring-less, the nails short and oval shaped and he had the urge to scoop them up into his hand and hold them, to put them to his lips. His whole body reacted to her, sparked into life.

"Thank you," she said, "For seeing me home."

He drew his arm away. "It's fine." He made his way back

to the hall and knelt to put on his shoes. He found his jacket and pulled it on, still sodden. Opening the door, he bent and picked up his wet socks.

"Thanks for the tea," He stepped out into the corridor, "And for the dry socks."

"It's still pouring," Kate said, "You don't have to go."

Nick looked at her. Her lovely, serious face had softened, and the frown had gone.

"Yes, I do," he said. He turned up his collar. "Bye." He walked off and heard the door close behind him.

KATE STOOD with her back against the door and listened to his footsteps recede. She closed her eyes, waiting for her racing pulse to slow, taking several deep breaths and hugging her arms about her. She was glad he had gone and disappointed and frustrated and relieved, all at once. She thought she remembered him – not that she was going to say – and she had a sense in her memory of his fierce passion and his gentleness. It was right that he had gone.

She sighed, moved away from the door, and had the sudden urge to be rid of the day. She unzipped her dress and shrugged it off, bent, rolled down her tights and knick-ers, unhooked her bra and naked, she gathered up her damp clothes to throw them into the laundry basket in her bedroom. There, she pulled on a long, soft sweater and sat on the edge of the bed in the dark, hoping that the longing to be touched and held, to be lost for however long in desire, would pass. She was alone and feelings of guilt and despair, feelings she knew only too well, threatened to descend. There was darkness in her peripheral vision, a darkness that rarely enveloped her fully now, but that she knew was perpetually there. She touched her neck with the tips of her fingers and shuddered.

The buzzer on the front door sounded.

NICK HAD STOOD in the meagre shelter of the entrance to Kate's building as the rain trickled down the back of his neck, thinking hard. He should walk away, he knew that he should turn on his heel and stride down the street as fast as the buffeting wind and rain would allow, but he couldn't. He had got to the corner of the street a few minutes earlier and felt a longing so strong and so physical that he'd stopped dead and instantly turned around, retracing his footsteps. He wasn't thinking; he was simply acting. He didn't want to be lonely anymore. He heard the door release mechanism, pushed it open and went inside.

Kate opened the door and heard Nick's footsteps on the stairwell. She knew what she was doing and yet she had no idea why. All she could think was that the thought of him stitched up her frayed anguish and that tonight she couldn't be alone. She didn't want to be.

"Hey," she said as he came into the corridor. He seemed momentarily shy, as if she reduced to him to someone boyish, inexperienced, then he smiled.

"Hey." He stepped inside the flat and enfolded her in his arms, kicking the door shut with his heel. He kissed her, lifted her, and carried her, still kissing her, into the bedroom. Placing her gently on her feet, Nick shrugged off his jacket and ran his hands over her bare thighs whilst she pulled his shirt off, still kissing him. Pressing her back against the wall, he lifted her legs up around his waist and Kate caught her breath. He held her hips, pulling her sweater off, releasing his trousers, his breath hot and intense. Naked and laying her head back against the wall, with half closed eyes she glimpsed the darkness outside, closing in.

Suddenly she screamed.

Nick froze. "What?!"

"There's someone out there!" Kate cried. "There on the balcony..."

Nick turned and saw a darkened figure through the glass doors, the light of a phone.

"Christ!" He released her thighs, righting her on her feet and fumbling with his trousers, he strode to the doors, struggling with the lock for a few moments until he got them open. He burst out onto the balcony. The figure had gone, disappeared into the darkness. Nick was sweating. He looked over the edge. There was nothing there. "I'm going after them!" he said.

"No don't!" Kate grabbed her sweater and pulled it on, following him as he pulled his shirt on and hurried to the front door. "It could be dangerous..."

But he was out in the corridor in an instant, running down it.

"Nick?!" She called after him, "Nick don't please!" But he had disappeared into the stairwell.

Kate hurried back into the bedroom and to the glass doors. She slammed them shut and locked them. Whoever had got up to her balcony had been determined; whatever they were doing it was done with purpose. She shivered.

A short while later Nick buzzed on the front door and Kate let him in. He was breathless and flushed; soaked.

"I saw someone dart down Webber Street and went after them, but they'd scaled the wall and gone by the time I reached the end." He stood dripping on the carpet and Kate fetched him a towel which he draped over his shoulders.

"Can I have a glass of water?"

"Sure."

He followed Kate into the kitchen, and she gave him a glass. He ran the tap and filled it, drinking it down in one go.

"Bastard!" he spat. He refilled the glass.

Kate stood behind him, watching his back still heaving with the effort of sprinting.

"What do you think they were doing?"

Nick turned. His face was ashen, despite the exertion. He looked at her. "Taking pictures," he said.

"What, of us?!" Her question was laced with scepticism. "Why on earth would they..."

Nick looked at her.

"Because you're an MP?" Kate shook her head. "Surely that isn't a good enough reason to..."

"Because I'm up for a shadow cabinet post," Nick said. "And I'm married."

Kate blinked rapidly several times as if she wasn't quite seeing the person in front of her. She felt a terrible thudding in her chest. She wasn't sure if she had heard him right. "Sorry? Did you just say that you're married?"

Nick continued to stare at her, and she noticed that the pulse in his neck was throbbing even though his face was completely still.

"Yes, I did." He looked down at the floor.

Kate took a step back. "And this fact, what, slipped your mind? Were you going to tell me? Or just fuck me and let me find out some other time?!"

Nick said, "It wasn't like that Kate, I didn't mean *not* to tell you, I..."

"You what? You forgot?" She shook her head. "You said to me in the bar that what I see is what I get." She threw her arms up in the air helplessly.

"I meant it…"

"What bit did you mean exactly?"

"All of it, it's just that… I just didn't think it was impor-tant," Nick said.

"What?! Not important?!" She slapped her palm against her forehead. "Jesus, I am so gullible. You know what Nick? I don't do this; I don't go round inviting men into my home and fucking them. I just don't! But tonight… tonight when I met you, I thought that you were…" her voice cracked, and she stopped speaking. She turned away. Why was she ranting at him when she should be ranting at herself? She'd been an idiot. Obviously he hadn't told her, why would he? This was quick, no-strings-attached sex and thanks very much; nothing more.

"Kate, I don't do this sort of thing either, I meant it when I said what you see is what you get, I'm not really married, I…"

"Oh please," Kate interrupted, "You can't be half married Nick, you either are or you aren't."

Nick's body slumped as he put his head in his hands. He didn't know where to begin. He was married, he was well and truly married, to Emma, whom he'd met at university and who was in the year below him and was waiting for him when he came back after his year out. Emma - the brilliant, bright, ambitious Emma and the youngest associate partner in her magic circle law firm; a woman who worked long hours, who travelled constantly and who barely realised that Nick existed. They had married straight out of univer-sity and spent the last ten years in separate spheres of life, coming together for family holidays and corporate events. He was married and yet he wasn't married at all.

"I'm married but…"

"No buts," Kate snapped. "You're married." She glanced

down at her semi nakedness and felt suddenly ridiculous. She said, "You need to go Nick. Please, just leave."

She walked past him and went into the bedroom, throwing on some sweatpants. He stood in the hall, watching her as she picked up his jacket off the floor. She held it out to him.

"Kate, please, will you let me explain? Please?"

She shook her head. "I don't want you to explain Nick, there's nothing that you can tell me that I want to hear."

Nick pulled his jacket on over his wet shirt, put his tie loosely round his neck. There was a lot more to explain, but it was pointless, she was right, why should she listen? It didn't make any sense to him so why would it make sense to her? He had never cheated on Emma, never given much thought to his ten-year marriage, except to realise every now and then that they didn't have anything in common, but he thought that happened in a lot of modern marriages; theirs wasn't rare. They worked hard, got on with it. He had never really considered that he was lonely, nor felt any sense of longing for something he didn't have - until tonight.

He opened the front door. "It's not what you think it is," he said, "I'm not what or who you think I am."

Kate shrugged. She didn't bother to reply; she didn't have the words to convey the overwhelming sense of disappointment that washed over her; the sense of despairing helplessness at being let down. It was all too familiar, and it made her very bones ache.

She watched Nick step out into the hallway and saw him glance back at her one last time. She stood tall, her face defiant, her chin tilted up. She looked right back at him in a way that she hoped was strong and fierce and without another word, he turned away and she closed the door behind him.

·   ·   ·

KATE STOOD in the doorway of the bedroom for some time. She seemed incapable of moving; there was a dullness and a heaviness in her body that weighed her down and made her want to sink to the floor and never get up. She knew the feeling; part fear and part despair and she knew what she needed to do. Taking a breath, she moved over to the chest of drawers and bent her knees, putting her hands under it and, taking the weight of it, she shoved it, bit by bit into position in front of the double glass doors. Once there, she wedged it into place, barricading the bedroom in from the world outside. In the hallway she did the same with the Edwardian desk, a heavier piece of furniture that made her grunt and heave with the effort of moving it. Once it was in position, sealing the front door, Kate drew the curtains in the sitting room, pulled down the blind in the bathroom and shut the night out as much as she could. She turned on all the lights, fetched her laptop and sat down at her small table to do some work. She would write the piece on homelessness using her notes from the debate and attach it to her application for lottery funding. She took a breath and said aloud, "I *am* fine, I *am* safe, I *have* control."

But, as she opened the lid of her MacBook, resting on the keyboard was a picture postcard; it was a view she knew well; blue sky, small boats dotted on the estuary. She reeled with shock at the sight of it. She had no idea how it had got there, and her hand shook as she lifted the card off the keyboard. She turned it over. There was nothing written on the back, simply the caption on the front. It said, *Welcome to Kingstanton.*

3

T HE PAST – *Kingstanton & Exeter, Devon, December 2008*

"A…"

The smaller girl had an elfin face with a small, pointed chin, which she lifted defiantly towards the bigger, older girl. "Nope," she stated, "No As." She wrote the letter down and drew a line from the gallows to the stick-man's throat on the notepad that lay between them on the bench.

The older girl raised her eyebrows and pretended to think. "Can you give me a clue?" she asked. "Let me see what I've already got." She leant over and her brow creased. "Hmmm… two Bs, with something in between, new word ending in E then another new word starting with a B, followed by U and I, with an E and R at the end. What's the clue? I'm nearly hung!"

"He's a cartoon character!" The younger girl could hardly keep the delight from her voice. She stared at the goldfish as it swam in its plastic bag, suspended by a piece of string from the arms of the bench. "Come on! He fixes things!"

The older girl shook her head. "No," she said, "I just don't know it. How about W?"

"No!! No Ws!" The younger girl drew a thick, circular line around the stick man's throat. "I won! You're dead!" She laughed; a short, sharp staccato noise. "Can I hold the goldfish?"

"No, not at the moment." The older girl moved protectively closer to the bag. "You can hold it if you tell me what you saw last night, down by the estuary."

The younger girl stared at the fish and her hand reached out towards it. "I can't. I promised I'd tell my mum when she gets in from work tonight. I told her I saw something, and she wants to know what it was. She said not to go mouthing off til I'd told her."

The older girl lifted the bag up and the water caught the last of the sunlight in the park. It sparkled tantalisingly. "You could tell me first?" She twirled the bag round. "Then I might let you have the fish."

"Nah, I promised." The smaller girl watched the bag and the slither of flashing gold in it. Her eyes grew wide with excitement. "I never had a pet."

"Goldfish make great pets. You don't have to do much, just feed them."

"Really?"

"Yeah." The older girl held the bag a bit closer to the younger girl's face. "Look, isn't it pretty?"

"It's lovely..." A small finger touched the cold, smooth plastic of the bag.

"I've got an idea." The older girl kept the bag aloft. "How about we play another game of hangman, and you could tell me what you saw, but I have to work out the words." She looked at the younger girl. "Then you haven't told me, have you? I've guessed and you've kept your promise."

The younger girl narrowed her eyes. She took several moments to digest the offer. "Can I have the fish even if you don't get the words, right?" she asked.

The older girl took her time in answering; it was all part of the game. "I'm not sure..."

"Oh please, go on, please, can I?"

The older girl shrugged.

"I can tell you everything..."

"OK then."

There was a gleam of triumph on the younger girl's face, and she laughed again, this time high pitched with glee. She took the pen and wrote the dashes of two words on one line, then the dashes of one word on another. She glanced up and looked at the older girl from under a fringe of lank, mouse-brown hair. "The last word is a name." she said.

"Is that right?"

"Uh huh. Bet you never get that though."

The older girl looked down at the notepad, her face grim, then she replaced the goldfish bag on the arms of the bench and zipped up her jacket against the cold. It was nearly dark; evening had fallen suddenly, like a great lump, cold and black from the sky, and pools of shadow spilled around their feet, dispersed every now and then by flashing red lights on the younger girl's trainers. As she went through the letters that she instinctively knew fitted the dashes - his name - the older girl wondered how long she had before the secret she had kept would be slashed open for the entire world to know. A few hours, she reckoned and at that point, she knew exactly what she had to do.

LYDIA KNOCKED on the door at number fifty-two and waited. She was a self-assured eleven-year-old but coming for her bi-weekly violin lessons had begun to worry her. From the bedroom above the porch, she could see a face peering out at her from behind the curtains. The face was always there, and it always made her wait. She knocked again, held onto her violin case a little tighter and hummed a few bars of her piece under her breath to calm her nerves. A few minutes later the door was opened and the same face that had peered down at her now stared at her blankly.

"It's me, Lydia," she said, "For Mr Hirsch?" She always had to say the same thing, even though she had been coming here for over a year now. "I've come for my lesson."

The face continued to stare and then turned as Mr Hirsch came into the hall.

"Ah, the wonderfully talented Lydia," he said, "Come in."

Lydia glowed at his address then stepped past the face which belonged to a skinny teenage girl, tall for her age and gangly, all bones at funny angles to her body. Lydia smiled at her, but it was not reciprocated.

Moving past her, she followed Mr Hirsch into the back room where he taught his lessons. She took out her violin and her music and placed it on the stand while Mr Hirsch stared out of the window at the small, fenced back garden. The radio news was on, reporting on the disappearance of a local girl and he seemed intent on listening to it. Lydia quickly tuned her violin and went over her music while she waited for him to begin the lesson. Finally, she said,

"Mr Hirsch?"

He turned. "Ah yes, Lydia." He went across and switched

the radio off, sitting at the table to face her. "Remind me of the piece Lydia?"

Surprised, Lydia looked across at him. He was fretting at the cuticle on his thumb, almost unaware of her presence in the room. She said, "I'm playing the Grieg Allegretto quasi andantino, the second movement."

"Good. Shall we start from the beginning? Or are we further on?"

Lydia hesitated; this was odd. Usually Mr Hirsch was prepared, gave her curt instructions, told her precisely where to start and how, stopping her to mark up her copy of the score. He praised her frequently, made her feel important. Today he hadn't even noticed if she had it open.

"Mr Hirsch, I think we are on the opening movement," Lydia said.

"Of course, of course." He got up and crossed to the music stand, having a quick peer down at the book that was open in front of Lydia. "Very good. Let's go from that first bar then..."

There was the bang of a door somewhere in the house and he glanced up, as if he had been startled but Lydia missed it. She had begun playing and all she could see and feel from that moment on was the music.

PROFESSOR RICHARD ROSS stood on the platform at Exeter St David's and waited for the 15.15 from London Paddington to arrive. It was a cold December afternoon; the platform was busy with Christmas shoppers and throngs of people milled about. He had left the university early, ignoring the three calls from Beth, not wanting to tell her what he was doing. She would be cross when he got home later that night; there would be sulking, maybe even a row, but he'd face that when he came to it. He was waiting for his daughter, and he'd missed her, or rather, he'd missed her as much as he'd been allowed to miss her. She was the grown-up product of a former marriage, she was at university in London and, even though he had a new family and his focus, Beth told him endlessly, was on them, not on a girl who was in her words, irresponsible, impulsive, and immature, Richard longed to see her. His daughter was all the things that Beth said she was, with the addition of stroppy and over fond of saying 'fuck' but she was also fiercely intelligent, determined, and curious – qualities he deeply admired. Beth was right, she wasn't easy, but she'd had a lot to deal with, and above all, she was still his daughter. He was looking forward to a weekend with her even though Beth had no idea she was on the way.

He glanced at his phone and wondered if calling Beth might be a good idea. He was getting cold feet about keeping the whole thing secret and besides, what could Beth say at this late hour except OK? He jiggled the phone in his hand for a few moments then, thinking that it *was* quite some time since the last incident with Katherine, he dialled home.

"Beth, Hi. Yeah, good, fine thanks."

He let her tell him about a problem she'd had at teatime with the twins and broccoli then he said, "I'm at the station. Katherine rang this morning. She's popping down for the weekend."

There was a silence on the other end. He'd used 'popping' to suggest something casual, unplanned; he lied about her calling that morning. Katherine had rung him on Monday, and she'd sounded so down that without thinking he had suggested they spend some time together this weekend. She'd been pleased; she sounded relieved. But that was four days ago, and he hadn't been able to face telling Beth. Richard hated conflict, he shied away from it and did anything for an easy life. He knew he should be more assertive with his wife, but it just wasn't in his nature. Richard was an academic, a thinker and an arch avoider.

"Where's she going to stay?" Beth asked curtly, "Because you know she can't stay here, not after the last time. I've got the twins to consider."

"Yes, I know. I've booked her into a hotel for tonight and then I thought..."

"A hotel? For God's sake Richard, how much is that going to cost?"

"It shouldn't be about money Beth. She sounded a bit low; she needs some moral support."

"She needs to be taught the consequences of her actions, that's what she needs!" Beth's voice had risen, and he heard her take a deep breath on the other end. She went on; "Look Richard, I know it's been difficult for her, I understand that, but hardship isn't an excuse. You know what she did..."

He knew; Beth had been reminding him at opportune moments over the past five weeks that he had spawned the child of the devil.

"We all make mistakes," he said wearily. God knows he was more guilty than most.

"Not mistakes that endanger the lives of young children." She snapped back.

"Beth, I don't think the twins were in mortal danger. Katherine had a few drinks, she went out for cigarettes, she wasn't a good babysitter, but we were only up the road and..."

"I can't believe that you're defending her Richard!! She was drunk!"

Richard glanced up and saw that the train was on time. He didn't want a row.

"Look," he said. "I'll drop her at the hotel, have a drink with her and be home for dinner."

There was a silence on the other end. "Fine," Beth said tightly.

"Beth, if she stays there tonight, maybe tomorrow she can come..." He stopped short; she'd cut him off.

"Bugger!" He said aloud. He put the phone back in his pocket. Professor Richard Ross knew when he was beaten – again. He knew that he couldn't take weeks of Beth ranting and giving him the cold shoulder, of her angst and jealousy erupting in a tirade of petty insults. He was on his second marriage; second family and he couldn't afford to mess it up again. He'd had enough emotion to last him a lifetime with Katherine's mother, so what else could he do? Take the easy way out, do what she said. Katherine would have to stay in the hotel tonight and go back to London tomorrow. It would be fine, at least she'd got away for the night and besides, she was young, she'd probably be dying to get back to the action after a few hours.

Moving towards the middle of the long platform, he stood back so that he was easily visible, watching as the train approached and scanning the windows for a glimpse of his daughter. He waited where he was as the train stopped and doors began opening.

"Dad?!" He turned. Striding towards him, carrying a giant bag was Katherine. She dropped the bag and rushed forward. Richard caught her up in a hug and squeezed her tight.

"Katherine," he said, "You are..." He stood back and looked at her. "Beautiful." He smiled and shook his head, "but bloody late! I was expecting you at lunchtime!"

"I know, I got caught up in something and well..." she shrugged. "At least I called..."

He caught a whiff of alcohol on her breath but said nothing. "Yes, true." That *was* a step forward. He thought back to when she lived with them, to the hours wasted waiting for her, not knowing where she was, driving round Exeter looking for her, dinners ruined, the twins' routine upset...

"And I'm here now."

"Yes, yes you are." He glanced behind her. "Here, let me help you with your..."

"Got it," she said. "No need."

Richard stood aside as Katherine lugged the bag up and onto her shoulder; independent to the last, he thought, stubborn, as Beth saw it.

"We'll get a cab," Richard said, "Into town."

"Town? Didn't you bring the car?"

Richard began to walk, and Katherine fell into step beside him, weighed down by the bag.

"No, I left it on campus, I didn't want to do all the rush hour traffic and there's no parking, so..." he stopped. "Look, I've booked you a room at the Royal Clarence in the Cathedral Square for the night. My treat, obviously. I thought we could have a drink and..."

"Beth won't have me." Katherine stopped. "I'm right, aren't I?"

"No, not at all, it's just that the twins have a routine and seeing as you're so late, Beth thought..."

Katherine's face changed. It had been open and smiling but now something in her expression closed against him. She was still smiling, but the smile had set blankly on her face. She was hurt; he could see it and feel it and he was helpless. He could do nothing about it. Richard's daughter stood between him and his new family like an impenetrable wall that they simply couldn't get over.

"Well, Beth thought it would be nice for you," he hurried on "to be in the centre of things, to have me all to yourself..."

Katherine interrupted; "You didn't ask her about me coming to stay, did you?" She stared at him. "And after the row about me drinking when I was babysitting..."

"You were drunk Hepburn, not just drinking..."

"I made a mistake, like ninety nine percent of teenagers do! I'm nineteen Dad, I'm supposed to mess up occasionally!"

"You messed up when you were looking after the twins!"

"Looking after the twins? They were in bed, fast asleep and you were half a mile away having a drink in the pub! It was hardly a major responsibility..."

"That's not the point!" Richard snapped.

"Really? What is the point?!" Suddenly Katherine cuffed her palm against her forehead. "Oh yes, I forgot, the point is that Beth hates me because I remind her of just how fucking awful she was to have an affair with my father and get herself up the duff while he was still married!"

Richard stared at his daughter. She was the image of the young woman he had fallen in love with thirty years previously. A woman he had married, betrayed, and let down.

He winced and felt his shoulders slump. "Hepburn," he said, "You've not been the easiest child to have around, even you would admit that."

"Like it was my fault?!" Katherine opened her handbag and began searching for her ticket.

"What are you doing?"

"I'm going to go back to London," she said. "I don't want to stay. You don't want me here."

She glanced up and her stare cut him to the quick. "If

you did," she said, "You'd have realised just how stupid it is to put me in a hotel. It's like..." She laughed, but he could sense the closeness of tears. "It's like the best snub. Mean, but covered up as thoughtful." She found her ticket. "Lucky," she said, "I don't need to change this, I..." She broke off and took a couple of deep breaths. There was a moment then when Richard could have changed it all, but he hesitated, he was too weak, and he knew it. The moment was lost.

"I got an open return," she finished, "Just in case." What she didn't add was in case you wanted me to stay longer. She held up the ticket and turned away from him. "The next train leaves in ten minutes," she said. She closed her bag and began walking towards the stairwell to the opposite platform.

"Katherine, please...." Richard hurried after her. "Come into town and stay the night, we can have a drink, spend some time together."

"And then you'll say good night and go back to your real family, the one that I'm not part of." Katherine laughed. "No chance." She walked away and upped her pace. Her father watched her go but he did not go after her. There really was no point.

As Abbey Salter's parents took their seats behind the table on the podium, Chief Inspector Derek Lewin waited for the rabble to calm down and glanced at the prepared statement that he had in front of him. Despite the cold outside, it was sweltering in there. There was something wrong with the thermostat in the room and that, combined with the number of people that were crowded into the small space, had raised the temperature to over thirty. He was sweating profusely and the tweed on his jacket was beginning to smell. He sighed, chewed the inside of his mouth and watched the sound and camera men checking their equipment. He hated the media circus that came with something like this. It was a necessary evil, but it made him sick with nerves; TV cameras, reporters, everyone looking to him, waiting for any tiny slip up or mistake. He caught the signal from the officer in charge of media and called for quiet. The TV news cameras began rolling.

"As you know, it is now two days since eight-year-old Abbey Salter went missing. She was last seen by her grandmother at approximately four fifteen pm on Tuesday the third of December when she left the house to go to the shop on the corner of Fore Street at the edge of the Halston Estate for milk. She did not arrive at the shop. Abbey regularly went to the shop for her grandmother and was known there, this was not an unusual trip for her. We are asking if anyone saw anything of Abbey or someone of that description in or around the Halston Estate on the afternoon of the third of December, or indeed if anyone saw her further afield. Her mother and her stepfather would like to make a statement."

Lewin glanced down at his script. Shit: he'd cut it short; he should have read it out. He took his reading glasses off and looked at Abbey's mum and nodded. She brushed the hair off her face, tucked it nervously behind her ear and leant towards the microphone in front of her.

"Abbey is my little girl," she said, there was a pause. She swallowed and the muscles around her mouth convulsed with the effort of trying to speak without tears. "My precious little girl and if anyone has..." she broke off and her face collapsed. "If anyone has seen my little girl or knows where she is then please... please come and tell us... Please let us know where she is..." She began to sob, and her partner leant forward.

"Abbey is only eight," he said, "She's a little girl, she's gonna be really scared so if you know anything..." He gripped the edge of the table and Lewin saw his Adam's apple bobbing in his throat as he struggled to get control of himself. "Please help us...please go to the police..."

There was an instant caw of voices, questions fired at Lewin and the other officers at the table. Lewin held up his hand. "So far we do not have any leads," he said loudly, "All we know is that Abbey left her grandmother's house in Barton Leigh Avenue, roughly two hundred yards from the shop she was going to and has not been seen since. We are urging the public to come forward with any information, anything at all that they think might be relevant to Abbey's disappearance."

Another question was fired at him. Christ, why the hell hadn't he just read it out? He should have said all this. He looked an idiot now. He began to sweat. "Yes... yes of course..." He cleared his throat. "Abbey was wearing a red jumper and jeans and a pair of white trainers with flashing lights." He held up a photograph of Abbey, in a skirt and crop top that her mother had taken at a family party a couple of months earlier. "Abbey is three foot eleven inches tall and weighs 5 stone. She has long brown hair which was tied into plaits on the day that she went missing." Lewin swallowed; he didn't need to read this; her innocent, smiling image was imprinted on his mind. His indigestion was killing him, and he needed to belch. He caught the eye of the media officer who was making cutting actions across her neck.

"Thank you. That is all we have time for now. Please contact us at Kingstanton Police on..." he glanced down at the statement and couldn't read the phone number. He patted his pockets for his glasses. Where the hell had he put them? He just took the damn things off... He lifted the statement up and held it closer to his face, finally reading the number out. There was a fifty second pause and then he stood up. He nodded at the WPC who helped Ms Salter and her partner up and off the stage. Once down Lewin belched loudly and rubbed his chest.

"Well done," the media officer said. There was no enthusiasm in her voice.

"Yes, well..."

"Sir?" Lewin looked across at his DC. "Calls coming in already sir."

"Righto." Lewin glanced at Ms Salter and caught her eye. The pain and despair on her face was palpable and when she looked away and he felt the familiar sinking in the pit of his stomach. He belched painfully again and followed his DC out of the press room.

4

P RESENT DAY – *London*
Tuesday – a.m.

KATE WOKE SUDDENLY; her phone was buzzing. It was still dark outside, and she was momentarily disorientated; she had no idea what time it was. As she glanced at the screen her stomach lurched; it was five am and Hannah was calling; the mother of Annie's friend.

"Hannah? Is Annie OK?" Kate couldn't keep the panic out of her voice.

"She's fine Kate. Look, I hope you don't mind me calling... your twitter account's been hacked. There's a video up there. I think you need to see it."

"Video?" Kate pressed speaker and opened her Twitter app. "Shit..." She watched the footage for a few moments with a sickening feeling of embarrassment. "Has Annie...."

"No, the girls are still asleep. We think your website's been hacked as well."

"What?!..." Kate jumped out of bed and, still on the phone, hurried towards the sitting room and her MacBook. The embarrassment turned to dread. She flipped it open and clicked on her site. "Oh my God..." She stood motionless and stared at the video footage. Her face was clearly visible, her head tilted back, her eyes half closed, her breasts were exposed and so was Nick's naked bottom, his thighs. Just before the footage cut out, he turned, and his look was unmistakable - full of longing and abandonment.

"Kate? Kate, you still there?"

"Yes..." Kate slumped into a chair. God, this was mortifying; she ran a charity – an ethical business, with sponsors. Kate put her head in her hands. She was applying for lottery funding...

"I've got Annie and Matilda's phones; we don't allow phones in the bedroom at night, so I'll hang on to them and hopefully you've a got a couple of hours to sort this out..."

Kate heard Simon's voice in the background. Hannah said, "Si says that Twitter will take the footage down almost immediately as its explicit content. You need to alert them though and then sort out your site security. Sorry, I'm sure we're probably telling you stuff you already know..."

"No... no, it's fine Hannah, thanks. I appreciate it..." Kate's voice trailed away. She was scrolling through her contacts on her phone. "I should go, get this sorted." She found the web management company she used. "I'll keep you posted. And thanks for having Annie..."

Kate pressed end and took several deep breaths. She suddenly remembered the fleeting idea that she'd had last night. Whoever it was who had climbed onto her balcony and taken the video had done so with rigorous purpose and, she thought, sitting alone in the dark, maybe this wasn't about Nick Farleigh, the married MP, but about something else entirely. She remembered the postcard and shivered. Dialling the emergency helpline for her website managers, she hung on the line and waited for someone to answer.

It was midnight in New York and on the seventeenth floor of the Madison Avenue offices of Mason, Pinter and Erics-son, Emma Smithson-Farleigh was still in a meeting, going through litigation documents with her client when she saw her assistant, Candice, through the glass wall holding her thumb and pinkie up to her ear, making the phone sign and pulling agitated faces. Emma frowned at her and ignored her; this was a hell of a big deal, she was exhausted, and it wasn't over yet, she didn't need any futile interruptions. However, a few moments later Candice opened the door of the meeting room and said,

"Emma, I'm sorry to interrupt you but there's a call for you. It's important."

Emma said sharply; "Please divert it, Candice."

"I can't." Candice shook her head. "It's urgent Emma. I'm sorry, but you really do need to take it."

Emma looked round the table and shrugged helplessly. "Sorry guys, will you excuse me for five minutes?"

She stood and made her way to the door. Once outside, walking with Candice down the corridor, she said; "This had better be good."

Out of sight of the meeting room Candice stopped. She handed Emma a phone. "There's no call. Your Twitter account's been hacked. This came up on my feeds..."

Emma took the handset and looked down. "Sorry, I don't understand..." She stared closely at the screen, watched for a few minutes then as the man in the footage turned, she saw Nick's face. "Oh my God," she said. "This is on my feeds? On my account?"

Candice nodded. "I've contacted Twitter and they've already been alerted to it, but they need to speak to you, the account holder."

Emma handed the phone back. "I need to call Nick," she said. "I've left my phone in my bag in the meeting room. Can you get it for me, and my laptop? I'll be in meeting room 7."

She walked down to the meeting room at the end of the corridor and went in, closing the door behind her. She picked up the phone, dialled 0, asked for an outside line and rang Nick's mobile. He answered immediately and she said, "What the fuck is going on Nick?"

NICK HAD BEEN UP since five am when someone from the press office had rung him. They'd had the footage taken off the party site and Twitter account and he'd dealt with his own personal account, but fuck knows where else it had been posted; he was still getting alerts. He'd tried to call Kate repeatedly, but couldn't get through and now, as soon as he saw the US number on his screen his stomach clenched. Now, Emma was involved as well.

"I said, what the fuck..."

"I heard you," Nick interrupted. He took a breath. "It happened last night. I met someone."

There was a pause on the other end. He wondered if she was looking at a screen; she usually did; she was the master of multi-tasking.

"Clearly. Who is she? Did you hire her?"

Nick took another deep breath. He had seen Emma as

combatant, and he knew the measure of her fight. "No Emma, I have never hired anyone, you know that."

"Really? I'm not sure I know anything anymore."

"Emma," he said gently, "I'm really sorry, honestly, I am. I mean that I met someone, last night, someone important, or at least someone who I think could be important to me."

"Good for you. And what, you felt the need to film your *meeting*?"

"No. We were set up, or I was. And it wasn't a meeting, it was an accident. It should never have happened...-"

"You're right there Nick!" she snapped.

There was a brief silence then she said, "Whatever it was it's going to be pretty bloody embarrassing for me. Whoever set you up, as you say, set me up too. My account was hacked, and it was posted on my Twitter feeds."

"Shit."

"Shit is right Nick. Have you any idea how this makes me look?"

"I know Emma, I..."

She didn't let him finish. "It's been taken down now, Twitter have just confirmed that on a live chat while I've been talking to you, but I'm an associate partner Nick, I've worked damn hard to get to this position and I have a repu- tation, the firm's reputation as well as my own. I look like an idiot, my husband caught with his trousers down...literally!"

There was a long pause with miles and miles of transat- lantic emptiness between them.

Finally, Nick said; "I'm sorry Emma; I didn't set out to hurt you..."

He heard Emma sigh. Her voice had altered when she said, "You know what Nick? You haven't *hurt me*."

He could imagine her putting the air inverted commas round those words.

"At least, not in the way that you think." There was another pause. Emma measured her words in the same way a chef measured ingredients; she knew exactly how much or how little needed to be said for the right effect. "You having sex with someone else I expected; I figured that we weren't having it with each other very often so there had to be an alternative, but getting caught is humiliating Nick. I can put up with it if it doesn't affect me…"

"Hang on a minute," Nick interrupted. "So, you're telling me that the fact that I almost had sex with another woman doesn't bother you? That you expected it, and you don't really care?" His voice rose. "Have you any idea how damning that sounds? What on earth are we married for if that's what you think?" He took a breath. "We've not been a couple for years Emma, not really, but I thought we were married, even if I didn't feel it, even if we spent most of our lives apart, I've stuck to it and now I find out that you don't really care as long as it doesn't fuck with your job!" He was breathing hard; his voice was raised and he wondered momentarily if his researcher in the other office could hear him.

"Excuse me? What, suddenly you're the victim?!" She said archly.

Nick held his tongue. There was a stretched silence then finally Emma said, "It's not that I don't care Nick, it's just that I care about different things. Yes, we're married, and we make a good couple. We have impressive jobs, a lovely house, and a comfortable lifestyle, we…"

"You know what Emma? Fuck the lifestyle!"

The silence fell again, and it seemed to echo.

Suddenly Nick said, "You just told me that as we weren't having sex there had to be an alternative. Did there? Was there one for you?"

Her reply rebounded off his words. "What we are talking about here Nick is you placing me in an embarrassing situation, a potentially damaging one career wise."

"You didn't answer my question, Emma."

"I didn't answer it because it isn't relevant. You've humiliated me Nick, that's what I'm concerned about."

"Clearly," Nick said.

There was a final moment of silence. Nick watched the clock on the wall ticking, each second marking the end of his marriage.

"I'm catching a flight home in a few hours. We can talk about this when I get in."

"What is there to talk about?"

"Don't make a fool of me," Emma snapped.

Anyone else, he thought, might have said, don't hurt me or even don't leave me, but not Emma. The clock ticked on.

"And don't make an enemy of me either," she said. "Don't underestimate me Nick."

"I don't even know what the fuck that means," he snapped then he pressed end without letting her answer him.

Nella arrived at the Costa across the road from the nick and got herself a drink, taking a seat in the window. She took out her phone and sent a text to her mate.

In Costa. Coffee?

Her mate, DC Mohammed Ahmad, was inputting the data he'd been given onto the system and to say he was bored would have been an understatement; he was brain-dead. Must be done, DS Waller said, Ahmad was new to the borough, had just done the eighteen-week foundation course after uni and was a trainee. *'You know diddily squat,'* DS Waller said, *'Fuck all compared to other members of CID who've come up through the force. Trainee is as trainee does. Inputting.'*

Mo finished the penultimate sheet and sat back in his seat for a few moments. His phone pinged. It was Nella.

Mo glanced over his shoulder at the semi-empty office – it was lunchtime. He exited his screen, tapped in; *Flat white – on my way,* and stood up.

"Just going to get some coffee boss," he called across to DS Waller. "Want anything?"

DS Waller shook his head without looking up and Mo left. Across the street, he waved to Nella, who had just picked up his coffee, and joined her at the window table. She was a couple of years older than him, and she'd done her stint in uniform - which she reminded him of constantly – but they got on, shared miseries and had teamed up pretty much on first meeting. Together they filled the station's ethnic quota.

"What's up? Thought you weren't on shift until later?"

"I'm not, but something's been bothering me, so I thought I'd come in a bit earlier and check the database. I had an odd call-out with DS Dennis yesterday – it was that poor bloke whose girlfriend died in the lift?"

"Yeah," Mo shuddered. He hadn't got a strong stomach and that one had been particularly grisly. He glanced at the coffee, but suddenly didn't fancy it. "It was sudden death, wasn't it?"

Nella nodded. "Apparently, yeah, but he had this thing about her not taking the lift, like not ever taking the lift."

"So?"

"Oh, I dunno, it just seemed weird, the whole thing. He says he thinks someone forced her into the lift."

"Is that a possibility?"

"DS Dennis says unlikely as CCTV for the road was checked and she was alone, but..." Nella shrugged. "Oh, I don't know...he was so adamant..."

"Are you sure it wasn't a bit of attention seeking? Nella, you are way too sincere, you take everything so seriously. People are full of shit. Fact. It may well have been just the need to talk to someone."

"Yeah, that's what DS Dennis said, but I don't know. I'm not convinced..." Nella shot him a look. "Oh, and by the way, you could have told me! I only went and asked about her husband."

"Idiot."

"Yeah, right. Anyway, I thought I'd come in and have a look on Intel, see if anything pops up."

"Like what?"

"I dunno. I did a bit of stalking last night, Facebook, google search... and Lydia, the girl who was, you know..." Nella didn't want to say decapitated, it sounded demeaning, a bit sensationalist. "Well, there are quite a few pictures of her as a musician and she's... well, she looks ill; anorexic. She's tiny, like a little girl and she wears these girly shoes and long skirts and she's painfully thin. She looks like... like she didn't grow up."

"So, she's eccentric; she's a musician. And she probably had an eating disorder, so do lots of young women. I should think the pressure to look good for a professional musician is pretty high." He looked at Nella. "What's your point?"

"My point is that doesn't something usually spark an eating disorder? What if she had history and her boyfriend was right, that someone was after her and..." She stopped abruptly; Mo was smiling.

"Nella, you read way too much shit fiction."

She frowned. "OK, clever dick. She was also opening a music centre for disadvantaged kids on the Belham Estate, the one that's just been bought for redevelopment into private housing... all except the community hub building which they couldn't buy because of the music centre. It's got lotto or some kind of charity funding. So, they've got the whole lot, bar that and its smack bang in the middle of the development."

Mo had stopped laughing. "OK, so you think it's worth having a nose?"

Nella raised an eyebrow. "Yeah, don't you?"

"I don't know Nels, only you can work out if you've got the time. Me, I'm swamped so I'd leave well alone." He shrugged. "But then again, what do I know? I'm just out of training and, according to DS Waller I'm useless." He stood up. "Talking of which, I've gotta get back. You coming?"

"Yeah." Nella stood and picked up her drink. She drank the rest down, wiped her mouth with a napkin and grabbed her coat. She followed Mo out of Starbucks and down the road to the nick.

KATE EMPTIED the left-over tea into the sink and rinsed the mug. It wasn't hers; she'd been too anxious to eat or drink since last night and now she was beginning to feel faint as it was already the middle of the morning. Mostly the fiasco with Twitter was sorted – mostly – but she knew she couldn't be sure for a while; things went viral for any reason, at any time. The post card... she stopped and opened the lid of the bin where she had put the ripped pieces last night. She saw the edge of one of the pieces, lurid blue sky, and her stomach lurched. The post card frightened her. She heard the irritating whistle of the bloke changing the locks and went back into the hall.

"Nearly done," he said, "Good idea to double lock. Mortice deadlocks, like this one, difficult to force. Good choice Katie, for front and back."

Kate bristled. "Kate," she said sharply, for the second time. "It's Kate, not Katie." He'd obviously been on some sales course that told him to use the customer's first name incessantly but hadn't told him to make sure he got the name right. She glanced at her watch.

"How long will you be?" she asked.

"Should be done in ten. Like I said, good choice and you can't be too careful nowadays. Terrible thing happened in my sisters flats up the road last week. Young girl was killed."

"Oh?"

"Yeah, terrible, it was. Police say it was accidental, her scarf got caught in the lift doors, but the girl was decapitated, her head was completely cut off from her body..."

Yes, I know what decapitated means, Kate wanted to snap. He stood straight and made a cutting motion at his neck, and she looked away. She had no interest in local gossip that was distorted at best, nonsense at worst.

"That wasn't no accident, I reckon, the boyfriend says she was forced into the lift."

"You seem to know a lot about it," she murmured, looking away.

"Yup, happened in the same block my sister lives in. My sister knew her, she did, says she was lovely. A musician; a violinist apparently. Terrible. Boyfriend's off his head with grief she said."

Kate looked up "A musician?" She could feel a slow thudding in her chest. "You don't know her name, do you?"

"Lydia Hel... something."

"Helston," Kate said instantly.

He looked up from the lock. "Blimey, did you know her...?" then he quickly stepped forward as Kate suddenly slumped back. "Christ! You OK?!"

She took several deep breaths and pressed her hands against the solid surface of the wall behind her, needing the concrete support.

"I'm fine," she murmured. "I just haven't eaten; I feel a bit faint..." She felt momentarily insubstantial, as if she wasn't there. "I haven't read about it... was it in the news?"

"Yeah, but only local cos it was accidental, like I said. You didn't hear about it then?

Kate shook her head and swallowed down the taste of bile. Her head swam with images, so she kept her eyes focussed on the Turkish rug by the door, counting the coloured triangles, the small diamonds in the pattern, the patches where the wool had worn away.

"Can I get you some water love? Shouldn't you sit down?"

"No." Kate stood straight and still holding the wall behind her, said; "No, it's OK, really."

"I'm sorry if I upset you, I shouldn't go on like that. My missus is always saying to me that I go on too much. Terrible business, that young girl though..." Now that he saw Kate had recovered, he went on; "You knew her then, did you? She a friend of yours?"

"No, no I didn't know her, I knew *of* her. I like music..." Kate's voice trailed away. She wiped a small beading of sweat from her hairline and moved away from the wall. "Are you nearly done?" Her voice was terser than she intended. "It's just that I've got to go to work, I'm pretty late already."

"Yup, all done here and in the bedroom. How do you want to pay? Cash or card?"

Kate went for her purse, handed over her card, but didn't wait for the transaction to go through; she put on her shoes and her coat, held her bag in front of her and made it plain she was ready to go as soon as the locksmith left. She keyed in her pin, took her card back and avoided his eye.

"Right, I'll be off then," The locksmith said, "Here's the keys, you'll probably want to get a spare cut, so here's our card as well. We'll give you a five percent discount on key cutting."

"Right, thanks. I'll remember that." Kate took the keys and tucked them into the pocket of her bag. She had her hand on the door ready to close it, but he still he lingered.

"Don't lose them now," he warned jokingly as he picked up his tool bag and stepped out into the corridor.

"I won't," Kate said testily. "Thanks." She shut the door without waiting for his reply and stood, breathing shallowly, waiting for him to exit the building before she left the flat in case she got caught up in any more conversation with him.

AN HOUR LATER, Kate rounded the corner from Wandsworth Road into Union Road and stopped. She stood opposite Kenvil House; her eye on the first-floor window that she knew was the window of Lydia's flat. She had been there before, just once, when she had found out that Lydia had moved to London and even though it had been dark, a thick winter night in the middle of February, Kate had seen her, Lydia, that fragile girl hurrying home after a concert, violin case clutched tightly in her small hand, her cloaked, child like figure unmistakable in the shadowy light. She'd watched her, scurrying across the road, darting around the side of the mansion block before being swallowed up by the dark building and Kate had remained standing there, lightheaded, as if she'd seen a ghost. Then by chance the light came on in the first-floor window, the one she stared at now, and she caught a fleeting glimpse of the pale, pinched face of a young woman who had never grown up.

Kate shivered, pulled her coat tightly around her body and crossed the road, going through the entrance into the courtyard that linked Kenvil House to the other Mansion blocks. She located Lydia's building and walked into the dark lobby. To her right was the stairwell; dank, grey concrete, damp smelling cut with the edge of something sharp and bitter; urinary. At the foot of the stairs were the flowers, a layered tribute of grubby cellophane, wilting flower heads. She knelt to read one of the messages.

"Can I help you?" The voice was flint hard and sharp.

Kate glanced up at a young man who stood halfway down the stairs.

"I saw you from the window, staring. There's nothing to see so you might as well fuck off."

Kate faltered. "I'm sorry, I didn't mean to intrude, I..." She what? What could she say that would make any sense at all to this young man, Lydia's boyfriend? "I heard about Lydia... I... I was a fan. I'm sorry."

"Yeah?" The young man seemed to slump slightly as his aggression weakened and Kate stood up.

"I didn't mean to be rude," he said, "I shouldn't have told you to fuck off. My bad. It's just that... well, word gets out and there's been some really sick people who wanted to take pictures of the lift, stuff like that. Lydia's parents are here for the funeral and its really upset them."

"I'm sorry," Kate said again, "It must be very hard."

"Yeah, its shit." He shrugged and turned to go back up the stairs.

"Was it an accident?!" Kate called out.

He glanced behind him and shrugged again. "That's what the police say... yeah... an accident."

"What do you think?"

The young man stared at her for a few moments. "Who are you?" he said warily, "Why d'you want to know that?"

"Just curious, that's all, I..."

A woman appeared on the stairs. "Matt, there's someone on the phone for you..."

She glanced down the stairwell; saw Kate and her face hardened, her mouth becoming a thin dark line. She was ashen, drawn. She turned momentarily to Matt.

"Go and take the call Matt," she said, and then she looked back at Kate.

Kate's heart began to smack against her sternum and her chest hurt. Breath constricted in her throat as Matt disappeared round the stairwell and the woman took a few steps down towards her.

"I don't know what you think you're doing here," she hissed through clenched teeth, "But you can piss off right now and don't you ever, *ever* dare to come back here again."

Kate took a step back, folding her arms across her chest defensively, as if holding in the pain.

"Go on..." The woman stepped down a couple more stairs. "Piss off! You've caused enough harm..."

Kate turned and fled. She hurried across the courtyard and out onto the street, the thud in her chest moving up to pulse urgently against the side of her neck. She began to run, down Union Road, darting past the pedestrians, along Larkhall Lane to the end and not stopping until she was several streets away. When she finally slowed, she bent double, her lungs burning, nausea rising in her throat. She stayed like that for some time, hot blood coursing round her body, cold fear lodged in her chest. It took some time to get her breathing under control and when she stood straight, she realised she had no idea where she was, except that she was outside a pub.

She thought about Annie, about picking her up from the bus, about dinner and about sitting with her daughter watching TV. She pictured it, felt it and, as she put some ground between herself and what had just happened, the trembling subsided. Only Annie had the power to save her, she thought. Of course, she had no idea, why should she, she was a child, but Annie was Kate's deliverer and, as soon as she had that thought, another more disturbing thought piggy-backed it. What if she didn't have the power to save Annie in return? She stopped dead.

If Lydia had been murdered, was someone else going to be next?

WHEN NELLA finally looked up from the screen and glanced out of the window, she was surprised it was dark. Winter did that, she thought, stole the day before you'd even had time to get on. She stood and stretched then wandered across to Mo, several desks along, still inputting information into the system.

"Her name came up in a CRIS report," she said.

"Really?" he wasn't listening. "Who's that?"

"Lydia Helston. The girl who was hung?"

Mo stopped typing and swung his chair round. "Say what?"

"Lydia Helston has at some point been interviewed by the police. Don't know any more than that – can't get into the data base."

"Where? By whom?"

"Devon and Cornwall Police," she said.

"Have you put a request in for information?"

"Somebody did their homework on the training course!" Nella grinned. "I'm gonna ring and find out what department and then I'll email and request the file."

"An idea what it might be connected to?"

Nella shrugged.

"Well don't get your hopes up, could be littering."

"Very funny."

"You asked the boss yet?"

"Nah, I'm about to do that now." Nella glanced briefly at DS Dennis as she chatted to one of the other officers.

"Good luck. Glutton for punishment."

Nella walked across to where DS Dennis was standing; she was showing photos on her phone.

"Sallie? Can I have a word?"

DS Dennis glanced over her shoulder at Nella.

"Sure." She held out her hand for her phone and someone passed it back to her. Nella tried to snaffle a look at the screen. "That your daughter?"

DS Dennis smiled. "Yes, here..." She held out the phone.

"Oh, how gorgeous, she's black..." Nella stopped; it was wrong – she knew it. Shit, why could she never think before she spoke? DS Dennis blinked then widened her eyes. She dropped the phone into her pocket and said, "You will clearly make an excellent detective DC Walsh. Our daughter is mixed race, and my partner is black. Well spotted." She eyeballed Nella. "What did you want?"

"I did a search – in my own time this afternoon - for Lydia Helston, the girl who..."

"Yes, I know who you're talking about..." DS Dennis cut in. "And?"

"She's come up in a CRIS report. Devon and Cornwall

police. I just wanted to check it's OK with you if I email for the file?"

DS Dennis continued to stare at Nella. "Not happy it's sudden death?"

"Not sure it is sudden death."

"You've got a desk full of proper cases DC Walsh, have you got time to look at something we've officially put to bed?"

"I think so."

"You think so?"

"I do have time Sallie, I'll make time."

"Fine. Just make sure you get your priorities right, OK?"

"Thanks Sallie, I will."

Mo was standing by the window when Nella came across to him. He'd needed a bit of a view, albeit just a street scene, with some desultory Christmas lights, after hours on the screen. Outside however, Mo had noticed a woman, late twenties, or early thirties, who had been standing on the other side of the road from the station for some time, her eye on the door, occasionally on the windows, once meeting his stare and turning away immediately. He got the sense that she wanted to come in, to make contact in some way, but she hadn't moved from her spot for the past half hour. He had a good mind to go down and see if she was OK when he felt Nella come and stand silently beside him.

"So?"

"So, I'll request the file and we can go from there."

Mo turned to her. "We? Not me DC Walsh, I'm up to me elbows already. There's no *we* in this one."

"Not even a visit to the lift company? See what they've

got to say? Or a sniff around the property development company?"

Mo narrowed his eyes as he faced Nella. He hadn't joined CID to input files - and she knew it; that wasn't his idea of real detective work. What Nella was suggesting was his – anyone's - idea of real detective work – and she knew it.

"One visit, one look at the property company and you can buy the coffees."

"Thanks Mo."

"Yeah, yeah."

He turned back to the window. "Here, see that woman over there? She's been standing looking at the station for the past forty minutes, hasn't moved from the spot. You think I should go and see if she's alright?"

Nella followed his gaze and clocked an attractive woman, early thirties, good winter coat, black suede trainers, wild hair and thought, time waster, wants attention.

"Nah," she said, "She'll come in if she needs to." She turned to him. "The world is full of crackpots Mo, people with time to waste and nowhere to go, especially at Christmas."

5

T HE PAST - *Kingstanton & Exeter, Devon, December 2008*

"RICHARD?!"

Beth hurried into the kitchen from the hallway where she was decorating the Christmas tree.

"Richard? Aren't you supposed to be keeping an eye on the boys?! I've been trying to arrange my glass baubles on the tree, and they keep interfering."

Richard held the phone in his hand. "I was about to make a call," he said.

"Who to?!" Beth held an ornate Venetian glass ball in her hand and Richard wondered why the hell she couldn't just have a pile of tinsel and a few plastic tree decorations and let the twins chuck them all over the tree.

"Sorry? I said, who to?" Beth had guessed who to and her tone was contemptuous. They had argued violently in the past week and finally Richard had told her, not asked her, what he planned to do. She was livid, but she was biding her time.

"Katherine. I was just going to..." Richard stopped mid-sentence as Beth rolled her eyes.

"It's hardly the most opportune time to ring," she said, "The boys really are making it difficult for me and I'm worried they're going to break something. These tree decorations are very precious; you know that Richard, I've been collecting them for years...

"From all over the world; yes, I know."

Beth glared at him.

"Look, why don't you stop what you're doing for five minutes, play with the twins and I'll be with you as soon as I've made my call." Richard's look was challenging. "OK? I want to catch Katherine before she goes out."

"While she's still in bed you mean," Beth said, "hung over," she added under her breath as she went back out into the hallway.

Richard let it go, but he closed the kitchen door and shut her out. He dialled Katherine's number.

KATHERINE ROLLED over in bed and looked blearily at the screen on her phone as it rang. She felt sick; her head was pounding. Recognising the number, she ignored the call and let it go to voice mail. When it stopped ringing, she lay on her back and stared up at the ceiling. She felt wretched. She had no memory of when or how she'd got home and the shame that gnawed rat-like at her insides started up again.

She dropped her legs over the side of the bed and got to her feet, walking unsteadily out of the bedroom into the

bathroom. There, she knelt over the toilet bowl and
threw up.

By the time she came to again, she was lying on the
bathroom floor, her face pressed up against the cold, slimy
toilet bowl and the acrid smell of stale urine rising up from
the tiles. Heaving herself up, Katherine stumbled back to
the bedroom, holding onto the wall for support. She made it
to the bed and looked at the room; dirty sheets, empty
bottles, ashtrays, pizza boxes and discarded grubby, crumpled clothes. She put her head in her hands.

This was a mess; her whole life was a mess. Where the
fuck had she been yesterday? It was now Sunday morning,
and she had a vague recollection of a party on Saturday
night, some of it anyway, but she was off her face and, even
though she did a fucking brilliant job at covering it, now she
couldn't clearly remember anything about the past twenty
four hours.

Katherine knew she was caught in a vicious cycle of
drinking to feel better but waking up feeling worse so
drinking all over again. Not massive amounts, she was small,
she got pissed easily on very little, but it was a mess. Her life
was a mess - more than a mess, she thought; her life was a
fucking train crash.

She reached for her phone on the unmade bed and
accessed the voice mail box. She heard her father's voice, his
concern and was almost seduced by it. Almost.

"Katherine, it's me, dad. I want to speak to you about
something. Call me, will you?"

The message ended and Katherine felt the familiar, dull
ache of disappointment. Whatever it was he wanted to talk
to her about, it wouldn't be good; it never was.

With her head still throbbing and her hands trembling,
a heavy feeling of nausea in her chest, she stood, pulled on

some jeans and a tee shirt and picking up her phone, she dialled her dad's home number. She might as well get it over with; he'd only keep ringing until she did. She waited until she heard his voice before she spoke; she always just hung up when Beth answered.

"Hey," she said, "It's me. You left a message?"

On the other end of the line Richard heard the sharp, brittle edge in her voice. He recognised it and it made him uneasy. "Hey. Are you OK?"

"Nah, not really, but who gives a fuck, eh?"

Richard heard her light up a cigarette. "I do," he said, but as soon as he did, he knew he shouldn't have.

"Really?" she said, "Who'd have guessed? No sir, I had no idea that you gave a fuck, it's certainly never looked that way to me, not from where I've been stand-...."

"- Katherine," he interrupted, "That's enough."

She was silent and he took a breath. "Sweetheart," he said, softening his voice, "Beth and I have had an idea about you coming home this Christmas."

"You and Beth? Really?" She blew smoke out of the side of her mouth. "And home? That's an odd word to use in the circumstances, isn't it? What did Beth say, she is never going to live under this roof again? Sorry, I thought home was somewhere where you lived and were always welcome, I thought..."

"Stop it!" Richard snapped. There was a silence.

Katherine said sadly; "Look Richard, please, just be honest, OK? You've had an idea about Christmas, some crackpot notion of a holiday or time together or some other crap idea because you feel guilty and you've managed to blackmail Beth into agreeing, as long as it doesn't involve her or the precious twins in any way..."

"Katherine, please stop this!" Richard snapped. "Shut up

for a few minutes and listen to what I have to say. If you don't like it then fine, but just be quiet and let me speak, will you?"

She took a long pull on her cigarette. "OK, speak."

He took another breath. He knew he didn't deserve any medals for parenting but by Christ she made it impossible sometimes.

"I want you to come down here for the whole holiday and stay; I don't want you on your own in London with nothing to do."

"Really. Why's that? Don't you trust me?"

"Oh, for God's sake Katherine, stop being so bloody childish! I'm worried about you, OK? I miss you; I'd like for us to try and spend some time together."

Katherine sat down on the floor and leant against the bed. He said he missed her. She stared at the wall. It was a start, but it was hardly a declaration of fatherly loyalty and love.

"I'm staying here," she said. "I've made my mind up."

"Well, I think you should reconsider. I made an enquiry, and you could have one of the student flats at the university; lots of them are empty all over the Christmas break. You could be near me, but still have your own space and..."

"Not get in anyone's way," Katherine finished.

"No, it's not like that Katherine..."

"Isn't it?"

"No, it's not! This time I'm trying to do what I think is best for you, not me. I want you at home, I'd like to know that I'm looking after you and it would certainly be a hell of a lot cheaper for me, but I don't think that will help you in any way. You and Beth can't stand the sight of each other, and you have nothing in common with your brothers..."

"Half-brothers"

"Half-brothers then…"

"Which is hardly surprising since they are seven and I'm nineteen."

"Look." Richard sighed heavily and Katherine heard his patience ebbing away.

"I'm trying to do something nice here."

"For a change."

"Alright! For a change, yes! But think about it Katherine, please."

Katherine dropped her cigarette into a mug and heard the damp fizzle as it went out in a pool of discarded wine. She looked down at her bare feet, dirty from the grubby floors in the flat and she flicked a dust ball with the tip of her toe. She didn't want to be alone, but she couldn't admit that.

"Where is this flat? In town or on campus?"

"It's in town, by the station." Richard heard a slight change in her voice. He forged ahead. "It's not luxury, but it would be your own space, like you have now, and I'll be in Exeter every day, on Campus working on my research project…" He knew he sounded eager, but for the past few days he'd thought of nothing but the dismal scene at the train station last weekend and the look of utter disappointment on his daughter's face. He was sick of failing her. "You'd be quite self-contained, and we could spend time together, have lunch most days and…"

"Dad…"

That was a good sign; it was a good sign when she called him Dad.

"I'll think about it," she said.

"I'll need to let the uni know that we'd like the flat…"

"I'll think about it, OK?"

Through the kitchen door Richard could hear the sound

of Beth shouting at the twins. "OK," he said. "I'll call you in a day or so when you've had time to consider."

Katherine heard the tension in his voice, the sound of Beth calling him in the distance.

"Yeah, sure." She said, and without waiting for him to reply, she rang off.

IT WAS SUNDAY, the day for Lydia's second lesson of the week and she stood outside number fifty-two and waited - as usual - while the teenage face peered at her from the small window above. Only today it was raining hard, and Lydia was cross at having to stand under her dripping umbrella while big splodges of water hit her shoulder and wet her coat.

In frustration, she kicked at a piece of tile on the step that was slightly wobbly, the only thing out of place in the front garden. She liked Mr Hirsch's house, it was neat and tidy, unlike her own, which was scattered with debris; music sheets, old instruments, clothes, discarded plates, and drinks half finished. Her parents were musicians, and they didn't ever seem to notice anything other than the pieces they were practising for performance. Lydia eased the tip of her shoe under the edge of the tile and wiggled it a bit. The rest of the front of the house was immaculate and as the tile came loose and shifted, Lydia felt a moment of panic.

The door abruptly opened.

"Don't do that. You'll ruin our house." The girl said.

"S'only a step," Lydia answered defiantly.

"Well, it's our step." The girl was angry, and Lydia was embarrassed. "You'd better come in and wait here."

Lydia fumbled with her umbrella.

"Leave it open," the girl ordered. "It can dry here on the porch."

Lydia left the umbrella outside by the front door and went into hall. She was damp and her shoes were wet. The girl pointed to a straight-backed chair in the hall. "Sit there, if you can be trusted." She waited until Lydia had sat then she said, "I'll tell father that you're here."

Lydia swung her legs defiantly and kicked the heels of her shoes against the chair leg. She watched the girl knock softly on the door of the room at the back and listened to the sudden hush of voices inside the room. The girl spoke quickly through a crack in the door then throwing a warning glare at Lydia, she left the hall and went back upstairs. A few minutes later the door of the room at the back opened and Mr Hirsch came out.

"Hello Lydia, why don't you come in? I have a young musician with me, an ex-student of mine. We are going over one of his pieces for performance. Come and listen, it'll be instructive for you."

Lydia stood, and swinging her violin and her music case boldly, just in case the face from upstairs was watching her, she followed Mr Hirsch into the back room. At the music stand stood a tall, dark, young man, violin held loosely in his hand. He was older than Lydia and she thought he must be almost grown up. His features were delicate, his cheekbones were set high on his face and his nose was thin with narrow nostrils. His hair was dark, slicked back with styling clay and he wore a slight beard that framed his chin. Lydia thought he was the most beautiful young man she had ever seen.

She stared at him, but he didn't say hello. He was marking up his music score with a pencil and seemed completely oblivious to her presence. Mr Hirsch nodded at a chair and Lydia sat.

"Lydia, this is Gabriel. Gabriel has just won a degree place at the Royal School of Music. He's been awarded a scholarship." Mr Hirsch smiled warmly as Gabriel glanced up.

"Gabriel, this is Lydia. She will be as good as you one day; she is a prodigious violinist and like you, she has a real connection with the music."

Lydia loved it when Mr Hirsch praised her; she felt special, chosen. Her parents rarely mentioned her talent; it was something they believed she had to work on, tirelessly.

"Let's take it from the third movement," Mr Hirsch said to Gabriel, "This time, I think you could place just a tiny bit more emphasis on lentando in the third bar to the eighth bar." He stood, leaning back against the table and waited.

Lydia watched the boy lift the violin, tuck it under his chin and take a breath. Then he began to play.

Lydia held her breath and sat completely still. When the piece was over, even at eleven years old she recognised that she had heard something wonderful. She glanced at Mr Hirsch, wanting to share her approval, but he was looking at the boy and smiling. He seemed to have forgotten that she was even there.

"That was very good," Mr Hirsch said, after a few moments. "I think the lentando works, don't you? It changes the mood, makes it far more moving."

"You're right," Gabriel said, "It felt a lot better than the way I had been playing it. Thank you." He smiled back at Mr Hirsch and Lydia, sitting quietly on the chair in the corner felt suddenly irrelevant, as if she had ceased to exist.

"I should go," Gabriel said. He began to put his music away and Mr Hirsch watched him keenly. The fine features were focused as he carefully laid the violin into its case. "I'm sorry that I've overrun into your lesson."

Mr Hirsch seemed to startle. "Oh yes, of course, my lesson." He turned to Lydia. "Would you like to start setting up Lydia? I'll see Gabriel out."

Lydia nodded and stood. Gabriel had pulled on a thin denim jacket and Mr Hirsch touched the sleeve of it. "You surely aren't going to walk home in just that, are you? It's pouring out. You should have something warm on."

Gabriel shrugged and they went out into the hallway. Lydia stretched her neck to follow them with her gaze.

"You should take my scarf," she heard Mr Hirsch say. "Put it over your head to keep you dry. You don't want to run the risk of coming down with something before the performance."

"No, honestly, I..."

"I insist," Mr Hirsch said. Lydia stepped forward a pace so that she could see them. "It's right here on the coat stand..." He lifted a couple of coats. "Or, it *was* right here," he said. He rifled through all the coats hanging up. "I'm sure I put it here..." he murmured, more to himself than to the boy. He stopped looking and shrugged. "Oh well..." he said.

Lydia took another step forward so that she had a better view.

"You'll have to do your collar up," Mr Hirsch said, and, as he did so, he reached out and pulled the lapels of Gabriel's jacket close together. He held them there, under Gabriel's chin for a few moments then he abruptly dropped them and stepped back.

"Good luck," he said, "For the performance tomorrow. You'll let me know, won't you?"

Gabriel nodded. "I will." he said. He opened the front door.

"Goodbye Mr Hirsch."

There was a silence and a shuffle and Lydia wished she could see the front door, but she couldn't; it would mean moving to the open doorway to spy. She daren't risk it.

"Goodbye," Mr Hirsch said. Lydia looked at the clock on top of the piano. She put her violin up to her chin and waited. They were already five minutes into her lesson and Mr Hirsch would want to get started right away.

But she was wrong. She stood like that for what seemed to her like ages and by the time that Mr Hirsch came back into the room that five minutes had expanded to ten.

CI Lewin sat in the office at his desk, hanging on the end of the phone and gestured to his DS through the glass that he was busy and would be a few minutes. His DS had a file in his hand and waited. A voice came back on the line and Lewin said,

"Do you know how much longer I have to hold? It's just that I've got someone waiting for me...." He listened to the reply. "OK, I realise that, but all I want to do is make sure that the district nurse goes over today. Can't I leave that message with you without having to speak to the doctor?"

He listened again. Procedure, he thought, can't live with it; can't live without it. He sighed heavily. "No, no of course not, yes, I understand, yes, I'll wait..."

He put his hand over the mouthpiece and called to the DS waiting outside his office, gesturing for him to come in, but just as he did someone came back on the line.

"Sir? I've got..."

Lewin cut him off and waved him out abruptly of the

room again. He waited until the DS had closed the door and then said:

"Yes, hello Doctor Pearson, I wanted to make sure that one of the district nurses will be over to see my wife this afternoon? It's just that I won't be able to get home at lunch and when I left her this morning, she was a little bit distressed." A little bit distressed was an understatement; she'd been in a state of confused high anxiety, and he'd found her impossible to cope with, but Lewin couldn't say that. He was a proud man and he hated to admit any weakness. He winced as a heavy pain momentarily constricted his mid chest and rubbed at his diaphragm. He belched quietly, holding the phone away from him.

"Oh, yes, erm sorry... Well, she was a bit weepy and didn't want me to go. Yes, she's more confused than when we saw you last month. I've turned everything off, you know, the gas and electricity and such like, but, well, I'd be grateful if someone could check on her.... Yes, that's what the home care team advised, no... quite right, I wouldn't want to take that chance doctor... not after the fire in the kitchen in February. No, I've left her sandwiches and cakes and a thermos of tea..." he belched again into his hand.

"Thank you, I'd be grateful. Yes, I think the number of the station is on file. Just ask for me." He stood up and motioned to his DS again to come in once more. "Thank you, Dr Pearson. Bye." He hung up and said, "Something come up?"

"Yes sir, the team down by the estuary, it's quite a way from the Halston Estate, but we've found a shoe..."

CI Lewin sat down. The pain came again, and an image of Abbey Salter came into his mind; she was smiling. "Have you got positive identification?"

"We're working on it, but it's a size three trainer with flashing lights."

Lewin left out a sigh. "Right," he said, "Let's get down there." He took his jacket off the back of the chair and pulled it on. He was exhausted; Barbara had been up for much of the night wandering round the house and for a moment the fatigue came up and slapped him in the face. He sighed again.

"Anything else turn up?"

"No," the DS said, "Not yet..." he shrugged, "But it's been pissing down all morning and..."

They both knew the end of the sentence. Abbey had been missing for three days.

"Come on." Lewin led the way out of the office. "Sandra," he called, "Radio if there are any urgent calls for me, will you?"

Sandra was a DS who'd worked with Lewin for years. She was the only one at the station, apart from the Chief Super, who knew about Lewin's wife. She nodded. They left the station and, as Lewin settled into the front seat, he popped a couple of Rennies into his mouth and chewed dryly and silently.

DOWN BY THE ESTUARY, the DS parked, and Lewin climbed out of the car. Forensics had already sealed off the area around where the shoe had been found and the twenty-five men on the search had been increased to forty. The place was awash with officers, the press had already got hold of it and there were cars parked up on the verge all along the road.

"Clear this place now, will you?" CI Lewin said to the officer in charge. "I want all those cars ticketed if they're not gone in the next ten minutes. Slap one on the first and the rest will come running. It's like a fucking circus down here."

He went across to the taped off area where the trainer had been found. "What's going on?"

Sam Finch, crime scene investigating officer, had been digging and he stood straight. "We need to get as much done as we can while the weather holds off. Apart from the shoe we've found some hair fibres on the bramble, so I'm hopeful..."

"Great, thanks." Lewin turned and looked across the ground down to the estuary, assessing the area. "Have we covered right down to the water? Isn't there a turning circle at the end of the lane there?"

"Yes, we've got a team of officers down there now sir and the underwater search team are on their way. The turning circle's got a bit of reputation, used for things other than turning the car round."

"I don't care what the hell it's used for Crowley, I want it checked. Understood?"

"Sir."

"We've checked that boat house have we?"

"On it now sir."

"Good. Let's take a drive down there, shall we?"

"Sir."

Lewin headed to the car. He was guessing that if they'd found a shoe here then she was carried across the fields down to the water; alive or dead. It was unlikely that she'd be anywhere in between, especially not if she was already dead. He felt a burning in his windpipe and rubbed at his chest.

"You alright sir?"

"Yeah; heartburn." He belched quietly into his hand. "Whatever I eat it feels as if I'm digesting a fucking donkey."

He opened the car door and climbed in. He took a bottle of *Gaviscon* out of his pocket, unscrewed the cap and took a large swig.

"Cheers," he said. The DS nodded, shoved the car into gear and they drove off, past an officer putting tickets on press cars, down towards the water.

An hour later Lewin stood with Sam Finch as the forensics team worked inside the taped off the area around the boathouse. It was a small wooden building, stuck out on the rocks with a sloping jetty that led down into the mud.

"My guess is that she was held here, and by the looks of things, for at least three hours," Finch said, "It's covered, so that's good news for us, and we should know exactly how long for by the end of the day."

Lewin saw that small, elfin smiling face and shivered. "What is there?"

"We've got a small piece of blue fabric that looks as if it's been torn on the door latch and it matches the description of her jacket, ropes there, possibly used to tie her up, plus hair fibres and some blood."

Lewin thought of his wife and her anxiety this morning. How odd it was that in the midst of her confusion she seemed to understand more acutely than anyone else the fragility of life. One minute a bored child is sent out for milk to keep her busy and the next...

Lewin said, "How dry is it in there?"

"Dry enough," Finch replied.

Lewin nodded and walked away. He scrambled down onto the rocks and made his way onto the sandy bank of the estuary. From there he looked up at the boathouse from the water. She could have been removed by boat, he thought, taken out to sea and dumped. It was easy to do, moor a boat on one of those buoys when the tide was in. He put his hand up to his eyes and looked out at the horizon. At this point, just before the estuary opened up into its mouth and the sea, it would take about an hour to get right out into the water. He waved at DS Crowley, who scrambled down onto the sand beside him.

"Sir?"

"Is there any way a boat would be seen leaving or entering the estuary here?"

"Depends on the size sir. All big boats coming in have to report to the coast guard and if they don't, they show up on the radar."

"What about small boats, a rowboat or a dinghy with an outboard motor?"

"Come and go as they like that size boat sir. Just looks like a wave on the radar."

DS Crowley looked at the boat house and then at the buoy in the water.

"Could she have been washed out with the tide?" Lewin asked.

"It's a possibility, especially in this rain. I'll get on to the divers," he said, "Get a team out there and we'll start a search round the coastal paths."

"Good. Something may have washed up on the rocks if she was taken out to sea." Lewin stared up at the boulders around the boat house.

"What's that?" He suddenly said, catching sight of something just below the boat house, caught on the rock.

Crowley followed his gaze then waved up at the officers on the road. "Get Finch!" he shouted. He looked at Lewin. "Looks like somebody has been careless..." he said, "Very careless indeed."

6

P RESENT DAY - *London*
   Tuesday – p.m.

"WE ALL MAKE MISTAKES NICK, that's a given..." The Deputy Leader shrugged and glanced out of the window in reflective mood.

Nick nodded; he'd spent the last few minutes locked in eye-to-eye contact with the woman and was relieved that she'd looked away. Awkward was the least of it.

"But sleaze we leave to the other side. You're in the running - in the front running - for a senior position in the shadow cabinet reshuffle and whilst we were able to hush this up pronto, that's not something we can do when you're in the full media glare. We're lucky that no-one gives a fuck about you..." she paused. "Yet," she added. "When things change, we won't be as lucky if anything untoward happens again, I can guarantee that."

She looked at him for some time, her gaze unswerving. He felt his right eye twitch slightly from the glare.

"I hope to God nothing like this ever happens again," Nick said, trying a half smile. It was not returned. "I'm solid, you know that. I've got an unblemished record with the party, I..."

She held her hands up to silence him. "You don't need to remind me of your virtues. Think of this as a stern warning, not a dressing down. I just want you to remember that bright futures are not guaranteed, they're hard earned. You've got a very bright future. I think you can join the dots."

She tapped her pen on the desk. The meeting was over, and Nick stood. They shook hands; Nick left the office and made his way along the corridor. As he went, he mulled over his position. He'd never been in politics for the glory; he wasn't interested in all the crap that came with the job, but he wasn't stupid, he knew that to make real change needed authority, a position of power. And he *was* interested in change, in making a difference. Politics was a corruptible and, at times, corrupted business, but his mother had told him grudgingly, that whilst she didn't admire the arena, she was proud he was up for the fight. But was he? Was he still up for the fight? His life since he'd entered politics had been all about the work. He liked looking after his constituents, he loved policy making, changing lives. He must be the only MP he knew who genuinely enjoyed his clinics, meeting people, solving problems... well, the ones he could do something about that is. Nick lived to work and that was fine - it was all he had. Only today he felt that something had shifted, something small, and internal, but something significant. What if there really was more to it than just

work? What if being married was more than just a conve-
nience and the odd night together when they were in the
right place, at the right time, in the right frame of mind?

He still felt the same about the job, of course he did - he
was sincere back there and you don't lose your principles
with a quick fuck – not even a fuck really. But what if finding
Kate meant more than just re-kindling an old flame? What if
the taste of her mouth, her skin, the feel of her thighs
wrapped round him were things he couldn't forget? What
would he risk losing to have more of Kate? Was it worth it?
Perhaps just even considering the idea gave it weight.

His thinking was cut short as he was stopped by a couple
of colleagues, and they chatted for a few moments. They
were backing one of his amendments to the homeless bill
and wanted to let him know. There was a joke about the
footage on *Twitter*, but he fielded it and was surprised not to
detect any judgement on their part; it was as if he'd
garnered sympathy, not lost it. As he moved away, he
realised that this is what came with rumours of a cabinet
post, influence. It was a game-changer.

Nick hurried along to his office, grabbed his coat and left
a hastily scrawled post-it note for his assistant. He would be
out for a couple of hours. There was only one way to find
out if Kate could be part of his future and not just part of his
past. It wasn't exactly prudent, but it *was* necessary.

AT SIX, Kate jumped off the bus on Westminster Bridge
Road, hurrying towards Lower Marsh and scanning the
road for Annie's figure. She had her phone in her hand, and
she kept glancing down at the screen, hoping for some

response from Annie, but there was nothing. She had sent a text an hour ago to warn her daughter that she'd be late to collect her at the bus stop, but the text hadn't been delivered - which was odd - then she had called Annie and the call went straight to voice mail – which was even odder. Now, five texts and two more calls later, also unanswered, Kate had begun to panic. Annie always waited at the bus stop if Kate was going to be late; the stop had a Perspex shelter, it was well lit and safe. They had an agreement; it was the best thing to do; Kate knew where Annie was, and Annie knew that Kate would come to the stop. *They had an agreement.*

Darting across the road, Kate dodged a car and dashed forward to miss a cyclist. He shouted over his shoulder that she was a fucking idiot, but she didn't shout back. The stop was deserted; she *was* a fucking idiot; why had she considered going to the police? She hadn't even gone in, wasted all that time and now Annie had vanished. Kate stood, wringing her hands, the panic rising hard and fast in her chest. She rang Hannah – again.

"We haven't heard anything yet Kate," Hannah said. "She got off the bus with Matilda as usual, but Mattie came straight home. I'm sorry Kate; I'll call if we hear from her. Try not to worry."

Kate rang off and stood staring up at the street. Try not to worry? Her face crumpled for a moment, and she put her hands up over it. Annie was a good kid, and she knew that Kate would come to the bus stop and that she'd be worried if Annie wasn't there. Annie would never just walk off, never break their agreement.

Kate took a couple of deep breaths and dropped her hands down. She was catastrophizing; she had to stop. Go to the office, she thought, Annie might have thought she was still at work. Seeing a break in the traffic, Kate ran back across the road and into lower Marsh towards her office. The dampness in the air had begun to freeze as night drew in and Kate's hot breath formed dense clouds that hung in front of her face.

Halfway up lower Marsh, still running, she heard her name.

"Kate?! Hey?! KATE?!"

She stopped and spun round. Kerrie, the Australian wait staff from the café stood in the road in her shirt sleeves and an apron.

"Kate?! You looking for Annie?! She's here in the café?" Kerrie motioned towards the door where Annie stood waving at Kate.

"Mum?!"

Kate stood for a moment looking at Kerrie, her hands on her hips, breathing hard. Her heart thumped against her ribs, and she had a pain in her side. Dragging the sleeve of her coat across her damp face, she glanced at Annie in the doorway and slowly began to walk back towards the café.

"God, its bloody freezing out here!" Kerrie called out, "The temperature has really dropped!" She rubbed her hands to keep them warm as she waited for Kate. "I'm so glad Annie spotted you. She's been waiting for you since five."

Kate nodded.

"Come on in. I'll get you a coffee."

Kate went past Annie into the café and waited by the table with Annie's things on. As Annie came in to join her, she turned and said sharply,

"What the hell do you think you're playing at?!"

Annie blinked and flushed. "What do you mean? I was at the bus stop, and it was freezing, and Kerrie walked past me and saw me and suggested that I came in here to wait in the warm, so..."

"So, you decided that rather than wait at the bus stop, as we agreed, as you always have, you would do exactly as you liked and bugger the consequences!" Kate's voice rose and the girl on the next table glanced over. "I've been worried sick Annie! What on earth were you thinking?! We agreed, we agreed that you wait at the bus stop if I am ever late to meet you, didn't we?"

Annie was staring down at her shoes. "Didn't we?!" Kate snapped.

"Yes, but..."

"Yes, but what?! I'm assuming now that your phone has run out of battery?! Even more reason to be where we agreed you'd be, isn't it? I've rung you three times and sent six texts. Christ Annie! I had no idea what might have happened to you, I..." Kate felt her voice tremble and stopped short. She was way out of kilter; furious and relieved and, although she couldn't recognise it, jealous. She swallowed hard.

"I was worried," she said again, more calmly, "Surely you can see that?"

Annie nodded, still staring at the ground. Kate felt a movement to the right and Kerrie stepped forward with a mug of coffee.

"Here," she said, "Thought you might need this? And look, don't be too hard on the kid, I mean, it was my suggestion, right Annie?"

Annie nodded.

"She looked pretty cold and miserable out there, so I reckoned she'd be better off in the warmth."

"I see." Kate glanced from Kerrie to Annie and saw a brief look pass between them. What was this? Collusion?

She had the distinct feeling that she was on the outside and the idea of that was so suddenly and acutely painful that all her feelings compounded into spite. "Well, I don't think what is or isn't good for Annie is any of your business."

Kerrie looked suddenly embarrassed but said nothing and put the mug down on the table.

Kate went on; "Actually, can I have it as a takeaway? And I need to pay for it as well as Annie's drinks."

"Oh no, that's OK, it's on the house and as for Annie..."

"No, it isn't on the house. Not this time," Kate interrupted. Her voice was curt. "And as for Annie, there'll be no more free drinks. I'll pay for everything we've had, thank you."

Kerrie took a step back, still holding the coffee. She looked momentarily puzzled and glanced at Annie who kept her head down. She shrugged in a way that said, weird, and Kate's hackles rose further. She rummaged quickly in her bag for her purse and followed Kerrie to the counter.

"In fact, I'll have one of your loyalty cards as well, with ten pounds on it, and then I won't worry about the number of free coffees that Annie is given - she can pay for her own." Kate handed Kerrie her debit card and took the takeaway coffee in return.

Kerrie rang up the coffees and tapped the card on the machine. She waited for a moment then said; "Sorry, the card's not authorised."

"What?!"

"Your card's been declined." Kerrie had assumed that slightly bored air that communicated deep offense and Kate felt like a heel. "I'll try the other machine." Kerrie disappeared for a few moments with Kate's card then reappeared with another card reader. She entered the details. "Nope.

Declined," she said. "It's probably our machine; it's been dodgy for a couple of days now."

"Shit," Kate pulled out another card. "Here, this one should work."

"We don't take credit cards."

"Oh, right...I..." Kate opened her purse, but she rarely carried cash – too easy to spend – so she started scratching around in the bottom of her bag for any loose change. Annie stepped forward and handed over a tenner.

Kate stared at her.

"Thanks," Kerrie said. "Do you mind if I give Annie my staff discount."

"Well...I..."

"It's my money mum." Annie looked at Kerrie. "Thanks, I'll take whatever discount you can give me." She smiled briefly at Kerrie then turned and walked away from Kate to the table to pack up her things while Kerrie recalculated the price and found Annie some change. Ready to go, Annie came back, took the coins and smiled again at Kerrie. "Thanks, it *was* warmer in here than out there at the bus stop." She turned and walked towards the door and, without a glance or a word to Kate; she went outside into the cold to wait.

The walk home was silent. Now that she had calmed down Kate felt stupid; she felt embarrassed. She knew that she had overreacted, it was hardly surprising after the past twenty-four hours, but she also knew that it was fear that had driven her behaviour; fear of losing Annie, both physically and emotionally. Annie was all Kate had and, regardless of how irrational it was, the feeling of jealousy that her daughter's friendship with Kerrie provoked, was painful and all too real.

Ten minutes from home, unable to stand the

atmosphere any longer, Kate said; "How was last night at Matilda's?"

Annie shrugged but didn't answer.

"Can I take one of your bags? You've got loads to carry."

Annie handed her sports bag over, still silent. Kate took it and said,

"Annie look, I'm sorry if you think..."

"No, you're not." Annie interrupted. "A sentence that begins with 'I'm sorry if you think' isn't about being sorry." She stopped and turned to Kate. Her face was flushed, and her eyes glittered with unshed tears. "You embarrassed me mum and you didn't need to do that. I know you were cross, and I'm sorry that I wasn't where I should have been, but you were mean to Kerrie and that wasn't right." Annie swallowed and Kate saw the effort it took to keep her sob down.

Kate took a deep breath. "You're right," she said, "I didn't behave very well."

"No, you didn't." Annie stared at her mother and for a moment Kate wondered where she had seen that earnest look before. Annie did everything with such conviction, such goodness. "I think you should apologise," Annie said.

Kate took another deep breath. "Okay..." A tiny spark of jealousy ignited, and Kate struggled to extinguish it. "Do you have Kerrie's number?"

"No. Call the café, they'll have it."

"Right." They stood there, face to face on the pavement and Kate just wanted to scoop her daughter into a hug, feel the comfort of her physical presence. "I'll send a text."

Annie turned away and began to walk. Kate started off behind her. "But Annie?"

Annie glanced over her shoulder. "Yeah?"

Kate took Annie's free hand and held it, stopping her

again for a moment. Annie squeezed Kate fingers. "I'm sorry too mum, I didn't mean to worry you."

"I know." Kate brushed a lock of hair off Annie's face; it sprang right back into place and Kate knew every strand as if it were her own. They turned and carried on the journey home, still not talking, but the silence was kinder now, more understanding.

At the entrance to the mansion block, Kate put down the sports kit she was carrying and opened the main door, letting Annie go ahead. She dug in the front pocket of her bag for her new flat key, not yet on a key ring, but her fingers were stiff with cold, and she couldn't locate it so she bent her head into the bag to see if she could spot it. When she glanced up, she saw a dark figure and started so violently that she let out a scream. She spun round.

"My God, you gave me such a fright!" Kate took a wary step back, away from the man. "What the f..." she stopped just in time, conscious of Annie inside the lobby and hesitated; collected herself. "What the hell are you doing here?!" she demanded.

"I came to apologise, about the fiasco, last night, this morning. All of it. I'm sorry."

Kate looked at him then glanced briefly inside the entrance lobby. She pulled the door a couple of inches. "Please," she said quietly, "Just go away. I don't want anything to do with you. I thought I made that clear."

All the way to the flat Nick had been rehearsing mentally what he would say, how he would explain to her how he felt, what she might say in reply, but now he stood there semi-mute; useless.

"You did, but... well, I feel..."

"Mum?" Annie opened the door and looked out. "Are you OK?"

Nick was about to say that he felt different, that he felt like this was something that he should pursue, that he was deeply regretful that he hadn't been completely truthful.

"Mum?!" He looked at Kate. "You have a daughter?!" He then looked at Annie and the likeness was unmistakable. She had the same features only magnified; the same wild hair, but more unruly and the same serious eyes, but more intensely brown; the colour of dark sherry held up to the light.

"Yes, I have a daughter," Kate said sharply, "And?"

"And you lied." Nick held her eye for a moment, but embarrassed, Kate glanced away.

"No, I didn't lie. You didn't ask me." She stopped short. "The difference is," she said quietly, turning towards him so that Annie couldn't hear. "The difference is that I wasn't deceiving anyone."

"Well nor am I. Emma, my wife, knows about you and how I feel..."

"Whoa, hang on a minute!" Kate suddenly snapped. "How you feel? Nick - that is your name - right?"

Nick stared at her.

"Nick, there is nothing between us and how you feel is nothing to do with me. Please, just go away, will you?!" Kate moved away from him towards the door, but he reached out and put his hand on her arm. She snatched it away.

"Look, I really don't know what you're doing here! I come home and you sneak up on me, giving me the fright of my life and now you're harassing me... Please..." She faced him square on. "Just fuck off!"

"Mum?!" Annie, who had been watching Kate, stepped forward. "Mum, stop! What's going on?!"

"Nothing!" Kate hustled Annie back towards the entrance. "This man, Nick, is just going."

Annie glanced back at the man. He caught her eye and half smiled. Inside the lobby, Kate slammed the door behind them and started towards the staircase, but Annie continued to look at Nick though the glass panels on either side of the main door.

"Mum?! He's still out there! What's going on?!"

Kate stopped. She caught Annie's question, but it was her own voice she heard, the same fourteen-year-old voice, tremulous with anxiety, raw with embarrassment and, as she closed her eyes, Kate saw herself, collecting her mother from the bus stop where she'd sat for the whole day in her nightdress and an old overcoat, cold and wet, speaking to the air.

"Annie..." Kate turned around and looked at her daughter. Tall and thin, spindly legs in heavy, black boots, saved from geekiness by her quirky beauty. Her face was dark with concern and Kate realised that she needed to explain.

She said, "Nick and I had a bit of a fling. I think he's more into me than I am to him, but it's really complicated, OK?"

Annie stared at Kate. "You had a fling?"

"Yes, and I'm really embarrassed about it, and like I said, it's complicated, so can we just drop it and get on with our night?"

She started again for the stairs and heard Annie trudge up behind her.

"A fling," Annie said as they got to their floor. Kate waited, but nothing else was forthcoming. She had located the new key and opened the front door, letting Annie go in first, but Annie stopped and turned, just inside the door.

"You know what mum; I think you have a real problem," she said. "He, Nick, he looked OK...actually, he looked nice, and he looked as if he liked you, really liked you and you were pretty horrible to him." Annie shook her head and turned, walking towards her bedroom. She stopped again as she got to the door of it and said, "You know what else? After tonight, I just don't think you're a very good person." She went into her room and slammed the door behind her.

Kate leant against the door frame and put her head in her hands.

7

P
RESENT DAY - *London*
Tuesday – p.m.

NICK'S WIFE Emma was back in England and, wheeling her *Away* cabin case behind her, she headed towards the meeting point for the car. As she walked, the managing partner she'd flown with was talking about the service in business class, but she wasn't really listening to him; she was thinking about the meeting they'd had yesterday or was it earlier that day, New York time? It didn't really matter when it was, she thought, what mattered was what was said. Emma caught a glimpse of her reflection in the big plate glass walls as they left terminal five and saw just how well she looked, in her suit and her long, camel cashmere coat. She was about to be made partner, a salaried partner. She was about to make it, to really make it and it was about fucking time, she thought.

Emma had texted her sister from JFK – she shared

everything with Caro - but she hadn't told Nick and she didn't know if she would tell him. If they weren't going to stay together then maybe it was better not to; she could hold the promotion off until after they were divorced. Why hand over more than she had to? She was a lawyer, and everything was a process after all.

Down the escalator and onto the concourse towards the collection point, the partner rumbled on, and Emma smiled politely, her mind somewhere else completely. They found the car, eased themselves into the back of it and with luggage stowed, the driver headed out onto the M25 towards central London. The comfort of it gave Emma a thrill. No looking for taxis or waiting for a train as she used to when she was on the bottom rung. None of that crap anymore.

Settling into the leather, Emma took the bottle of water from the side pocket of her door and opened it. She sipped as the managing partner said, "Welcome aboard. Life gets a little bit easier from here on in, or at least life outside the office does!"

Emma laughed respectfully.

"You know, having such a close connection to the next government in waiting is going to be a real boon for us Emma. When Nick's position as shadow chancellor is announced I guarantee that you'll be making the firm a considerable amount of money."

Emma turned to him. "How did you...?"

The managing partner smiled. "We have many friends in many places, a firm our size Emma, and we keep our ears to the ground."

You talk a lot of platitudes Emma thought, imagining stepping on this particular ear, hard. She felt a sudden burst of anger. Emma was usually lightning-quick on the up-take, but she had missed the point here; it had gone right over her head – like the interminable fucking glass ceiling, she thought.

"I expect he'll be delighted, your husband."

"Yes," she replied flatly, "he will." She turned to stare out of the window as West Drayton rolled past in a suburban blur of grey tile and brick. She had already moved beyond divorce, that wasn't going to happen, not now, and she had begun to think about the conversation she'd had with Nick last night, or was it earlier that day? What did Nick want, she wondered, sipping and staring blankly at the dreary outskirts of London? What was it that would really convince him to stay? Whatever it was she needed to deliver it otherwise... She felt the warm cream leather under her fingers... Otherwise just wasn't an option.

It was late by the time that Kate finally dialled the number she'd got from the café for Kerrie. She was hoping that the call would go straight to voicemail and then she could leave an apologetic message and be done with it, but the call was answered on the second ring.

"Hi Kerrie, its Kate Ross, Annie's mum."

The reception was cool; no more than Kate expected.

"Look, I was in a flap today, I'd had a rotten day, I got myself in a state about Annie and I took it out on you. I'm sorry, I was rude to you, and I shouldn't have been."

There was a hesitation on the end of the line and Kate wondered if Kerrie had hung up.

"Kerrie, are you still there?"

"Yes, I'm here. Listen, it's cool, about today, really, it's fine. I get it, you were stressed."

"Yes, well, thanks."

"Sure."

Kate felt she should say something more but was at a loss to know what. There was a brief silence then Kerrie said,

"Look, I was gonna let Annie handle it, but I'm guessing after today that I should really talk to you..."

Kate felt herself bristle.

"It's just that I was telling Annie about a lecture I'm going to at Imperial college, its free and she said she'd like to come, with that loopy mate of hers, what's her name?"

"Matilda,"

"Yeah, Matilda. It's on astrophysics."

"Right. I see."

"I've got a ticket, but I can get a couple more."

"Well, that's really nice of you but it's a school night and she doesn't usually go out late in the week..."

"It's six til seven, on Friday."

"Right." After years of therapy, Kate could recognise the feelings even if she couldn't compartmentalise them. She was being left out and that was right; it was natural, but she felt it.

"If you wanna come I could get three more tickets?" Kerrie said.

Kate took a breath. That was a nice gesture; it was kind. The whole thing was a nice gesture, she reasoned, Annie had asked to go along to a lecture that she was interested in, and Kerrie had agreed. Maybe Annie was right; maybe Kate didn't give enough people the benefit of the doubt.

"That's a nice offer," Kate said, "but it's not my thing; I wouldn't understand a word of it."

"OK. I'll get two more tickets then, but if you change your mind let me know?"

"I will...and thanks, you know for understanding about today."

"Cool."

Kerrie rang off and Kate sat for a moment. Then she heard Annie's steps in the hall and called out, "I just rang Kerrie, and she asked about the lecture at Imperial. I said you'd love to go. That's right, isn't it?"

Annie appeared a few moments later, grinning ecstatically and Kate told herself that there was really nothing to be afraid of.

EMMA HAD BOUGHT a chilled bottle of champagne from *Wine World* on St John's Hill and some takeaway nibbles from *The Good Earth,* as well as eggs and smoked salmon for Saturday morning breakfast and she tucked them all away in the fridge in the kitchen while she showered in anticipation of Nick's arrival home. She had texted him to make sure that there wasn't a vote in the house this evening and now, as she shaved her legs and armpits, she thought about how she would do this; what she would say and what would be the most persuasive argument for staying together. She had to be careful; she needed to show him the future he wanted without making specific promises. But then Emma was an arch negotiator; she had been talking her way to what she wanted since she was five years old and had realised that her father held all the power in the family.

An hour later, in a silk shirt dress easy to slip off if the mood took them – and bare feet, she sat in the sitting room, the gas flame effect fire lit, her legs tucked up under her, reading some papers, but not reading at all. She was like a leopard waiting to pounce. She heard his key in the lock, called out to him and smiled, tilting her face so that she was looking up at him as he came into the sitting room – slightly submissive, a powerful ploy.

"How was your day?"

"OK. Considering the shit involved." Nick remained just inside the room. He knew Emma's pose on the sofa; she'd used it before; she looked almost tame - almost.

"I'm assuming it was all sorted by the powers that be. From my end it was a storm in a teacup. Twitter took the video down immediately and no-one seemed to notice."

"That's fine then." He walked back into the hall and took his shoes and jacket off; only it wasn't fine – it was terrible – he felt terrible. He'd stood where he was for a few moments, too exhausted to go back into the sitting room but as he began to climb the stairs Emma came into the hall.

"Nick? Can we talk? I want to apologise for this morning. I want to try and work things out."

Nick's shoulders sagged as he felt the weight of that comment. He sat down on the stairs and put his head in his hands. When he'd been with Kate last night, when he'd touched her and kissed her, he felt alive, for the first time in years, he felt truly alive. Not going through the motions, doing what he thought he should do, but light and free and unburdened. He pulsed with life every moment he was with her. But she didn't want him, she'd made that absolutely clear and the sight of her daughter, that tall, gangly teenage version of Kate filled him with such sadness that he could barely speak. Of course she didn't want him; she already had everything that she needed or could ever want. And he had a job, a new job, a chance to change things. But that was all he had.

He took his hands away and said, "What can you

possibly say Emma that would make a difference to our marriage now?"

Emma took a step towards him. "We should start a family," she said, "I want to have a baby."

Nick stared at her. He was incredulous. "That's..."

"Ridiculous?" She took another step and sat down on the stairs below him. "Is it? I'm thirty-six Nick. The job isn't everything..."

"Ha." Nick shook his head. "Emma, stop this, please. The job *is* everything, of course it's everything; it's all you've ever wanted..."

"Yes! You're right, up until today that is. Nick, I know that I nearly lost you last night. You met someone and you're prepared to give all this up..." She glanced around at the spacious hall, "Our life, the things we've been through together, our home... all of it and..."

She swallowed hard, surprised at the strength of her emotion. "I don't want to lose our life Nick; I want to cement it and I think we can do that with a baby." She reached up for his hand.

Nick held Emma's neat, square fingers and looked down at her. Her face was flushed, and her eyes glittered with the hint of tears.

"I bought some champagne," she said softly. "I thought we could drink to a new beginning."

He shrugged. He wasn't convinced by her, but he was too exhausted to examine it all, to pick over it in an argument. "OK. I could do with a drink. I'll get it."

"No." she stood up and bent over to kiss his lips and her hair fell in a curtain round his face. "I'll get it; you stay there. I've always wanted to have sex on the stairs."

She disappeared and mechanically, Nick untied his tie. There was a buzz on Emma's phone on the console table and a text message flashed up on the screen. He knew he shouldn't, he knew it wasn't the right thing to do, but he couldn't help himself. Nick never looked at Emma's phone, he simply wasn't interested, but after what she'd said this morning, he couldn't let it go. He stood and descending, he picked up her phone. It was Emma's sister. He unlocked the screen with her passcode and read.

The text said, *"Just got your voice mail! How bloody brilliant - You super star! Forget the fact that they need Nick and focus on just how fucking amazing it is that you've been offered a partnership..."*

There was more, but Nick didn't bother to keep reading. He put his shoes back on, grabbed his jacket and left the house. When Emma came back with the champagne, the hallway was empty, and when she saw her phone, she knew why. The text from her sister had been read.

8

P RESENT DAY - *London*
Friday – p.m.

"YOU KNOW WHAT REALLY ANNOYS ME?" Nella said, as she shifted into reverse to bay-park the squad car.

"Quite a few things I'd say." Mo was watching the wing mirror on his side; she was bang in the lines, three inches either side *and* she was talking. He couldn't bay or parallel park to save his life.

"Yeah, well, the thing that really annoys me about this is the amount of time it's taken us to get here, to this point. A girl has been murdered…"

"Had a fatal accident."

"Yeah, OK, fatal accident, murder, whatever, but seriously? It's been nearly a week since I called the company to make an appointment…"

"Two days, it's now Friday lunch time and you spoke to *Stairaway Lifts* on Wednesday."

"Ok, two days then to get to interview the lift company – it's still too long Mo. Has the MD really been out of the country, or do they just not want to talk to us?"

"Who knows, but we're here now so come on, stop being arsey and let's get on with it."

"And don't get me started on the file from Devon and Cornwall. How long does it take them to respond to a request for God's sake?" She stopped. "I'm not arsey, am I?"

"Yes." He looked at her before they climbed out of the car. "Do you really have to ask?"

"Nah. You're right. I'm arsey."

He opened the door and got out, checking the front. The bumper was nestled up to the barrier without touching it; both back wheels were inside the line. Bloody perfect.

NELLA AND MO were shown into the MD's office right away; they were expected, and no-one liked a couple of coppers hanging round reception. Nella had a theory that you could spot CID at ten paces: plain clothes, party clothes, even naked. There's something shifty about us she thought; always looking to catch people out.

Standing as they came into the office, the managing director of *Stairaway Lifts* held his hand out and shifted his weight forward. He looked nervous, Nella thought, probably wondering if they were investigating a bloody great compensation claim for faulty mechanics.

"So, Detective Constable Walsh and Detective Constable Ahmad, how can I help you?"

He offered them a seat in front of his desk; he sat behind it. Nella took out her MacBook and opened it. She glanced up.

"It's just a courtesy call really Mr Gibson,"

"Jack, please."

"Jack, we'd like a bit of information about lift safety please."

"Right. Lift safety. Well of course *Stairaway* is all about lift safety."

"Not exactly," Mo said.

There was an uncomfortable silence.

"We take our lift safety very seriously indeed, DC Ahmad. In our new lifts, we install several cross beams that are sensitive to any object that might obstruct the lift doors. In a matter of milliseconds, the lift doors will open when the smallest object is detected in the beam pattern."

Nella typed then glanced up. "But the lift at Kenvil House is an older hydraulic lift, isn't it? I'm assuming that it was only fitted with sensors, not the cross beams, and had door interlocks that stop the lift from moving if the doors aren't properly closed?"

Mo glanced at her. He could see that she had some kind of technical drawing open in a window on her document as she typed. She went on; "Are the interlocks both mechanical and electrical?"

"It's standard safety nowadays to have mixed interlocks."

Mo said, "How old was the lift mechanism in the lift in Kenvil House where Lydia Helston was killed?"

"Died," Gibson corrected him.

"Yes, died."

"Not that new, 1993, but not outdated and serviced regularly."

"Was it faulty?" Nella glanced up from typing and looked directly at Gibson.

"No, no it wasn't faulty when it was last checked. However, having said that, we can't be held responsible for faults that occur in between services. If no-one reports a fault DS Walsh, we are not contractually obliged to a, know about it, or b, fix it. That is our legal position."

Nella made a mental note; he'd been to the lawyers; that explained the delay.

"It definitely wasn't faulty then?" Nella probed. "I'm assuming that you sent in an engineer to check it after the accident."

"No, the lift wasn't faulty, but the sensors weren't working..." Gibson shifted in his seat. "For the accident to happen, the sensors had to, erm...malfunction, to stop the lift door opening again when something was caught in it. It appeared that this is what had happened because they technically weren't faulty; they just didn't come on that once when they were supposed to."

"Oh? Were there just sensors or door bumpers as well?"

Mo looked at Nella, but she seemed completely genuine. How the hell did she know all this?

"The lift was installed in the 1990's when the building went from council to private and it was just sensors. They were independently powered by an electrical unit, and it appeared that this unit didn't connect for some reason."

"So technically, either they were faulty, which you say they weren't, or someone could have tampered with the electrical unit to disable the sensors?"

Gibson shrugged. "Technically..."

Nella raised an eyebrow and stared at Gibson.

"Technically, of course, but realistically, it's highly improbable. To be honest, this whole thing is so extraordinary it feels like one of those bizarre accidents that sometimes happen in life. It could have been a freak power break that disabled the sensors, for all we know. He shrugged. "When your number's up, you know?"

"No, not really." Nella said, "There's not usually much serendipity about murder."

"Murder? Nobody has mentioned murder. You think it was murder?"

Mo shot Nella a look. He said, "Not currently Jack, no. We're looking at all the possibilities of what might have happened."

"Right, I see..." He shook his head. "Murder," he murmured.

"Mr Gibson? Jack, why is it highly improbable that someone might have tampered with the lift mechanism?"

"Well, quite simply, it's a technical job; he or she would need a good level of technical knowledge, be a lift engineer. What are the chances of that?"

Nella looked up. "Could we please have the full list of your employees?"

"Why? You don't think..."

"It's procedure," Mo said quickly. "We need to be thorough. Check all avenues."

"I see. Right, I'll get that organised." Gibson stood and walked to the door. Before he left, he said; "Just the engineers?"

"All employees please," Nella said. Mo shot her another look and she shrugged.

"Might as well." She saved her notes and slipped her MacBook into her bag. "Beats inputting data Mo." She stood and took a cursory walk round the office.

"You don't really think that this is connected to a lift engineer, do you?"

Nella shrugged.

"Come on DS Walsh, over eighty eight percent of female murders are domestic violence related."

"So, you admit it could be murder?"

"No, not at all! But I'll admit that I think this is a bit of a wild goose chase! What are you trying to prove? We both know that you only have to look at the statistics."

"We also both know that seventy five percent of statistics are made up on the spot."

"Ha." Mo turned as Gibson came back into the room and handed over a manila folder with the employee list in.

"Thanks."

"Is there anything else I can do for you DC Walsh and DC Ahmad?"

Mo tapped the folder. "This is enough for now, thank you."

Gibson opened the door for them.

"Any of your employees particularly interested in music Jack? That you know of?" Nella asked.

"Possibly. To be honest, apart from the Christmas party and our summer family day, I don't have much to do with our employees, not personally, anyway. We've got a hundred and fifty staff on our books and with the best will in the world…"

Mo nodded.

"I can ask, if you like? My management know their teams well. I'll give you a call if anything comes up."

Mo handed over his card. "Please do," he said.

They left the office and made their way down the stairs.

"A hundred and fifty staff!" Mo said, shaking his head. "Thanks DC Walsh, I was due to finish at lunch time and that's my afternoon buggered."

"If we get back in time."

They hit the ground floor and left the building. Mo said, "What do you mean 'get back in time'?" He was almost afraid to ask. "We're heading straight back, right?"

"Almost straight back," Nella said.

"Great."

"With a small detour to Lydia Helston's funeral."

"You're not serious?" He glanced sidelong at her as Nella began to reverse, neatly and expertly out of the bay. "Shit, you are serious! Are you sure? The funeral?"

"Yes, I'm sure. To pay our respects."

"Pay our respects? Yeah, right."

"We're both off duty; it's in our own time..." She shifted gear and drove off.

Mo wasn't at all happy, nobody was going to like police presence at a funeral, but he knew better than to argue with Nella, and in truth, at least it was proper detective work. He also knew that if the shit hit the fan, which it almost certainly would with DS Dennis, he was going to get covered, alongside DC Walsh. That was a given.

AT PUTNEY VALE CEMETERY, Nella parked the car right at the end of Hayward Avenue and she and Mo climbed out, the hum of the A3 like a low mourning wail behind the gates. The chapel was packed and a small crowd - unable to get in for the ceremony - stood outside in winter coats, shifting from foot to foot, and hands dug into pockets, noses red in the cold. They were an arty crowd, Nella thought, clocking the fur collars and trilbies, a few carried instrument cases, on their way to or from rehearsals or performances. There was a loudspeaker mounted on the corner of the wall and a choir sang something she recognised, a hymn from her childhood, but rearranged into varying harmonies so that it felt spiritual and melancholic. She stopped for a moment suddenly aware of their intrusion. Mo sensed her hesitation and said,

"Shall we give it a miss? Not sure this is the best idea."

"We're here now; we should at least have a wander round the crowd outside." She buttoned her coat up. "We won't give it long."

But, as soon as she said this organ music came over the loudspeaker and the crowd began to shift. There was a muffled murmur in response to a prayer that was intoned and then a general sense of movement. Nella wandered round the back of the throng and scanned some of the faces while she had the chance, but before she could get a good look, the doors of the chapel opened, and a couple Nella assumed to be Lydia's parents came out. The woman wore a long black coat, tightly belted in around her thin, small frame, falling to just above her ankle, the hem uneven, and a pair of red T-bar shoes on her feet, the type that a tap dancer might wear. She seemed to sag as she hit the cold air and the man behind her stepped forward and took her arm, holding it just under the shoulder, lifting her slightly to keep her standing. He was tall, nearly a foot taller than the woman, but he too looked weakened, as if he had just the frame of a body with all the bulk dissolved.

Nella took a step sideways, behind a large man in a hat, suddenly acutely aware of their intrusion, but Matt had come out onto the steps, and he caught sight of her shifting stealthily. He looked, whispered into the woman's ear and she then turned and stared directly at Nella; stationary for longer than she needed to be as a queue began to form behind her. Nella moved into sight and Matt made his way across to her, the small crowd of mourners was silent in his wake.

"Why are you here?"

He stood opposite Nella, hostile, overbearing. This was not the emotional, quivering mess they had seen earlier in the week. Nella noticed a livid bruise on the side of his neck that she hadn't seen before. It wasn't fresh; the colour was too deep, too mottled. A struggle, she wondered, some sort of abuse?

"We came out of courtesy."

Matt moved a little closer to her, leaning his face in. She caught the faint whiff of sour breath, but she didn't lean back; Nella didn't flinch at intimidation. She stood a little straighter and looked directly back at him.

"Well fuck off... out of courtesy." He swallowed hard. "This is a private funeral. I don't know what you thought..."

"We thought that you had reported a possible murder." Nella said tightly. "This is part of our investigation."

"Really? Well, I made a mistake. Lydia's death was an accident." Matt glanced over his shoulder at the sea of faces spilling out of the chapel. "It was an accident," he said again. "OK?"

Nella shrugged. "Fine; an accident. We won't waste any more police time then." She stepped back and squared up to him. "And nor, I hope, will you."

She turned, caught sight of Mo at the edge of the crowd and made her way towards him. Together they walked to the car, climbed in and sat, hidden along the avenue of trees, while the coffin left, and the tide of grievers began to seep away.

Nella had turned the engine on and had the heater up full blast. There was a fug in the car and Mo wound the window down. He hadn't spoken, but he knew that she knew what he was thinking. As several of the funeral goers found their cars parked up by the squad car and began to leave for the wake, Mo and Nella continued to sit there, waiting until the place had cleared completely. Finally, when the chapel was deserted and the endless rows of grey headstones cast shadows over the ground, Nella shifted into gear and began to back the car out of the parking space. As they moved off respectfully slowly down the long drive towards the exit, Mo said,

"Not your finest hour."

"Possibly not," Nella replied, "but worth it."

Mo shook his head. "You can't be wrong, can you Walsh? You can't admit that this was a bit of a cock-up."

"Because it wasn't."

"Really?" He snorted derisively. "We've been shamed into hiding in the car and you say it wasn't a cock-up. Did you see the way they looked at us?"

"Yes, but Matt's changed his stance. He no longer thinks it was murder. He's now convinced that it was an accident."

"So?"

"So that's pretty odd, isn't it?"

Mo shook his head again. "No, not really. He changed his mind Nella, he was upset, hysterical perhaps and now he's had time to consider, he thinks he made a mistake."

"Did you see the bruise on his neck? An old one, a week old maybe?"

"No." Mo looked at her profile. She was concentrating and her face had a fierce quality about it. Sometimes he admired her and other times in all honesty, she scared him. "He's got a bruise, so what?"

"So..." Nella indicated and turned left at the first round-about and then left again. "Maybe he got that bruise in a struggle with Lydia. Maybe he forced her into the lift?"

Mo shook his head. "Oh, come on Nella! Why? Why would he do that and why would he alert us to the fact that he murdered his girlfriend when it had already been filed as an accident? That's just bizarre. It's not like we've found anything that clearly points to murder, is it?"

"No, but maybe that's the point. He needed to know if we'd come up with anything and now we haven't, he can relax."

Mo looked across at her. "You don't know when to stop, do you Nella?"

"No. Why should I stop?"

"Because no one apart from you seems to think there's anything suspicious in Lydia Helston's..." Mo suddenly spotted a lone figure walking along Central Drive towards the exit and, out of curiosity, turned in his seat to look at her. There was something about the hair that was familiar.

"Stop..." he said.

"Stop what? Looking for the truth?!"

"NO, STOP! That woman, back there. Just stop a minute, will you? I think I recognise her."

Nella slowed to a standstill and Mo climbed out of the car. It had begun to rain, and the woman had put up an umbrella so that Mo couldn't clearly see her face, but he recognised the hair; it was distinctive. She turned right, across the graveyard and headed towards the pedestrian exit, but when Mo called out to her his voice was lost in the wind and rain. He watched her for a few moments then opened the car door.

"S'up?" Nella asked as he climbed back in.

"That woman, the one over there? She's heading off towards the gate, there. I think I know her."

"Really? How?"

Mo shook his head. "That's the problem. I can't remember. But I've seen her before, I'm sure I have."

Nella raised an eyebrow. "Well," she said. "If it's not murder then it's certainly a mystery."

"Yeah, maybe." Mo kept staring at the retreating figure trying to place her. "Or maybe not."

KATE SAT on the sofa with her laptop beside her, work abandoned, listening to the mindless chatter from the kitchen as Annie and Matilda made themselves something to eat before the lecture. They had been ready to go within half an hour of arriving home and now waited for Kerrie - who had insisted on collecting them from the flat – clomping around in *flatform* trainers and ripped skinnies, Annie in a cloth cap with a peak, Mattie with her hair in a long plait wound round her head. They both looked dazzlingly fashionable for a lecture on astrophysics at Imperial College, heavy on the mascara and lip gloss, nails painted blue and purple. But their excitement was palpable, and science could do with a bit of glamour, Kate thought.

The buzzer for the main door went and Annie rushed to the intercom, a peanut butter and banana sandwich in her hand. She pressed the button.

"Hey Kerrie, we'll be right down!" She grabbed her coat from the back of the chair and called to Mattie who appeared a moment later, stuffing down the last of her own sandwich, parka already on and zipped up.

Kate stood. "I'll come down and see you off," she said. She crossed and followed the girls out of the front door, down the stairs to the main door. It was cold, so she stayed on the step, just inside.

"It's very good of you to collect the girls," Kate said to Kerrie, "They could have caught the bus."

"No worries, I don't live too far away." Kerrie dug in her bag for her phone. "Give me your numbers girls; I'll text you the tickets."

Annie read hers out and then Matilda and Kerrie sent the tickets via text. She glanced up when it was done and said, "You could always come you know? It's not full; I checked online."

Kate hugged her arms around her. "Thanks, but I really don't think that I'd understand it."

Kerrie smiled. "Nor will I, but it's a night out, isn't it?!" She dropped her phone into her bag and said, "We'll be finished around seven forty-five, so if you fancy a coffee later?"

"Oh thanks, but I..." Kate glanced over Kerrie's shoulder and saw Annie nodding theatrically. She hesitated. "Well..." The nodding became more pronounced. Kate didn't fancy a coffee; she didn't want to even leave the flat, but Annie was her Achilles heel; she was impossible to refuse. "OK then," Kate said. "Where shall I meet you all?"

"Let's meet at the South Ken Campus and go from there? There are a few places near South Ken tube."

Kate nodded. "Fine." She caught sight of Annie again. "Great!" She added a little more enthusiasm to her voice. "I'll see you all later then. Annie? Hug?"

Annie stepped forward and hugged Kate. "Thanks mum," she whispered, and Kate smiled, properly, it felt, for the first time in days. She waved them off down the road to the bus stop and went back inside.

As she closed the door, she leant against it and let out a long, tense breath. She'd had tightness in her chest for the past week and the only thing that seemed to ease it momentarily were these deep, long breaths that also seemed to zap all her energy. Exhausted, she laid her head back and closed her eyes. Today had been worse than she'd expected, even sadder and more dispiriting than she'd thought it would be, but at least she hadn't seen anyone she recognised, which was a good thing, she supposed. Stepping away from the door she rubbed her arms and reckoned on a piece of toast and some scrambled eggs before she'd need to set off for Imperial College to meet them. She headed up the stairs and was almost at the top when she heard a loud rap on the main door.

"What have you forgotten?!" She shouted, as she made her way back down again. She opened the door, but no-one was there. She saw the back end of a florist's van head off round the corner and thought, bloody deliveries, not even stopping to make sure they'd got the right flat. She bent and saw a big card box. It had her name on it. Flowers? There was no florist's name or address, just the word in capitals along the side of the box and 'THIS WAY UP.'

Peeling the tape off the top of it, Kate peered inside. She lifted an arrangement out and stared at it, the tightness in her chest escalating to a sudden sharp pain. There was a message, in a small, plain brown envelope attached to the bottom of the funeral wreath. With trembling fingers, Kate opened it and pulled out a card. It said, *With Deepest sympathy. RIP*

9

T HE PAST – *Kingstanton & Exeter, Devon, December 2008*

"WITH DEEPEST SYMPATHY...?!!" Abbey Salter's mother, Donna, stood in the hall in a grubby towelling robe, her face stricken. She held the card out to Gary and her hand trembled as she did so. "She's not dead Gary; tell me she's not dead!" A pleading look came into her eyes, as if Gary somehow had omniscient power, then her face crumpled, and she began to cry.

He came across to her and awkwardly put his arms around her; he wasn't good at emotion. He wanted to tell her the truth, tell her that by now, four days in, her little girl probably was dead, but how could he do that?

He said, "As long as they haven't found her body there's still hope."

"Why do people do this?! Send things like this?!" She

pulled away from him and shook the card at him. "This... this is awful..."

He took it and opened it. There was a message of support inside, from the neighbours. Nothing sinister, just thoughtless perhaps.

"They mean well," he said wearily, "Its sympathy for what we're going through babe, that's all."

"WE?!" The word came out as a shriek and he wondered how long he could stand it, this irrational, chameleon grief. "She's *my* daughter Gary! She's *my* child!"

He turned away, still holding the card and went into the kitchen to put the kettle on. He held the spout under the tap and filled it, his hand shaking. He heard Donna come in behind him, but he didn't turn round.

"I'm sorry," she said falteringly, "You're a good stepdad. I know you love her too."

He replaced the kettle on its stand, switching it on and reached up for a couple of mugs from the cupboard. Was he really? Was he a good stepdad? A good person? He didn't know; he'd lost sight of whom and what he was in the past four days.

"We should ring the man in charge," she went on, "Whatshisname, Detective Inspector something...we should speak to him, make him tell us what's going on Gary... we should..."

Gary turned. "I rang this morning, Donna. First thing, remember? You told me to ring as soon as we got up?"

"Then ring again! Ring him again now. Make him tell us Gary, please....?"

Gary looked down at his hands, which had begun to shake again and dug them deep into the front pockets of his jeans. "CI Lewin isn't in this morning," he said. He kept his head down because he couldn't bear to look at her and see his own pain reflected.

"The duty sergeant said he'd call us as soon as he could." Finally, he glanced up. Donna had begun to cry again.

~

CI Lewin sat at the kitchen table and waited for the phone to ring. His wife was in the front room, safe for now, in front of the television, but he couldn't leave her, not until their daughter arrived from Taunton. He glanced at his watch; ten a.m. Two minutes later, the phone rang.

"Got the results," the DS said, "And they're odd, but not conclusive I'm afraid."

"Go on."

"There's semen on the item and we found a couple of hairs that match with one found in the boathouse. So, whoever wore this was also in the boathouse. However, there's nothing to link Abbey to it, no trace of her DNA anywhere near it."

"Bugger. Have you run a screening test? Does it match any other DNA we have on record?"

"We're just doing that now boss. How's Mrs Lewin, by the way?"

"Oh, she's erm..." Lewin sighed. "She's a little confused, but thanks for asking. Our daughter is coming from Taunton so that I can get in. You did cross check the DNA with the stepfather, didn't you?"

"Yup, no match."

"What about time frames? How long has our item with the semen been there?"

"Now there's another oddity. Finch reckons three days,

which puts it there at the same time Abbey was held at the boat house."

"So, it has to be linked. It has to be our first piece of evidence in the case."

"I don't know sir, I'm not convinced."

Lewin heard shuffling from outside the kitchen. "Look, I've got to go. Can you fax me the full report then I can be up to speed to meet Finch this afternoon?"

"OK, I'll do that now."

Lewin rang off and opened the door of the kitchen. His wife was standing there, looking lost.

"Hello love, would you like a cup of tea?"

"Oh… yes, please, tea. We had tea once at the Ritz. It was lovely, we had bubbles and I ate five cream cakes. I never had to watch my figure in those days; I was as slim as a pin. Five cream cakes and not an ounce of weight put on."

Lewin nodded; he held out his hand. "Five and not an ounce of weight, eh? You must have been a beauty."

"Oh, I won contests. Ask my Derek, he'll tell you. I was Miss Paignton and then Miss UK." Barbara Lewin took his hand and walked slowly. "I had to be ever so careful of my crown, it slipped off so easily," she said as they came into the kitchen.

"Sit there, former Miss UK and I'll make us a cuppa."

Lewin pulled out a chair for her. There was a copy of *Hello* Magazine on the seat with a celebrity on the cover in a ball gown wearing a tiara. That made sense, he thought. He took it up and shoved it under a pile of old newspapers.

"Have you seen my Derek recently?"

Lewin poured some boiling water into the tea pot and swirled it around, emptying it out before he spooned the loose-leaf tea in. Barbara had never allowed tea bags and now he was used to it. He brought the pot over and put it on the table, far enough away that she didn't burn herself on it.

"Where's my Derek gone?" she said. "I told him to be back for tea."

Lewin brought mugs over and sat down next to his wife. "I'm here love," he said, "I'm back for tea."

"Oh Derek, I wasn't sure where you'd got to. I don't like it when you're not here."

The doorbell rang and Lewin got up to answer it, leaving the kitchen door open so he could see Barbara. "I won't be a tick, Barbara."

Their daughter Debbie was at the door. "Hello Debbie love," he said. She came in and hugged him tight.

"How are you dad?" She stood back to look at him. He looked exhausted, she thought.

"I'm with the beauty queen of Devon again," he said, smiling.

"I don't know how you put up with it," she said. "All the lies,"

Lewin looked at her. "They're not lies Debbie love, they're stories. Stories in her mind of what she might have been or wanted to be or dreamed about doing. I quite like them to be honest. Apparently, we went to the Ritz for tea, and she ate five cream cakes."

Debbie smiled. "How many did you have?"

"None, on account of my indigestion."

"That still bothering you?"

"Something chronic," Lewin said. "All day pain." He followed Debbie into the kitchen.

"Debs is here love?" he said to his wife, "She's going to look after you for a few hours while I go to work."

"Debs?" Barbara looked up. "Who are you?" she said.

Lewin watched his daughter falter for a moment then

she took a breath and smiled. "I'm Debbie," she said, "I've come to keep you company for a while."

That's my girl, Lewin thought. He patted her on the shoulder. "I've made Mum a brew, but I have to go and read a fax and then get to work. You all right with that Debs?"

"I'll pour it and bring you a cup," she said. "How's the case going dad?"

He shrugged. "Some progress yesterday, but its bloody awful. I never wanted to finish my career with something like this Debs. It's crippling to see the pain on that poor woman's face. It's a bloody gruesome job at times."

Debbie reached out for her dad's hand and gave it a squeeze then she turned to Barbara.

"Would you like some tea Barbara?" She had stopped calling her 'mum' a few months ago on the advice of the specialist. It upset and confused Barbara to be called mum by someone she didn't recognise as her daughter.

Lewin left them to it and went into the back room that he now used as a home office. The fax had come through and was piled up on the table. He took it off the machine and sat down at his desk to read it.

He was on the final page when the phone rang again. It was his DS.

"Finch has found more semen," he said, "Inside the boathouse. It matches what we've already got."

"Jesus." Lewin felt a band tightening around his gut. "So, the same place that Abbey was held also has DNA that matches what we've found on our item of clothing."

"Yes."

"Then we need to find out who owns it," Lewin said. "I want every scrap of CCTV looked at and every known user of our little meeting place at the end of that lane tracked down and interviewed. And I don't care who they are, is that clear?"

"Yes Sir."

"Good. Someone must have seen him wearing it; it's distinctive. I'll be in in the next half an hour." Lewin rang off and folded up the fax. It had been almost five days with nothing at all, but now they'd got a link and he was going to make sure that they used it to find their killer. Whoever it was had made a mistake. Make one and you can make another Lewin thought. He was going to make damn sure he caught his man on the next one.

THE ATMOSPHERE WAS TENSE.

It was clear when Richard had picked his daughter up from the station at eleven am that morning that she had been drinking on the train down from London. She had that dishevelled look that drunks have as if the alcohol has unravelled them – which it had. He'd taken her to the student flat in Exeter, a sterile, boxy three rooms that smelt of bleach and fried onions, where she'd abandoned her luggage just inside the door and slumped down onto the sofa.

"Beth has made lunch," he'd reminded her anxiously.

"Oh? Am I invited?"

"Yes, you're invited!" he'd snapped.

Katherine had raised an eyebrow in that disconcertingly astute way that she had, letting him know that she saw right through the bullshit.

"Really? You sound very sure." She'd fumbled in her pocket for a packet of cigarettes and found it, crumpled and battered. "That makes a change."

Richard had moved swiftly forward and swiped the cigarettes out of her hand. "It's a no smoking flat," he'd said. He crunched the packet in his hand.

Katherine had looked at him. "You've got to be fucking joking," she said.

"No, I am not *fucking joking* and you are going to go to the bathroom, wash your face and teeth and then we are going home for lunch."

"Fuck, Richard shows some back-bone... at last."

Richard had had to bite down his anger, but she had stood, unsteadily, and found her washbag in the giant holdall she'd brought down. They had left for Compton Combe in hostile silence; a hostile silence that now invaded the kitchen where they sat for lunch.

The atmosphere was so tense that it felt physically cold in the room.

However, the twins - who had broken up already from their smart prep school – were oblivious to the strain and intoned a litany of Christmas presents they wanted while Beth sat with a fixed smile on her face, the bottle of wine planted firmly at her right hand, away from Katherine and nodded every now and then in response to their chatter.

Katherine ate very little, gulped down water - having topped it up unseen from a vodka miniature she'd got on the train - and feigned excessive interest in the twins' list, knowing she was being too subtly offensive for them, but not for Beth. Richard throughout chewed his lunch with a pained expression and kept glancing across at Katherine in nervous anticipation.

Finishing his mouthful, and unable to bear Beth's scowl any longer, Richard said,

"Oh, I didn't tell you did I, darling, that the police were

on campus yesterday?" he addressed his comment to Beth, but it was aimed to shut Katherine up.

"Really? What for?" Beth asked. She poured herself more wine and replaced the bottle at her elbow.

"In connection with this Abbey Salter thing. Apparently one of our maintenance team was being questioned."

"Oh God, how awful. He's not connected, is he?"

"I don't know. I think not because they left him alone after they'd interviewed him. The whole thing is just terrible though and so close to home."

"What whole thing?"

Beth held her wine glass and looked at Katherine over the rim of it. "Goodness, where've you been for the past week Katherine? I thought you were supposed to be sharp, ahead of the game; it's all over the news."

Katherine blinked. Beth was rarely openly hostile; she preferred the cold war approach. "I've been pissed and fucking my way round LSE," Katherine said. "I seemed to have missed the news."

There was a sharp intake of breath and the twins started giggling.

"There's no need to use that sort of language, not in front of the twins." Beth said. She stood and began to clear the plates even though Richard was still eating.

"Sorry." Katherine shrugged. She had a warm buzz in her head as the vodka kicked in.

"I told you this was a bad idea," Beth said to Richard as she scraped the leftovers. "I told you that she doesn't have the maturity or the respect to even sit nicely through a meal with us. I told you that..."

"She? Don't talk about me as if I'm not here!" Katherine interrupted. "It's so fucking rude."

"And you'd know all about that, wouldn't you?" Beth spat back. "You are the…"

"Stop it!" Richard rarely raised his voice, and it was enough to silence Beth. He dropped his knife and fork onto the plate with a clatter and turned to Katherine.

"It is December the 8th and you are here until January, and I will not have another lunch, dinner… another moment spoilt by you." He turned to Beth. "Take the twins into the other room to watch TV."

"No Richard, I think I need to…"

"Take the twins out!"

Beth's face set, her mouth had disappeared into a hard thin line, but she ushered the boys up out of their seats and over to the door. There she stopped for a moment and glowered at her husband, but he missed it. He had turned towards Katherine.

"You have had a shit time of it," he said, when the door clicked shut.

"And who's fault is that?!"

He held his hands up. "I know that, Katherine; you don't have to keep reminding me."

At this sudden understanding, Katherine felt the on-rush of tears, drunken tears, self-pitying and gushing, but still tears and she never cried in front of her father; she didn't want to give him the satisfaction of knowing that he'd hurt her. She bit her lip and stared down at her plate.

"But shitty time or not, my fault, Beth's, whatever, this has got to stop Kat. It has got to stop." He picked up her glass and sniffed it. "This self-destructive path that you've decided to take. It's leads nowhere." He stood up and crossed to the sink, pouring the vodka water mix away. He turned. "It leads to the dead-end of a ruined life; is that what you want to do? Sabotage your life?" The words too little too late flashed into his head, but he came back to the table and said,

"I'm going to drive you back to Exeter now Katherine and when you sober up you are going to have a long, hard think about your life and how you fill your time. I don't want to be witness to any more drugs and booze. You are at a top university, you're a clever young woman, too clever perhaps at times, and you need to straighten out. Find some purpose Katherine, use your intelligence for something other than thinking of not very smart ways to keep drinking at lunch so that we don't know. It's beneath you."

Katherine looked up. "Fucking hell," she said, "I don't think I've ever heard you say so much." She stood up, holding the table for support, now suddenly conscious of how drunk she was. "I don't know what gives you the right to lecture me Richard, the great moral role model, but..." She shrugged, "Maybe you're right, and maybe I do need to have a look at my life." She raised an eyebrow, but her face didn't look ironic, just lopsided in her drunkenness. "Trouble is that the sight of it and the people in it just makes me want to drink all the more to obliterate it."

LYDIA HAD the morning off school for her grade eight violin practical exam. She had done the theory exam some time ago and passed it with the highest mark it was possible to award. Now it was the recital element - the easy part in her view - and she was looking forward to it. Lydia wanted to be a violinist when she grew up, to play in a string quartet, and she'd been playing in front of people since she was four years old. At an early age she'd shown a gifted flair for music, her parents had encouraged it and now, as she packed her music and checked her violin strings, it felt natural to be doing what studying music required: performance.

She did some homework, practised her pieces twice and was ready early, making her way downstairs for lunch. She could hear her parents in the kitchen talking and she stopped as she heard Mr Hirsch's name. She stepped silently up to the door and put her face against it. The door opened.

"Were you snooping Lydia?" her father said.

"No, I just heard you talking about Mr Hirsch, and I wondered what you were saying."

Lydia was an only child and a clever and precocious one. She was rarely excluded from adult conversation, whether it was good for her or not. Her father looked across the table at her mother who said, "We were just saying that he's improved your pieces immeasurably Lydia."

She saw her father's eyes widen quizzically for a moment.

"No, you weren't, you were saying something private. I should be able to hear it, he is my violin teacher; it may concern me. Besides, I adore Mr Hirsch!"

Her parents exchanged glances. "Don't be melodramatic Lydia," her father said.

Her mother poured her a glass of water. "It does not concern you," she said. "And you should not be able to hear everything we talk about."

"I do usually."

Again, her father looked at her mother. She got up and went across to the fridge to get some more butter, passing a murmured comment to him as she did so. Lydia strained to catch it, but she didn't manage to. Her father came and sat at the table as she started on her soup.

"So, are you ready then?"

"Yup." Lydia put far too much butter on her bread and waited for her mother to protest. She didn't.

"We'll leave in about ten minutes," he said. "The exam is one fifteen, isn't it?"

"Yup." She finished her water, poured milk into her glass, added chocolate *Nesquik* and stirred, spilling some of it over the edge of the glass onto the tablecloth. Usually there would have been a comment, but this afternoon there was nothing. She ate, her mother read the paper and her father cleared away their lunch things.

"Finished?"

She put her spoon in her soup bowl. "Yup."

"Get your stuff for school too then. We'll go straight on."

Lydia stood and hurried out of the kitchen. As she shut the door behind her, her father said; "I think we should say something, I really do. At least to the boy's parents."

Her mother hushed him. "No," she said, barely audible. "It is none of our business; we don't want to get involved."

Puzzled, Lydia went upstairs to get her instrument and her bags for school.

WHEN KATHERINE WOKE up it was dark. Her head was thumping, and her mouth was dry and sour. She was disorientated for a few minutes then she rolled over on the hard, thin mattress and remembered where she was. She sat up and dropped her legs over the side of the bed. She was an expert at this feeling and, on her way to the small kitchenette to get some water, she knelt, rummaged in the handbag she'd abandoned just inside the front door and found some ibuprofen. She would alternate that with paracetamol for the next few hours and things should be fine, or at least fine enough to get back on the train and get the fuck out of there.

She ran the tap, filled a glass and swallowed down the pills. She switched the kettle on and rubbed her hands wearily over her face. She didn't feel bad about the scene at lunch or about being brought home and she certainly wasn't going to feel bad about doing a runner from this institution-alised box. Richard, her father – although she rarely called him that – would be relieved. He could get his money back on the flat, spend it on some expensive skin cream for Beth – although she'd need more than a bit of posh unguent to sweeten that sour face – and he could have himself a merry little Christmas without all the aggro of a daughter he didn't want.

The kettle boiled and Katherine realised that she didn't have any coffee or tea or milk or sugar. "Fuck", she said aloud, and she opened the cupboard to see if one of the students before her had left anything.

Taken aback, she stared at the white MDF shelf for a few moments, at the unopened, newly bought tea, coffee, sugar, *Coco Pops*, hot chocolate, peanut butter, jam and ginger biscuits. There was a card propped up against all this and in her father's handwriting, scrawled and difficult to read, it said:

"For last year's words belong to last year's language
And next year's words await another voice.
And to make an end is to make a beginning."
T.S. Eliot

Then the words; See Fridge.

Katherine opened the fridge and found milk, butter, eggs, bread, cheese, apples, grapes and orange juice. She also found several small pots of *Ambrosia* creamed rice pudding – her absolute favourite and a bar of *Cadbury's* fruit and nut chocolate – her father's favourite. She bent, took all three pots of rice pudding out, found a spoon and went back into the bedroom, climbed back into bed and there she ate them all, one after the other, her tears soaking into the scratchy poly cotton duvet cover, turning the violet flowers purple.

10

PRESENT DAY - *London*
Friday – p.m.

KATE HAD LOST track of time. She heard a door open along the corridor and looked up, remaining pressed against the wall, not moving, the main door still open, the wreath back in its box, outside the building. As she lifted her hands off the wall, she realised they were shaking so she pressed them together tightly.

The sound of the dog came first, a scampering, breathless sound then Marcy's heavy plod behind it, the rubber soles of her trainers squeaking on the polished floor. Kate stepped forward and knelt to stroke the dog. She didn't, as a rule, like little dogs, but she liked Marcy's - a Norfolk terrier - a smart and affectionate dog that Annie had played with when she was younger to get her used to animals. It was fiercely loyal to Marcy; Kate appreciated that fact.

"You all right Kate love? You look a bit peaky."

"I'm fine," Kate said. She remembered the therapy; FINE; fucked up, insecure, neurotic and emotional. She stood again as Marcy opened the door and the terrier pulled out in front of her, sniffing the night air.

"Oh flowers! Who are they for?"

"Me," Kate said flatly.

"Lucky you," Marcy said, "Somebody cares."

Kate nodded. "Marcy, could you hold the door for me for a moment? I haven't got my key."

"Course love."

Kate stepped out, just in her socks and lifted the box. She carried it round the side of the building and opened one of the big communal bins, dumping the box inside it, letting the lid bang shut. When she came back Marcy was staring at her, puzzled.

"Not somebody you want to care?" She probed.

Kate shrugged. "Something like that."

Marcy raised an eyebrow. "Shame to waste a nice bouquet."

Kate shrugged again, "Not really," she said.

Marcy patted her shoulder, as if she wasn't well, and headed off down the street, the terrier walking smartly at her heels. Kate watched her go. The constant churning in the pit of her stomach had moved up and felt like the painful flapping of wings in her chest. She found it hard to breathe and had to keep expanding her lungs, sucking in great mouthfuls of air to try and get enough breath in them. She stood like that for a while, seeming to gasp in the cold then the phone in her pocket buzzed and she saw a text from Annie.

"Interval. This lecture is AMAZING!!!!! Kerrie's got a voucher for Venchi!!!!! She says shall we meet you there? It's just by South Ken Tube."

Venchi? Venchi; an expensive ice-cream and chocolate shop; Kerrie had a voucher. That figured. Kate felt suddenly lightheaded, as if she was losing control of her senses and she struggled for a few moments to get any air into her lungs at all. She began to panic and put her hands up to her face, inhaling deeply and breathing in the air she exhaled, trying to increase the carbon dioxide in her body so that she could use the oxygen she had. She did this for a few minutes and slowly her head cleared; her pulse rate began to slow. When she dropped her hands down, she was cold. The icy night air had crept in around her and the hallway was cold too. The lights – on a timer – had switched off.

Pushing the door shut, Kate slowly made her way back up the stairs to her flat. Suddenly exhausted, she went inside and into her bedroom, curled up on her bed and closed her eyes for a few moments. The wreath, the card with its neat black handwriting, the empty faces at the funeral today punctured the blackness behind her eyes and she sat up. Her phone buzzed again. Annie.

Her text read: *???*

Kate typed; *Will be there at 7.15. xxx*

Kate put the phone down and again, images of the day crowded her mind, elbowing each other hard, jostling for space. She should never have gone. Lydia's mother would have seen her, possibly her father. Perhaps the wreath was from them? A message to stay clear, to stop hankering after the past, trying to off-load her guilt. RIP it said. Leave Lydia alone. Let her rest in peace.

Agitated, Kate stood up and, hugging her arms around her, she stared out of the window at the darkness beyond. Or maybe, she thought, shivering, maybe it was nothing to do with them at all. No matter how hard she tried to dismiss it, how many times she told herself that accidents happen, that it had to be an accident, she couldn't stop the small growling niggle of doubt that started up somewhere in her unconscious and gnawed its way to life. Maybe, she thought dangerously, maybe there was someone else at the funeral that had seen her, maybe her boyfriend was right and maybe Lydia had been murdered. Kate felt the panic rise again in her chest. And if she had been, then what did that mean? Kate crossed to the window and swiped the curtains across it to cover the darkness. What could it possibly mean for her?

NICK STAYED at the end of Sancroft Street, just round the corner from Kate's flat, watching the window from a distance; watching the outline of Kate's figure as it moved across the room, mesmerised by her. He wasn't sure what he was doing here. The last thing he remembered he'd been sitting in the Chamber after lunch for the second reading of an amendment to a healthcare bill and suddenly it didn't make any sense to him at all; none of it made sense. So, he'd left - abruptly. He had wandered aimlessly for a couple of hours, round Westminster, down to Lower Marsh where he knew that Kate worked then when it got dark, he'd perversely found his way to Sancroft Street and Kate's building. He'd been there for over an hour; he'd seen everything and now he was even more conflicted than before.

He stood where he was until the light in the flat went out and Kate left the building then he made his way to The Duchy Arms and ordered himself a pint, taking it outside and sitting in the cold at one of the deserted tables to think through what to do next. Nick was usually a cautious man, often too cautious, he knew that, but standing in the dark and staring at the home of a woman he'd almost had sex with wasn't cautious at all. It was a bad idea and if she found out, she certainly wasn't going to be impressed by it. Stalking was what she'd think and even though he should have gone to the flat and asked if she was OK when he'd seen the wreath delivered, even though he should have given her the number of the van he'd memorised then tapped into his phone, he hadn't. But he had seen, and known instinctively, that something was wrong; something was very wrong. Who the fuck sends a wreath to someone? And what the hell was it supposed to mean?

Nick looked at his phone, at the number of the florist he'd found on-line - a small exclusive outlet in Marylebone High Street, a long way from SW8 - and he pressed call. The number rang, clicked to voicemail, but he immediately cut it. He'd sit and wait, see that Kate got home safely and maybe, if he had the nerve, he'd approach her and tell her what he knew. Nick went and got another pint and nursing it, he sat at the empty tables on the pavement outside the pub and felt as adrift and alone and he appeared.

NELLA HAD ZONED OUT. She was listening to the rant about the complaint that Lydia's boyfriend had made that evening both online and in person at the station; heavy handed, embarrassing, distressing, blah, blah, blah. She was listening, but she heard nothing. Her mind was elsewhere.

When DS Dennis had finished speaking, she said; "So?"

And Nella came back to the room, narrowing her eyes, processing the last few sentences as quickly as she could. "So, in hindsight boss, it wasn't well thought out and I've no excuse really. I was trying too hard."

"As usual." DS Dennis said.

Nella nodded. A year ago, she would have argued, but she'd learned the hard way; arguing with superiors just created more shit on top of the shit they were calling you out for. Arguing was double shit.

"Nella?"

"Yes?"

"I said, even though you weren't supposed to be there, and you were hardly discreet, did the funeral raise any issues?"

"No."

"Are you any further along in the investigation into this accident?"

"No."

"Have you got hold of the file from Devon and Cornwall?"

"No."

DS Dennis raised an eyebrow.

"But we did see the lift company earlier today and they admitted that the door safety mechanism must have malfunctioned, but that it wasn't faulty the last time they serviced it. They said it could have been tampered with, but apparently that needs a level of technical knowledge, so we've got a list of employees and we've been ploughing through them this afternoon, cross checking with our data bases.

"Has anything come up?"

"No. I mean… not yet anyway."

"The property development company?"

"No… Nothing odd there, except of course the fact that the building that Lydia secured a five-year lease on is right in the middle of the development and can't be touched."

"So, hang on a minute... what I'm hearing mostly is, *no* and *no*, is that right?"

"Yes."

There was an uncomfortable silence.

"And the only concrete thing you seem to have is this idea about the music centre lease?"

"Yes."

"Which is a community project that could be seen as positive to the development company – open to all, with a professional musician at the heart of it? Could even be marketed as an attraction to new buyers, buyers with young families?"

"Could be..." Nella was wondering how many of the new apartments were aimed at people with young families. At nearly a million a pop, very few, she thought. "Good point, Sallie." She added.

"Thank you."

"You're welcome." The sarcasm went over Nella's head.

"So everywhere you've looked you've come up with nothing. We've had a complaint about you, and you've wasted your time off this afternoon and plan to waste more *of your own time* sifting through lift engineers and cross checking our data bases. Right?"

Nella stared down at her shoes. "Yup, I think that's about the sum of it."

"So, from where I'm standing, there is really no reason to carry on with this investigation, is there?"

"No."

"You have enough to do – we're all stretched, so put it to bed."

"Yes, I will." Nella wondered how she had become so proficient at lying.

"Good, well, that's all, thank you."

"Boss."

Nella turned to leave the glass walled office. DS Dennis called,

"When I say put it to bed Nella, I mean it. Don't pay me lip service – just do as I tell you, OK?"

DS Dennis was sorting through papers on her desk and didn't even look up. Not as proficient at lying as I think I am, Nella told herself as she left the room. She a saw a few smirks as she crossed the incident room to Mo's desk. He glanced up from his screen and pressed escape as she perched on the edge of his desk. She didn't wait for him to speak; she launched straight in.

"What the hell was Matt doing here at the station a couple of hours after the funeral?" she whispered, "When he should have been at the wake with Lydia's family, grieving, like any normal boyfriend?"

Mo shrugged. "Maybe we pissed him off so badly that it couldn't wait. People do weird things when someone's died."

"Or..."

Mo shook his head, but he had to admire her tenacity; that's probably what made her parking so brilliant. He would have put money on the fact that she'd practised parallel and bay parking relentlessly when she took her test.

"Or what?"

"He's done with our sniffing round; he knows that we haven't got anything on him, and he wants us off his back."

Mo looked at her for a few moments then shook his head a second time. "Really?"

Nella shrugged. "I've got him in my sights," she said. She looked at him for a few moments then she stood up and walked away.

⁓

It was after nine and Kate walked with Kerrie down towards the Cut while Annie and Matilda walked up ahead. They had met for ice-cream - which Kerrie had bought with a voucher she had - and now they were on their way to catch the bus back home. It had been easier than Kate had thought it would be. The girls had had a good time and Kerrie was open and friendly; she'd grown on Kate as the evening wore on.

"It's amazing what ice-cream can do," Kerrie said suddenly, breaking the silence, "You look calmer than you did earlier."

Kate hesitated before she answered. She glanced momentarily at the girls ahead, linking arms and chatting gaily and guarded, she said; "Really? Why do you say that?"

Kerrie shrugged. "Oh, I dunno, it's just that when you arrived you looked kind of upset... not in a major way, don't get me wrong, but pale, a bit frantic and aloof, like there was something bothering you."

Kate was caught off guard. She didn't like to be analysed; to have her behaviour dissected.

"Well, I'm sorry if I..."

Kerrie reached out and touched her arm. "Hey, I'm only saying you look better for a bit of chocolate ice-cream." She smiled. "That's all." Leaving her hand for a moment longer on Kate's arm, she said,

"Besides, a bit frantic and aloof is attractive."

Kate stared for a moment at the hand then turned to Kerrie. She was about to speak when Kerrie said,

"It's OK, I'm not hitting on you. I mean, I would, if I thought there was any chance, but I know a straight girl when I see one. The lady's not for turning, eh?"

Suddenly Kate smiled.

"Phew! You got the joke. Good to see you smile at last."

Kate shook her head. "Come on, I'm not that miserable."

Kerrie shrugged and again Kate smiled.

"Look," Kerrie said, "I don't know what's going on in your life and I know we've only just met, but if you ever want to talk, to share anything then let me know, OK? Sometimes just an ear can help."

Kate stared straight ahead when she answered. "That's nice of you, but... well, I'm a private person and my life's a bit of a muddle now. I don't know you well enough to burden you with all that."

They were almost at the stop and had caught up with the girls.

"Well, it's up to you," Kerrie said as Annie turned to them, "I'd be glad of a friend myself. London can be a cold and lonely place for a warm and friendly Aussie at times."

Annie looked challengingly at her mum. Kate didn't answer so Annie said, "Mum could do with a friend too. She doesn't really see anyone or go out. She works like all the time."

"Hey! Not all the time."

"No, not when you're sleeping," Annie said.

Kate nudged her. "Thanks for the support daughter."

"S'OK." Annie shrugged and held her fist out to Kerrie.

"See ya," she said, fist bumping Kerrie, who then did the same with Matilda.

"See ya homies."

They all laughed and outside the fist bumping circle, Kate watched them. "That's my bus," Kerrie said, "But remember what I told you about independence ladies." Kerrie shuffled into the queue.

"Sure. See you at the café next week?"

Kerrie held up her hand in a salute and boarded the bus.

They watched her settle in a seat by the window and Annie and Matilda waved at her as the bus pulled away.

"Ah, here's ours," Kate said with relief. "Come on girls." She marshalled them into the queue. "What was that about independence?" she asked, as casually as she could muster.

"Nothing." Annie said shrugging. Kate turned to Matilda who crumbled more easily. She raised an eyebrow and Matilda said,

"Kerrie just reminded us that we're nearly fifteen and going to a lecture at Imperial College is the first step on being independent, living our own lives."

"Did she now?" Kate said coldly. "For nearly fifteen, read just fourteen and plenty of time to be independent." Her voice was snappier than she'd intended and Annie ahead of them in the queue glanced back and shot Matilda a look. Kate caught it and felt a shift inside her. It was a look that completely excluded her, and it cut her to the quick.

On the bus the girls sat together, and Kate sat on her own. Independence, she thought, at fourteen; really? But she knew, looking at the two girls, that possibly Kerrie was right. Kate was holding onto something that wasn't going to last very much longer and the thought of that filled her with dread.

KATE STOOD outside the flats with Annie and Matilda, waiting for Hannah to collect them. They had come up with the idea of a sleepover at Mattie's on the bus instead of at Annie's because Mattie had two cats and a dog and Annie loved animals and Mattie lived closer to the shops and the girls could go and get breakfast in the morning at Gail's Bakery. Kate had little argument against it, except that she didn't like Saturday mornings on her own. They had somehow badgered Matilda's mother, Hannah, into coming to pick them up and now, with a small bag packed, Annie chatted excitedly with Matilda while Kate wondered how she was going to fill the time from waking in the morning to collecting Annie from Matilda's.

A car drove up and pulled into the parking space in front of the building and Hannah pressed the window down.

"Hi Kate. Shall I drop her back at lunch time?"

"No, I'll come for her."

"Sure?"

If Kate collected Annie, then she was in control of the timeframe; she hated waiting on other people's agendas.

"I'm sure," she said. She turned to Annie. "Hey you, hug?"

Annie stepped forward and hugged her mum and Kate gave her an extra squeeze before she released her. Annie climbed into the car, sliding along the seat to sit close to Matilda, and pressing the window down, she called; "Missing you already!"

Kate smiled, waved and turned towards the flats, waiting by the door until the car drove off down the road and disappeared round the corner.

AT ONE OF the tables outside The Duchy Arms, Nick stood up. He'd been watching Annie hug her mum, already four inches taller, having to bend her long giraffe legs at the knee to be the same size as Kate. He saw the same hair, the same smile but he also saw something else, or at least he thought he did; something intangibly familiar about Annie. He glanced momentarily at the four empty pint glasses and four shot glasses, holding onto the edge of the table for a few moments as they blurred and then came back into focus again. Shit, had he drunk that much? Nick wasn't a drinker, rarely went past two and now his head swam as he tried to put his phone in his pocket but kept missing. How the fuck had that happened? He'd been nervous, agitated, he'd lost count and the barman had kept popping out with refills, or had he gone to the bar? Shit, he couldn't remember. He let go of the table, staggered back a pace or so then staggered his way towards the flats where Kate was just turning inside after having waved goodbye to Annie.

"Kate?" Nick missed the kerb and lost his step. He lunged forward a few paces but managed to right himself. "Katewaitwait!" It came out garbled; the intention and the action misconnected.

Kate turned. She saw the tall, suited figure stumbling towards her and felt caught. She wanted to get inside, but she didn't have time before he reached her, swaying precariously as he tried to focus.

"Look, I don't know why you keep stalking me like this," she said coldly, "I thought I'd made myself clear the last time you were here." She turned on her heel.

"S'abouttheflowers..." Nick slurred.

Kate stopped. She turned back to him. "I'm sorry? What did you say?"

Nick opened and closed his mouth, but the sound that came out didn't make any sense to him. He tried again. "Isawthewhatsit...theflowersyou...Isawyou...FLOWERS!" he finally managed. "ME, I..."

"You?!" Kate said. Her amygdala lit up and anger rose suddenly and violently in her chest. She was incredulous. Why? Why on earth would he send something like that?

"You sent that wreath?!" She stepped forward, but Nick was unable to shake his head: he suddenly felt very sick. He stumbled towards her and without thinking Kate shoved him hard, backwards, with all her force.

"Hey!"

She turned towards the cry and saw Kerrie running up the road towards her.

"Hey Kate?!" she shouted, "Are you OK?!" She arrived, breathless, panting hard.

"What's going on? Who's this fucker?!"

Nick had hit the ground with a crunch, but he was too drunk to feel it. He was trying to get up, but he couldn't see anything clearly.

Kate was shaking her head, backing away from him. "He's someone I had a fling with, a few days ago... he's warped, mad!" her voice trembled.

Nick got onto his knees, pressed his thumb down onto his phone and unlocked it, but unable to see the screen, he held it out to Kate, waving it, dropping it, slurring something. He tried to get onto one knee, but, as he heaved himself up, nausea rose in his throat and, still on his knees, he vomited up half the beer he'd drunk. He dropped his phone, hung his head as a second wave overwhelmed him and was violently sick a second time.

Kerrie bent and picked up his phone. She held it, pressed the button down and said,

"Siri, call Emma." The phone flashed, dialled and rang. A woman's voice answered. "Hi, your husband is outside The Duchy Arms on Sancroft Street, and he's paralytic," Kerrie said coolly, "I think you need to come and get him. He won't make it home on his own." She pressed and put the phone down by Nick. She glanced at Kate who was at the entrance to the flats.

"Go on in," she said. "I'll wait with the bastard just in case."

Kate frowned. "What are you doing here?"

"I've got Annie's bag. She kept losing it, in the auditorium and then in the toilets, she left it hanging on the door! I said I'd put it in my rucksack for safe keeping." Kerrie smiled briefly. "Go on, go in. I'll ring on the bell when he's gone."

Kate went inside and shut the door. She stood for several moments in the sterile lobby, cold and trembling then made her way up to her flat and sat in the dark, waiting for Kerrie to let her know that Nick had gone.

P RESENT DAY - *London*
Saturday – a.m.

KATE WOKE WITH A START. She heard the toilet being flushed and it took her a few moments to realise who it was and to remember what had happened last night. She rolled over onto her side and listened for more sound. The flat was small, the walls thin but the habitual noises that Annie made Kate barely noticed; she was used to them. Now she heard the running of the tap in the kitchen, the pad of footsteps around the sitting room, the squeak and dull thud of the sofa bed and finally, a knock on her door.

"Hey." Kerrie put her head round the crack in the door. "I'm making some tea. Is that ok? Do you want some?"

"Yeah, sure." Kate sat up slightly. "I'll get up," she said. "See you in a few minutes?"

The door clicked shut and she lay down again in the dark. Kate wasn't good with spontaneity, she wasn't good with people in her space – it was all to do with control, losing it, needing it - and yet even though she wasn't exactly comfortable with Kerrie staying, she was glad of the company. The physical presence of another person was reassuring. She heard the cupboard in the kitchen open and close and, dropping her legs over the side of the bed, she stood up, pulled on a bath robe over her pyjamas and made her way to the sitting room and the small galley kitchen off the end of it.

Kerrie was sitting at the table and had made a pot of tea. She was dressed, the sofa bed had been put back and the cushions on it were righted and plumped. Her presence last night was undetectable. She had her scarf on, and her bag was by the door.

As Kate came in Kerrie handed her a mug and Kate pulled out a chair.

"You're all ready to go."

"Yeah. You need your space."

Kate had the uncanny feeling, for the second time since last night, that Kerrie knew her, in a strangely close way; knew what she was thinking, feeling; what she wanted. It felt good to be on the same level as someone else. It was friendship, in the best sense.

"I'm OK. You don't have to go so early."

Kerrie shrugged. "Yeah, I do." She poured herself another cup of tea. "It was nice of you to let me stay."

"Well, it was so late when we'd finished talking."

"When I'd finished talking, you mean." Kerrie looked at Kate with amusement over the rim of her mug. "You'd have made a great spy. You hardly give anything away."

"Not true, I..." Kate accepted defeat and smiled.

"Kate, hey look, it's none of my business, OK?" Kerrie shrugged. "I'm just saying that... well, like I said last night, if you need someone to talk to, you can call me, right?" She stood and took her mug to the sink where she washed it, dried it and put it back in the cupboard. How many people did that, Kate thought? It was a small gesture, but Kate felt the solidarity in it.

"That business last night, that guy," Kerrie said, "I don't know what it's all about, but I've got your back. You need to know that."

Kate stood up as well. "Thanks," she said. She walked with Kerrie to the front door and there Kerrie pulled her coat on and slung her bag over her shoulder.

She said, "Any time." Then stepping into the hall, she added; "You've got my number, right?"

"Right."

"Good. See ya then."

Kerrie turned and walked away; Kate watched her go. She glanced back, waved when she got to the stairs and then disappeared. Kate went back into the flat, suddenly aware of how empty and quiet was. She went to the bedroom, found her phone by the bed and on impulse she brought up Kerrie's number then sent a text. It said,

Thanks for the offer of support. I really do appreciate it.

Kerrie responded immediately and an emoticon came back – a flexed and pumped-up bicep. Nothing else, but that small, graphic image made Kate feel suddenly safe.

NICK WAS aware of his body first, a cramp in his right arm and leg, a dull ache in his back, a weird furriness in his mouth. Then his head kicked in, a sharp pain banging against his temples and finally, as he shifted slightly, now conscious of where he was, an empty, gnawing sickness

rose in his chest. He opened his eyes; saw the washing up bowl on the floor, leant forward and tried to retch. He couldn't. The sickness was cloying, but there was no relief from it.

A minute or so later Emma came into the sitting room. She was in her pyjamas and carried two mugs of tea. She put one on the side table and sat down on the sofa opposite Nick.

"How are you feeling?"

Nick sat up. He was still in half a suit, his shirt crumped, his tied had been removed – that must have been Emma – and his suit trousers were sweaty and creased.

"Like shit," he said.

"Not surprising. You drank around sixteen units of alcohol. Not bad for someone who rarely touches the stuff."

Nick dropped his thumping head in his hands. "Only you could have calculated my alcohol intake Emma," he said through his fingers. "Analytical to the nth degree." He glanced up. "What did you do? Count the empty glasses?"

"No, you forgot to pay. A young girl came out of the pub with your tab while you were lying on the ground; apparently you left your card behind the bar." She frowned. "Really? What were you thinking Nick?"

Nick stood up. He felt unsteady, weak and pathetic. "I don't know what I was thinking Emma, it's been a shit week, one of the worst since my mum died and you know what, I wasn't thinking, OK?"

Emma sipped her tea as he walked across the room. "Where are you going?"

At the door he turned, holding onto the door handle for support. "I'm going to get some water." He felt the nausea rise and stooped over. "Is that OK?" he added sarcastically.

Emma stood. She put her tea on the floor and said, "Go

and sit down Nick. I'll bring you some water and some paracetamol. You've got a hangover. Get over yourself."

She brushed past him and went into the kitchen. Nick staggered into the downstairs toilet and locked the door. He sat down on the toilet seat and tried to remember what the fuck he'd been doing last night. He heard Emma call him; her voice was tender, maternal but then it would be, he thought, she wants to keep me on side; she has a motive.

He closed his eyes and behind the lashed shutter he saw Annie and Kate, just for moment then he saw the ground, the vomit splashing onto the concrete, Kate's face, angry and distressed. He pressed his fingertips to his eyes and tried to think back, to evoke his memory. He remembered the van, trying to tell Kate about the van and the florist in Marylebone High Street, but what had happened next? How did Emma get there? Did he call her?

Suddenly Nick stood up. He heard the words, the voice. "Siri, call Emma." Call Emma, call, Emma... How did that woman know who Emma was? Did he say her name? Did she ask him who to call? The voice went round and round his head and his heart started to thump. Call Emma... He was pretty sure he hadn't said anything; fuck he hadn't been *able* to say anything. Whoever was with Kate, whoever had arrived, had called Nick's wife and somehow... Nick bent forward over the sink and splashed his head and neck with cold water to wake his thoughts up... somehow, she had known who Emma was; she had known Emma's name.

He looked at himself in the mirror above the sink as the cold water dripped off his face. There was something else that was niggling at him, something more important than the young woman last night, something that he needed to consider. He glanced down at his body; long legs, very little extra weight - apart from the beginnings of a small no exercise belly - two inches too tall to be fashionable, too gangly to be athletic, too thin to be imposing, but it was a body he was comfortable with, familiar as he was with its shape and height; familiar as he was with the look of it. He saw Kate and Annie again in his mind's eye; Annie stooped, bent slightly at the knees to hug her mum; tall thin legs, no weight. Annie was fourteen, he thought, fourteen.

Nick unlocked the door and walked out into the hall. He put his head round the door where Emma sat with the Saturday FT and her cup of tea. He saw the two white tablets on the sofa table with a glass of water and his own undrunk mug of tea. He crossed, popped the pills into his mouth, washed them down with the water and then swallowed some tea.

"Thanks," he said. He crossed back to the door, and she glanced up.

"Why don't you go back to bed, I mean our bed, not the spare room put-you-up and then if you feel a bit better later, I thought we might go over to Borough Market, get something for dinner, Sunday lunch..."

Nick shook his head. "Not today, Emma," he said, "I need a shower then I've got something I have to do."

At the door he turned. "How long have we been together?" he asked.

Emma lowered the paper again. "Fourteen years," she said. "We met right at the beginning of the first year, your second year technically, just after you came back from... from taking the year out to be with your mum..."

Nick nodded. "I'll see you later," he said. "Not sure when."

Emma pressed her lips together as if she had wanted to say something but decided against it. Nick left the room and headed up the stairs.

"Fourteen good years," Emma called after him. Her voice was controlled, overly bright.

Fourteen, he thought, there's that number again. Had they been good? He honestly didn't know.

Dr Jane Hardman let her springer spaniel off its lead just inside the gate of her large, winter-pruned front garden on Blomfield Road W9 and dug in the pockets of her waxed jacket for her house keys. She made her way along the black and white tiled path to the steps of the house, calling her dog to heel as she climbed them and put the key in the lock, opening the front door. She pulled off her wellies - damp and muddy from walking along the canal path – and, holding the dog by his collar with one hand, she leant just inside the door to grab the towel off the chair in the hallway and wiped his feet. She let him in first, followed - the cold from the tiled floor seeping up through her socks - found her slippers and made her way into the kitchen.

The house, a white fronted Victorian villa was too big for her really, but she loved every square, fully-paid-for inch of it. It marked a turning point in her life; it marked her success. Her first book, 'the Power of Shame' published ten years ago had been on the Sunday Times best seller list for fifteen weeks – enough time to carve out a media niche, with interviews and expert opinions – and it made her name. The rest, she told people - not seeing any reason why she shouldn't quote platitudes – is history.

In the large kitchen at the back of the house that overlooked Little Venice Gardens, Jane went to the fridge for coffee and spooned some into her Moka pot, putting it on the hob. She called to the dog - Ari, short for Aristotle, pretentious, but she didn't care – and when he didn't arrive, went out into the hall to find him. They had a Saturday morning routine, walk, coffee for her, biscuits for him then work.

"Ari?" He was sniffing the floor, trailing his nose from the front door to the door of her study. Jane watched him for a few moments then she looked closely at the door of her study. It was closed, but not shut; she always kept it shut; firmly shut. Going back to the kitchen for her phone, she found her neighbour's number and kept it on screen as she headed back to her study. She opened the door and went in, her heart thudding.

Inside, the room was in semi-darkness; the white wood shutters were still closed from last night. Jane turned the overhead light on and scanned the room as Ari trailed his nose all over the wooden floor, from her desk to the book-cases and back to her desk. He had picked up a scent, someone had been in here. She watched him again then she followed him to the point he kept going to at the bottom of the bookcase. She stood and reached up for a box file on the shelf directly above the spot that Ari kept sniffing. Jane didn't label anything – she was well known now with some important and celebrity patients - and she needed to protect their identities. But even without any labels, she knew exactly what each box file contained, whose client notes were where. She took the file she'd retrieved over to her desk and opened it.

Katherine Ross. She knew it as soon as she saw her own handwriting. There were no names, no times or days, just one date on the front of the file that told her what it contained. Jane looked at the date. Fourteen years ago, she thought, all in the past, but she knew, as she leafed through the papers, reading her scrawled black script covering the pages, she knew that it wasn't in the past at all. Not now. Someone had been here, someone had carefully and meticulously been through these notes, been here, in her house, this morning.

Jane walked across to the window and opened the shutters. She looked out at the gardens. She'd been watched - easy to do – and when she'd left for her walk someone had come in. She wondered how, but then she knew enough about psychology to recognise that the how was irrelevant; it was the why that mattered. And, going back to the file, looking again at her notes, Jane could hazard a guess why. Someone had unfinished business and that someone was going to bring all the pain that Jane had helped to bury, back to life.

12

T HE PAST – *Kingstanton and Exeter, Devon, December 2008*

It was Monday morning; Richard stood at the entrance of the university library and watched Katherine, easily visible across the space at one of the desks, her wild hair tied back off her face with a rubber band in a messy top knot, an old, frayed, red jumper swamping her. She looked tired, her skin had a grey pallor, but she was focused on something, chewing the end of her pen and reading. That was a first, he thought; she was naturally bright, but she did bugger-all academic work, probably to annoy him, which it did – continually. She always only just scraped by, he thought, when she could have won prizes. He saw the pile of books and academic studies stacked up beside her, some open, others discarded, and intrigued, he made his way across to her.

"You look busy?"

Katherine glanced up.

"Hi. Yes, I am, very busy." She sat back in her chair and looked at him. "Thanks for the supplies."

"My pleasure."

"I had *Coco pops* this morning for breakfast. Two bowls *and* I drank the chocolate milk straight from the bowl." She smiled and raised an eyebrow.

"Good for you." Richard ignored the challenge. She couldn't do it, he thought, she couldn't just say thank you and leave it at that; she had to have a dig. It used to infuriate Beth when Katherine was bad mannered at the table in front of the twins; drinking the left-over milk from her breakfast cereal straight from the bowl was one of Katherine's best provocative moves. It had created caustic rows.

"What are you doing?"

"I have a summative to do by Easter, so I thought I'd make a start."

"Really?" Richard was taken aback. "What's it on?"

"Ah ha!" Katherine handed him one of the studies from her stack.

"*Brown and Polk, Taking fear of Crime Seriously*. Great." Richard glanced at the rest of the stack. He saw Bannister and Fife, *Fear and the City*, and a Home Office research study on the cost of crime. He felt a niggling sense of alarm. "What's the essay on?" he asked.

Katherine looked across at the Librarian. "Let's go and grab a coffee," she said, "We can't really talk in here." She stood. "I mean, if you have time?"

Another challenge, but again Richard didn't rise. "I've got time," he said. He followed Katherine out, down the stairs and into the cold morning air. It was bright and she immediately put on a pair of large, dark sunglasses that she pulled from the back pocket of her jeans. She also produced a packet of cigarettes and lit up as they walked towards the coffee bar in Devonshire House. She was posing to annoy him.

"I was thinking, last night," she said, "A lot, about what you said and how, well...how I need to get my act together and..." she took long drags of the cigarette as she spoke; she had a faintly frantic air about her. "I thought about the child abduction case in Kingstanton, the one that Beth was talking about at lunch yesterday and I looked it up on one of the computers in the library today, I looked at some of the press reports on the microfiche and I had this idea, so I rang my tutor..."

Richard looked at her. "You did all this this morning? It's just after eleven."

"I got to the library when it opened, at eight and then I rang my tutor an hour ago and well, it's all decided, and he thinks it's a great idea..."

Richard interrupted her. Katherine could be impulsive and thoughtless; she ran at things, sometimes blindly. "What is a great idea Kat?"

"A socio and economic study into the impact of crime on the community – that's the title of my summative essay. It struck me that I had this great opportunity staring me in the face! Just up the road there is the scene of a crime that is one of the worst imaginable; the abduction and possibly murder of a child and..."

Richard stopped and put his hand on her arm. "Kat, stop a minute, will you? Have you really thought about this?" He looked at her animated face; her eyes were bright and full of life, and he held down the comment on the tip of his tongue. He hadn't seen that face, heard this enthusiasm for years.

"Yes! Yes of course I've thought about it; I've been

thinking about it all night! I want to get over to Kingstanton and start interviewing people, find out from local businesses how they feel and if there's been an impact on spending. Is the community suppressed by what's happened? I thought I could speak to people about how they feel, about the abduction, about the atmosphere in the town. I thought I could maybe even talk to some of the friends of the family, I..."

Again, Richard interrupted her. "Hang on a minute Katherine..." He paused and for many years afterwards Richard wondered about that pause. He wondered if he'd just said, 'stop right there, this is not the right thing to do' would any of it have happened? But he did pause; he stopped himself from blurting out his natural reaction to her plan. He hesitated, he thought, and in that moment she said,

"I know that you think I'm a light-weight dad – a bit of an academic failure next to the great professor Richard Ross." She glanced at him then looked down at the ground. She never called him dad; his resolve faltered.

"You're right," she went on, "I am, and I've been pretty crap up to now.... but I think this is a good idea and..." she shrugged. "You never know, I might just make a good job of it."

Richard looked at her face once again. Behind the dark glasses he saw how fragile she was, how she was poised on the edge of either opening up or closing down and seeing her like that, knowing that he was responsible for so much of his daughter's anger and pain, he did what he was so often inclined to do, he took the easy way out. He didn't challenge her, he said nothing; nothing of any value anyway.

"Just go easy, will you sweetheart?"

Katherine nodded and flicked her cigarette end into the bushes, but Richard knew she hadn't heard him. They arrived at Devonshire House and Richard went up to get their coffees. When he came back to the table Katherine was talking to a post grad student on the table next to her and the question of her essay and its research was never raised again.

CI LEWIN RUBBED his hands wearily over his face. His meeting had just finished, the incident room was clearing, and the mood was tense. The divers had been at it all day yesterday, but there was nothing out there, sweet FA, he thought, bugger all. Wherever Abbey was, she wasn't dead and dumped at the bottom of the estuary. DS Crowley thought that was hopeful, Lewin thought Crowley was deluded. He knew that the chances of finding Abbey alive were diminishing incrementally as each day passed and he knew that it was his fault. He rubbed his gut and brought up some wind. Recently his arm had started to ache as well; a tight, dull throb all down his left side and he was chewing *paracetamol* as well as *Rennies* by the pack load, washed down with mint tea which Sandra insisted on making him. Christ, he hated mint tea; not more than he hated the job though.

Next thing was a house to house, which he had to sign off by the end of day. It was a huge drain on resources and expensive, but there was nothing on the DNA on the scarf, could've been dropped by aliens as far as he was concerned. The only flagging hope they had on it was that one of the men using the area recognised it, but that was a dead end, he thought. Who would seriously own up to having seen someone in that scarf when they were having sex with other men in the bushes or down on the beach?

Lewin picked up the phone and pressed nine for an outside line. He had to speak to Donna Salter, and he had nothing to tell her. He moved his mouth from side to side as the line rang, trying to loosen his jaw before he spoke but it made little difference. There was nothing that was going to make the next few minutes any less tense, nothing he could say that was going to make it any easier at all – for either of them.

It was early evening and Katherine sat in the pub on the quayside in Kingstanton with a pint of cider. She had told herself that she wouldn't drink today, that she needed a clear head, but the afternoon had been so dismal that just the one would lift her spirits, give her a bit of Dutch courage to approach a couple of people in the bar. She sipped and made some notes, conscious of the time, of having to get the bus back to the station and the train back to Exeter. She had quickly realised that 'I'm a sociology student from LSE writing a paper on the effects of crime' wasn't going to wash with anybody so she changed it to 'I'm a journalist,' which was even worse. No-one wanted to speak to her and after several hours traipsing around the town and the housing estates, she had given up.

She had documented the refusals she'd been given though, so that was something, and she had the beginnings of some research in the lack of responses themselves, in how dismissive people were, how closed and guarded they appeared. But that wasn't going to be enough; she needed interviews if the essay was going to come to life.

Katherine looked up from her notebook and realised that she'd drunk her pint. Just one more, she thought and then I'll get going. She saw a space at the bar next to a young man with a pint and a cigarette. She needed a drink and a light, so she left her notebook and squeezed in beside him to order.

"Do you have a light?" she asked after ordering her pint.

The young man dug in his pocket for a lighter and glanced at her to decide whether he'd flick the flint or hand it over. He smiled; she was worth flicking the flint for.

"Here." He held the small flame out and Katherine bent to light her roll-up.

He had a weakness of scruffy girls, the student type. "You here on holiday?" he asked.

"Sort of," Katherine said. "I'm here doing some research for a paper at uni."

He took a cigarette out of a smart black packet and lit it. "University, eh? Smart as well as pretty."

Katherine smiled. She had never known why men used such inane comments in their pick-up lines, but she went with it. He was attractive, in a clean-cut, square and solid way. Her pint arrived and she fumbled in her jeans for some cash.

"Here, let me buy you that. I shouldn't think you've got a lot of cash to flash, not with you being a student."

"Thanks!" Katherine smiled at him. "That's kind of you." She took a large gulp of cider; it was local and strong, and she hadn't eaten today, not since the *Coco Pops*. She was beginning the buzz stage. "I take it you're not a student, seeing as you *have* got cash to flash?"

The young man held out his hand. "I'm Mark; I'm one of the local police officers here."

"Katherine Ross," Katherine said, her interest sparked at the words, police officer. "Nice to meet you, Mark." She took another two big swigs of the cider, and the buzz became the familiar warmth, a lightness and an easing of her angst.

"God, you must be up to your neck in it at the moment," she said. "This whole abduction thing is terrible, isn't it?"

"Yeah, tell me about it. The atmosphere here is impossible," he lifted his pint. "Hence the relaxation." He nodded at the table with her notebook on and her coat over the chair. "Shall we sit down?"

"Sure." Katherine picked up her drink and held her cigarette between her lips as they made their way back to the table. They sat and she relaxed back in her chair, looking directly at him. "Tell me," She said, "I'm a good listener."

"I bet that's not all you're good at," Mark said.

Katherine didn't smile. Instead, she ignored the crass comment and gave him the once over. Why not, she thought? He could be useful and, if we have another couple of pints, I'll have missed my train home anyway.

13

P RESENT DAY - *London*
Saturday – a.m.

NICK MADE his way along Marylebone High Street looking for the right shop number. He found it easily, a fragrant, cream fronted shop with an old bicycle parked outside it, its basket piled high with blooms. He looked at the buckets of flowers in the window. He'd never bought flowers - Emma considered them a colossal waste of money – but he could see now why other people would. There was something wild yet elegant about the flowers on display here, as if the florist had taken a handful of nature and arranged it artfully and of course very expensively. These flowers shouted good taste.

"Sorry," a girl said, lifting a bucket of roses off the display. "We're closed. We close at one on a Saturday."

"Oh, that's OK; I don't want to buy anything."

The girl glanced at him and then at another of the girls

also clearing buckets of flowers from the display and a brief look was exchanged that made him uncomfortable.

"I'd like some information, about one of your deliveries. It was sent to a friend of mine and she's a bit upset."

An older lady came into the shop from the back. "Can I help you?"

"Yes, I hope so. You delivered a wreath yesterday, early evening, to an address in SE11, a home address."

Her face was blank. "We deliver hundreds of bouquets, floral arrangements and wreaths each week," she said. "Was there a problem?"

Nick drew himself up to his full height. "There was actually. No-one had died and the wreath was delivered to a young woman, my friend. She was pretty upset, and I don't blame her. It was ordered either by someone with a very bad sense of humour or as some kind of sinister message. I'd like some details about who ordered the wreath, please."

The woman blinked several times. "I'm very sorry, but don't think I can give those details out."

"Oh. That's a shame, especially seeing as you or someone here didn't bother to check who the wreath was going and as a result caused enormous distress to my friend."

There was a moment of silence between them then she said, "Of course, terrible thing to happen. Let me look at the order book."

"Thank you."

She pulled it out from under the desk and opened it at the beginning of the week. "A wreath to Sancroft Street, SE11?" She ran her finger down the page. "Here. Here it is. It was ordered on Monday and was paid for in cash. We attached a card, but that's it; there are no other details. We usually take a contact number, in case there's a problem with the delivery, but there's nothing here. That's Shelly's handwriting; it looks like she took the order. She's not in today, but if you come back on Monday, she works on a Monday."

"So do I," Nick said. "Can you give me Shelly's number and I'll give her ring and see if she remembers anything about the person who made the order."

"No, I'm sorry, I can't do that."

Nick looked at her, but he said nothing.

"Let me give her a ring myself and you can speak to her. OK?"

"Great." He waited while the florist found the number on her mobile and dialled.

"Shell? Sorry to bother you darling, but there's someone here who wants to know about an order you took on Monday? ... Yes I told them that, nearly three hundred orders this week... yeah, only... well apparently this was for a funeral wreath and it was delivered to a home address where no-one had died, to a young woman... yes, she's pretty upset. Yeah sure, I'll put them on..."

She handed the phone over and Nick said, "Hi Shelly, thanks for speaking to me. Do you remember anything at all about the person who placed the order on Monday? Were they male or female, young, old? I'm just trying to find out who it was... it was probably someone we know... and if it is then I can find out what on earth they were up to."

On the other end of the line Shelly had been bent over the washing machine, but now she stood straight and tried to remember Monday. It had been busy and there were some odd ones; a man who sent the same flowers to his girl-friend and his wife and an order for an expensive potted cactus garden with a card that said, 'for a big prick,' - which they'd all found hilarious in the shop. She didn't remember the wreath though. God, she should have checked. They usually always went to the funeral directors, so she didn't know why this didn't ring any alarm bells. She tried to think back.

"I'm sorry, but I don't, not at all. I was on my own that day, one of our girls was off sick and I took so many orders that day," she said, "I honestly don't really remember any of them. There were two funerals as well, so that's probably why I don't recall it..." She bit her fingernail and looked across at her husband who was feeding the baby. "I'm ever so sorry," she said, "That's an awful thing to receive." She remembered the card; it said RIP. She shuddered.

Nick handed the phone back to the florist and she hung up. "Thanks," he said. "If Shelly does remember anything else, can you give me a call?" He handed her his House of Commons business card.

She glanced at it then at him again. "Of course. Thanks Mr Farleigh. And I'm sorry, you know, for the upset."

He left the shop and made his way back down the High Street towards Oxford Street and the tube. Saturday in the West End was grim; he'd forgotten just how grim, so instead of elbowing his way through the crowds, he took his time and window shopped. He was only four doors away when the florist came up behind him and tapped him on the shoulder. She held out her phone.

"It's Shelly," she said. "She's remembered something."

Nick took it.

"Hi," Shelly said, "I do remember something now. I don't know if the person was male or female, but they were young, and I'm leaning more towards male as I remember dropping my pen and I think he, or she, had on some of those really expensive trainers; you know, the ones that you can run and climb in, with the special sole. I recognised them because I just bought a pair for my husband for his birthday. They're NIKE, they're called NIKE Metcon."

Nick glanced down at his feet. "OK, well thanks." He handed the phone back to the florist for the second time and she said, "Can we send some flowers? To make up for the mistake?"

"No, thanks, that's really nice for you, but I don't think she's going to welcome any more deliveries at the moment."

The florist nodded, turned and made her way back to the shop. Nick went on his way. Trainers, he thought, that's all she remembered.

KATE LEFT the flat and turned down Sancroft Street towards Black Prince Road on route to Albert Embankment, taking the scenic walk to Lower Marsh where she had arranged to meet Annie and Kerrie in the café. As she walked, she wondered how this had all come about, meeting them both, lunch then on to a Christmas open day in Lambeth Palace Gardens, finishing with a takeaway in the evening. One minute she had texted that she was happy to have a friend and the next she had one, *fulltime*. Annie was delighted of course; she thought Kerrie was cool, but Kate - ever wary - had agreed to Kerrie and Annie's suggestion with misgivings.

Kate wasn't sure why Annie had been hanging around in the café in the first place this morning; they had gone there from Mattie's house, they both had some sort of addiction to the place, or to Kerrie. Kate thought back to herself at that age, but she couldn't remember anything except loneliness and a swamping feeling of helplessness. What she would've have given for a cool older friend who worked in a café and gave her free drinks. Grudgingly, she could see the attraction and well... Annie was right; Kerrie was cool.

Having cut down Hercules Road, when she arrived at Lower Marsh, Kate's misgivings had subsided, and she strode towards the café feeling – if not excited – then at least comfortable. She skirted past her office – the shop – always worried that someone would be waiting outside with a weekend problem that she couldn't solve, but couldn't ignore, and made her way to the café. Inside it was busy and Annie sat with her book at a shared table in the window. Kate knocked on the glass and Annie glanced up. She was embarrassed and Kate wished she could retract the knock. She kept forgetting that her daughter had entered that teen self-conscious stage when everyday actions became acutely awkward.

"Hey." Inside, Kate stood next to Annie's table. Do you want another drink?"

"No thanks Mum, I'm good. I've had two hot chocolates already." Annie put her hand up to cover her mouth conspiratorially and hissed, "Freebies!"

"Great. I'll get a coffee then." Kate made her way across to the counter where Kerrie was serving. Kerrie turned from the coffee machine and saw her.

"Hey! How are you doing?"

"Fine. Could I have a latte please?"

"Coming up, on the house." Kerrie turned to her colleague. "Can you do me a latte hon? I'm off duty as of now." She untied her apron and came round the counter to Kate.

"Look Kate, can I have a quick chat, you know, about last night?"

Kate was puzzled. "Sure. What's up?"

Kerrie moved in closer so that their shoulders were

touching. Kate always felt uneasy about physical contact with anyone else but Annie. She said nothing though and simply edged back an inch or so. "The thing is," Kerrie began, "I've been thinking and I just wanna say, that bloke last night? Well, he shouldn't have been round your place, you know, at your home. That's pretty much stalking and you were really upset about it. Right?"

Kate nodded, tight lipped; she knew this was concern, but she couldn't help feeling the edge of intrusion.

"I'm guessing it's not the first time either, right?"

Kate hesitated. She looked at Kerrie, but saw only worry and recognised that she was too closed, too guarded, so she took a breath and said,

"No, no it's not the first time it's happened." She felt a sudden relief at being able to confide in someone. "He's been round before. We knew each other – a long time ago, we met briefly at university...and I guess he thinks he knows me, but..." She felt her voice falter. "I think he did some-thing really weird yesterday..." she trailed off and took another deep breath. "He sent me a wreath, or at least I think it was him."

"Excuse me? He did what?"

Kate said, "Oh thank God you look so shocked – I thought maybe I was overreacting because it really upset me." Kate didn't mention exactly why, the funeral, Lydia, her moment of overwhelming fear.

"Fucking hell Kate, I'm not surprised. That is fucking weird." Kerrie was shaking her head. "It was definitely him, right?"

"Well yes, I think so. The wreath was delivered around five, just after you and the girls left for the lecture and then when he turned up later, drunk, he was garbling on about flowers and..."

"Yeah, sounds like it was him. God, the bastard! You need to report this Kate, to the police. You really do."

"No." Kate chewed her lip and looked away. Going to the police would only complicate things, she thought, and they were complicated enough as it was. "I don't want to do that. I don't think it'll do any good, not in my experience."

But Kerrie didn't seem to hear her. "God, this is terrible. No wonder you were so upset last night. You should have told me..." She broke off, then a few moments later said; "You are definitely going to the police and I'm coming with you."

"No, no honestly Kerrie, you don't need to do that."

"But you are going? You should log it at least Kate, just in case anything else happens. I think you're right; I don't think they'll do anything, but if you've made a complaint then it's there in writing, you're in the system. Right?"

"I don't know..." Kate felt suddenly hemmed in. "What about our plans?"

But Kerrie missed the end of what Kate said because she turned to get the latte that was ready.

"Here, I'll take it over to Annie's table for you."

"No, you don't have to do that, I..."

Kerrie set off and slightly bamboozled, Kate fell into step behind her. When they reached Annie, Kerrie said,

"Hey sweetness, there's been a bit of a change of plan. Your mum has to do something this afternoon, so you and I are going to hit the Gardens for a couple of hours on our own."

"Really?" Annie looked up from her book.

Kate frowned; she wasn't going to be pressured into anything. "Well, I had wondered about doing it, but not if you're looking forward to..." She broke off as Kerrie took a pair of headphones out of her pocket and held them out to Annie.

"This little baby..." she said, holding up a dual headphone jack on the end of them, "means that we can both listen to the latest Taylor Swift album which I only downloaded this morning!"

"No, seriously?!"

"Uh huh!"

"Wow! Amazing."

Kate felt suddenly superfluous to requirements, and it hurt. She said, "Look, I honestly don't have to do this thing right this minute, I'll can come with you guys and do it on Monday instead."

Annie looked at her mum. "It's not a problem with me mum, honestly. If you have somewhere else to be then that's fine; I'm happy to go with Kerrie and we can meet you later. Especially seeing as I can listen to *Reputation*."

Kate knew that she was reserved, but she had no problem with being assertive – usually. She was strong and she knew her mind... only Annie was her Achilles heel. Annie she couldn't confront, refuse or lose face with. Kate had spent too many years as a teenager wanting attention, needing someone who wasn't there and now she overcompensated for that. If Annie wanted to listen to Taylor Swift, then Kate wasn't going to interfere. She wondered momentarily how all of that had happened so quickly then she said,

"OK, great. Taylor Swift. Right... as long as you're sure?"

"We're sure, right Annie?"

"Right." Fait accompli. Now if she insisted on going with them, she would look difficult and needy.

Kerrie scooped up Annie's mugs and said, "So if you're ready to go Sweets, we might as well head off now before it gets dark and leave your mum to her coffee. I'll pop these in the kitchen and grab my coat."

"Great!" Annie got to her feet and took her jacket off the back of the chair. Before she pulled it on, she leant forward and planted a kiss on Kate's cheek. "I'm glad you and Kerrie are friends," she said, "She's really nice, isn't she?"

Kate held out her arms and Annie stepped into a hug. We are still close, Kate thought, she is still mine. Annie stepped back from the embrace as Kerrie signalled from the door.

"I'll see you later," Kate said. "Text me?"

Annie made her way across the café and stopped to blow Kate a kiss at the door. She disappeared out into the cold December afternoon and Kerrie followed her, looking across at Kate before she did so and giving her the thumbs up.

Kate watched them go down the street through the window then glanced at the latte on the table; she didn't fancy it anymore. Moments later, she too left the cafe, heading in the opposite direction to Annie and Kerrie, down towards Southwark and the Police Station.

EMMA WAS STILL in her pyjamas mid-afternoon. She had made herself the smoked salmon and scrambled eggs she had bought to have with Nick for breakfast and now lay on the sofa, the faux fur throw over her, her weekend work completed on the floor beside her and her MacBook open on her lap as she scrolled through Kate's Twitter feed. It was all very dull stuff, she thought, far too PC to be even remotely interesting. The woman clearly had enough social conscience for half of London, lobbying MPs, outing bad landlords, doing her bit for the good and poor in the community. Quite frankly it bored Emma to death, and so far, it had proved distinctly unfruitful. It was time, she decided, to try another tack.

Reaching for her phone, Emma rang one of the trainees assigned to her team. She was hoping the girl would answer with her name because she couldn't quite remember it. She did and Emma said, "Sophie, glad I caught you. I'm not interrupting anything am I?"

Emma knew of course that she probably was, and that Sophie would never say so. Shit job, trainee, but excellent prospects, especially if you killed yourself to get on.

"Good," Emma said. "I've got a small job for you this weekend, if it's not too much trouble?"

Emma waited for Sophie to assent that it wasn't too much trouble, which she did just moments later and then continued; "There's a charitable organisation - London based - that we're thinking could be a good target for our CSR initiative, maybe some investment? It's called *Legalhub* and I'd like you to do a thorough investigation into its legal and financial history please."

It was hardly a small job, not now she'd articulated it, but Emma didn't care. Weekend or not, work had to be done. "If I could have it by Monday, please Sophie? Monday close of day will be fine and that should give you ample time Monday a.m. to check with any regulatory bodies that might be closed over the weekend, the Charities Commission and the like."

Emma shut her laptop and placed it on the floor. "Good, that would be great, thank you Sophie. Yes, I'll put a meeting in my diary for the afternoon on Monday and send you an invite."

She heard a muffled silence and knew that Sophie had

her hand over the microphone, probably explaining to the boyfriend that she had to go into the office. Emma waited. Thank God those days were over, the groping, gofer days. "Thanks Sophie," she said, cutting short the silence. "See you on Monday." And she pressed end. Not my problem, she thought, and she stood up to get herself a glass of wine.

KATE SAT opposite a female police officer in a small interview room and waited while the woman made notes.

"OK, so this is what we've got so far." The police officer glanced up at Kate and smiled reassuringly.

"You met Nick Farleigh five days ago at a drinks party at the House of Commons, you went to a bar and had a couple of drinks – you don't drink alcohol - and he came back to your flat for a cup of tea. Then you don't hear from him again until last night when he sent you a funeral wreath with a card attached that had the letters R.I.P on it. Is that right?"

Kate nodded, but she glanced away. Of course, it wasn't right; it was only a fraction of what had happened in the last five days, but Kate had no intention of sharing that. The truth - her fears that this man, someone she hardly knew, had almost had sex with, and who she thought had some knowledge of her, wanted in some way to damage her - seemed bizarre in the cold light of a police interview room. God, it sounded ridiculous, even to her. This had been a stupid idea, she thought, to come to the police; how could she possibly explain her suspicions, her anxieties? They needed to stay where they belonged - in the past.

"And you've no idea why he might have sent you a wreath?"

"No." It was the day of Lydia's funeral, but Nick couldn't have known about that. She thought back to some of the things they'd chatted about when they went for a drink, his constituency, his clinic, problems in the area. Did he know about Lydia and the music centre? Could he have been at the funeral? She glanced up. The police officer had asked another question and was waiting for an answer.

"I'm sorry, I missed that," Kate was momentarily caught off guard. "What did you say?"

"I was asking if you're sure it was him? Did he tell you he'd sent it?"

"No."

"Did you check with the florist?"

"No, I..." It must have been him, Kate thought. "I think it was him, but I didn't see the florist's van and the flowers didn't have a label to say where they were from."

"Were they addressed to you?"

"Yes."

"Was the card handwritten?"

"Yes."

The police officer looked at Kate. "So why do you think it was Nick Farleigh?"

"He was at my flat last night, sometime after they'd been delivered, and he was drunk. He kept going on about flowers..."

"Were you together?"

"No, he was outside the block of flats I live in."

"But you took him 'going on about flowers' to mean the wreath?"

"Yes. He was very drunk, and my friend had to call his wife to come and collect him."

"His wife? Nick Farleigh is married?"

"Yes..." Kate faltered.

"But there's nothing between you, no relationship?"

"No" Kate's voice was sharper than she'd intended. She took a moment then said; "Why are you asking that?!"

"I'm just wondering if there might have been a mix up at the florist. If he had sent you flowers, but the order was wrongly delivered?"

Kate swallowed down a response. Yes, that *might* have happened, but she wanted to say that she'd felt it was deliberate, that the card and delivery had felt malicious, although she couldn't explain why.

"Look, Kate, I'm not sure this is a crime or that we can help you in any way. What I suggest is that you stay here for a short while and I'm going to run this past my boss and see what we should do next. Is that OK?"

Kate nodded. The police officer stood. "I won't be long. If you need to use the ladies, press the green button here to get out and they're at the end of the corridor."

"Thanks."

The officer left and Kate sat for a few minutes more. Then without thinking any further, she stood, gathered up her things and pressed the green button, exiting the room, the corridor and the station as quickly as she could. Once out in the cold night air she felt a sudden relief. She should never have gone to the police, of course they couldn't help, and the PC had clearly thought it was all an over exaggeration. Same lack of understanding, she thought, just a different time and place. Brushing past someone going into the station – which she barely registered – Kate turned and strode down the street to the tube, texting Annie as she went. If she hurried, she might just catch the end of their walk in Lambeth Palace Gardens and the afternoon wouldn't have been a complete waste of time.

Mo STOOD JUST inside the door of the station reception area and wondered why the woman he'd just caught with his elbow as she brushed past looked so familiar. He darted back out again and watched the back of her for a moment, walking purposefully down the street. It was the hair; he recognised the hair. Back inside, as he was about to tap his electronic ID onto the keypad, he saw PC Taylor on the other side of the door coming out so waited for her to release the door lock.

"Have you just arrived in Mo?"

"Yes."

"You didn't see a woman leaving by any chance? Mid length hair, slim build, in a black coat?"

"Yeah, I passed her on my way in. Why?"

PC Taylor shrugged. "She was in making a complaint about someone sending her a wreath." She shook her head. "Never mind. There wasn't much we could do about it anyhow - sounded like a cock up at the flower shop to me."

"A wreath? That's weird."

"Yeah, if that's what really happened. She was vague about the details so who knows. Don't forget it's Saturday afternoon, near Christmas and it's cold out. I'd say there were mental health issues."

Mo held the door open for her and they both went through into the station proper. He made his way up to the incident room, sat down at his desk, and found the report that PC Taylor had just filed on the system. He rang Nella.

"Hey, you ok? Yeah, I'm at work. Where else would I be?"

He skimmed through the report as he listened to her banging on about her mum and when she drew breath, he jumped in with; "You know the Lydia Helston accident?"

Nella shut up; he had her attention. "Well, I just remem-bered where I'd seen that woman I saw at her funeral. I saw her here, at the station, a few days ago. She didn't come in, but she stood across the road for ages. Remember? I told you about her?"

Mo clocked the name from the file. "Kate Ross, that's her name and she's been here again today. Allegedly someone – according to her, Nick Farleigh the MP for Lambeth - sent her a wreath last night, after the funeral, with a card attached that said R.I.P. They had a fling and she said he's been harassing her ever since and..." he kept the best bit 'til last. "It turns out that she runs a legal charity."

He waited for Nella to speak and when she did, he wished he'd been able to bet a tenner on her response. "Yup, that's what I thought..." he said, "The development is in his constituency. It's potentially a big boost for the area..." He stood up and went over to the window. "My guess is Kate Ross is connected to Lydia in some way and that's why she was at the funeral, maybe even why she was here a few days ago but didn't come in. Yeah...music centre, leases... some sort of legal advice?" He could hear the rustle of keys and the slam of a front door as Nella left her house, still talking on the phone. "Yup, done it; I've requested his phone records, Kate Ross's, Lydia's and the boyfriend's too..." He heard her get into her car; she was on her way in. "OK, I'll start checking as soon as they come in. Great! See you in half an hour." He pressed end and looked across to check that DS Dennis was not in the office.

Nick took his shoes off at the front door and hung his coat up. The house was in semi darkness, so he wondered if

Emma was out. He switched on the hall lamp and went into the kitchen to make a piece of toast and some tea. He hadn't eaten all day and now he was tired and hungry.

"Nick?"

He turned as Emma came in. She stood just inside the door. She was wearing jeans tucked into boots and a silk shirt.

"Where have you been?"

"Out."

"Don't be facetious Nick. I was worried. You looked terrible this morning and I..."

Nick turned away and continued to make his tea. He went to the fridge for milk and butter and the toast popped up.

"I wondered if you'd like to go out; maybe get a drink, something to eat?"

He buttered his toast and cut it on the bread board. He took a mouthful.

"No thanks, Emma."

Emma came forward. "Look, Nick, I'm sorry for not telling you about the associate partnership, I..."

"It's OK." He bent in the cupboard for a plate.

"It is?"

"Yeah, it is. You don't tell me lots of things Emma because you're never here and when you are, I am irrelevant. That's why I'm going to move out. I'm going to live with Caro for a while."

"Your sister?"

"Yes. She said I can have the sofa-bed until I sort myself out."

"Is that where you've been this afternoon?"

"Yes. There and round and about."

"With Kate?"

Nick blinked. He stared at her for a few moments, directly at her as if he was seeing her for the first time in ages. "No, not with Kate," he said.

"I don't want you to leave."

"I know, but for the first time it isn't all about you Emma. I need to focus on work - I want this job and what's more I'd be bloody good at it, so that's my priority, that and trying to sort out how I feel about..." he stopped and looked at her. "... About everything really."

Nick picked up his mug and plate of toast and moved past her out of the kitchen. "I'll carry on sleeping in the spare room until I go," he said, and he climbed the stairs turning the lights on as he went.

It was approaching midnight when Nella sat back in her chair and stretched.

"Great way to spend a Saturday night," she said, "Hanging round here waiting for phone records and trawling social media."

Mo glanced across at her. "What else would you be doing Nella? Eating a *Dominoes* and watching the X factor, sobbing into your free garlic dip?"

"Very funny. I don't like Dominoes."

"Papa John's then or are you a posh Pizza Express girl?"

"Neither. Local pizza place does for me - the one up the road." She went back to the screen and clicked on another contact for Annie Ross. "Tell you what; Kate Ross and her daughter are poles apart. Kate's contacts are all connected to the charity – no personal presence on *Facebook* or *Twitter* or *Instagram* at all – just loads of business stuff and Annie has hundreds of people. How the hell can you know that many people at fourteen?"

"Dunno..."

"How are you doing on Lydia?"

Mo was clicking through photos on the screen; they had split the job; Mo got to scroll through Lydia Helston's social media and Nella was going through Annie and Kate Ross's. "Lots of contacts, no sign of Kate Ross or Annie Ross and no friends in common so far... See what you mean though about the eating thing. In some of the older pictures she's tagged in from college she looks ill."

Nella pushed her chair back and stood up. "Road to nowhere, this, I think. They don't seem to be linked in any way. We now know that the music centre used a big legal firm so how come Kate Ross was at Lydia's funeral and how come she's being stalked by Nick Farleigh?"

"No idea."

"Me neither." She crossed to his desk and peered at the screen. Mo was scrolling down the list of Lydia's friends. Nella watched the feeds for a moment.

"Hang on a minute... Stop. Scroll up...Go back to that one..." She pointed to the screen. "There. Who's that?"

Mo clicked on the image. "Laura Warren."

"That's odd..." Nella leant forward and stared at the image.

Mo shifted to glance at her over his shoulder. "What?"

She hurried back to her desk. "That's really odd... Wait a minute... she's here somewhere...I've seen her on Annie's contacts..." Leaning forward, she clicked and scrolled through several screens. "Here! Here she is...I thought I recognised her! Same person... Mo? Come and have a look at this..."

Mo stood and came across. "Is that the same person? But

that's the profile picture for Kerrie Hart? Can you screen shot the picture Nell?" Nella took a screen shot and sent it to Mo's phone. He opened the link and went back to his PC. "Yup it's the same person... Isn't it?"

Nella wheeled over and had a look. "Yeah, same person, different profile. Or same photo, different profile."

"So, we've got a *Facebook* and an *Instagram* profile that links Lydia to Kate Ross's daughter? Could be a paedophile, couldn't it? Annie's fourteen and Lydia looks like a young girl..."

Nella shook her head. "It could be... It doesn't feel like it though. It's too much of a coincidence; grooming two young women who don't know each other, and we stumble across it."

Unable to stay seated, she stood and paced a bit then said; "There's something else, something we're missing... Someone has befriended them both using one or more fake profiles. Is Lauren real or is Kerrie? Are either of them? And why? Why Lydia and why Annie?"

Mo shrugged.

Nella sat down again and clicked on Kerrie Hart. Not much there, a few selfies, some shots with a couple of mates in a bar – all posted in the last year. She clicked on *about*, but that just said, *female* and the *Instagram* handle.

"Anything unusual for Laura Warren?"

"A few photos, mostly posted in the last year - not much history."

"Classic." Nella said. "New profiles, recent activity only..." She sat back.

"We need a warrant for Meta Mo. We need to find out who's set up these profiles." She looked at him and raised her eyebrow. "And considering we're not supposed to be spending any time or resources on this, do you want to ring the DS for the warrant or shall I?"

SALLIE DENNIS WAS WATCHING Netflix with a box of *Maltesers* open on the arm of the sofa and the sound of Rosie's gentle snores coming from the baby monitor. Sarah was in the kitchen making tea; she'd lost interest in the Norwegian cop drama; too much like real life, she said. I need escapism from my telly not more of the same. Her phone rang in the kitchen where she'd left it and Sarah appeared in the doorway a few moments later.

"Sal? Phone. It's work."

Sallie sighed. Nearly one a.m. and her phone was ringing; shit, that meant trouble.

The phone continued to ring, and Sarah walked into the sitting room holding it. "Do they ever leave you alone?" she said flatly,

"No." DS Dennis took the phone. "Dennis."

She listened and sat forward. "OK... yes...Let me make a couple of notes. Hang on..." She stood and went into the kitchen. She found a notepad on the table and picked up a pen.

"OK Nella, fire away..." She began to write, "Yes, start with the boyfriend, Matt. OK, you've matched his number to who? Let me write that name down. And he's a director at Unicorn Properties – the developer at the estate. Ok, got it. There were how many calls? Five... OK... How often? OK, good work, yeah, agreed, a very interesting link. And the other? We need a bit more to justify a warrant for Meta." Dennis looked up at Sarah who had followed her back into the kitchen and was shaking her head. They both knew where this was going to end.

"And when was this? The call to Farleigh's constituency office from Unicorn Properties? OK, that recent? Yup, you're right, I agree that merited the request for phone records. How many profiles? Yes, could be a paedophile ring... for all we know there could be more, yes, apply for the warrant for Meta and I'll come in and sign it. I think we could do with some surveillance on the boyfriend too, starting tomorrow..." Sarah passed her a cup of tea as she sat down at the kitchen table. "Good work Nella," she said, glancing at her notes. "You're right; there's a connection here somewhere and we need to find it."

IT HAD BEEN a long drive and it was very late when Dr Jane Hardman pulled into the parking space in front of the small cottage that sat back from the lane on the outskirts of Kingstanton. Behind her on the back seat of the car Ari was agitated; he could smell the sea air and the fields. She switched the engine off and sat for a few minutes looking up at the house. It had belonged to her mother, and she had inherited it. Once an old, dilapidated farm cottage, now it was a pristine, modernised, 'stylish, bolt hole' which the letting site rented out for most of the summer. Jane climbed out of the car. God, what she wouldn't give to have it messy and cold and ramshackle and her mother still alive to welcome her home. She unlocked the front door and left Ari to sniff round the outside of the house for a few minutes. No wonder she'd ended up a psychologist, her own attachment issues were complex and deep; still missing her mother at nearly sixty.

Throwing her coat over the bannister, she looked round. A cleaning lady in the village came in twice a week and did a good job; the place was spotless. The cream woodwork was without a scuff and the cushions were plump, the throws neatly folded. Jane called Ari in and went to make some tea. In the kitchen, here again, the surfaces gleamed, and she stood for a moment surveying the room. All was in perfect order. She went back and closed the front door, locking it and bolting it. Why then, she wondered, did she feel so odd? Why could she feel an air of unsettlement all around the house? Walking across to the bookshelf she ran her finger along the titles. She always kept a copy of her first book in the house; it was a tribute to having written it here. She followed her finger all the way down the shelves, past the walking guides, the recipe books, the paperback novels that holiday makers left, right to the very last book on the bottom shelf. It wasn't here.

Jane started over, running her finger along the spine of each book, this time more carefully and thoroughly. It was here the last time she stayed, just a few weeks ago and the house wasn't let in winter. If it has been taken, she thought, it will have been replaced. She stopped running her finger over the books three shelves down. Her book had been removed from between two paperbacks and something else had been placed there. It looked like a book spine from the side, but as she pulled it out, she saw that it was a book sized black board with a thin wood frame. She looked at the blank side of the blackboard and, turning it over, felt a sudden chill. On the other side, drawn in chalk pen was the stick figure representation of a childhood game. Hangman.

14

THE PAST – *Kingstanton, Devon –December 2002*

KATHERINE SAT ON THE TOILET, seat down, with her head in her hands. She needed to get dressed, get out of there and get to a phone box to call Richard, but she didn't move. She could hear Mark moving around in the bedroom next door, his electric razor, the tinny sound of the radio, but still, she couldn't raise herself up. Shame, she thought, was a great paralyser.

She had managed a shower, standing in the bath under a meagre jet of water with a damp smelling, mildewed shower curtain pulled across. But now, naked, having dried herself on a stiff towel that she'd found on the radiator, she was shivering and felt sick. Five pints of cider softened and warmed the night but made the mornings cold and hostile. There was a bang on the door.

"Katherine? You all right in there? I've got to leave for work in ten minutes. You need to be ready by then."

"Yeah" she called out, "I'm good. I'll be out in a tic." Then she stood up, lifted the toilet seat, leant over the bowl and threw up.

MARK PULLED into the bus stop, a hundred yards up the road from the Kingstanton police station and Katherine climbed out of the car. He pressed the window down on the driver's side as she walked round onto the pavement.

"Will you be in the pub again tonight?"

She shrugged. She felt terrible; her phone had run out of credit, she was nauseous and hungover. So much for good intentions, she thought, twenty-four hours and it had all gone down the toilet - literally.

"I'll probably take a walk, get some breakfast then head back to Exeter. I need to check the bus timetable."

Mark reached into his pocket for his wallet. He took a twenty pound note out and handed it across to Katherine. "Look, put some credit on your phone so I can call you and get something to eat. If you can hang on, my shift finishes at eight this evening."

Again, she shrugged. She really needed to get home; she felt sicker than she ever had before and wondered if perhaps her liver was giving out, or if she was going down with something.

"I've got your mobile number; I'll call you," she said.

He reached out and took her hand. Mark was familiar with one-night stands, but there was something about Katherine that made him loath to leave it casual.

"If you head down Fore Street and take a right, that'll bring you into the square. You can get some breakfast there and I'll see if I can pop out in an hour or so, check on you."

Katherine gently pulled her fingers away from his and dug both her hands into her pockets. "Look, don't worry, I'm fine." She stepped back from the car. "Go to work! You'll be late if you keep hanging round here talking to me."

"Yeah, sure." He shifted the car into gear.

"You sure you're OK?"

She nodded. "Go."

"Right, yeah." Putting the window up, Mark indicated and pulled out. He glanced in his mirror as he drew off and saw Katherine still standing there, hands in her pockets, swamped in her big coat and scruffy scarf. He waved, watching her in the rear-view mirror, but she didn't see him. She had turned away and was walking in completely the wrong direction for the town square.

FIFTEEN MINUTES LATER, Katherine stopped. She had been walking with her had down, glancing up occasionally and now she realised that she had headed right out of town and was lost. She had no idea where she was. She was in a lane that followed the estuary, fields on one side, and the sea on the other. Up ahead the road split and if she took the right fork it looked as if it wound back towards town, via some allotments. She decided to do that rather than go back on herself. It was still early, and she was still feeling sick.

LYDIA WAS UP EARLY, far too early according to her parents, whose bedroom door she had knocked on five minute earlier, but she couldn't sleep. It was always the same on results day. Her parents were nonplussed, told her to expect the best - they knew what a prodigy she was - but their lack of excitement only escalated her own and, in spite of the fact that she usually had to be dragged from her bed at seven forty-five, she was up, dressed and running through her scales in her bedroom at six thirty.

By eight am, she was waiting in the hall for the post. Both her parents had left for work and had allowed her to wait until the letter arrived with the post man anywhere between eight and nine am then she was to go straight to school before Mrs Gurney came in to clean. If they heard from Mrs Gurney that she'd not done as they asked, she would be in a great deal of trouble.

Lydia paced the hall carpet. She watched her feet in brown school shoes, one in front of the other, as she walked. She wished the post man would hurry up.

At eight fifteen the letters came through the door and Lydia bent to scoop them up. She found the one in the brown envelope and discarded the others, dropping them back on the floor. She looked at her name on the front of the envelope and slowly, her heart hammering in her chest, she opened it. She pulled out the sheet of paper and read it; Grade eight violin; distinction; mark – one fifty out of one fifty. There was only one person who would know how much this meant, who would praise her and tell her what she wanted to hear so seconds later, she had grabbed her bag and dashed out of the front door. Down the street she ran, her socks slipping down her shins, her brown shoes, too loosely tied, slapping against the pavement. She sprinted along her street, up to the crossroads and along the next two streets to Mr Hirsch's house. There she repeatedly pressed the doorbell until Mrs Hirsch came to the door.

"Goodness me Lydia! What on earth is all this about?!'"

"Is Mr Hirsch here?" Lydia asked, between gulps of air. "I really want to show him my exam!"

Mrs Hirsch smiled. She wiped her hands on her apron. "He's at the allotment Lydia. You know where that is, don't you?"

Lydia nodded and turned to run off.

"Lydia dear? Can't it wait? Shouldn't you be at school?"

Lydia didn't reply. She was off down the street, her bag across her shoulder bumping against her hip as she ran.

AT THE ALLOTMENTS, Lydia let herself in through the gate and looked around. She was breathing heavily now and small beads of sweat had formed on her upper lip. There was no-one here and she had no idea which allotment belonged to Mr Hirsch. She scanned the small plots of land and then she saw his sweater, the one he always had on the back of the chair as he taught. It was hanging over the handle of a fork that was dug into the ground. There was a shed next to the allotment and Lydia assumed he must be in there. She took several deep gulps of air and made her way along the rough grass between each plot to Mr Hirsch's patch. As she approached, she could hear voices in the shed, some knocking, loud breathing. Yup, he was almost certainly in the shed.

At the door she put her hand on the latch and called out, "Mr Hirsch, I..."

She pulled on the handle and peered in.

It was dark inside the shed, but a shaft of light penetrated the gloom as she opened the door, and she could just make out two figures. Mr Hirsch was leaning against the wooden wall; his head was thrown back, and his trousers

were round his ankles. Someone knelt in front of him, a
man, and she could see Mr Hirsch's hands buried deep in
the long dark strands of the man's hair.

She stood there for a moment, no longer than a couple
of seconds, and then Mr Hirsch gave a cry. "Oh Christ!"

The head stopped moving and turned and Lydia saw Mr
Hirsch's penis, angry and red, glistening with saliva.

She uttered a small howl and turned. Leaving the door
wide open she ran, stumbling over the clumps of grass
between the plots, out through the gate and into the fields.

"Lydia?! Lydia, come back?!" She heard Mr Hirsch's
voice.

She ran.

She ran but she didn't know why or what she was
running from, she only knew that she was afraid. She could
hear her breath; sharp, quick and rasping in her throat. The
flesh on her face tightly stretched across her bones as the
fear deepened. She could hear him behind her. She could
hear his breath too, harsh, heavy and desperate. He would
catch her, she realised that as she stumbled over the tree
roots, the brambles of the woodland at the edge of the field.
The light rippled down through the trees making patterns
on the ground and she felt as if she ran through a kaleidoscope. He would catch her and the only thing she could do
was run.

Her shoes were too loose, she kept tripping, stumbling
and behind her his breathing got louder as he got closer.
She caught the strap of her bag on a branch. It unbalanced
her. She fell, her hands hitting the ground and the skin on
her palms grazing. She looked behind her as she scrabbled
to her feet and saw him just metres away. He was red faced,
determined to catch her. His trousers were undone, and she
could see what she had seen just a few minutes before. She

screamed, shrugged off her shoulder bag and ran on, faster than she had ever run in her life before.

KATHERINE WAS MAKING her way alongside some fields when she heard the scream. She turned and saw a girl running towards her across the field, a look of terror on her stricken face. Behind her a man followed, but when Katherine called out, he stopped. She saw him, about a hundred yards away, stop dead and watch the girl run towards Katherine. His face was a mixture of panic and despair. His trousers were undone, and his penis hung out, limp and flaccid.

Katherine hurried towards the girl, fumbling with the gate catch and finally running into the field. They met head on. She held out her arms and the girl ran into them, no shoes on - left behind in the chase - her socks filthy and bedraggled. She clung to Katherine, her whole body shivering with shock. Katherine hugged her for some time, soothing her, trying to calm her down.

"You have to come with me," Katherine said, standing back and looking at the girl. Her face was still ashen and now tear stained. "We need to get you to the police. Can you tell me what happened?"

The girl shook her head and began to cry.

"Come on." Katherine took her hand and began to lead her towards the edge of the field and the gate. She found herself walking quickly as if the fear had spread from the girl to Katherine through their fingers.

At the gate Katherine looked up and down the lane praying for a car. She held on tightly to the gate and finally one came round the corner. She walked out into the road to flag it down.

"Can you take us to the police station?"

The driver looked at Lydia and nodded. "Get in the back," she said.

Katherine climbed in with Lydia and cradled the girl in her nook of her arm. At Kingstanton Police Station they got out and walked into reception. Katherine told the duty sergeant what had happened and immediately there were officers all around them. Lydia was taken away, Katherine saw Mark, but as she tried to smile her face collapsed and she began to cry.

CI Lewin walked along the corridor to interview room four where the young woman who had brought the little girl in was waiting. They'd got nothing out of the girl, she was in shock and wasn't able to speak. They had her name from the name tag on her school sweater and had contacted her parents; they were on their way in. In Lewin's experience things like this happened in a case. There was nothing for days, weeks even, no leads, nothing to go on and then suddenly, out of the blue, something unexpected happened and the whole thing kicked off. This was one of those moments. He pushed open the door of the interview room and knew he was about to make progress.

"Good afternoon, Katherine, isn't it?"

"Yes, hi."

"Katherine, we'd like you to make what's called a witness statement. We'd like to record your statement so that we have the exact nature of what you say. Are you happy with this?"

"Yes."

"Good. I will be interviewing you and taking your

witness statement. My name is Chief Inspector Derek Lewin, and my officer number is 74353. Shall we begin?"

"Fine." Katherine was nervous. She had been waiting for some time, going over and over what she had to say.

"Well, if you could begin, in your own words, by telling us where you were and what you were doing this morning when the incident happened."

"Yes. Erm..." Katherine cleared her throat. "I was walking. It was about nine thirty am, maybe a bit later. I'm sorry, I can't be exact as I don't wear a watch. I came here from Exeter last night and I erm... I met someone in the pub and stayed over. I was walking, I'd got lost and I was down by some fields, in a lane by the estuary..." Katherine broke off; her voice was wavering with nerves. She swallowed.

"Anyway, I was walking when I saw this little girl running towards me. She was terrified, running for her life. She had a shoe missing and her clothes were all twisted, like she'd been in a bit of a wrestle with someone. She was running towards me, and I ran towards her."

"Was she alone?"

"No." Katherine swallowed again, knowing the magnitude of what she was about to say. "There was a man chasing her. He had almost caught up with her when he saw me. He stopped then and I looked across at him."

CI Lewin waited. He watched the young woman, trying to remember the detail. "Can you describe this man for me?"

"He was tall; he had brown hair, longish, but pushed back off his forehead. He was wearing a shirt; it was unbuttoned at the neck and his..." She took a breath. "His trousers were undone, at the zip and button. He had a belt on, and it looked... well, it looked as if he'd just pulled them up suddenly and belted them and left the rest. I could see his..." Katherine blushed and again she took a breath. "I could see his penis... it was hanging out."

"Was it erect?"

"No... at least I don't think so."

"What happened next?"

"I think he was chasing the girl because when he saw me, he stopped. He looked, well, sort of desperate and then he was gone. I didn't see him go, but maybe he went back to some allotments maybe? I'd passed them earlier. Or out onto the road. I don't know. I didn't see."

"Then what happened?"

"The little girl held onto me and started crying. I thought that she'd had some kind of assault, or something like that so I just hugged her and then told her that we had to go to the police. I held her hand and we crossed the field to the gate and onto the road where we flagged down a car."

"Can you be more specific about what the man was wearing please?"

Katherine closed her eyes, thought back and then said; "He was wearing a checked shirt, it was blue and brown, and he had on brown cords, those baggy heavy ones. And his shoes were..." She stopped. "I'm sorry; I don't know what his shoes were like. I don't think I looked."

"That's OK, you've done really well to remember that much."

"He looked, Oh I don't know, sort of arty, like a professor or an artist or something."

Lewin glanced at his DS. "Is there anything else that you'd like to add?"

Katherine shrugged. "I don't think so," she said.

Lewin reached over and turned off the tape. He held out the statement and pointed to where Katherine should sign, which she did.

"Is this connected to the murder of Abbey Salter?" she suddenly blurted.

CI Lewin glanced up at her. "I'm afraid that I'm not at liberty to say."

"But it could be the same man, couldn't it? Making another attempt?"

"DS Crowley, could you escort Katherine out please?"

DS Crowley stood and so did Katherine. She watched CI Lewin carefully as he read through the statement and made some notes. She felt sure it was connected; it made her feel dismal.

In the reception area she saw two people sitting together in silence and wondered if they were the girl's parents. The woman had been crying and held a crumpled tissue, rubbing it between her fingers nervously. Katherine sat down and waited for the duty sergeant to make her call.

BETH TOOK the call because Richard was putting the boys in the bath. She called up to him.

"It's the Police," she said. She carried the phone up and passed it to him as he dried his hands on a towel. She watched him as he spoke briefly to the duty sergeant and glanced at his watch. "If you could let her know that I'll be there as quick as I can," he said. He finished the call and looked at Beth.

"Kat's in Kingstanton police station. She's got no credit on her phone so she couldn't ring herself. She's been witness to a crime apparently and ..."

"And what Richard?" Beth's lips were compressed as she waited for his reply.

"And she needs collecting," he said, hanging the towel

up. He didn't want to look at his wife; he didn't want to see her barely suppressed anger rising to the surface.

"I see." But she didn't see at all. She stood in the doorway of the bathroom, not moving. "So, Katherine has got herself into trouble and you are going to rush over there, miss putting the boys to bed, miss dinner and bail her out – yet again!"

Richard said, "She's in Kingstanton Beth."

"And how did she get there? I presume she got the train and the bus because she didn't ask us for a lift." She raised an eyebrow.

"I don't know how she got there, but I am assuming that you're right. It's quite a journey."

"Exactly. So, if she can make it there on her own to do whatever reckless, poorly thought-out scheme she had embarked on then she can fucking well make it back, can't she?"

Richard glanced at the twins who were watching them silently from the bath.

"On her own." Beth finished. She walked out of the bathroom and Richard followed her.

"Beth, Kat has been involved in some kind of incident..."

"And what's new?" She turned. "That girl is a magnet for 'some kind of incident'!" She did the air quote marks when she said that, and Richard could feel his temper bulge suddenly at the edges.

"Maybe she is, but right now she is in a police station in Kingstanton, and I am going to collect her."

Beth looked at him. He wondered if he imagined it or whether she really did puff herself up, swell almost imperceptibly and harden as she faced down the challenge.

"You go if you want to Richard, but I won't be here when you get back if you do."

"What the hell does that mean?!" He was angry now and his voice was raised. "Don't threaten me!"

"Oh, it's not a threat Richard, I mean it. If you leave and pander to that wilful girl, that rude, spoilt, unhinged girl, who couldn't give a flying fuck about you or me or any of us then I will go to my parents for Christmas and take the boys with me. You can stay here and rot in hell for all I care!" Beth had her hands on her hips, and she was breathing hard.

Richard said, "Beth... Beth please. Why are you doing this?"

But Beth couldn't articulate the jealousy and spite she felt when she encountered the product of Richard's first marriage. She couldn't vocalise the threat she felt from a young woman who was beautiful and intelligent and who desperately needed Richard's care. And even if she had been able to put it into words, she would never have been able to admit it to her husband because that made her less of the woman that she thought she was.

So instead of answering him, truthfully, she said; "Your place is here, with us Richard. We are your family, and the boys are your responsibility, not Katherine. She's a big girl; she'll figure it out."

Richard sighed. He dropped his head and Beth knew she'd won. She took a step forward and touched his arm. "Tough love," she said, "It works."

Richard glanced down at her hand.

"Yeah, maybe." Had she ever shown Kat any gentle love, he wondered. "I'd better ring the station and let them know I can't get there."

"I'll do it," Beth said. "You carry on bathing the boys."

He nodded, handed the phone to her - he still held it in his hand - and she took it, heading down the stairs with it.

He turned towards the bathroom and took a big breath. Bath-time noise had resumed, and the boys were shouting and laughing as they splashed. It was a joyful sound, but he heard it now without any joy whatsoever.

KATHERINE PULLED on her coat and found the twenty-pound note that Mark had given her in the pocket. She rubbed it reassuringly between her fingers as she headed for the door; at least she could get back to Exeter.

The duty Sergeant watched her and felt terrible; she looked like so many of them that ended up on the other side of that dividing wall between the nick and reception - lost and forlorn.

He called out to her. "You sure you're all right to travel home on your own? You've had a difficult day. If you don't mind waiting for a while, a couple of hours max, I can probably find a squad car to drive you back to Exeter."

Katherine shook her head. "Thanks, but I'm fine."

Fine, he thought, she was a long way from fine. The woman who'd rung the station had been harsh. Katherine had got herself into the mess, she'd said, and she could get herself out of it. Please tell her to make her own way home. Home: he wondered what that looked like.

"Where do you have to get to?"

"Exeter."

"You alright for money?"

Katherine nodded. She felt close to tears and the offer of help made it even worse. She sniffed and turned away. "I'd better get going," she said. "Thanks."

The duty Sergeant came round the desk and opened the door for her. He had a grown-up daughter, married, and a granddaughter. This whole Abbey Salter case had been grim and sending a teenager home alone after a day like she'd had really upset him.

"Mind how you go love," he said.

Katherine nodded again, not trusting herself to speak. She stepped out into the cold, dug her hands deep into her pockets and made her way towards the bus stop in the town square.

A few minutes later, a hundred yards up Fore Street she heard the beep of a car. It slowed and she saw Mark. Katherine stopped walking and he pressed the window down.

"Boss let me off a couple of hours early. Said I should run you back to Exeter." Mark indicated and pulled in. "I don't know what you said to that gruff bugger on duty, but he rang up and told DS Crowley to let me go." He looked at Katherine and saw that she had her chin down and her wild hair had fallen over her face. He yanked on the hand brake and climbed out of the car.

"Katherine?"

Stepping in close to her, he folded her into a hug and felt her shoulders shake. "Come on," he said gently, "You've had a hell of a day. Let's get you back to your flat." He found his handkerchief and handed it over to her. Then he manoeuvred her into the car and in silence, they set off for the city.

CI LEWIN CAME out of the incident room where they were in full swing to take the call that confirmed they'd got him and were on their way in. It hadn't taken long to find him; Lewin hadn't expected it to. It was just as he'd thought; something clicks and the whole investigation connects, like joining the dots.

They'd started earlier with a list of allotment holders and Lewin had sent officers to interview each one. A couple of hours in, there he was, having dinner with his wife, still in the checked shirt and baggy brown cords that Katherine had described. As soon as he was in, DI Lewin was going to charge him with attempted assault and start the process. Lewin had a good feeling about this. He was going to connect Ellard Hirsch to the murder of Abbey Salter; he was sure of it; he could feel it in his bones.

15

P RESENT DAY - *London*
Monday – a.m.

IT WAS seven thirty on Monday morning when Annie called out to Kate from the kitchen.

"What, no bircher? Homemade muesli? Like nothing healthy at all for my breakfast?"

She picked up the loaf of bread that Kate had left by the toaster and held it theatrically aloft. "I think like you're taking this whole 'independence thing' a bit too seriously mum."

Kate was packing her bag for work in the sitting room, and she glanced up. "Annie, I didn't think you liked all my homemade healthy food. Besides, I've got three messages on my phone from people who've been evicted over the weekend and that is just the beginning of all the stuff I'll have to deal with today..."

"So, change jobs."

"Excuse me?"

Annie sighed. "Mum, you've got a first-class degree in social sciences from the Open University, you're a trained solicitor and you like run rings around the law firms you deal with. You could get any job that would earn you tons of money and save you tons of shit."

"Don't say shit, but thanks for the vote of confidence. I don't want any job Annie; I like what I do. I worked in a law firm after I qualified, when you were little and then I wanted to make a difference, right a few wrongs legally. Now make toast. It's not hard."

"What be a social warrior? Mum, it doesn't challenge you, it makes you like all stressy and we're always like strapped for cash."

Kate left her bag and came into the small galley kitchen. She flicked the switch on the kettle, took the bread out of Annie's hands and put two slices in the toaster.

"Where's all this come from?" Kate continued to fix breakfast, not wanting Annie to see that she was hurt. When had she gone from being Annie's hero to someone who doesn't quite measure up? I do my best, she thought; I do my absolute, fucking best.

"Oh, I don't know." Annie took a jar of jam out of the cupboard and put it on the table. "I just think you're like really smart mum and well...Kerrie and I were like chatting and we both like thought that you could be like running Google if you wanted, not just a charity in South London."

The toast popped up and Kate put it on a plate. "Don't say like," she said, handing the plate to Annie. "I counted at least five, you don't *like* need them in your *like* conversation."

Annie was spreading peanut butter on her toast. "Ha."

Kerrie, Kate thought. "It's not *just* a charity in south London. What I do is important, I..."

Annie had placed her hand on Kate's arm. She said, "Yeah, I know mum. You don't have to keep telling me."

"Right, yes." Kate turned away and went back to the sitting room to finish packing her bag.

"We'll be leaving in ten minutes," she called, "make sure you're ready." But her voice sounded emptily bright and, leaving her things in the hall, she went into her bedroom and closed the door behind her. There she sat down on the bed and wondered if all the careless things she had said to her father so many years ago had been just as painful for him.

NICK WATCHED THE CLOCK. It was just behind Clive Haroldson's head and once or twice he'd caught Haroldson's eye as he glanced up at the hands ticking round. These meetings of the Housing, Communities and Local Government Committee – a committee he'd elected to be on - and wanted to stay on – always seemed to run over. This was never usually a problem for Nick, he'd very little else to get home for, but today he needed to be away. He glanced at the clock again - the third time – and Haroldson, the committee chair, said,

"Are we keeping you Nick?"

"No, no not at all. Sorry, just conscious of time and making sure I brief my assistant this afternoon before she leaves on the deadline for evidence submissions - seeing as it's only a couple of weeks away. She's leaving early; doctor's appointment." He'd been caught and he merged a waffled excuse with a blatant lie. His assistant barely left the office, as did he.

"Well, you should have said, and we'd have wrapped the meeting up early to accommodate you."

His sarcasm wasn't lost on Nick who shifted uncomfortably in his seat. He'd never felt any conflict of interest before; he was a dedicated Member of Parliament who was married to a dedicated and ambitious lawyer and between them work was the only thing that really mattered. This past week the structure of his life had been turned on its head and now, sitting here waiting for the meeting to end, all he could think about was making sure he got to Lower Marsh when she came out of school. He had to see her; he had to know.

"So, our key question outstanding, which is fed by all the others; sustainability, short and long term of the children's services, innovative approaches to deliver of children's services, etc, challenges to those..." Haroldson went on, "Our key question answerable is; will the funding for local authorities' children's services be sufficient to enable local authorities to fulfil their statutory duties?"

He closed a manila folder and tapped it on the table in front of him.

"Let's make sure when we meet next week that we've got a good handle on the evidence. Liz, you've got the oral transcripts in hand, haven't you? Jeff, if you can bring all the Ministerial correspondence and likewise, Nick, all the written evidence submissions to date. Jessie, can you email the minutes to all of us by the close of day please and can you brief the press officer? I think we should have something out about this inquiry pronto, let the media see that it's all in hand before they ask. I think that's it. Meeting dismissed." Haroldson stood up. "Nick, can I have a word?"

The committee members filed out and Nick hung back. It was two fifteen, he had time in hand.

"Glad to see that your profile has been raised Nick," Clive Haroldson said, "Good people are hard to come by. I expect they'll want to announce shortly?"

"I think so, but nothing is confirmed yet Clive, still a bit in the balance. I think my name's in the hat with a couple of others."

"Then don't lose sight of this inquiry Nick, or what you're doing here at Westminster. Dodgy posts online and failure to pull your finger out on a select committee inquiry, especially one as important as this one, will result in your name staying in that hat."

Nick looked at Haroldson. He was old school Labour; worthy, only there for the common good. He was a decent MP. "Point taken Clive," he replied. "Thanks."

Haroldson opened the door for Nick. "Don't thank me, Nick; listen to me, that's all."

They went their separate ways and Nick, hearing, but not listening at all, collected his overcoat and immediately left the building.

AN HOUR LATER, Nick was standing in the cold grey light of the fading afternoon near Annie's school on Lower Marsh. He was chilled; he'd been hanging around, walking up and down, trying not to be conspicuous. He was waiting - having taken an educated guess that Annie would come this way on her way back from school to meet her mum from work - waiting for Annie to appear. It was just after four p.m. and the schools in the area mostly got out around three thirty so if she was going to come, it'd be in the next hour. Nick was nervous. He didn't have any real plan or proper explanation for being there, all he knew was that he wanted to see Annie – from a distance, nothing more.

Ever since he'd caught sight of her at the flat, he'd been in a state of perpetual tension. He'd done the maths, it all added up, or at least it added up the way he desperately wanted it to. Nick had not always been aware that there was something missing in his life; caring for his mum, being beside her while she died had left him numb, not just unable to feel, but not even wanting to. He supposed that explained Emma. She had never asked much of him, and she had never given much in return. But now, completely unexpectedly, his emotions had erupted, lava like, unstoppable and threatening to burn everything along the way. All he knew, as he stood there in the cold, was that he had to find out if Annie was his. And he thought, foolishly, that he would be able to tell as soon as he properly saw her.

Annie walked down Lower Marsh, headphones on and her phone in her hand as she messaged the group chat from school that she was about to get to the café and have a large Mocha with whipped cream on top. She popped her head round the door of the job centre as sometimes Kate was in there with a client, but it was empty, so she carried on up towards the café where - they had agreed with Kerrie at the weekend - Annie would now wait daily for Kate after school. Well, not exactly agreed, Annie thought, pushing open the door of the café, more badgered Kate into it.

Annie waved to Kerrie who was serving behind the counter and found an empty table by the window. She unbuttoned her coat and un-wrapped her scarf, hanging them both on the back of her chair. It was warm and steamy in there and Annie felt very mature as she took her seat, waiting for Kerrie to come over. It felt good to have an adult friend, one she could discuss things with, in a way that she couldn't with her mum. Annie was able to chat freely to Kerrie, to say anything at all and know that there would be no repercussions. Not that Kate was a difficult parent, God no; Annie knew how lucky she was compared to some of the girls at school. It was just that, well, sometimes, Annie thought, Kate cared just a little bit too much.

She scrolled down her playlist and found *Glorious*, by Macklemore, turning the volume up a notch as she stared out of the window at the darkening street. Just across, standing with his back to the men's hire shop, she thought she caught a glimpse of someone she recognised, looking directly at her. She thought it was the bloke who'd come round to see her mum last week, but she didn't get a good look at him and, as she held up her hand to wave - in case it was him - he turned and walked away. She glanced round as Kerrie arrived at the table.

"Hey. How was school?"

"Fine."

"What'll you have?"

"Mocha please."

"Cream?"

"Do you have to ask?"

Kerrie smiled. "Who were you waving at across the road? Wanna ask them in?"

"Nah, it was just someone I thought I knew..." Annie shrugged, "But I don't think it was them and I don't really know them anyway."

"Really? Who was that then?"

"Oh, just some bloke who came round to see mum last week."

Kerrie peered out of the window. "Really? Tall guy, thin?"

"Yeah. Do you know him?"

Kerrie shook her head. "No, but mum told me about him." she cleared away an empty plate and cup from the table. "One Mocha coming up," she said. She moved off, then turned and took a step back. "Hey look, I've been meaning to ask you, do you see much of your dad at all? I mean, if you do, you're welcome to bring him here for free drinks if you want to, any time."

Annie suddenly flushed. She looked away, staring at her phone for a few moments then she glanced up and said, "I don't see my dad, but thanks anyway." She avoided meeting Kerrie's gaze.

"No worries." Kerrie took a step closer. "Look, sorry," she said gently, "I didn't mean to upset you. I just didn't think..."

"No, it's OK, you didn't upset me." Annie swallowed down a painful lump in her throat. "It's not an issue, honestly."

Kerrie said, "I'm gonna add extra chocolate to the Mocha and extra whipped cream and then I'm gonna come and sit and talk to you." She looked round the busy café. "Nothing better to do, so I might as well." She smiled ironically and Annie smiled back.

"Maybe you can tell me about your dad... I mean, if you want to."

"Yeah, maybe." It was difficult to talk about someone you had never met, Annie thought, or even seen a picture of. The truth was that Annie had absolutely no idea who he was.

∾

Mo HAD JUST SIGNED on when Nella called. They were both on late after yesterday spent in the car outside Matt Brennen's place. Fifteen hours of boredom and more of it today.

"Hey."

She sounded rushed. "I'm gonna have to bail on you this afternoon. I'm gonna head down to Devon. They've got the file but its sensitive and it's been held back by someone in Exeter, so they won't release it - they want me to go down to read it. The DS has sanctioned it so I'm shoving some stuff into a bag as we speak..."

"Really? That's a bummer."

"Yeah. The weather's shit and I've got to take two trains. Still, it's a day out and my electronics weekly has just arrived, so...."

"You sure know how to have a good time, don't you?" Electronics weekly. Really? He heard the sound of toilet flush and shook his head. She just didn't operate on the same level as everyone else.

"Any luck on the warrant for Meta?"

"Still waiting. I guess I'll have to buddy up with Carter today for surveillance."

"Take some mints."

"Cheers." Carter's breath was legendary.

"Let me know if you get anything will you?"

"Yeah. Thanks for the call, Nella."

"No probs Mo. Laters."

He pressed end and looked at his phone. Who the hell said *'laters'*?

Dr JANE HARDMAN carried the glass of white wine she had just bought at the bar over to a small table, tucked away in the corner of the pub, near the fire. She set the drink down and took her coat off. It was warm in there; the fire was roaring, and she wished she hadn't worn a sweater. Sitting, she took out the paper and turned to the crossword. She was early; he had said four thirty p.m.

Twenty minutes later, on the dot of four thirty, she saw him come in. He hadn't changed but he had filled out and now carried himself with an air of importance. She waved and he came across to her.

"Jane," he said. "It's lovely to see you again." They shook hands.

"You too. What would you like to drink?"

"No, it's fine. I'll get it. Would you like another?"

She shook her head. "Driving."

"Yes. This place is out of the way. I'm assuming you didn't want to run in to anyone in Kingstanton?"

"No."

He raised an eyebrow. "The plot thickens. Let me get a pint and I'll be right back."

Jane watched him go to the bar, order his drink then come back empty handed. "They'll bring it over," he said. He pulled out a seat.

"So?"

Jane said, "Lydia Helston is dead."

Mark looked at her. "Ah. There was a request from the MET for the Abbey Salter file, so that makes sense now. I held it back knowing we were meeting. I'm guessing she didn't die of natural causes?"

Jane took up the iPad she had on the table and unlocked it. She'd got the screen up already and she passed it across to him. He read the news article from the Metro online.

"Hung?"

"A tragic accident, apparently. Someone has been to my

house Mark and to my cottage. She took the iPad from him and brought up the pictures. Whoever it was left me this."

She handed it over again and showed him a photo of the chalk board she had found. He stared at it and then at her. "What about Katherine?"

Jane shrugged. "That's exactly what I came to ask you."

Mo SAT in the passenger seat with DC Carter and stared out of the window at the pub. It had begun to sleet making what was already a dull job even greyer. DC Carter was not Nella and for all her weird nerdiness, and the fact that she could irritate the hell out of him, he missed her.

Mo glanced across the street at a man in a pin stripe suit, a bit out of place, he thought, for a Monday afternoon in Stockwell. He watched him go into the pub then took out his phone, bringing the web page for the property company up on his screen.

"John Sachs, director of Unicorn Properties has just gone into the pub."

"Really?"

"Yeah."

He watched the pub for a few minutes. It was dark outside, and the pub interior was lit like a stage. Through the plate glass windows he saw the man order a drink at the bar, pay for it then turn as he was joined by Matt Brennen, Lydia's boyfriend. They shook hands and Matt pointed to where he was sitting. Mo leant forward and stared, but they disappeared out of view.

"Are we going in?"

Mo shook his head. "No."

DC Carter ate another of the mints from the packet that

Mo had put on the dashboard. "Bit of a waste of time this, I reckon."

"Oh yeah?" Mo was watching the pub again.

"You reckon he really murdered his girlfriend for money?"

"I don't reckon anything," Mo said, "But people murder for a lot less than standing to make a wad load of cash by handing over a lease."

EMMA STRODE into *Benugos* holding Sophie's report under her arm. She saw Sophie at a table in the corner and went across.

"Hi," she put the folder down on the table. "This was good work," she said, "Very thorough, thank you. Do you want a coffee? I'm going to grab one to go."

"Yes, thanks, Soya Latte please. Triple shot." Enough to keep me awake, Sophie thought, considering that I spent most of the weekend researching this crap. CSR my arse. Sophie had recognised the name of the woman as soon as she'd started researching the charity – it was the woman Emma's husband had been shagging - as seen by everyone on Twitter last week. It made Sophie feel kind of sad. Is that what happened when you ran your life into the ground for a senior associate partnership? Your husband shagged around, and you got trainees to do your revenge dirty work?

Emma left her bag on the chair and went to the counter. Sophie watched her queuing for their coffees. Emma was impressive; blond, trim, very well dressed and the Birkin bag on the chair, left so casually - not chained to her wrist for fear of it being nicked – told everyone that she had made it. But she was pathetic too; she had to be, going to all this trouble to find out who it was her husband was probably going to leave her for.

Sophie checked her phone. She'd had to lie to come out of the office and she couldn't stay too long. Emma was important, but she wasn't a partner yet and Sophie still had to answer to the partner on her current team.

Emma, in the queue, thought about why she hated these synthetic coffee places, uniformly designed so that you could be anywhere in the world. Perhaps that was the point, she thought, no surprises, like fish and chips in Benidorm. It was anonymous though and that's what she needed. Picking up the two coffees she'd ordered, she took them over to Sophie.

"Here, one soya latte." She sat. "How did you get hold of the accounts by the way?"

"The charity has an annual income of over twenty-five grand, so they have a duty to file accounts. I asked a mate at KPMG if they could access the accounts filed online for me and they did. Voila. The charity has an open book policy for transparency, so it was all right and proper."

Emma had opened the folder. "Like everything else, by the looks of it. They've got several main sponsors, which all look fine, including Devon and Cornwall Police…" Emma glanced up. "Unusual…" She was running her finger down the page, "but not beyond believable…" she stopped suddenly and looked at Sophie. "But there's also this? Did you notice this?"

Emma had her finger on the name of an offshore company. "This one here isn't incorporated in the UK. Any ideas?"

"No. Is that important, an offshore trust?"

"I don't know; it could be."

Clutching at straws, Sophie thought.

"The Charity gives out quite a lot of financial aid so I was thinking that this could do with a bit of investigation. It might not be legitimate."

Hence the coffee, Sophie thought. It left a bitter taste in her mouth. "If it doesn't look right, we should report it to the Charities commission," she said, "Leave it up to them. I think that's about as far as we should go."

"Yes, good point, but for now I'd like you to do a little bit more digging – just so we have something concrete to take if we need to. It's Australian so I'd start with the ASIC, if I were you."

But you're not me, Sophie thought, and if you were, you wouldn't take this kind of shit. But she glanced away knowing that she'd never have the nerve to say that out loud.

"When?" Sophie asked. "When do you want it? I'm really snowed under."

"Time management," Emma said, "It's the pathway to success."

Sophie stood and picked up her coffee, glad now that it was in a take-away cup. "So that was...?"

"Mid-week? If you're snowed under."

"Right." Sophie tucked the folder under her arm and wished she'd taken her mother's advice and gone to work in the Foreign Office. "Thanks for the coffee."

Emma shrugged. "S'ok," she said, "I charged it."

ANNIE AND KATE walked from the tube to Hartington Road in silence. Kate had tried a couple of attempts at conversation, but now she had slipped into her own thoughts, wondering what it was that seemed to be upsetting her daughter. The problem, she thought, was partly of her own making. She had no friends to speak of; she didn't have time. She had a coffee with Matilda's mum, Hannah, every now and then, but she didn't really have anyone to confide in, to talk to, another mother who might know the pitfalls of an adolescent girl. That, coupled with the fact that her own teenage experience had hardly been usual meant that she was batting in the dark most of the time, trying to guess where the ball was coming from.

"So," Kate began when the silence got too much for her, "School was '*same*', you had a Mocha at the café which was '*fine*' and you hung out with '*everyone*' at school. Result I'd say."

"Mum. Don't say stuff like 'result', it sounds a bit lame."

"Oh, right." Kate put her arm through Annie's and said, "So I'm not running Google and I say things that are a bit lame. Anything else bothering you?" She thought she'd kept her voice neutral, but Annie took her hand out of her pocket and let Kate's arm drop, breaking any physical connection. They walked on another fifty paces or so then Annie turned to Kate.

"Who's my father?" she said.

Kate stopped. Annie stopped too. Kate faced her daughter and looked at her. She was beautiful, intelligent and kind and Kate wondered how she had managed to create something so amazing out of all that crap. She said, "Annie, I don't think this is the right time to talk about all this. Not now."

"But I want to know."

Kate could see the position of Annie's mouth, how it had puckered slightly the way it did when she cried and how her chin had dimpled because she was close to tears.

"Why do you want to know now Sweetheart? Why suddenly do you want to know about your father?"

"I just do,"

"OK, but not now. This is a discussion we need to have quietly and reasonably at home; not suddenly, out of the blue, on the Stockwell Road, walking home."

"Don't Mum!"

"Don't what?!"

"Don't make excuses."

Kate put her hands on Annie's arms and held her steady. She could see the tears in her daughter's eyes.

"I am not making excuses," Kate said, "But I need some time to..."

"To what? Make something up?"

Kate reached up and wiped a tear from Annie's face. "No, to sort things out." She sighed and kept holding Annie. She said, "The name of the father on your birth certificate is Mark Heddon. He lives in Devon and he's a police officer. And I think if we are going to have this discussion, he needs to be there." She reached for a packet of tissues from her pocket and handed it to Annie. "OK? That's all I want to tell you..." She watched Annie blow her nose. "For now, at least," she said.

Annie nodded, but she stiffened as she pulled away from Kate and they carried on walking in silence as if nothing had been said.

JANE STOOD and buttoned her coat. Mark was on his feet already and she noticed how tall he was. She bent and picked up her bag. There was something about tall men, she thought, height seemed to give them an innate power – true or imagined – she wasn't sure.

"I'll send someone round tomorrow," Mark said, "and we'll see if we can get anything from the black board, but I don't think we'll come up with much – if anything at all. Whoever it is who's stalking you Jane is meticulously careful by the sound of it."

He picked up their glasses to hand into the bar on the way out and they headed towards the exit.

Outside in the car park, Mark walked Jane to her car. She pressed unlock on her key fob and the car bleeped.

"Are you sure you're ok going home on your own? The offer to camp out on your sofa-bed is still there if it'd make you feel safer."

"No," Jane smiled. She had been living alone since her mother died, she didn't even holiday with other people and the idea of someone in her personal space didn't appeal. "Thank you," she said, "but I'm fine."

She opened the car door. She had something to say before she left, and she'd been trying to lead up to it all evening without success. She decided to just say it.

"Mark, do you see anything of Annie?"

He hesitated for a few moments then he said, "No, I haven't seen her since she was tiny. Once they were settled in London Katherine wanted it that way."

Jane watched him; he seemed to be cogitating on something then his face closed so she didn't ask any more.

"Mind how you go," Mark said, slamming the door once she was in the driver's seat. Jane pressed the window down. "I think I might come along tomorrow," he said, "Just have a look and see how they might have got in."

"You don't need to."

"No, but I'd like to."

Jane started the engine. "Thanks." She thought that he had probably been in love with Katherine, possibly still was, and then she thought how sad it was that Katherine had not seen that. But, as she drove off, she remembered that Katherine had not been in a fit state to see anything at all, let alone someone who loved her.

WHEN SHE'D LEFT London this morning, Nella had planned that she would get into Exeter, look at the file and get out of Exeter and back to London as quick as she could. That was before snow and ice, road closures, a flat tyre on the side of the A303 and a two hour hold up on the M5. Fat chance of that now, she thought, heading through the outskirts of Exeter towards Devon and Cornwall police headquarters in Middlemoor. She was tired and hungry, despite the two packs of plastic sandwiches from the service station, and as she drove, she wondered briefly about stopping at a drive-thru MacDonald's, but it was already five and she wanted to get back to London before midnight, so she'd have to go hungry. Nella wasn't happy when she was hungry.

At the Middlemoor headquarters she was shown into a waiting room, where she texted Mo to say she'd arrived and shortly after that she was taken upstairs into an empty office by a DC.

"You can use this for as long as you like," the DC said. "File's on the table. D'you want a coffee?"

Nella glanced at the table and her heart sank: there were four boxes full of paperwork.

"Shit," she said.

"Yeah." The DC followed her gaze. "Abbey Salter case;

the little girl that disappeared in 2002. Unsolved; bit of a disaster for the team that handled it."

"Lydia Helston is connected to that case?"

The DC shrugged. "I'm afraid I'm the wrong person to ask. I don't know much about it. We've got a DI here who was around then, he's just back from holiday but I can check the rota, see if he's coming in?"

"Yeah, thanks, that'd be great." Nella walked across to the boxes and lifted the lid of the one nearest. She checked the date; it was the third of four. Jesus, there was no hope of getting out of here by nine, she thought, checking the dates on the boxes and moving to the first. She sat down. It was going to be a hell of a long night.

16

THE PAST – *Kingstanton, Devon, December 2008*

CI LEWIN WAS in his office looking at the DNA report on Hirsch that had just come in. He had called a meeting and was about to brief the team when the phone rang. He hesitated before picking it up; he didn't have time to be answering calls – he needed ideas, they needed to brainstorm this, get it right, and so, walking towards the door, he let it ring.

In the incident room, he waited for silence and then said; "We've got semen on the scarf and hairs in the boathouse that belong to Hirsch." There was a murmur. "It's promising, but we need to make sure we can link it unequivocally to Abbey Salter. We haven't got her DNA on the scarf so we can't link that, and the hairs are older, probably several weeks old so there's nothing to tell us that Hirsch was in the boathouse at the same time as Abbey that night.

We need to place Hirsch at the scene; we don't want any slip-ups with the CPS. We know he wasn't in because his wife confirmed it, but where was he?"

Lewin took a breath. He found speaking to the team much more stressful now than it used to be. He was having difficulty distinguishing the voices when they came at him.

"Hirsch still isn't giving us any answers, so we need to make sure we've got them for him."

He glanced across the room as a uniformed WPC came into the room. She held up her hand to catch his eye. He motioned to her, and she walked around the throng to the front, leaning in to speak quietly to him. His chest tightened.

"Sir, a call just came in from the information room. Mrs Lewin was found down on the beach at Munster Head about ten minutes ago in her nightdress. She's been taken to Kingstanton General."

The tightness in his chest moved down to his gut and the old ache started up. Christ, how had she got out? Where was the district nurse? He rubbed his chest and called to DS Crowley.

"My office, Bill. Now please." Crowley was a safe choice; promotion to DI was long overdue.

Crowley followed him into the small fishbowl that served as his office and Lewin turned.

"I'm going to hand this over to you Bill; I need a couple of hours out this morning." He belched quietly behind his hand and the pain deepened in his belly. "I want to be able to place Hirsch at the scene, down by the boathouse in a two-to-three-hour window of Abbey being there. Get everyone on it. I want anything we can find, anything at all that can link him to Abbey's disappearance."

"Right boss." DS Crowley looked at Lewin. "Everything OK, boss?"

"Nah, not really. It's my wife," Lewin said, "She's not well, she's been taken to Kingstanton General." Lewin had only told a couple of people about Barbara, but he was sure station gossip had increased that to more than a handful. Still, he felt no compunction to enlighten DS Crowley any more than he had done.

"I'm sorry to hear that, sir. Give her my best, won't you?"

Lewin smiled grimly. DS Crowley clearly wasn't one of the handful then; Barbara didn't know her own daughter, let alone some of the team she'd met several years ago at the Christmas party. He sighed, rubbed the area beneath his chest that ached the most and picked up his jacket.

"I'll be back around one," he said. He made for the door. "Thanks Bill," he added, and he left the office.

～

As MARK PULLED up in the market square in Kingstanton and killed the engine, Katherine made no effort to move.

He said, "Come on, out you get. You need to get going!"

She looked at him and then out of the window, chewing her lip, not moving.

"Look, from what you told me last night, your research idea is a good one, Katherine, you just need to get on with it and..." He gave her a little prod, "Now is as good a time as any."

Katherine opened the car door but still she didn't get out. Mark had stayed in Exeter with her last night and heard the message that Richard had left on her phone. What had he said? *I'm just wondering Katherine, if this whole thing isn't just going to be another mess for us to clear up?* She looked again at Mark.

"I don't know..." She begun, "I'm not so sure it's a good idea now and I..."

"You've let your dad put you off," Mark interrupted. "And you shouldn't. You're smart, Katherine, and if you do this properly you could even get your research essay published. I'm pretty sure that the police force would like to know the impact of something like this on the community!" He gave her another gentle prod and smiled. "Go on, I've got to get to work."

Katherine climbed out of the car and leant back in. "Thanks," she said, "For the moral support."

Mark smiled and slid the gear stick into reverse. "See you later?"

"Yeah. I'll call you when I'm done. And thanks, for the money for my phone and lunch and blah blah blah..."

Mark revved the engine; Katherine slammed the door shut and he pulled away. He tooted her and pointed up the hill. They'd agreed last night that the best place to start was the road where Hirsch lived, talk to some of the neighbours, and see what a direct impact the news circus had had on them in the past twenty-four hours, how they felt about their neighbour, what effect it might have on their immediate community. But this morning Katherine had lost her nerve. She didn't feel well and, if she was honest, part of the whole reason she was doing this, a big part of it in fact, was to impress her dad. Clearly that had already been an epic failure. She set off slowly, following the directions Mark had given her – off the record.

HALF AN HOUR LATER, when she found Hirschs' address there was a small crowd of press - photographers and reporters - camped out in the road, hanging around the front garden, smoking and chatting, littering the place with their drink cans and cigarette butts. Katherine looked at them and walked past, heading up the street. As she went, she kept an eye on the front windows of each house, looking for lace curtains, china ornaments, a well-kept front garden. A few doors up, on the opposite side of the road, she found exactly that. Older people, Mark had told her, especially people who lived on their own, would be much more likely to want to talk.

Katherine knocked at the door, waited, saw the lace curtains move in the front window, the shadow of a face behind them and she held up her hand in a little wave. She continued to wait - not knocking again - with a benign look on her face.

The door opened a crack.

"Good morning," Katherine said, "I'm sorry to bother you, but I was hoping to speak to you about your neighbour, Mr Hirsch? I'm not a news reporter."

The door opened a little bit wider. "I've had lots of them fellas here. Trying to push in," a voice said.

Katherine shook her head. "That's terrible. I just wanted a few minutes, just to try and get a picture of what's happened and how you feel about it. This is more about the impact of the crime than anything to do with your neighbour."

The door opened more, and Katherine could see the figure of an elderly lady. She stood behind the door defensively and held it firmly in her hand ready to shut in an instant.

"Well... I don't want to be talking to those newsmen, they're pushy, but..." The lady stopped and looked Katherine up and down. "I don't mind if you want to come in for a chat. Not too long mind, I've got to make a phone call at ten."

She shuffled to one side to give access; Katherine stepped over the threshold and offered her hand.

"Katherine Ross," she said. "I'm doing research for a project at London School of Economics on the impact of crime."

"Oh, research you say. That's very important, dear. Come on in to the front room and I'll make some tea."

Katherine followed the lady into a cold sitting room so little used that there were still marks from the vacuum cleaner on the carpet. She turned to look at the ornaments on the mantelpiece and waited for the lady to come back with the tea.

"I THINK I've got it, Bill," DC Wittard called out. He was sat at a computer at the back of the incident room. "I've got footage from the Texaco garage at the corner of Druid Street."

DS Crowley hurried over. "Let's take a look." Druid Street was two roads down from the estuary road that led to the boathouse.

Wittard re-ran the CCTV footage; they looked hard at the grainy images.

"Seven forty-five, he goes into the garage. The car's parked over there, see..."

DS CROWLEY NODDED. They watched the tape. "Seven forty-seven, he comes out. He's wearing the scarf, it's clear there in the image... then he drives off in the direction of the boathouse and..." DC Wittard ran the tape forward. "He comes back for a can of drink just over an hour later, that's five past nine and he's not wearing the scarf."

DS Crowley looked at Wittard. "Nice work," he said. "So we can pin down the fact that the scarf went missing somewhere between seven forty-five and five past nine and that Hirsch was within a one mile radius of the boathouse..." He looked up. "Can someone read me out the time that Abbey was in the boathouse?"

"A window between eight to midnight."

DS Crowley patted Wittard on the back. "Looks like we've got him," he said.

"A LOVELY MAN, ELLARD HIRSCH," Mrs Cushing said, "So kind and gave up so much to teach those little kiddies." She shook her head and Katherine shifted in the small, hard Victorian armchair she'd been seated in. This wasn't useful and she was looking for a kind way to cut it short. She didn't want to talk about Hirsch, only the impact of his crime, but Mrs Cushing was so grateful for the company that she hadn't drawn breath since she'd returned with a tray of tea things.

"He was a very good musician in his own right," Mrs Cushing went on, "Of course that showed, particularly with Gabriel. I heard Ellard play, years ago, and when I listen to that young man, I can hear the same nuances in the pieces. Not that I'm an expert, mind, but Ellard gave that boy all his genius." Again, she shook her head.

"Gossip is a dangerous thing," she continued, "I fathom that there was nothing more to it than the love of music. Of course, the boy was brilliant. Now at the Royal College of Music, one of their young Fellows."

"Oh?" Katherine feigned interest.

"Yes, well... I shouldn't be repeating things, but some said that Ellard gave a bit too much of himself to that boy, if you know what I mean." She paused and let the comment sit there for a few moments. "Well, it wouldn't be the first time a musician has been found to be homosexual; I think it goes with the creative mind, don't you? Anyway..." Mrs Cushing took a breath and a sip of tea.

"People talked quite a bit and the rumour was that there was something more than just a love of music in their friendship." She sighed. "I didn't believe it, it was all nonsense as far as I was concerned - utter nonsense. Jealousy, I'd say, people have got dirty minds, they don't like success and that boy was successful, even at eighteen. I've got one of his CDs here. Let me show you. It's called Gabriel..."

Mrs Cushing screwed her face up trying to think of the name. "Oh, it's erm...Oh dear, I can't for the life of me remember it... hang on..." She eased herself up slowly from her wing chair and walked across to the display cabinet that housed her cut glass, china and a small selection of CDs. She ran her finger along the spines of the CD cases. "Radley," she announced. "Gabriel Radley. He's here, on this CD." She pulled one out and held it up for Katherine to see. "He was eighteen when he made this, and Ellard was coaching him for the Junior Fellowship to the Royal College..." She stopped suddenly. "That poor family..."

Katherine looked at the CD. Gabriel Radley was featured on the cover; a beautiful dark boy and then just named BBC young musician of the year. "Is he still at the Royal College of Music?"

"Yes. Comes back regularly to see Ellard though." Mrs Cushing looked at the clock on the mantelpiece. "Well..." she began to shuffle towards the door. "I must make my call. It's to my sister and she'll be waiting by the telephone."

Katherine stood up. She'd only asked two of her research questions, but Mrs Cushing was clearly now in a hurry to get rid of her. She followed Mrs Cushing to the front door and waited for her to open it, sliding the chain across and unlocking the Chubb lock before pulling back the catch.

"How would you describe your feelings about what's happened?" Katherine asked quickly, before she was ushered out.

"Me? Oh very sad. Very sad indeed," Mrs Cushing said, "Ellard Hirsch is such a nice man. I just can't believe..." She sighed as her voice trailed off and Katherine stepped out onto the front step.

"Thank you for your time, Mrs Cushing, I'd like to..." She had been about to ask for another interview, but she didn't finish her sentence; Ellard Hirsch's neighbour had closed the front door and Katherine made her way back down the street, past the reporters, towards the market square and along Fore Street towards the train station.

DI Lewin switched on the tape in interview room four and leant forward.

"My name is Chief Inspector Derek Lewin, and my officer number is 74353. Also present is Detective Sergeant Bill Crowley, officer number 65521. The date is the fifteenth of December two thousand and two and the time is thirteen hundred hours. We are interviewing Ellard Hirsch and also present is his legal representative, Michael Goode. Ellard Hirsch, you do not have to say anything, but it may harm your defence if you do not mention, when questioned, something which you later rely on in court. Anything you do say may be given in evidence."

Lewin leant back and looked at Hirsch. He wanted this godforsaken case over with and he wanted Hirsch to confess. He took a deep breath and felt the air burn in his oesophagus as it went down.

"Mr Hirsch, Ellard, I'd like to ask you again. What were you doing at the boathouse?"

Hirsch sat, slightly hunched, his face pale and drawn. His composure was intact, but his hands, folded on the table in front of him, trembled. He didn't look at Lewin, but he shook his head and stared down at the Formica table between them.

"For the purpose of the tape the suspect is shaking his head." Lewin glanced at DS Crowley. "Ellard, can you tell me when you first met Abbey Salter?"

Again, Hirsch said nothing.

"Why were you chasing Lydia Green? Why were your trousers undone and your penis clearly visible? What had you been doing?"

Hirsch looked up at this point. He bit his lip and Lewin saw his hands shake. He clasped them together and put them down under the table onto his lap.

"Ellard," Lewin said quietly, "I would implore you to speak to us. Right now, you are the chief suspect in the disappearance of a little girl, eight-year-old Abbey Salter. We can place you at the boathouse within hours of Abbey being there. Please, Ellard, do yourself a favour, talk to us, talk to me."

Hirsch sat mute. Lewin saw the muscle in his cheek

twitch with the effort to control himself, and he leant forward towards the tape recorder. "I am terminating this interview at thirteen ten," he said, and he pressed the stop button. Without another word, he stood and left the room.

Outside in the corridor, Lewin sucked in some air to try and ease the tightness in his chest. He had to get back to the hospital that afternoon and that fucker was wasting his time. Barbara had been hypothermic and confused when they'd brought her in, and she was seeing a neurologist on the ward at three. Lewin needed to be there for the meeting. He looked up as DS Crowley came out.

"The bastard's hiding something, I know it," Lewin said.

"How's your wife, Sir?" Crowley asked.

Lewin looked at him. It was subtle, but he picked it up. "Not good," he replied, "I've got to get back to the General in half an hour or so."

DS Crowley glanced behind him at the interview room. "Sir, he's not going anywhere for now so let's leave him to sweat a bit. There's no rush."

Lewin nodded. Of course, there was no rush. Why then, he thought, as he made his way up the corridor, did it feel as if time was silently and rapidly slipping away from him?

KATHERINE HAD GONE STRAIGHT from Kingstanton back to Exeter after she'd spoken to Mrs Cushing. She hadn't bothered to wait for Mark or to do any more research. To be honest she'd completely lost all heart for it. But something was niggling her and, as she sat on the train and mindlessly watched the rolling green fields of Devon stretch to the grey horizon, it began to grow to more than a niggle, it began to really bother her. It was something that Mrs Cushing had said, about Hirsch and Gabriel. At Exeter St Davids station, instead of heading straight home, she checked in her purse and saw the £20 that Mark had given her yesterday, along with another twenty he'd given her today. She stood just outside the station looking at the ticket office and wondering what to do. However, impulsive as always, Katherine went to the counter, enquired about the cost and without any more deliberation, she bought herself a return ticket to London.

On the platform as the train came in, she sent Mark a text. It said,

"I don't know if you've got the right man. Have gone to London to find out."

CI Lewin sat with his daughter in the hospital cafeteria and drank tea from a plastic cup. He stared blankly at the display opposite him; limp, ready-made sandwiches, buns going stale, everything beige, but he wasn't seeing any of it. Early onset Alzheimer's, with a rapid decline, was what the consultant had said, but 'take early retirement effective immediately and prepare yourself for a life of loneliness' is what he heard. Debbie reached out and touched his arm.

"Dad? We should go back and see Mum before we head off."

He sighed. "Do you think it'll make a difference?"

Debbie looked at him. "You can't start thinking like that, Dad. She's still Mum, no matter what."

He nodded and got to his feet. Debbie took his arm.

"How is the case going?" she asked as they headed back up to the ward.

"Not great." He thought briefly about Hirsch, about the

missing body of Abbey Salter. He hated calling it a body, but that was almost certainly what it was by now. "But we might be close to charging someone," he said.

Debbie glanced sidelong at him. "Will you find her?"

Lewin rubbed his chest and took his indigestion tablets out of his pocket. He popped two in his mouth and began to chew. "Yes," he said. But neither his face nor his voice held much conviction.

It was early evening as Katherine waited at the Royal College of Music. Gabriel Radley was easy to find, she had simply asked at reception where he was and had been told that as a Junior Fellow he was teaching a workshop. She located the room and waited for him outside it, blending in with the other students. At six thirty, three violinists came out and left the door open. Katherine knocked and, without waiting for an answer, went inside.

She didn't need to ask if he was Gabriel, she recognised him from the CD cover. He was beautiful, tall and fine-featured, with long dark hair.

"Gabriel," she said, "I'm Katherine Ross. Please could I talk to you for a few moments about Ellard Hirsch?"

She didn't know what she expected when she mentioned Hirsch's name, but his reaction startled her. The thought that had been bothering her came to the fore. Gabriel had been packing up his music and his hands slipped so that he dropped the sheets, and they scattered all over the floor. Hurriedly, his hands shaking, he knelt to pick them up and Katherine could see all the colour had drained from his face.

"I don't have anything to say," he murmured, without looking up. "Please, go away and leave me alone."

"Look, I'm sorry, I know this is a huge cheek, coming here like this, but I heard that Mr Hirsch taught you for several years and that you were friends and... well, I wanted to ask if you'd seen him recently." She dropped her voice and said quietly, "I just wondered if you could tell me what happened yesterday?"

Gabriel kept his head down and stacked the sheets of music. He got to his feet and still kept his face averted, stuffing them into his music case, his trembling fingers struggling with the metal clasp.

"Gabriel, please? Ellard Hirsch is in custody, I helped to put him there, and... it doesn't feel right. I just keep thinking that he wasn't chasing Lydia, but..." She sighed. "Oh, I don't know what. He's in trouble, Gabriel... and I... I just wondered how close you were."

When Gabriel finally looked up Katherine saw that his eyes were wet. He was embarrassed and put the back of his hand up to his face to wipe them. He sniffed, pulling the sleeve of his shirt down over his wrist and wiping his eyes with it.

"He's a wonderful man..." Gabriel said and then his voice broke. He picked up his music and his violin case and went to move past her, but she put her hand on his arm. He stared down at it for a few moments, but he didn't pull away. Then pleadingly he said, "I can't tell you anything. I won't. I promised him..." he pulled his arm away from her. "Please, let me go." Katherine nodded. She looked at his face one more time and moved out of the way as he left the room.

She stood where she was and stared after him. The idea she'd had was now a terrible certainty and she simply didn't know what to do with it. She listened to Gabriel's footsteps as they hurried along the corridor and faded, then she sat down on the edge of the desk and put her head in her hands. The impact of an action, she thought, is far deeper and wider than any of us ever realise. But the action that she was thinking of was not the abduction of Abbey Salter; it was the love affair between a student and his teacher. The knowledge – the truth – she understood at that moment, was that Gabriel Radley loved Ellard Hirsch.

17

PRESENT DAY - *London*
Monday - p.m.

IT WAS MONDAY EVENING, and, pleased to have company on a weekday, Nick's father, Daniel Farleigh, carried two cups of tea up the stairs, placed them on the table by the window and went to the bottom of the drop-down ladder that led to the attic, now right in the centre of the landing.

"Nicholas? I've made tea." He called up. There was silence up there, then he heard his son's heavy footsteps and Nick appeared at the hatch.

"I'll come down," he said.

A few minutes later they stood companionably, drinking tea at the top of the stairs.

"What exactly are you looking for?" Daniel asked. "If it's something specific I might know where it is."

"No, nothing specific, I just wanted to go through a few of my things from uni. See what's there, files and stuff."

"What is there?"

"Bugger all. Did you remove all trace of me when I moved in with Emma?"

"No, but I had to make room for Mum's things up there... I couldn't throw them out; you know that, so... I put them in the attic." Daniel shrugged and Nick realised that his father felt guilty.

He said, "It's not a problem, Dad – I was only joking."

"What do you want with uni files anyway? They're not any use to you now, are they?"

"No, they're not, it's just that I... well, I wanted to check on some dates of something, when I met someone, that's all. I thought I might have kept my planners – they had everything in them - I was anal about being organised."

"I remember." Daniel smiled. "When was it, roughly, that you met this someone?"

"November 2008, in my first term. At least I think it was November, but I honestly can't be sure. It might have been October or even late September. That's what I wanted to check."

Daniel looked at his son. "Why?"

Nick avoided the look. He turned to stare out of the landing window at the orange street lamps, the splatter of icy rain outside.

"What's so important about the date you met this 'someone'?" Daniel persisted.

Nick turned back. "The someone is called Kate; Kate Ross and I fell in love with her. We only spent one night together, but I've never forgotten it and..." Nick felt his throat close. He swallowed hard. "She, Kate, has a daughter who's fourteen."

"I see." Daniel looked down at his cup. "Is she the woman you were caught with on Twitter?"

Nick suddenly flushed. "Fuck. You didn't see it, did you?"

"No, but your sister told me. Is she, Kate, the reason you're leaving Emma?"

"No." Nick moved away from where they had been leaning against the banisters.

He said, "Not exactly anyway. She is and she isn't, if that makes sense. Kate isn't interested in me, I fucked up by not telling her I was married, but meeting her, feeling like I do, it's just made me realise how little I love Emma and..." he shrugged, "how little she loves me back."

"Well, I'm glad you've reached the conclusion that Caro and I reached several years ago. Emma loves herself and her work, in that order. Don't get me wrong, she's perfectly nice, but she's not the partner you deserve, Nick." Daniel put his tea down on the table. "Come into the bedroom for a tick, I've got something that might help."

Nick frowned. "Like?"

"Just come into the bedroom," Daniel said.

Nick followed his father into the bedroom that Daniel had shared with his mother; the room she had died in. It was unchanged; she could have been downstairs reading the evening paper right now. Nick stopped and looked round. He had thought when she died that he would never be able to come in here again. He'd slept on the floor by her bed night after night when the cancer had gone to her brain, and he felt as if he knew every rose on the wallpaper and every thread of weave in the rug. But it was comforting, now, to feel her presence all around him.

"Sit on that chair," Daniel said, "It's under the bed."

"What is?"

"Your mother's calendar." He knelt and lifted the cream-pleated valance up, revealing a divan with two drawers in it. He pulled one open and took out a carrier bag. Inside there was a monthly planner, the sort they sold in Marks and Spencer, and Nick had a sudden memory of the calendar stuck on the fridge door in the kitchen.

"I look at it often." Daniel said, getting stiffly to his feet. "It's full of nonsense; reminders about the milk and Sunday papers and so forth, but I find it comforting."

Nick wondered what it must be like to love someone that much. He stood up and gave his father a sort of awkward man/bear hug, but it only lasted for a few moments. His father was old school proud; he didn't like his children to see his loneliness and pain.

"Here," he said, handing the bag across to Nick. "She wrote herself lots of notes – especially during the chemo when her memory got bad."

Nick looked inside the bag and pulled the planner out.

"Read it here, will you?" Daniel said, "And put it back when you're done?"

"Yeah, of course..." Nick flicked through a few pages. He didn't think this was going to be any use, but he wasn't sure how to tell his father. He had the strongest inclination to replace the calendar without reading a word, but his father was watching him, so he sat back down on the bedroom chair and flicked through to the month of September. Suddenly he laughed.

His father smiled. "Yes, I know. *'September 1st - putting Viagra in Daniel's coffee'.* It was a joke – she never did that." He moved towards the door. "I forgot a dinner she'd arranged, and I pretended that I'd read the calendar and that it was her fault because she hadn't put it on there. She knew I never read it, so she wrote that to catch me out."

"Did she catch you out?"

"Of course. There was no getting one over on your mum,

Nick." He opened the door and stepped out into the hall. "I hope you find what you're looking for."

He was gone, and Nick went back to reading September. His father was right, each day had some kind of note or comment on it; his mother must have used the planner like some kind of personal diary. He read; *'Remind Nick to wash bed linen in halls – smelly.'* Then a small note by the side of that that said, *'No, don't – interfering!!'* Then one more underneath that said, *'Buy Febreze.'*

KATE WAS WASHING up and Annie had gone to her room. That wasn't the usual situation, they usually washed up together, but Annie had been so silent over dinner that when she had mentioned a headache and asked to go to her room, Kate had agreed. It wasn't worth the aggravation to insist that she dried up. Now, Kate stood alone at the sink and noticed the silence. She thought about their earlier conversation and realised, with a heavy, sinking feeling, that she would have to call Mark. She felt alone. That was what she had always wanted of course, but this kind of alone wasn't the same. It didn't speak of choice and independence, it was simply lonely alone, and that was wholly different.

Kate's phone rang. She pulled off her rubber gloves and crossed to the sofa where she had left it. She glanced at the screen; it was Hannah.

"Hey," she said, "How are you?"

There was a brief silence on the other end then Hannah said, "Is Annie around?"

"No, she's in her room. She's not feeling too well - she's got a headache."

"Good."

"Good?" Kate said, "Hannah, are you OK? You don't sound..."

"No Kate, I'm not OK. It's good that Annie's in her room because what I have to say isn't particularly nice, I'm afraid, and it concerns her."

Kate could feel herself stiffen. "What are you talking about, Hannah?" Any semblance of friendliness had disappeared from her voice. "What concerns Annie?" Kate heard Hannah take a breath.

"Matilda was wearing a bracelet on Friday when the girls went out. We bought it for her when she passed her piano exam. It was loose on her, apparently, and she was worried about it slipping off, so she put it in her purse which she gave to Annie to look after as she didn't have a bag with her. Annie kept the purse until school this morning and... well..." Hannah hesitated. "The bracelet's gone missing...."

"Hang on a minute..." Kate said, "what exactly did Annie say?"

"When Matilda got her purse back this morning she asked Annie for the bracelet, and Annie said she didn't have it. She said it was Matilda's problem and that if she'd put it in her purse for safe keeping then that's where it was. Only we've checked the purse, all the pockets, and it isn't there."

Kate took a breath. "If Annie said she doesn't have it then she doesn't," Kate said. "The only thing I can think is that it's fallen out of the purse, and it might still be in her bag, at the bottom somewhere, or it's fallen out of the bag at some point." Kate felt sick. "Annie doesn't steal," she said.

"I'm not suggesting that she stole it Kate, I'm just saying that it was something that both the girls wanted, and Mattie got it first and well... you know how girls can be?"

"No, no I don't. I know how Annie can be and that's

honest and kind." Kate could feel her hands begin to tremble. She needed to get off the phone before she said something she regretted. "I'll go and speak to Annie now, but
Hannah, I believe my daughter. Annie doesn't steal and she
doesn't lie either." Kate didn't wait for a response. She
pressed 'end' and dropped the phone onto the sofa.

She stood for a few moments and felt her heart thudding in her chest, then she walked along to Annie's room
and knocked on the door.

"Yeah?"

Kate put her head round the door. "Annie, can I
come in?"

Annie shrugged. She was sitting in bed hugging her
knees, watching something on her phone.

"Annie, Hannah just called. Matilda has lost a bracelet
and she thinks you might still have it."

Annie glanced up from the screen. "I told her I don't
have it."

"OK. Have you any idea where it might have gone?
Could it still be in your bag?"

Annie glanced away. She shrugged again.

"Annie, this is quite important. Matilda has lost something that's valuable to her and she thinks you're involved.
Have you checked your bag?"

"I told you mum; I haven't got it." Annie finally looked at
Kate. Her face was so easy to read, too easy, and Kate saw
hurt and confusion there, but as she stared at her daughter,
she also saw something else, longing and loneliness. She
recognised them because she knew the feelings herself.
"You know what, Mum, I can't believe that you're even
asking me this." Annie's voice wavered. "If I said I haven't got
it then I haven't got it."

Kate came to the edge of the bed. "I know you haven't,

sweetheart, of course I know that and that's what I told Hannah."

"Then why are you asking me?"

Kate thought back to the missing photo in her drawer, to the postcard, the wreath, and she knew that she was asking because she was afraid. Nothing was as it had been, and it made her fearful and suspicious.

"You're right; I shouldn't even be asking. I trust you Annie, you know that, but please remember that if you ever do anything that maybe you're not sure of, or that you regret, you can tell me, OK?"

"Like you did you mean?"

Kate blinked rapidly. "What?" She took a step back. "What is that supposed to mean, Annie?"

"Having me," Annie said, "You must be ashamed of it because you've never told me who my father is, and I've never met any of your family. It's just us, like you want to keep me secret, keep me away from everyone."

Kate caught the breath in the back of her throat. "Annie, that's not true! Where on earth did you..."

Annie got up off the bed and headed towards the door.

"Don't, Mum," she said. "Don't make any more stupid excuses."

"Annie?!"

The bedroom door opened, Annie left, and Kate heard her go into the bathroom and lock the door.

"Annie?!" she shouted, "Annie, come back here..." But the shower was running, and Annie couldn't hear her. Knowing she was defeated, Kate shut up.

∿

Nick had lost track of time; he started when Daniel knocked on the door.

"Can I come in?" his father called.

"Sure…" He placed the calendar on the floor beside him, still open at October, 2002.

"Ah…" Daniel sat down on the edge of the bed and looked at his son. "You saw it then."

Nick nodded; he didn't trust himself to speak. There were three comments on three dates, more or less a week apart, all in his mother's spidery handwriting. Just a few words in each date box that spoke volumes.

October 18th – *To Nick for dinner – student flat – eat first! Nick distracted. Girl on scene? Take nice wine? Check with D. not too much…* Then on November 8th, her writing said; *Nick home – get treats.* There was a sad face next to that line and, finally, the following week, she wrote, *Call Jen – Nick bad – heartbreak?* Jen was his mother's oldest friend and a GP in Surrey; she was her go-to person for his or his sister, Caro's health.

Daniel and Nick sat there in silence for some time, the lamp on the bedside casting a warm, soporific glow, Nick counting the rosebuds on the wall opposite as he'd done so many times in that room in the past, until finally Daniel said:

"So, you met Kate in October, that's the 'Girl on scene,' right?"

Nick nodded.

"And the cause of the heartbreak?" Nick winced at the choice of word, but he remembered the pain and nodded again. "And Kate's daughter was born the following year." Daniel took a deep breath. "You know Kate may well have met someone else after you, or just before you?"

Nick swallowed. "Annie is five ten I'd say, and still growing." He motioned to his chest. "She has legs up to here and she's..." He broke off. There was another silence. Nick cleared his throat. "She's absolutely beautiful," he said, then he smiled wistfully. "That is clearly not something she might have got from me. She reminds me of Mum, there's something about her."

Daniel shifted position. He took another breath. "Nick," he began, but he had to pause to phrase his words, "Do you think that you might be getting this a little bit out of proportion? Don't you think that somewhere along the line Kate might have contacted you if she thought you were the father? Doesn't this all feel a little bit coincidental? Perhaps a little wishful? I mean, I see your mum everywhere, in so many people, or rather, I don't see it, I imagine it because I miss her so much."

Nick didn't answer. He continued looking at the rosebuds, but he'd lost count. There was another long silence and then he answered his father.

"I don't know what I think Dad." He uncurled his legs and stood up. He was stiff and his legs hurt as he straightened. The whole lot of him hurt. "I couldn't believe it when I saw Kate in the gallery at the House of Commons, I recognised her immediately and.... Well...I know this sounds stupid, but when I met her, when I was nineteen, she blew me away - she completely blew me away." He shrugged. "And she did it again, the second time I met her, which in itself was a meeting that was completely serendipitous, seeing her at a drinks party in the Strangers' Dining Room just hours after noticing her in the gallery but..." he broke off. "You know what, Dad, I can't explain it or fathom it, me, Captain fucking Sensible, feeling like this, but that's what it is and then..." He chewed the inside of his lip, "Then I find out that she has a daughter, and when I see her daughter, I realise that she reminds me of myself, and mum, and that the dates fit and I feel awed and frightened and absolutely fucking livid that she might be mine and I've missed all that time. She might be my daughter and I don't even know her."

Daniel stood as well. "But she might not be your daughter, Nick, and..." he looked across at his son. "Well... to be realistic, the chances are that she isn't." He pressed on. "You are on the verge of a big job Nick, a real opportunity in your career, a chance to make a difference to society. Surely that means something to you?"

Only Daniel didn't get an answer and, looking across at Nick, he wasn't expecting one. He knew his son wasn't listening; he knew that Nick had been looking and longing for something since his mother died and that he hadn't found it, not in his work and certainly not in his marriage. Daniel didn't think he'd found it now, either, but Nick was beyond hearing what anyone had to say.

"So," Daniel said, as Nick passed him the calendar and he put it back in the carrier bag. He left it on the bed to read again later. "What now?"

Nick shrugged. "I don't know." They walked out of the bedroom. "See Kate, I guess, try and find out what's going on."

On the landing it was dark, and Daniel turned the main lights on. They stood in the glare of electric light and Nick said, "I should go; it's late."

"Yes. Do you want something to eat before you go?"

"No thanks." He looked at his father. "I think I should go over to Kate's now, get this thing sorted."

"Are you sure? You said yourself it's late and I wonder if this might not look better in the morning?"

"No time like the present."

"Right."

The moved down the stairs and Daniel wondered if he should break the habit of a lifetime and tell Nick not to go; insist that he leave this alone for the time being. He said;

"Nick, I think a few days to cogitate on this would be advisable. Don't go rushing into things, it's never wise."

But Nick had already reached for his jacket from the coat stand and begun to pull it on, and Daniel knew he'd wasted his words.

"Mind how you go," he said as Nick opened the front door.

On the step Nick turned. "I will, Dad, and thanks, for letting me see the calendar."

Daniel watched Nick leave, saw him wave as he turned and went on his way and wondered what Fi would have made of it all. He had no idea, but he realised that she would know exactly what to say and do, and that was one of the things he missed about her most.

KATE WAS WORKING on a report when the buzzer for the main door went. She walked into the hall, pressed the intercom and heard Nick's voice.

"Let me in Kate, I need to talk to you."

She froze for a moment. She had no intention of letting him in. The buzzer sounded again, this time for longer, and she glanced behind her at Annie's closed bedroom door. God, this was the last thing she needed now. How the hell the bastard thought he had the right to come here and start causing havoc she couldn't fathom. On an angry impulse, and to shut him up, she grabbed her front door key, threw a jacket round her shoulders and left the flat.

Down in the hallway, she yanked the main door open and snapped,

"What the fuck do you think you're doing? How can you even show your face here after all that crap you've dealt me?" She held onto the door, keeping it half closed. "Go away Nick!" She hissed angrily. "Please, just go away."

Nick stared at her. He'd been about to rant, to start demanding, but suddenly he lost his nerve. "The wreath was nothing to do with me," he said. "I've been looking into it and..."

Kate began to close the door, but Nick stuck his foot out to stop her.

"Hey!"

"I need to talk to you about Annie," Nick said. "Please!"

Kate stared at his foot and pressed the door hard against it.

"Ouch, fuck!" He kept it there and continued, "I'm not going anywhere until we talk about Annie."

"Annie has nothing to do with you," Kate said, "There is nothing to say."

But she hid behind the door and her heart pounded in her chest. Annie? He wanted to talk about Annie?! She began to hyperventilate and had to breathe into her cupped hands.

"Kate?!" He waited. "Kate there *is* something to talk about and Annie *is* something to do with me, or at least I think she is. I want to see her." Nick gave a shove against the door with his knee and opened the gap. "Let me in, Kate, we need to talk."

"No!" Kate pushed the door, trying to shut it, but Nick pushed back.

"Let me in!" Nick pushed hard and suddenly the door

gave. He saw Kate spring back, but she took up a position, arms out either side of her.

"You are not coming in!" she cried. "This is my home, and you are not coming in!"

"MUM?!" Annie stood on the stairs in her pyjamas. "Mum, what's going on?"

Kate glanced briefly behind her at her daughter, but she maintained her position. "Annie," she called over her shoulder, "This is nothing to do with you, please, go back to the flat."

"But Mum, I..."

"I want to see her," Nick insisted. He called out, "ANNIE?!"

"Annie, please go back love," Kate cried, "Go back to the flat and call Kerrie. Tell her to come over. Now!"

"ANNIE?!" Nick shouted. He tried to get past Kate, but she held her position. "ANNIE?!"

"She's gone!" Kate snapped, "Stop shouting!"

"Fuck!" Nick turned away, but he stood his ground. They stayed like that, at an impasse; Kate guarding the hallway, Nick prowling the front step, militant, furious. After some time, he finally left the front door, walked a few paces away then suddenly he turned and came back as Kate was looking behind her up the stairs. He pushed his way into the hallway past her.

"Get out!" Kate spat. She gave him a shove.

"No! I'm not going anywhere Kate! I'm going to stay here until you at least let me see her, until you tell me the truth, tell me what the fuck you've been thinking all these years!"

"I don't know what you're talking about," Kate cried desperately, "Annie is my daughter, and she has nothing to do with you Nick. She's mine, I gave birth to her, I nursed her and I've raised her. She has *nothing* to do with you! Do you hear me?! NOTHING!"

Nick shook his head. He had gone past reason, past any kind of self-constraint. His emotions churned inside him, and he felt sick. He had spent the last ten years in a cool, unemotional marriage and now, unused to feeling - to experiencing - anything like this he had no idea what to do, how to control himself.

"You're lying," he said vehemently, "You think you can treat people any way you want, take what you want and..."

"MUM?" Annie called down from the top of the stairs. "Mum, I called Kerrie a while ago and she's just texted. She's almost here. She's rung the police as well. Mum?"

Nick leapt forward towards the stairs and Kate grabbed his coat, pulling him back.

"Annie?" he called. "Annie, my name's Nick and I'd really like to meet you! Annie, I..."

Suddenly there was a screech of tyres in the parking space outside the building and flash of blue lights. Nick spun round.

"POLICE! Stay where you are please sir." A uniformed officer came into the hall. "Let's take this outside, shall we sir?"

"I'm not doing anything wrong; I'm just talking to this lady here, I..."

Nick turned as a young woman rushed into the hall.

"Kate?!! Are you OK?" She turned to the police officer. "I'm Kerrie Hart, I called the police. This man's been causing a disturbance and it's not the first time. He's an absolute menace. He needs locking up!"

She spat that at him, her face distorted with anger then suddenly, and without warning, Kate began to cry. Nick felt a heavy weight hit his chest and he turned away. Staring at the ground, he walked out of the building and into the cold night air. He could hear her sobs, a great heaving sound that seemed to wrack her and he could hear the soothing voice of the young woman. He leant against the wall of the building and closed his eyes. What the fuck was he doing? Nick Farleigh - sensible, reasonable, boring Nick. Eight years an MP and never a foot wrong, one week after meeting Kate and his life was a fucking mess.

He opened his eyes and saw the young woman talking to the officers by the car. He went over.

"We'd like you to come down to the station with us please sir."

"Are you arresting me?"

"Yes. The young woman says she saw you kick the front door. Name please."

"Nick Farleigh."

"Nick Farleigh, I am arresting you for damage to property. You do not have to say anything. But, it may harm your defence if you do not mention when questioned something which you later rely on in court. Anything you do say may be given in evidence."

Nick was silent until the officer started to handcuff him. "Is that really necessary?"

"Yes it is. It's for our safety and yours. In the car please sir."

Nick glanced up at the building one last time as the officer opened the squad car door. He saw a figure at the window. Annie. He held his hand up in a brief wave and she waved back. He bent to climb into the back seat and as he did so he saw Kerrie's shoes.

Trainers; fancy; Nike Metcon.

KERRIE HANDED Kate a cup of tea, strong tea, with sugar in it.

"Drink it hot," she instructed, "You've had a shock and an upset." She pulled on her coat. "You sure you don't need me to stay?"

Kate nursed the cup; she was cold and her hands trembled. "No, I'm fine, thank you though." Kate needed some space; she felt crowded and confused. That scene had been ugly; ugly and frightening. Kerrie was right, Nick *was* mad, he needed locking up.

"Is Annie OK?"

"I think so, but..."

"But what? What's up?"

Kate stared down at her tea. She hesitated for a few moments, but the urge to tell someone was too strong. She couldn't do this all on her own. She said,

"Apparently Matilda gave Annie a bracelet to look after on Friday and it's gone missing. Mattie and Hannah, her mum, think Annie might have taken it."

"Did she?"

"No!" Kate took a swallow of tea. She closed her eyes. "At least, I don't think so."

"Did you check?"

Kate opened them abruptly and looked at Kerrie. "No, and nor should I. If Annie says she doesn't have it then she doesn't. I trust her."

Kerrie shrugged. "Your call," she said.

Kate wavered. "Do you think I should check?"

"Perhaps?" Kerrie hovered in the doorway, uneasy, and Kate watched her for a few moments then said, "What? What is it you want to say?"

Kerrie came into the room and perched on the edge of the chair opposite Kate.

"Sometimes growing up is hard, especially without a

dad. Maybe Annie feels a bit jealous of Matilda? Of her family set-up?"

"No." Kate's voice was cold. "No Kerrie, I don't think you've got that right, not at all."

Kerrie stood. "OK, sorry. I shouldn't have said that."

"No, you shouldn't. Annie has wanted for nothing, Kerrie, even without a dad. In fact she's had more love and attention than millions of kids who've grown up with both parents." Kate stood as well.

"I should go."

"Yes."

Kerrie headed to the door. She stopped and turned and said, "They fuck you up, your mum and dad." Kerrie smiled, "I read that on Instagram,"

But Kate didn't smile back. She stood in silence until Kerrie had left the flat and closed the door behind her, then she went to Annie's bedroom and knocked gently on the door.

It was after eleven and there was no reply, so Kate pushed the door open and crept into the room. Annie was asleep, curled onto her side, one arm over her body, and Kate smoothed the duvet, tucking it up round her daughter's shoulders. Annie didn't wake.

Kate stared down at Annie's face - the features now smooth and peaceful - and remembered the look of loneliness and longing she'd seen earlier on those same features. What had she missed? What was it that Annie longed for? She wondered if Kerrie was right and that Annie longed for a father, for a family. Kate wouldn't know what that felt like; how could she? Her own family, her strained, broken relationship with her father and her mother, ill, unbalanced and not able to look after herself, let alone a teenage daughter. And Beth, the second wife, mean and territorial, the twins, innocent pawns in a jealous 'who-do-you-love-the-most' game. It had all been so fucked up that Kate had longed to be rid of them. And now, she wondered, had she made Annie suffer like she did, but in a different way? Had she inflicted the same isolation and loneliness on her own daughter?

Kate touched Annie's hair and moved away, back towards the door. Then suddenly, on impulse, she crossed to the chest of drawers by the window and slid the top right-hand drawer open, the smallest one where Annie kept her private things. Silently, she rifled through the papers and photos there, shifting things, searching and finally, under a pile she found a folded handkerchief. Inside it was the bracelet.

18

PRESENT DAY – *London*
Tuesday – a.m.

IT WAS JUST after 5am when DS Dennis called Mo and DC Carter into her office by banging on the plate-glass wall and beckoning with her hand.

"She looks pissed off," Mo said.

They went in. She was looking for something under a pile of papers.

"Ma'am."

She glanced up. "Farleigh, the Right Honourable; have we charged him?"

"Not yet, but we're…"

"Get rid of him then." She continued to riffle. "I don't want him cluttering up the cells on my watch and I don't want to leave here in an hour and find half the fucking press on the doorstep braying for a scandal."

She found what she was looking for, put it between her lips, inhaled and blew a cloud of vapour into the air.

"Plus, his wife is a shit-hot lawyer for some top legal firm, and she'll have the crème de la crème of criminal law down here before you can say Member of Parliament."

She removed the vape and held it. "What have you got anyway?"

"Disturbing the peace, entering without permission, harassment..."

"Bugger all then." DS Dennis sighed and ran her hands wearily over her face. She was tired and she couldn't wait for the shift to end. It was her second night in a week, and she was hacked off with the whole fucking thing. "Why are we keeping him, might I ask? Technically you should have released him hours ago."

"The boyfriend, Matt Brennen, links to Unicorn, we've got positive ID of them together this afternoon. The director of Unicorn, David Sachs, called Farleigh's office last week, Farleigh has been harassing Kate Ross and Kate Ross knows Lydia Helston - she was at the funeral."

DS Dennis took another long drag on her vape. "It's not enough to hold him, Mo, you know that."

Mo bit the inside of his lip. "Yes Boss,"

"Like I said, bugger all. Get him out of here."

Mo sighed. "But Farleigh is linked, I'm sure of it. He won't admit to knowing Unicorn, but he is linked in some way."

DS Dennis shrugged. "How?"

"Everything that's happened is on Farleigh's patch – he could have a finger in the pie? If there is something between Brennen and the developers, maybe Farleigh is in on it too? Maybe he's harassing Kate Ross because she has some legal knowledge, access to the lease..."

Mo's voice petered out. There was a silence. DS Dennis took a long drag on the vape, blew a cloud of vapour into the air but still she said nothing. Mo was beginning to feel uneasy. He shifted position again.

"Any further on the link between Kate Ross and Lydia? The fake profiles?"

"No."

"Still no warrant for Facebook?"

"No."

"Then do what I've told you; get rid of Farleigh. I'll chase up the warrant."

"Yes, Boss."

The interview was over.

It was their usual early morning walk to the office and the bus for school, but Kate had given up trying to make conversation with Annie. The atmosphere was miserable; tense and hostile and Kate was at a loss. She hadn't mentioned the bracelet, she didn't know how to. It meant admitting to not trusting her daughter, to snooping in Annie's private things, and those two ideas were almost as bad as taking the bracelet. Kate and Annie had been so close; it was always just the two of them and what had - even just a week ago - been intimate now felt suddenly claustrophobic. A chasm had opened between them, and Kate kept asking herself how that had happened and why Annie might have lied and taken the bracelet in the first place – but she had no answers. Of course, Annie had the usual teenage moods and sulks and sometimes they were hard to navigate but she was, unequivocally, Kate's chief joy in life - she was everything Kate had hoped she would be, had strived to make sure she would be. She was kind, clever and honest. Honest. Kate fretted over that word. Annie had none of Kate's bitter complications, none of Kate's angst – at least she hadn't had, until now.

They walked in silence and Kate longed to hook arms with her daughter, to find some of that warmth that they had shared so often, but as they approached the office, they did so apart. Annie stared at the pavement, headphones in; Kate chewed the inside of her mouth – a nervous habit she had - unspoken words of reproach and remorse on her lips. Annie has done wrong, she kept telling herself, but it is my fault - it must be.

Turning into Lower Marsh from The Cut, Kate saw several people outside the office, and her heart sank.

"Looks like I'm needed," she said, offering Annie a smile.

Anne shrugged and kept her head down.

When they arrived at the office, the several people turned out to be a family - parents, grandfather and a small child; they spoke very little English. Kate opened the door and ushered everyone inside, then turned to Annie who stood forlornly by the door. That was unusual; normally Annie would have played with the little girl, tried to make people comfortable.

"Annie, I'm going to have to sort this out I'm afraid, you OK to go down to the bus?"

Again, Annie shrugged. She didn't look at Kate; she simply turned and walked away. Kate went to the door and called after her. "Annie?"

Annie stopped, glanced back and Kate felt desolate; they always walked to the bus together; it was part of their morning ritual.

"Hey, don't go without a hug?"

Kate walked across to her daughter and hugged her, but the embrace was awkward and stiff.

"I'm sorry about this, love, I really am. You don't mind, do you?"

Annie shrugged once more, put her earphones in and moved off. Kate's phone rang; it was social services. She took the call and Annie carried on down Lower Marsh.

IT WAS JUST after seven thirty when Nella woke. She came to suddenly as someone pulled open the blinds. She had fallen asleep with her head on the desk and now, as she looked up, she had a stiff pain in the side of her neck. She sat up and rubbed it, blinking wearily. She picked up her phone. Four missed calls, two texts from Mo.

"Shit, sorry I must have conked out."

"Would you like a cup of coffee DC Walsh? Our DI is in the office this morning and he wants to have a chat."

Nella stood stiffly and stretched her shoulders and back. "Yeah, thanks, milk and two sugars. I'll just pop along to the toilets and freshen up."

She picked up her handbag and phone and headed to the Ladies. There, she washed her face with the hand-soap and dried it, bending down to get it under the hot air hand-dryer. She rinsed her mouth with cold water and re-tied her hair back into the knot she wore at the nape of her neck. Respectable, just, never gonna be a looker, she thought. She took up her phone and dialled Mo. The screen lit up for a few moments, trying to connect, then her phone promptly ran out of charge. Bugger: she should have called him last night as soon as she'd seen it. Making her way back to the office, she saw a tall man waiting by the desk, flicking through the file she'd been looking at. Nella knocked, went in, and the man, on seeing her, stepped forward.

"Detective Inspector Mark Heddon."

"DC Nella Walsh."

They shook hands; Nella always gripped as good as she got.

"How are you getting on?"

"OK."

"What are you looking for?"

Nella sighed. "We've had a sudden death in London, accidental on the file, but I've been looking into it and..."

"Lydia Helston." Mark said.

"Yes!" Nella stopped and looked at him. "You know about it? It's a bit off the radar for Devon Police, isn't it?"

"Yes, but someone recently told me, an old colleague. I worked on the Abbey Salter disappearance; the case Lydia was involved in."

"Ah, right. She was hanged, did they tell you that?" Nella asked, "Her scarf caught in the lift doors, doors that should have been working, but weren't. She never took the lift. I thought maybe it was her boyfriend, that he had something to gain, financially, but now..."

"Now you know you don't think so."

Nella shook her head. "No, I don't think it has anything to do with him at all."

EMMA HAD PARKED some way from the police station, and she and Nick walked to the car in silence. It was cold and grey, and Emma was in no mood for conversation. She pressed the key fob when they reached the car, the light flashed, and the doors unlocked. Nick climbed into the passenger side and waited for Emma to get in.

"Thanks," he said. "For collecting me. I appreciate it."

Emma started the engine. "Well don't," she shot back. She indicated and pulled out into the traffic. "I didn't do it for you Nick; I sorted your little mess out because I don't want you fucking up my chances of a partnership. Until I can file for divorce we're still connected."

Nick looked at her. "You're filing for divorce?"

"Obviously." They pulled up at some traffic lights and she glanced across at him. "Don't look so shocked, Nick. What on earth did you expect? You've moved out and you're harassing another woman, a woman you had sex with."

"It's not like that Emma, it's..."

She held up her hand to stop him. "I have no desire to know what it's like, Nick."

"Of course not," Nick said coldly, "If there's nothing in it for you, you're not interested."

Suddenly Emma veered left and, hitting the kerb, swung into a side road. She slung the car up onto the kerb, yanked on the handbrake and turned to him.

"You don't get it, do you?!" she snapped, "You just don't get it? In your smug little white-man world you just can't see how fucking hard it is to be a woman, to do a job – mostly better than everyone else – and to have to claw your way to the top!" She was so angry that she banged the steering wheel with the flats of her hands. "Fuck!" She was breathing hard, and Nick could see the pulse in her neck throb.

They sat in silence for a while then, more calmly, she said,

"I'm selfish, self-interested, hard, cold, self-seeking... yeah, I know, I've heard it all. Christ, it's even what your father and sister think..."

Nick winced.

"But really, you know what I am? I'm simply acting like a man, that's all. I act like a man and that's not allowed. How many men do you know who put their jobs first? Who have endless midweek dinners with clients? Who work over the weekend? Yeah, quite a few, but that's OK, isn't it?"

Nick turned to look at her as she stared out of the windscreen at the rain.

"Why is it so important to get on Emma? To make partner?"

"See?" she said. "You'd never ask that question to a male friend, would you? It's taken for granted that men want to be successful, to get on." She looked at him. "I'm very, very good at what I do, I really love my job, and it's the unfairness of it Nick, that's what rankles. We've both put our jobs first, but I'm the one who gets criticised for it."

He went to reply, to argue that she had been prepared to use him to get on, to use the idea of a family to keep him, but he realised that her actions weren't unique. How many of his colleagues had used their marriages that way? He sat there mute, feeling stupid and embarrassed because she was right.

Emma shifted in her seat. She let out a sigh.

"I thought we were OK," she said, "Not La La Land romantic but OK - muddling through. I thought we'd have a family one day."

"Really?" Nick turned to her in disbelief, and she shrugged, then offered him a sad smile.

"OK, probably not really, but I thought it was a nice idea, hypothetically."

"Emma, we weren't OK, you know? We've been separate people sharing a house for years. Come on – you're a lawyer...-"

"A very good lawyer..."

"Yeah, a brilliant lawyer. You can see the facts."

She nodded, they were silent for a while - the low hum of the Mercedes engine and the whirr of the car heater felt like an appropriate swansong – then Emma gathered herself together and said, "We should get going. I need to get to the office."

Nick smiled ruefully. "Where else?" he remarked.

Emma glanced in the rear-view mirror and indicated to pull out. They took a few right-hand turns and ended back on the main drag again.

"By the way," she said, as they drove, "if you look in my bag there's a file in there you might want to see."

"Really? What file?"

"It's a report on Kate's charity. I had one of the trainees do it."

"You're fucking kidding me!"

"No. Calm down Nick. I was looking out for you, protecting my interests, you could say. I was just making sure that there was nothing there that could bite you on the bum when you were least expecting it."

"I don't believe you, Emma." Nick was suddenly angry. "What the fuck did you think you were...?"

"Save the indignation Nick. Read the file. There's a company in Australia you need to check out – sooner rather than later."

He shut up and reached behind him to her bag on the back seat. He lifted a clear plastic folder out of it. "Australia?" He felt suddenly uneasy.

"Yeah, offshore investment – check out the director – not sure how kosher it all is."

Nick opened the folder and flicked through the report. He stopped, looked up and suddenly said, "Emma, can you drop me off here?!"

"OK... I thought you wanted to go to Caro's?"

"No, here's fine. Anywhere here..."

Emma indicated and pulled up alongside the kerb. "Nick, are you OK? Is there something in the report?"

Nick unfastened his seatbelt. "Em, you've got several pairs of trainers, haven't you?"

"Yes...?"

"Nike Metcons. Are they any good?"

"Yes, very. Lots of people have them for climbing – you know, on the climbing wall? They've got great grip apparently. Why, do you..."

But Emma didn't finish her sentence. Nick had climbed out of the car and was hurrying up Westminster Bridge Road towards Lower Marsh.

KATE WAS STANDING with the interpreter, watching and listening, while she spoke in Arabic to the family who had arrived earlier that morning. The waiting room was full, and her colleague Luke was already working flat out, using the office to see clients while the family were in the waiting area so that their daughter could play with the toys. Kate, who had been taking notes with her iPad resting on the corner of the reception desk, was now trying to make sense of their situation. Her phone rang.

It was in the drawer of the desk for safe keeping, and she hadn't looked at it since she'd arrived that morning. Now, snatching it up, she saw it was the school and, like most parents, her stomach lurched.

"Hello?"

"Hi, this is Southfields Academy. Annie isn't in school

this morning and she hasn't been registered by you as absent, so we're just checking that she's OK?"

Kate floundered for a moment. Her mind went blank. "I'm sorry? Did you say Annie wasn't in? I sent her to school this morning; she came with me to work and then went on to catch the bus..."

"She hasn't signed in I'm afraid, and she isn't on the late list."

"Are you sure she's not in her lessons? Maybe the bus was late, maybe she just went straight to her classes?"

"No, she's been marked absent for period one this morning. We did email you at eight fifty, but we've not had a reply, so I thought I'd give you a call."

"You emailed me?" Kate looked at her watch. It was nine fifteen and panic immediately rose in her chest. "I haven't checked my emails; I've been so busy..." She realised how inadequate she sounded - how lame. "I have no idea where she is. I sent her to school, she should be there, I just don't know."

The voice on the other end was calm. "I'm afraid we'll have to mark her down as absent without authority."

"Absent without authority...?"

"Yes. I'm afraid that we're required by law to make a note of any truancy."

Kate felt a sudden spurt of anger. Did this person even know Annie? Annie a truant?

"Annie doesn't truant," she said coldly. "Annie's a good student, she's a top student, she..." Kate stopped as an image of the bracelet came into her head.

"Ms Ross, if you could let us know when you've located Annie by emailing the school via the absence link on our website, we'd appreciate it. Someone from our home liaison team will be in touch with you by the end of the week. Thank you."

"But can you...?" Kate broke off; she was wasting her breath.

"You OK, Kate?" Luke had been seeing his client out. "Kate? What's happened?"

Kate was ashen, stricken with panic. She was dialling Annie's number, it rang, and Luke heard the voicemail click in.

"I'm fine, really, it's..." She faltered. "It's Annie," she said in a small voice. "She's not turned up at school. They've just rung... I don't know where she is..." She was texting now, intent on the phone.

The interpreter had stopped talking and was looking at Kate.

"She's never done this before... she's not like that... she's..." Kate looked up. "The text is undelivered."

Luke said, "Have you got a neighbour you can call? See if she's gone home? If not, I can ride over there on my bike and see if she's there?"

"Yes, yes, I'll call Marcy." Kate scrolled through her contacts and found her neighbour. She pressed 'call'.

"Hi Marcy, it's Kate. Please could you knock at mine and see if Annie's there? Yes... That would be great if you don't mind...You've still got the key? Yes, I'll hold... Thanks..."

Luke held the office door open, and Kate went in, biting her nail, holding on for Marcy. He followed and waited with her.

A few moments later, she exchanged a few words with her neighbour and pressed 'end'. She looked at Luke and shook her head.

"OK, is there anywhere else she might be? Starbucks? A café close to home?"

"She might be at the café; the one at the end of Lower Marsh."

Kate began scrolling through her recent calls, looking for Kerrie's number.

"Shall I run up there?" Luke asked.

"No, I'll call..." She found it and dialled. It rang for some time before Kerrie answered it.

"Hi Kerrie? Are you at work?" The line was muffled, a bit unclear. Kate went on, "Oh, no, it's just that...well Annie's not at school, they just rang, and I wondered if she might be at the café..." Kate glanced at Luke and shook her head. "She didn't? What time did you leave?" Kate felt her stomach drop. "OK, thanks, I know... but..." She stared at the ground.

"She *is* a good kid Kerrie, I know, you're right, but I'm worried... I... Do you think I should call the police? She's not answering her phone..."

Kate listened and chewed her nail. "Yes, you're right, I know I did, but that was different... I think... OK, OK right... I will... thanks..."

Kate pressed 'end' and continued to stare at the ground.

"So?"

She looked up. "She isn't at the café. Or at least she wasn't there this morning when my friend Kerrie was working her shift. Kerrie said that she left forty minutes ago and Annie wasn't there. She said I should relax, that Annie's a good kid and she's probably just gone walkabout... needed a bit of space, teenagers do that, don't they? They..." Again, Kate faltered, and Luke stepped forward. He put his hand on her arm.

"She's probably right, Kate. Maybe Annie just needed a bit of time out – maybe things got on top of her a bit?"

"Yes...yes...I do tend to panic; Kerrie reminded me that

when Annie wasn't at the bus stop last week, I got pretty uptight, and she was fine... She said to give it a few hours..." Kate spoke as if she wasn't thinking – wasn't taking any of it in.

Luke said, "Why don't I just sprint down to the café and check Annie isn't there? She might have called in in the last half hour."

Kate didn't seem to hear him. "Do you think I should report her missing? Kerrie said not, she's only been gone a couple of hours, but..."

Luke was pulling on his coat. "You stay here, Kate, I'll..."

His action seemed to galvanise Kate. "No, it's fine Luke, I'll go. I should be out anyway; I should be looking for her... I..."

Kate walked out of the office and found her coat and bag. She put her coat on, her bag over her shoulder. "I'll be back in a while. Call me if..."

She strode out of the office, barely aware of the interpreter, the family or Luke who watched her go.

Halfway down Lower Marsh Kate broke into a run. She kept telling herself as she ran that it was all going to be fine, she was catastrophizing; Annie was fine, it was all going to be fine, but as she got to the cafe, breathless, her heart thudding in her chest, she knew instinctively – the way a mother does – that something was wrong. She went in.

"Hey," she held on to the arm of a passing waitress, interrupting her. "Have you seen my daughter here today? I'm sure you know her, Annie? She's tall, very slim, she..."

"Yes, Annie! I know her – she's always in here! She was here this morning, came in about 7, usual time and she left around eight with Kerrie. She seemed upset. Something about a bracelet?" The girl shrugged. "Anyway, Kerrie cut her shift short, which was fine as she was owed a few hours anyway..." The waitress stopped.

"Are you OK? You don't look very well..." She put both hands on Kate's arm and led Kate to a table. "Here, sit. Shall I call Kerrie?"

"No!" Kate fumbled in her bag for her phone. "No, she's..." Kate looked up abruptly as the door to the café banged open. "Nick?!"

In one stride he was at the table. "I called at your office. I've run here. Where's Annie? Have they seen her?"

Kate shook her head. She was shocked, she couldn't think straight. "What the hell are *you* doing here?!"

"Look, Kate, don't worry about that for now. What about Annie?"

"No! This is nothing to do with you. You must go!"

"Kate, please?" Nick's voice wavered; he stared at her, and Kate caught a hint of something in his look, something familiar - something so painfully familiar that she caught her breath.

"Please Kate, please let me help?"

"Annie left with Kerrie..." She glanced at the waitress. "Are you sure she left with Kerrie?"

"Yes. Annie came in, like I said, chatted to Kerrie for a some time, she seemed upset and then Kerrie came out into the back, took her apron off and said she was owed a few hours and she was taking them now. It was OK 'cos we had enough cover, so..."

"But Kerrie told me she hadn't seen her, when I rang her, just a few minutes ago she told me she'd only just finished her shift and that she hadn't seen Annie..." Kate began fumbling in her bag for her phone. She found it and dialled

Kerrie's number. The call went straight to voicemail. She dialled again and then a third time.

Nick said, "Kate, how well do you know Kerrie?"

"Quite well... I... she's..." Kate looked at the waitress. "How long has she been working here?"

"'Bout three months."

"Annie and I come here a lot and we've got friendly. Recently more so... she's been nice, kind, she..."

Kate put her hands up to her face.

"Kate? That night, the night we were filmed?" Nick pulled a chair out and sat opposite her. "Kate?"

She removed her hands and looked at him.

"I ran after the person," he went on "but they were too fast, I didn't get near, but I did catch a glimpse of their shoes as they climbed over the wall. I remember it, but I didn't think anything of it at the time. Then I went to the florist, the one that sent the wreath, after that night - when I was off my face - I thought I could help. They didn't remember much about the order except that the woman remembered the person's shoes – said she'd just bought them for her husband, and she recognised the make. Kerrie was wearing those trainers the night the wreath was delivered. I remember them, in my pissed state it was pretty much all I remembered, but I looked down and saw those trainers; really flash trainers; Nike, Metcon. I saw them again last night. I wasn't mistaken, or drunk. Kerrie was wearing Nike Metcon trainers... good for climbing..."

Kate was shaking her head. "Nick, stop it! Stop this please! This is crazy! Trainers? What the fuck are you saying? Kerrie's a waitress; she's here from Australia, travelling the world. She's a friend, she..."

"She's lying..." Nick took his phone out. "We need to call the police."

"Maybe Annie asked her to lie? Maybe she's covering to give Annie some time out…"

"Call the police, Kate."

"What? Because of a pair of trainers?"

"Yes, because of the trainers. Please Kate, call the police."

Kate looked down at her phone.

"At least report Annie as missing…" He still held the clear plastic folder he'd got from Emma and suddenly remembered it. "Did you know that you have an Australian sponsor, through an offshore trust?"

"Yes, I…" She didn't know much, just that the trustees had said the sponsor wanted to keep their identity private, so she hadn't asked too many questions. She ran a charity; money was money.

Kate glanced up at Nick. She pressed 999 on her keypad. The line connected and rang.

"Does the name Kerina Hirsch mean anything to you?" Nick asked.

Kate started. She dropped her phone.

"Kate?"

The line was answered. "Emergency services, which service would you like?"

"Kate?" Nick bent for the handset. "Police," he instructed, then, "Kate?"

"I need to call Mark," she said, "I have to call Mark now."

Nick looked at her. "Who's Mark?"

Kate took the phone and cut the emergency call. "He's Annie's father," she said.

Nick walked out of the café.

19

T HE PAST - *Kingstanton – December 2008*

KATHERINE RANG on the doorbell and stood back to look at the tall, rambling house in front of her. It had been neglected; the window frames were rotting; the paint was blistered and the cracks in the stone path were filled with moss and weeds. She saw a figure come into view behind the stained-glass panel in the front door and she stepped forward. The door opened and a woman stood there, blinking in the sunlight. She was young looking, her hair fell over her face, and she pushed it back with a long, thin hand.

"Yes?"

"Hi," Katherine said, smiling. "My name is Katherine Ross; I was the person who found Lydia. I came to see if she's all right?"

"You OK, love?" A man appeared behind the woman. He

put his hand on her shoulder, and she glanced back at him. "This is the girl who found Lydia," she said. He nodded and looked at Katherine.

"I came to see if she's all right," Katherine repeated.

"Right." They both stared at her for a few moments.

"Could I see her?" Katherine asked.

They glanced at each other, and the man said, "OK." The woman opened the door for her, and Katherine stepped inside. The door was closed swiftly behind her.

In the darkened hall Katherine could see the walls had been painted a bright yellow to halfway up the stairs, then they were a dull, dirty grey. It was as if someone had run out of paint and energy before they got to the top.

"She's watching TV," the man said. "She won't talk to you, by the way. She doesn't seem to remember what happened, but she hasn't spoken to anyone, not even us."

"Not since..." the woman broke off and looked down at the floor. "She's not played either." They exchanged another look.

"Not played?"

"No, not at all." The woman looked at Katherine. "She's a violinist, you know - gifted."

Katherine nodded. She did know; she'd read about it in the newspaper, but she realised that the woman had needed to say it – to reassure herself of her daughter's talent.

Lydia's mother opened the door to the front room of the house and Katherine went in. Lydia sat curled on an old, winged armchair that had been stripped back to the hessian, but never re-covered. The arm rests had been clawed by a cat, and dirty tufts of grey wool felt padding bulged from the gashes. She stared blankly at the television, watching children's BBC and continually picking at the wadding.

"Hi," Katherine said.

Lydia continued to stare at the screen.

"I just came to see if you're OK. I was the one who..." Katherine stopped. Lydia had lifted her hands up to her ears and placed them there, shutting out Katherine's voice. Katherine watched the little girl awkwardly for a few minutes, aware of her intrusion, then she turned and left the room.

In the hallway Lydia's mother closed the door after her, shutting Lydia in, or out of their view, Katherine wasn't sure. "Do you want a cup of tea?" she asked. "We should thank you. You were kind to Lydia."

"No, I'm fine thanks." Katherine stood uncomfortably in the hall. "I wanted to ask Lydia about someone she might have met. You don't know Gabriel Radley, do you?"

The atmosphere in the hallway changed; Katherine could feel it. Lydia's mother looked away and her father said, "We've met him a couple of times, we're all musicians."

"Do you know anything about his friendship with Ellard Hirsch?"

Lydia's parents exchanged one more glance, but this one was heavy with anxiety. Lydia's mother shook her head and stared at the ground. Lydia's father dug his hands into his pockets. Katherine waited for a few moments then she said, "Is there something that you know that you're not telling me?"

Lydia's father went to speak, but her mother said; "Don't, Colin, please."

Lydia's father shrugged. He said, "There were lots of rumours in our music circle that Ellard Hirsch and Gabriel Radley were lovers and had been for over a year. Gabriel was always with Ellard, practising with him, hanging round him down at the allotment, Ellard goes to all his concerts.

Gossip spreads easily; it's a very small world, the world of performance."

His wife looked accusingly at him, and he shrugged again. "Why shouldn't I say it, Ellie?

She shook her head.

"Was Lydia fond of Mr Hirsch?" Katherine asked, "As her teacher?"

"She adored him," her mother said. She folded her arms across her body almost defensively. "She couldn't wait to tell him that she'd got her distinction, in her grade eight exam, that's why she went to the allotment – or at least that's why we think she went – she won't tell us... she just won't speak..." her voice faltered and as she turned away, Lydia's father opened the front door.

"We won't keep you," he said.

Katherine stepped out, stumbled momentarily on a loose front step, regained her balance and turned to thank Lydia's parents. The front door had closed. Standing on the path, she looked at the half-closed shutters in the front room and saw a small, pale face peering out; the eyes staring, but unseeing.

Lydia had witnessed something in the shed at the allotment and that's why she ran, Katherine thought. She turned and walked down the path, her mind somersaulting over events. Had Lydia seen Ellard Hirsch and Gabriel together? Had she seen them having sex? Now Katherine's mind ran on so quickly that her thoughts left her almost breathless. And if she had, had it shocked her so much that she blanked it out? Katherine saw the memory of Ellard Hirsch in her mind's eye, running after Lydia, his face a mixture of humiliation and despair. She saw his trousers, but this time she saw them as not unzipped, just not zipped up. In his panic to catch Lydia, to reassure her, to silence her, had Hirsch failed to do his trousers up? Was there nothing more to it than that? Katherine stopped at the end of the path and the urge to go back to speak to Lydia, to wrestle the truth out of her, made her stand there, indecisive, for quite some time, but she knew it would be pointless. In the end she turned towards the town and the police station; that was where the truth needed to be told. Hirsch wasn't a paedophile, an abductor; he was a married teacher having an affair with his student. Hirsch, Katherine realised, wasn't chasing Lydia to harm her, he was chasing her to explain.

CI Lewin was going over the case for the CPS when he was told that Katherine Ross was in reception and wanted to speak to him. They had placed Hirsch near the scene with the CCTV footage from the garage, they had his semen on a scarf found near the boathouse, it had been discharged within a three-hour window of Abbey being in the boathouse, and they had several of Hirsch's hairs inside the boathouse, albeit out of the time frame. They were going to argue that Hirsch had taken Abbey to the boathouse, sexually assaulted her and left the scarf at the scene. It wasn't great, but the attempted assault on Lydia Green could be worked into the case. He finished making a couple of adjustments to the notes and went down to meet Miss Ross.

Katherine had been shown into an interview room. She sat waiting for CI Lewin with the truth whirring round her head and the anxiety of that churning in her stomach. She had stood up several times and paced the floor whilst she'd been waiting, and now she sat, her arms folded tightly round her body, chewing the inside of her lip. The door opened and she abruptly stood.

"Hello, Chief Inspector Lewin? I've been looking into this case, speaking to people and I've…"

Lewin held up his hands to stop her. "You've been looking into this case and speaking to people?" he said. "I'm not sure I understand you, Miss Ross. Do you have our authority to get involved in this case?"

"No, but I…"

"But you thought that you would go ahead anyway and get involved in what is a highly sensitive police investigation, regardless of the damage you might be doing."

Katherine stood and stared at him.

"You do understand that I could have you arrested for hampering an investigation?"

"No, I…" Katherine looked down at her hands. "Chief Inspector," she said quietly, "I'm sorry if I've done something wrong, but I honestly don't think that Ellard Hirsch is involved in the Abbey Salter case. I know I gave a statement, but I think you've got it wrong, I think that…"

"You think…" Lewin interrupted. He sighed heavily and shook his head. "You are a young woman of what, eighteen, nineteen?"

"Nineteen," Katherine said.

"And you think you know more than the entire Kingstanton CID, do you?"

"No, but…"

"But what?"

"But I spoke to Lydia's parents, and someone called Gabriel Radley and I think that Ellard Hirsch was with him, that's why Lydia fled on the day that I found her, with Gabriel in the shed on the allotment, they were involved, in a relationship…" It came out in a rush; words tumbling after each other in a breathless stream, she was so desperate say it all. "And I also went to the garage and asked the man there if he knew Ellard Hirsch, and he said he did and he looked pretty embarrassed, so I asked him what the problem was and he said that he thought Ellard Hirsch was gay, and that's why he didn't understand all this because Hirsch sometimes bought condoms there on his way to the place down by the estuary where..."

"Stop!" Lewin snapped suddenly. Katherine did stop, mid-sentence. She took a breath and looked at him. "Stop all this gibberish right now!" Lewin felt a sudden moment of intense anger. All the work his team had put in, all the hours of grind, of answering calls, door to door enquiries, searches, watching CCTV footage and now this stupid young woman thought that she'd solved a murder case by asking a few questions. "We have run a highly professional and detailed investigation into the disappearance of Abbey Salter, but you think that teams of people working day and night on this, qualified, experienced police, have got it wrong? Really?"

"But..."

"But nothing. Stop wasting my time, Miss Ross; our interview is over." He was incensed. He walked to the door and opened it. He had enough on his plate without this rubbish.

"Please keep your crackpot theories to yourself," he said, "We are not interested."

Katherine walked towards the door, but she stopped when she was level with Lewin. "Please Chief Inspector; I don't think it's Hirsch."

"And I don't care what you think," Lewin retorted. He saw her down the corridor, out into reception, then went silently seething back to his desk.

∽

KATHERINE STOOD IN THE LADIES' toilet of the Duck and
Ferret in Kingstanton and stared at her reflection in the
mirror above the sink. It was after nine pm, she was still
sober – highly unusual – and she knew that her actions
were the result of some clear thinking and not five double
vodkas – even more unusual. As she looked at her face, a
pale oval, her dark hair as wild as ever, she saw her mother
gazing back at her and the image momentarily filled her
with despair. She was *not* her mother. Her father loved her;
he *did* love her. He would be proud that she was doing the
right thing for once.

There was a bang on the door.

"You all right in there, love?"

"Yeah," Katherine called out, "I'll be done in a minute?"

The journalist she'd been speaking to was impatient; he
wanted to file his copy, get it in the morning papers and he
wanted her to sign something he'd had faxed through, some
sort of legal document that verified her as a source. Still
feeling sick, Katherine splashed her face with some cold
water and went back into the pub. The journalist was at the
bar with some other men, and he moved away from them as
she approached.

"Got this," he said, holding several sheets of fax paper.
"The pub B&B has got a fax. Hardly state of the art, but it
did the job. Come over here, love, and let's take you through
the document."

Katherine followed him to the small table in the corner
that they'd sat at earlier. The man unfolded the paper and
smoothed it on the table. He took a pen out of his pocket
and handed it to her.

"So...." He ran his finger down the words. "Here it says
you agree that to the best of your knowledge this statement

is true and... here it says that you agree to take full responsibility for your statement."

"What does that mean?" Katherine was trying to speed read what was in front of her, but the journalist had his hand on the paper, blocking her view. "I take full responsibility?"

"Standard stuff," he said. "Shows I'm not making it up. That's all." He turned to her. "Just sign here, Katherine, on this page. I've pretty much told you everything you need to know."

He was a big man, thick set with a belly, and his breath was heavy and wheezy; Katherine felt uncomfortable. She said:

"Can I just read it through, please?"

"Of course, but hurry it up a bit, won't you? I've got a deadline and if we want the truth to come out then I'm going to have to get this filed and over to the paper sharpish." His face was smug. "Don't mind me, with my law degree from Oxford, I'll sit back and let you go over the document. You must be some kind of legal expert, are you?"

"No, I..."

Katherine was young. She was half his size and later, when she went over and over that moment in her head, even though she knew it shouldn't have made a difference, his physical bulk intimated her, and his manner made her feel stupid.

She looked at the document, but the type was small, and she knew it was going to take her some time to get through it.

"How long do you need, 'cos we're running out of time?"

"It's OK," she said at last, "I'm done. I trust you; I'm sure it's fine. We both want the truth to be published, that's all

that matters." She turned the pages over and found the
dotted line to sign on, doing so and dating the document.

The journalist stood, collected up the papers and said,
"Thanks Katherine. I've got your phone number, so I'll be in
touch if I need anything." He didn't look at her again, he
headed back to the men at the bar, and she realised that she
had been dismissed. A sense of unease began in the pit of
her stomach, but she quashed it. Gathering up her coat, she
pulled it on and left the pub to make her way back to the
bus station and to Exeter.

20

T HE PAST- *Kingstanton – December 2008*

KATHERINE WAS UP EARLY, waiting outside the newsagent at the station for it to open. The journalist she'd met in the pub in Kingstanton had sent her a message late last night to say he'd filed his copy. He had promised that he would run the story past her before he did so, but his text said he'd run out of time and that the story would be out this morning. As soon as Katherine had a copy of the paper, she wanted to take it directly to Chief Inspector Lewin. She was nervous, it wasn't over yet, but the battle was under way. Truth will out, she thought.

A delivery van pulled up, the driver jumped out, went round the back and took a bundle of papers from the truck, chucking them onto the steps of the station shop. He threw out two more bundles, climbed back into the van and drove away. Katherine waited for him to go and hurried across to the papers. She found the stack of copies of The Times and turned it over. She stood, staring down at the front page and her whole body jolted. There was a picture of Ellard Hirsch on the front page, alongside a picture of Gabriel Radley. The headline read, *PAEDOPHILE MUSIC TEACHER IN GAY RELATIONSHIP WITH PUPIL*. The subheading read; *Ellard Hirsch, suspected of abducting Abbey Salter and Lydia Green is a predatory paedophile in an illicit gay relationship with a pupil twenty years his junior.*

Katherine ran to the two other bundles and turned them over. Different papers, different words - same slant. She didn't read on; she couldn't. She tore a paper from the stack and held it, her hands trembling as she flicked frantically through it. Where was her article? Where was the truth? The truth she'd shared with the journalist. She began to panic. It wasn't there. Surely it was. Surely it had to be there, he'd reassured her, told her what he was planning to write. Kneeling, she put the paper down on the ground and began to slowly turn the pages, a terrible fear gnawing at her. She worked her way through the paper, scanning each page, then she went back to the front page. She read the article with a sense of mounting despair. It was accusatory and damning. It created a monster out of Ellard Hirsch and implicated him even more deeply in Abbey Salter's disappearance. Katherine turned the page, and her eye went to the end of the piece. There, next to the journalist's name was her own. She was cited as the source.

CI Lewin's meeting with the CPS was interrupted by two phone calls from the hospital and DS Crowley putting his head round the door to ask for a few minutes. He dealt with the hospital quickly and efficiently, but the bottom line was that he had to collect Barbara by five as they needed the bed. Christ, he wanted shot of this case. If he'd been a swearing man he'd have exhausted his supply of expletives by now; he was sick of it and the only way he was going to get the location of Abbey's body was to wring it out of Hirsch; physically, if he had to.

When the meeting was finished, he called Crowley into his office. DS Crowley was carrying a newspaper and he laid it on the desk. DI Lewin looked down.

"What the hell...?"

DS Crowley pointed to the source.

"Oh Christ, that's all we fucking need." DI Lewin said.

"KERINA?!" Melanie Hirsch stood at the bottom of the stairs and hollered. "Kerina?! Come down here now!" She turned to her younger daughter, Sofia, who was kneeling on the floor, a great mass of books scattered all around her, flung from the shelves. She was sifting slowly through them, making two piles.

"All these books!" Melanie said, wiping her hand across her sweating brow and leaving a smear of dirt there. "All these stupid, ugly books!" She looked at Sofia. "Why is that pile so big?! Hmm?! I told you to get rid of most of them, only keep one or two!"

"But Mumma... I...-"

"She's doing the right thing, Mum." Kerina appeared on the stairs. Even at fourteen she had presence; she spoke in a calm, measured tone that implied authority.

"I don't want them, Kerina, I want them out of here,

gone! I can't bear to look at his things; I just can't bear it... I..."

"Sofia, keep making your piles. Mum, go and lie down. You're upset. It's no good trying to do this if you're upset. Papa hasn't been charged yet. We must be sensible."

"Sensible?! Sensible?!" Melanie Hirsch's voice rose distressingly. "How can we be sensible, Kerina? He's been in custody for two days – they'll charge him, I know they will!" She threw her arms up helplessly. "Sensible... after what's happened? How can we be?! Tell me?"

Kerina crossed the hallway to her mother. "I don't know," she said quietly, "But we have to try, Mum."

Melanie put her hand on her elder daughter's cheek. The flesh was cool – she was always so cool to touch. She had worried, earlier, when Kerina was small, that there was something amiss, that her lack of emotion signalled some-thing else. She had worried that her daughter - even as an infant - was too detached; cool inside and out.

"I'll make you a cup of tea," Kerina said. "Go and lie down, Mum, please. Let Sofia and me do this." Melanie stroked a strand of Kerina's blonde hair from the side of her face and felt her daughter stiffen; it was too much. She stepped back.

"Did you manage to fix the heater?" she asked.

But Kerina had walked away into the kitchen and didn't answer, so Melanie went into the front room, turned the heater on and felt warm air blow against her hand. Kerina had fixed it. She crossed to the window and pulled back the net curtain, peering out at the street. A couple of neighbours had stopped in the middle of unloading shopping from their cars for a catch-up and a gossip. They glanced across the street every now and then and Melanie thought they were probably talking about her – them – that family. She dropped the curtain, suddenly filled with shame and self-loathing.

She bent and dragged the heater as near to the door as the cord would allow so that it blew warm air into the icy hall. She hadn't had the heating on since he'd gone – she didn't want to waste money. In the hall she looked again at the heaps of books. Ellard had collected so many books, she thought, so many bloody books and each one just another way to escape his marriage, his life. He played his violin, tended his allotment, read his books. He also, she now knew, did other things that were so disgusting that she felt sick at the thought of them. She stepped over the books and put her foot on the stairs. Kerina appeared with a mug of tea.

"Here." She held it out for her mother then she bent and picked up a book on Beethoven. Her hands were long and thin, Melanie thought, watching her, like her fathers, but she wasn't musical like him. Instead, she had all his technical skill in the shape of a mechanical mind. It was early days, but she was just as brilliant, just as distanced.

"I'll get some rest," Melanie said. Sofia glanced up and smiled, but Kerina was absorbed in the book. Melanie's gaze swept the chaos in the hall, and she thought; we will have to leave, that much is obvious, but for now we'll purge his presence from the house. For now it would have to be enough. She climbed and left the mess behind her, hearing the low murmur of Kerina's voice as she instructed her sister, feeling the dull ache of humiliation and grief heavy in her limbs. At the top of the stairs, she turned and looked down at both her daughters. Kerina had put the book down and had her coat on.

"Where are you going?" Melanie called.

"For a walk."

It was typical of Kerina not to ask permission, to just

assume she could come and go as she pleased. Melanie said nothing. She should have argued, told her to stay put, but she didn't have the energy. She watched Kerina button her coat and leave the house without another word, then she carried on to her room to lie down.

It was nearly dark when Kerina Hirsch stood on the edge of south-west coastal path, round the headland from Stare-hole Bay and looked out at the sea. She knew the path well; she had come here often with her family when she was a girl, her parents believing that fresh air and exercise were all the entertainment a child needed. She'd walked here a lot recently too, on a Sunday when her father was at the allot-ment and couldn't be disturbed, wandering the cliffs, aimless and anxious. She knew; she'd known for longer than anyone what was going on, what *not to be disturbed* really meant. She knew, and despite everything, so now did everyone.

She walked on for fifty yards or so then stopping at the low wall that intersected the land, Kerina turned, and, instead of going over the stile, she followed the wall down towards the edge of the cliff. The land was rocky here, but over the wall it sloped gently for a few yards, before drop-ping away steeply to the rocks below. Kerina took the ruck-sack off her back and hunkered down in the shelter of the wall, out of the wind. She unzipped the bag and took out a sheet of paper. She didn't know why she'd kept it, fear mostly, fear of not knowing what to do with it. She should have burnt it, but there never seemed to be the right moment. Now she glanced briefly at it, at the stick figure hung on the scaffold, the wobbly letters of a small girl's handwriting – then she ripped it in half, then in half again and again and again until it was in tiny little fragments. The ground was muddy all along the wall and there was a thin trench that had filled with water from all the recent rain. Kerina scrunched all the small pieces together and dipped them into the water. It was icy cold. She mulched the fragments into a ball of mush then she went back to the rucksack. Taking a small white trainer out of it, she tucked it into her pocket and stood up. She made her way along the wall to the very edge of the cliff and climbed over it. Looking down, she stared at the grey sea below, frothing and crashing onto the rocks and she could hear the endless crying in her head. It had started to rain again, and the screech of the gulls merged with the howls of the little girl.

"Stop it!" she had shouted, "Just stop it! You are in such big trouble, and you have to come with me so that they don't find out! Stop crying! Stop it!"

But the little girl hadn't stopped crying and Kerina had grabbed her, on the edge of the estuary bank and had shaken her. She had shaken her so hard; she was so angry that this little girl was going to tell everyone about what she'd seen; *that* music teacher, down by the river with *that* boy. She had shaken and shaken so that the little girl's head lolled backwards and forwards like a rag doll while she stared wild-eyed and terrified. And then she had let go and Abbey, stupid, stupid little Abbey had fallen backwards, limp and lifeless, into the water.

Kerina took the trainer out of her pocket. The other one was lost; it had come off while she hid Abbey in the boathouse, looking for ways to weigh the body down. It was raining heavily, the child was small, there was no fat on her and if she was weighted Kerina knew there'd be a good chance that overnight she'd get dragged out to sea.

Kerina lifted the shoe, and the red flash on the heel lit up. She threw it carefully, not far out, but in an arc so that it would land on the rocks and get wedged, hidden, buried. She threw the ball of mulch after the shoe, then she turned and made her way back to the wall and began the long journey home.

21

P RESENT DAY – *Kingstanton*
Tuesday - a.m.

MARK WAS in Jane's kitchen when he took the call from Kate. Jane had been making tea for the officers who he'd brought with him – including Nella. She stood, watching him.

"Kate? Kate, slow down, please. Tell me everything in order." He motioned to Jane to get him a pen and he took a notebook out of his pocket. Nella heard the name, Kate, and came to the doorway of the kitchen.

"OK, right, Annie hasn't shown up at school this morning. And that's not usual? Hang on a minute Kate; I'll put you on speaker so I can make notes."

Mark pressed the icon on the phone and Kate's voice filled the kitchen. She went on,

"Mark, she's never skipped school before. We'd had a row about a bracelet that her friend had accused her of stealing and I confronted her, I didn't trust her – God, I even went looking for it last night..."

"And she didn't take it?"

"No, but I found it in her drawer..."

"I'm not following you, Kate. It sounds like she took it and she's lying. Might that be the reason Annie skipped school?"

"No... well at least I don't think so. Annie's a good kid, Mark, she's really honest. She gave her purse to Kerrie last Friday, when they went out with her, to look after. It had the bracelet in it and Annie left her purse in Kerrie's bag..."

"Hang on...who's Kerrie?"

"She's a friend, a waitress at the café up the road from my office. We've become friends recently - Annie's taken a real liking to her... well, I thought we were friends, but now..."

They could hear Kate blowing her nose and when she spoke again, her voice was cracked.

"Look, Mark, Kerrie lied to me this morning, said she hadn't seen Annie when she had. She finished her shift early and went off with her. And there are other things too – things that Nick is saying and now this bracelet thing..."

"Kate," Mark said gently, but firmly, "We need to find out where Annie might have gone with this Kerrie person. Have you any idea?"

"No."

"OK, tell me what you know about Kerrie? You say she's a recent friend?"

"Yes, but I don't know much. She's Australian, late twenties, maybe early thirties, I don't know, travelling and working as a waitress; she did a degree in some kind of engineering which is why Annie and she..."

"Is it Kerrie Hart?" Nella said.

Mark turned to her. "What...?"

Nella stepped forward and said, "Kate, this is DC Nella Walsh from the Met CID. Is it Kerrie Hart you're talking about?"

"Yes, but why are you...?

"Don't worry about that now. Is Kerrie blonde, about five eleven and quite pretty?"

"Yes... yes she is..." They could hear the panic in Kate's voice.

Nella said, "Kate, where does Kerrie live? Do you know her address? Can you find it?"

"Oh God... no, I don't know where she lives, wait... I'll ask..."

Nella had begun to write something on her notebook. She held it up for Mark to see. In black capitals she had written,

I THINK THIS IS AN ABDUCTION.

Mark said, "Kate, can you send us an up-to-date picture of Annie please, right away. What was she wearing this morning?"

"Yes, yes, I'll do that. She was in her school uniform. I've got a picture of her in it – it's a couple of months old, but I can send that along with one of her a few weeks ago... wait, here... I've got her address..." They heard talking in the background. "I've got it from the café owner... We'll go there now."

"No, you stay there Kate...We'll get on the line to the local CID. Someone will be on it right away, OK?"

Nella had walked out to call Stockwell.

"It's much quicker that way Kate," Mark went on, "You need to sit tight and wait. Go to the office, maybe go home, but keep your phone on..."

"Mark? Mark what's happening... Please... tell me what's

going on? Is something going to happen to..." Kate's voice broke, and she began to cry.

"Kate? Kate, just try and keep calm, OK?"

"Yes..." They could hear Kate take several deep breaths then she came back on the line and read out an address. Mark wrote it down and passed it to Nella.

"We're on it now Kate, OK? Try not to worry. Make sure that we can contact you. Is there anyone with you?"

"Yes, I've..." She looked out of the plate glass window at Nick, standing in the cold. "I've got someone with me."

"OK text us their number and keep the lines open."

"OK..."

Mark went to press 'end' when Kate said, "Mark? Kerina Hirsch has been donating to my charity, through an offshore trust... You don't think..."

"I don't know," Mark said. "But don't think about that now, Kate. Just focus on keeping calm, OK?" Mark ended the call and Jane walked into the sitting room and opened her laptop.

She was typing into Google when Mark came in.

"Schoolgirl German," she said, "Never leaves you." She turned the laptop screen towards him. "Melanie Hirsch took the girls to Australia after the whole fiasco, where her brother had emigrated ten years earlier. She changed their name, remarried, I think. I kept up with them, originally for research, then simply because I thought it was prudent. The English translation of Hirsch..."

He looked at the screen. Google translator had; Hirsch – kind of deer/hart.

"Kerina Hirsch is Kerrie Hart," Jane said. "She has a degree in mechanical engineering and a PhD in electrical engineering. She is an extremely intelligent and, I would hazard a guess, an extremely vengeful and dangerous young woman."

Mo and DC Carter had been sitting at the end of Lower Marsh waiting to see what Nick did next - Mo just couldn't give it up – when they heard the call over the radio - missing teenager - Annie Ross – suspected abduction.

"Shit, is that the same Kate Ross?" Carter could see Nick leaning against the wall outside the café. They'd watched him go in and come out again. "What the ...?"

Mo was already on it. He picked up the radio and spoke into it. "Unit 457, we're right on top of it, in Lower Marsh right now. Yup, will do..." He motioned to Carter who had his notebook out. "Kerrie Hart, 7, Somers Road, SW2. OK, got it."

Carter closed his notebook and opened the car door. "Come on, let's get up to the café and see what's going on, then we'll take a look at that address." He climbed out and leant his head back into the car.

"Mo?"

"Kerrie Hart," Mo said, "The social media profile – it was Kerrie Hart. She was the link between Kate Ross and Lydia Helston..."

"Really? Get onto Sallie Dennis now, I would mate."

"Yeah, I will. At least it doesn't look like Farleigh. He's got us as his alibi."

Mo called DS Dennis, spoke briefly to her then climbed out of the car and together they headed up Lower Marsh. At the café they nodded to Farleigh and went inside. Nick followed them in.

"Ms Ross?"

Kate looked up. She had been alternately dialling and re-dialling Kerrie's number, then Annie's. There was nothing from either number.

"Good morning, Ms Ross. I'm Detective Constable Mo Ahmad and this is Detective Constable Carter. Can you tell us in your own words what's happened this morning? We're about to head over to Somers Road and see if we can get hold of Kerrie Hart, but if you could just run us through the events that would be helpful."

"Oh, yes, erm..." Kate closed her eyes for a moment and rubbed her hands over her face. She took a deep breath and dropped them away. "Annie, my daughter..." she began.

Nick walked away again.

Outside in the cold, he watched Kate through the window and wondered for the hundredth time what the fuck he was doing here. What masochistic tendency was it that made him come back, watching with increasing dismay as she shunted him aside? His father was probably right; the chances of him being Annie's father were slim; there was no reason for Kate to keep lying to him. So why was he here? Why was he hankering after something that was never going to happen, after a connection that they simply didn't have? He rubbed his hands wearily over his face and went back inside.

He caught the tail-end of the conversation.

"Have you any idea why this friend, Kerrie Hart might have lied to you?" Mo was taking notes.

"Because she's not a friend," Nick interrupted: he couldn't help himself. "She's someone Kate's just met, and she can't be trusted. She tried to get me arrested last night, to get me out of the way..."

Mo turned. He said, "I'm sorry Mr Farleigh, but what is your position here?" He glanced at Kate.

"Annie...she's... I'm -" Nick broke off.

"He's a friend," Kate said. "It's OK, he's here for me."

Nick stared at her, but she didn't meet his gaze. She looked down at her hands. Mo exchanged a glace with Carter.

"Right, well, we'll get across to SW2 now and speak to Kerrie Hart, and in the meantime, if there's anywhere else you think Annie might have gone, or if you hear from a friend or from school then please could let us know right away? My officer number is DC 8170 Ahmad, and this is DC 9224 Carter. We'll be in touch as soon as we can."

Mo opened the door and waited for Carter to exit before following him out. As they headed back to the car Mo said, "What the hell's going on there?"

Carter shook his head. "Nowt so queer as folk."

In the car as they drove off, Carter put his foot down and said, "Lights and siren?"

Mo nodded, flicked the switch and the police siren started on the unmarked Audi, the lights flashing.

"Whoever this Kerrie Hart is," Mo said, "She's linked to Lydia and to Annie Ross. One of them is murdered and the other goes missing."

Mo held onto the ceiling handle with his left hand as Carter began to weave through the traffic, and with his right he took out his phone and dialled Nella. "Doesn't look like a coincidence," he said. "Doesn't look like a coincidence at all."

"OK, listen up everyone. Thanks for getting here so quickly."

DS Sallie Dennis was knackered, but the adrenaline had

kicked in and so had the four coffees since five am. She stood at the front of the incident room and addressed the team that had rapidly assembled in the last hour.

"So, Lydia Helston, hung by her own scarf, caught in the lift doors and decapitated..." DS Dennis pointed to the visuals from the coroner.

"What we originally thought was sudden death is now a murder investigation and is connected, we believe, to the abduction of this person here. This is Annie Ross, aged fourteen. Annie went missing this morning, she didn't turn up for school, she has no truancy record, and she was last seen leaving Browns Café on Lower Marsh just after 8 am with this person here...." DS Dennis pointed to the Facebook photo of Kerrie.

"Kerrie Hart, who probably came into the country with a British passport in the name of Kerina Hirsch, has been working at Browns for the past three months and has befriended Annie and her mother Kate Ross. The link is this..."

A picture of a smiling eight-year-old in school uniform came up on the screen.

"Abbey Salter. Eight-year-old Abbey disappeared in 2002 in Kingstanton, Devon - a small town on the Kingstanton estuary. The body washed up some months later further down the coast, but there were no convictions. Kerrie's father was wrongly accused of abduction and murder. Lydia Helston was responsible for his arrest, along with Kate Ross, Annie's mother. There are some notes for you on the case that DC Walsh has just sent though from Exeter where she's currently going over the casefile – I'll leave the sheets here." DS Dennis paused. She let that sink in, then she went on.

"Mo and Chris have been along to Kerrie's address, and

she's cleared out. A neighbour saw her getting into a white Ford minivan this morning at around eight thirty, but they didn't get the registration. They didn't see any sign of Annie. We've got a team of forensics down at the flat now, but I want to find that van. The neighbour thinks it was hired, so I'd like Jenni and Rob, you two on that please. We also need to check CCTV, traffic cameras, anything in the SW2 area to see if we can spot the van. I want to know where Kerrie is headed."

There was a murmur around the room. "We've every reason to believe that Annie Ross is still alive... for now. So, let's go, everyone."

The lights came on and the meeting broke up. There was a flurry of activity and chat. Everyone knew what 'for now' meant; it meant get a fucking move on because time is running out.

"Mo?" DS Dennis was heading back to her office. "A word?"

Mo followed her into the glass-walled room, and she rooted around on the desk for her vape.

"We've got a facetime meeting in ten with DI Heddon and Nella in Exeter. Can you be around for that?"

"Course."

"Thanks..." She found it and took a drag. "And good work Mo, you and Nella. She's as annoying as hell, but that was good work, from both of you. We wouldn't be as far along as we are without it."

Mo smiled. "Thanks... I..."

The meeting was over; DS Dennis had picked up her phone and was texting. He left the office.

～

KATE TORE another small piece off the croissant that Nick had bought her and left it on the plate. She had worked her way through most of the pastry, but she hadn't eaten any of it. It lay in honey-coloured shreds, flakes of it scattered on the table.

"What do you think is happening?" Kate asked. The question had become her mantra, repeated over and over for the past hour.

"I don't know, but we'll find out as soon as they know anything." Nick glanced at his phone on the table. The unanswered calls were mounting up; his arrest last night would be all over party headquarters by now and the shit would have hit the fan. His phone had been buzzing every few minutes, but the agony of each call or text not related to Annie was almost unbearable. At this moment he cared about nothing else.

"You don't have to stay," Kate said.

"No, but I'd like to."

She glanced away. They sat in silence for a few minutes, then Nick said, "Kate? Would you come with me to see something? I've got somewhere I'd like to take you."

She shrugged. "I don't think I should leave here, in case Annie comes back."

Nick said gently; "I understand." He let a few moments pass then said, "There's a police officer in Lower Marsh though, keeping watch for Annie. If she does come back, there's someone here who'll call you right away."

Kate sighed. She stared out of the window then she said, "Where do you want to go?"

"It's not far. We can get a taxi."

"But where?"

"Dean's Yard. It's near Westminster Abbey."

Kate shrugged again. "I don't know..."

"It would be good to get out of here for some air, just for half an hour."

She picked up her phone and looked at the screen. It was a selfie of her and Annie, taken in the summer. She closed her eyes and held it in the palm of her hand.

Nick stood up. "Come on," he said, "Let's go – just for half an hour...?"

Kate opened her eyes and looked up at him. His face was determined, serious and for a moment it looked so familiar to her that she caught her breath. She got to her feet.

"OK," she said, "Just for half an hour?"

"Less if you want."

Kate pulled on her coat and followed him out into Lower Marsh. They headed towards the Westminster Bridge Road where Nick hailed a black cab and, giving instructions to the driver, climbed in after Kate and sat opposite her.

"I used to go to Dean's Yard with my mum," he said, "When I was young."

Kate stared out of the window as they drove across Westminster Bridge.

The driver put the screen down and said, "Shall I drop you at the Abbey?"

"Yeah, that's good, thanks."

The bridge rolled away then they turned into Broad Sanctuary and then The Sanctuary, and all the time Kate was silent while Nick glanced back and forth from the window to her face. At Westminster Abbey the cab stopped, Nick opened the door for Kate to get out and climbed out after her. She stood on the pavement while he paid, looking round blankly, her face ashen, and her eyes unseeing.

Nick joined her and said, "This way, it's through here."

He held out his hand and amazingly, Kate took it. He noticed the slimness of her fingers, how cold her skin was, how good it felt to touch her. They crossed to Westminster Column and went through the arch into Dean's Yard. The noise of the traffic fell away as the square opened; a green, Dickensian space flanked by eighteenth and nineteenth century buildings and watched over by the north tower of the Abbey.

Kate stopped. "It's beautiful," she said. "I had no idea it was here."

"Here, come over here." Nick led the way onto the grass and across to a large London plane tree. "Look, this is where I used to sit with my mum."

Kate looked and saw that the roots of the tree rose into its trunk, thick and muscular, like arms. There was a space between the roots to sit. Nick took his jacket off and put it on the ground.

"Come on, sit down."

"You'll freeze," Kate said, "Your jacket will get filthy."

Nick shrugged. "I'm hardly the picture of sartorial elegance now, am I?" He glanced down at his sweat-stained, crumpled shirt and trousers. "I've had a night in the cells, and I smell; might as well add damp and muddy into the mix."

Kate sat, leant her head back against the tree trunk and Nick sat down next to her. She shifted a bit to make room for him and they sat close. Nick said, "It's nice, isn't it? It feels like the tree is hugging you."

Kate nestled back. "Yes, yes it does." She closed her eyes and Nick saw tears slide out from under her swollen lids.

"It will be OK." he said gently, "I'm sure it'll be OK. They will find Annie."

"Yes..." Kate murmured. Her nose began to run, and she sniffed.

Nick dug in his pocket and brought out a handkerchief.

Miraculously, it was clean. He handed it to Kate. "My mother said a handkerchief was nicer than tissues, softer on your nostrils."

Kate smiled through her tears as she blew her nose. "Your mother was right." She went to hand the damp hankie back to him but thought better of it and held on to it.

"I don't know why I'm crying," Kate said. "I never cry. It doesn't change anything."

"No, but it helps sometimes." Nick hugged his arms round his chest. Kate was right; he was fucking freezing. "I blub all the time," he said. "My mum used to say that I'd cry at the opening of an envelope."

Suddenly Kate laughed. "Oh, Annie cries like that. She cried so much in one episode of *Call the Midwife* that she had to lie down afterwards..." She laughed again then she began to cry, openly this time, hiccupping sobs, her face contorted. Nick put his arm round her and hugged her into his body.

"I've waited fifteen years to do this," he said gently, "And now you're making my shirt all wet."

After a while Kate began to calm, exhausted by her distress.

"What do you mean?" she asked quietly, "About waiting?"

"God... long story..." Wrong time and place he thought, for the lonely-hearts club.

Kate said, "Tell me?"

Nick sighed heavily. "Really? Now?"

"Yes."

"OK... I looked for you Kate, after the night we spent... well... day and night. I looked everywhere and I couldn't find you. You disappeared and then I wondered if I'd imagined you, but I couldn't have because it hurt so much to think about you." He took a breath. "I was an awkward, spotty, giant nerd and you were... well you were everything I'd ever imagined sex and love and desire to be, and you blew me away. Then you disappeared."

He could feel Kate's breathing against his chest. "The following year my mum got sick and I... well you know what I did and then, when I came back to the LSE, Emma was waiting for me. I was never in love with Emma, but she didn't seem to care about that, and I was lost and lonely and grieving... The next thing I knew I woke up fifteen years later and I saw you...It feels like I've been waiting for you all this time..."

He touched her hair. "I'm sorry Kate," he said. "I should have told you the truth, you know, about being married, but when I met you again, I couldn't see anything other than you... I didn't even think about..." he stopped. He took another breath. "Kate, I..."

Kate's phone rang. She started and jumped forward, scrabbling in her pocket for it.

"It's Mark" she said anxiously, looking at the screen. "Annie's dad." She accepted the call, stood up and walked off to speak.

"Sal? Traffic cameras have picked up what we think is the van on Hogarth Lane, heading up towards Chiswick. We've got a couple of stills here... Looks like a white female driver."

"What time was that?"

"Over an hour – an hour and twenty-eight ago. We've got a time of... 9.42am."

"Registration?"

"Not got it yet. We're working on it."

DC Dennis brought a map of London up on the screen. "Let's check traffic cameras for M4, South Circular and North Circular. She's headed out of town – we need the direction – Jenni? Anything yet on the rental?"

"Not yet. There are hundreds of rentals. I've covered the local ones, checked some of the bigger ones, but she's not on their databases. My guess is she's gone small and local and much further afield. Could be anywhere."

"OK. I want everyone on it. We need the registration of that van." DS Dennis looked across at Mo and tapped her watch. She'd had to put the meeting with DI Heddon and Nella on hold while she spoke to the SOCO guy down at the flat. Annie Ross had been there - they'd got hair and what looked like fibres from her school uniform, all currently being checked with DNA samples they'd picked up from Kate Ross's flat – but where the hell she was now they had no idea.

DS Dennis sat down, opened her MacBook and dialled Nella. Mo tapped on the door, and she beckoned him in. The screen bleeped then Nella came on.

"Nella. What have you got?" DS Dennis said.

"Dr Jane Hardman is here with DI Heddon, and she's drawn up a character profile of Kerrie Hart. She's here..."

Jane came into view and Mo moved behind DS Dennis so that he could see the screen.

"Hi, so..." Jane put her glasses on and looked down at her notes. "During the investigation into her father, Kerrie Hart, or Kerina Hirsch, was interviewed by the police and then seen by a child protection officer and finally by me, in my capacity as a psychologist. The reason she was passed on to me was because she wasn't demonstrating any percep-tible signs of stress or grief. She was completely unemotional, acting as if nothing had happened. I diagnosed PTSD and she went on to CAMHS for some treatment, but I don't believe it was very successful – I think she refused to cooperate. In my notes I record that she had an exceptionally high IQ and that she was maths and science orientated. I would now say that she was probably demonstrating the first signs of sociopathic behaviour, an inability to empathise...." Jane looked up at DS Dennis, nudging her glasses down to the end of her nose. "Kerrie has a degree in engineering and a PhD in electronic engineering. She's highly competent technically and the modus operandi of the lift killing fits her profile. She would have been quite able to demobilise the sensors on the lift, and quite capable of chasing Lydia into it."

"The CCTV footage showed nothing unusual."

"How far back did you go? Lydia's killing had been planned - possibly for years. Kerrie wouldn't have slipped up by being seen on camera a few hours before the killing."

DS Dennis glanced over her shoulder. "Mo, can you get one of the lads onto that now? Go back several days, a week if necessary."

Mo nodded and left the room.

"What about Annie?" DS Dennis chewed the tip of her vape.

"Killing Annie is about Kate Ross."

"You think she's killed her?"

"No... not yet, anyway. This murder won't be quick. She's got us running scared and she knows that."

"Christ... Any idea of how or where?"

"No."

DI Heddon came into view. "Any sightings of the van yet?"

"We think it was headed out towards Chiswick at 9.45

this morning. We're trying to trace the reg now for a positive ID, but nothing apart from that."

"We've got to find that van," Mark said, "while there's still time."

KATE STOOD IN THE HALLWAY, outside the front door of her flat and waited for the police officers to leave; she didn't want to be in there with them. They'd taken away DNA samples from Annie's toothbrush and hairbrush some time earlier, but now they were back, checking her room, looking for evidence, links, anything that would help. There was a determined intensity to their searching that filled Kate with despair.

Nick was in the flat making tea, and Kate stared blankly at the empty corridor, her mind full of images of Annie as a baby, here in this hall, sitting in the pushchair while Kate struggled to undo the stiff old plastic clips on its harness; as a toddler, lining up her tiny red wellies covered in mud next to Kate's big blue ones, making sure they were neatly aligned, nestled together; Mummy's and Annie's. As a little girl, with her *My Little Pony* rucksack bobbing emptily on her back, worn everywhere, full of nothing but a reading book and her pencilcase; and, as a teenager, hockey bag dumped in the corridor until Kate nagged and moaned and it was finally moved three feet to inside the front door. All that love and care...What a different home it had been to the one she had shared with her own mother.

Nick came out with tea.

"Here. It's full of sugar – supposed to be good for shock."

Kate took the mug and wrapped her hands round it; she

was cold, trembling. Glancing at Nick, she said, "Would you like something warmer to wear? Your jacket's really damp."

Nick shrugged. It was damp and muddy after sitting on it in Dean's Yard, and the wet had seeped through to his shirt. "Actually, yes, if you've got something."

"I've got the box in the cupboard. It's got a few sweaters in it."

Nick thought back to the night they'd first met. "Oh, right, yes, the box."

Kate went into the hall and opened the cupboard. She bent and lifted the plastic box out and unclipped the lid. She began to riffle through it.

"I keep thinking about Annie as a baby..." she murmured, "growing up... just the two of us." She was turning over items of clothing, not really seeing them. She handed Nick a wool sweater.

"We've always been alone... and... I kept thinking - you know - all the time that I had to do a better job than my own mother..." She swallowed. "Protect her, look after her." Her voice wavered. "I was so damaged by everything, by all the people in my life, that I thought if I kept everyone out then..." She broke off. A few moments later, she said, "I didn't manage it – to keep everyone out – to protect her..."

"Kate, this isn't your fault."

Nick pulled the sweater on and then knelt next to her.

"It really isn't."

"No?"

"No." He took her hands. "Look at me, Kate. This isn't your fault."

She shook her head. "Nice try, but it is." She put the lid back on the box and stood up. "I trusted someone, Nick, for the first time in years, well, two people actually..."

Nick winced; he deserved it.

"But Kerrie... Kerina Hirsch as she really is ... I thought she was my friend, our friend, mine and Annie's, and yet all she wanted was to do me harm, to do us harm... a kind of perverse revenge. How could I have been so stupid? So unguarded?"

Nick took a breath. "What happened to you, Kate? What happened that meant you've had to spend your life guarded? Can you tell me, explain?" Bad timing, he knew, but he had to say it anyway. "It's just that I want to be in your life and...well..." He looked down, unable to face her. "I guess I just want to understand why I can't be."

22

T
HE PAST- *Kingstanton – December 2008*

KATHERINE GOT off the bus at Kingstanton and walked quickly and determinedly towards the town centre. She knew where she was going; she knew how to get there from memory, and she knew that this was something that she had to do. The images in the paper, the nasty headline, the horrible accusations burned behind her eyes as she walked. They had to know it was a mistake, that she was trying to help.

As she arrived at the turning to Ellard Hirsch's Road however, she stopped, shocked by the crowd gathered outside his house. It was noisy, some people were shouting and there was a general sense of confusion and anger. It was more mob than crowd. Pushing on, she walked to the edge of the throng and slipped through, her head down. At the gate to the front garden Katherine hesitated, suddenly aware that the faces around her had stopped moving, the voices had stopped braying. She opened the gate and walked down the garden path, holding her breath.

At the front step, she reached forward and rang the bell. The house was tidy, neatly kept, the glass panes in the front door were clean and the brass key plate had been polished, the door freshly painted. She waited but there was no movement inside the house.

"You're wasting your time love!" Someone called out. "They're not gonna answer."

Katherine held her nerve, stepped forward and rang a second time. She felt the eyes of the crowd at her back and stood straight, her heart thudding in her chest. There was still no movement inside the house.

Standing back, she looked up to see if there were any signs of habitation, but the house was dark, the curtains drawn. She felt thwarted, ashamed. They would never know what a terrible error it all was, how she'd been duped, how sorry she felt. Turning, she glanced momentarily at the crowd then dropped her head down and pushed her way through. On the edge of it, a few yards from the house, she turned for one last time and looked up at the window. There she caught the shadow of a face behind the net curtains, and she felt, even at that distance, the impenetrable glare of hatred.

ELLARD HIRSCH WAS CURLED up on his side on the hard, plastic-coated mattress in the cell, facing a cold, grey wall. He stared at a small spot where someone had carved their initials; RW. How could anyone have the energy to be bothered to carve their initials into the paint on a police custody cell wall, he wondered? He could hear footsteps along the corridor and then something was slid under the door. Hirsch turned his head and saw it was a newspaper. He sat up. He smelled bad, he could smell himself and his mouth was sour. Perhaps, he thought, this was the beginning of a reprieve... perhaps a newspaper – a small sign of humanity – meant that somehow, they'd found out it wasn't him. Standing, his legs felt weak, and he had to hold onto the bunk for support. The metal grille over the bare lightbulb on the ceiling meant that the harsh electric light fell in bars on the concrete floor – a pattern of confinement. He crossed to the cell door and picked up the copy of the paper. It was a tabloid rag, but it would do. He turned it over.

KERINA HAD BEEN WAITING all morning. She sat in the reception of the police station, a forlorn, awkward adolescent girl, silent, watching. It made the duty sergeant uncomfortable – he had no idea what to do with her.

"You really should go home," he said, "They're not going to let you see your dad, I'm afraid, not at the moment anyway."

She looked at him, but she didn't move. She continued to sit there.

A short while later he heard the custody sergeant in the back office, so left the desk for a few minutes to speak to him.

"Is there any way we can bend the rules a bit, Jerry and let Hirsch's daughter in to see her dad? The boss doesn't need to know, does he? Even if we just let her have a glimpse of him though the viewing slot? She's been here for an hour and quite honestly, she gives me the willies. She just sits there, silent, staring at me."

"I don't reckon so, Bob. Boss wanted to let him stew this morning, so no-one's been down there. There'll be real shit if we do, and he finds out."

"I'm not gonna tell him. Are you?"

The custody sergeant shook his head. "Sorry mate..."

"Jobsworth," The duty sergeant muttered under his breath as he went back into reception. He stood at the desk and did a double take. It was empty; finally, she had gone.

AROUND THE BACK of the station, one of the squad cars had just come in and parked up - the gate was open. Kerina walked into the car park and saw the back entrance to the station; it had been left propped open with a heavy box; someone was clearly in the process of unloading supplies. She hesitated, but only for a moment. Unseen, she walked into the back of the station where the cells were, the custody sergeant was up in the back office, and in one of those rare moments of uncanny timing, the place was empty.

She made her way along the corridor. There were only three cells and two of them were empty. At the end, the cell on the right was shut fast and locked so Kerina put her head to the heavy metal door and listened; there was no sound.

"Papa?" she said quietly at the door. "Papa? It's me, Kerina."

There was still no sound. Unfastening the catch in the viewing slot, she yanked it back so that she could see into the cell.

"Papa?" she whispered.

She put her head to the grille and peered inside.

"Papa?"

She saw his feet, just half a metre from the floor, dangling, lifeless... and then she began to scream.

KATHERINE WALKED along Duncombe Street from the park towards the police station. She had been sitting in the rec, in the freezing cold, for a couple of hours, not knowing what to do. Now, as she made her way through town, she thought that she had to try and see Mark, to try to explain things to him, to make some sense of it all if she could. However, as she trudged and the gloom of the winter morning closed in around her, she began to feel odd, to have a sense of impending disaster. It was strange; she had never been someone who believed in all that psychobabble, yet the closer that she got to the police station the more she felt it, and a fear began to grind in the pit of her stomach. Turning into Fore Street, she heard ambulance sirens, the blaring screech of them cutting through the fog like a knife edge, the shrill screaming getting closer and closer. Katherine turned. From behind her she saw an ambulance and two squad cars racing towards the police station. She stood for a moment and watched them hare past, then she looked up the hill towards the station and without knowing why, she started to run.

At the station there was chaos. A small, gawping mob crowded the pavement and there were officers everywhere. Katherine caught sight of Mark as he ran into the station, but she didn't call out and he didn't see her. She edged her way to the front.

"What's happened?" she asked.

"The bloke that they were holding, the teacher, he's topped himself."

"What...?" Katherine felt suddenly as if all the air in her body had been smacked out of her. She bent double and began breathe heavily.

"You all right?"

"Yeah... I..." She huddled over, wrapping her arms across her. Nausea rose in her throat. "Are you sure...?"

The woman next to Katherine snorted. "Sure?! Yeah, just saw them take the body out - a few minutes ago - and good fucking riddance is what I say." She turned and looked at Katherine. "Took the coward's way out... You sure you're all right, love?"

Katherine nodded, still half bent over. "How...?" she managed through gritted teeth.

"Hanged himself with his belt," the woman said, matter of fact. "His daughter found him, poor love. She's in the back of the ambulance, in a terrible state apparently..." She broke off and, just as she did so, Katherine bent further forward and retched violently on the pavement.

23

T HE PAST – *Kingstanton, Devon, December 2008*

RICHARD ROSS COLLECTED his daughter from Kingstanton later that day. She was white-faced, tearstained. He opened the passenger door for her, and she slumped into the seat, her shoulders hunched and her hands still trembling. He didn't know what to say to her.

They drove back towards Exeter in silence. He watched the road, but glanced sidelong at her every now and then while she stared blankly out of the window as the country-side slipped past. He was both furious with her, with her stupidity and her naivety, and he was desperately sad for her, hurting as only a parent can. She had made a terrible, tragic mistake, but it was still a mistake, an error of judgement.

"Do you want to talk?" he asked her, twenty minutes or so into the journey. She shook her head. "OK...." He hesitated. "I think you should come back to the cottage. I don't think you should be alone."

Katherine chewed the inside of her mouth for a moment, then she shrugged. They drove on in silence.

As he pulled into the lane for the cottage, he saw several cars parked along the verge and a small crowd up ahead waiting outside the gates to the cottage; press, he assumed. He carried on, stopped the car and climbed out to open the gates. People started shouting to him.

"We've got nothing to say!" he called loudly, "Please just GO AWAY!"

He parked outside the cottage and went round to open the door for Katherine, but as she climbed out of the car, the small crowd moved forwards, shouting, calling out. Her face was a mixture of shock and despair as Richard took her arm, guiding her towards the front door.

"GO AWAY!" he shouted, "WE HAVE NOTHING TO SAY!"

They made it inside, and in the hallway, Katherine stood just by the door, her shoulders hunched over, and began to weep. Richard guided her towards the sitting room, taking her to the sofa and pulling the curtains. He could hear the dull murmur of voices outside. Beth appeared in the doorway.

"Thank God the twins are at school," she said. "This is a bloody fiasco."

Richard nodded towards Katherine and Beth's face tightened. Her mouth puckered into a thin, mean line. She stepped further into the room and said, "I hope you're satisfied."

Richard stared at her. "Beth, I don't think..."

She cut him off and spoke directly to Katherine. "What in God's name did you think you were doing? You got involved in a police enquiry for what; a bit of attention, to impress your father?"

"Stop it, Beth," Richard warned.

Katherine looked up. "I thought that..." but Beth cut her off.

"You thought what?! Thought that you knew what you were doing, did you Katherine, thought that you knew better than anyone?"

Katherine had gone back to staring at the ground. She said, "I never meant for any of this to happen, I just wanted to tell the truth, I wanted..."

"You wanted!" Beth jeered. "Oh, how familiar that sounds. It's always what you want Katherine, isn't it...?"

"BETH!" Richard suddenly shouted. "LEAVE IT!"

Beth's chest was heaving, and her face was flushed. "No, Richard. She has to hear this, it's about time that someone..."

Richard moved across to her and stood right in front of her, very close. He said, "Not now. She doesn't need this... or you now. I told you to stop it." His voice was low and hard and as he hissed the words at her a small blob of spittle landed on her cheek. He watched as she struggled to control herself.

"Yes now! We need to discuss this!" She was defiant, but an edge of wariness had crept into her voice.

Richard put his hands on Beth's shoulders, very gently, but his face was fierce.

"Then we do it privately," he said.

"Fine." Beth turned and walked into the hall; Richard followed her. He closed the door and when she turned, her face had hardened.

"I thought, the other day, when Katherine was at the police station, I thought that you understood me, Richard, but now I'm not so sure. Your daughter has been a destructive element all our lives - she's done everything in her power to make us miserable and still, still you give in to her."

"She's my daughter, Beth."

"No Richard, in name only. She has never acted like a daughter to you. I meant what I said a few days ago. She can't stay here. If she does, then I go."

"Don't be stupid Beth, you can't walk out; you can't take the boys a week before Christmas."

"Yes, I can. I can do whatever I bloody well want to, Richard. Katherine does."

"She made a mistake, Beth."

"And she has to pay for it – like we all do."

Richard suddenly put his hands up to his face. God, he knew enough about mistakes and paying for them. Katherine, he thought, had paid for his mistakes too.

"Let her stay tonight then I'll take her back to Exeter in the morning," he said. "She's upset..."

"So she should be."

"Just tonight, please Beth?"

Beth looked at him, challengingly. "I'll go and pack then," she said.

Richard stared back at the woman he had married and wondered who she was and why he had married her. Her rigidity, her lack of kindness still shocked him seven years on. He had made his bed, that's what Katherine's mother had told him - in one of her more lucid moments - and no matter how hard and cold and uncomfortable it was, he had to lie in it.

He sighed and after a long silence, said; "I'll drive Katherine back to Exeter. I'll settle her in and be back for bathtime."

Beth raised an eyebrow. Any wariness had disappeared; she knew her strength now. "Make sure you are," she said, and she walked away.

Richard stood where he was for some time. He felt – as he had so often felt in the past ten years – bewildered by his life, by the complexity of emotion that surrounded him. He was an academic, a historian. He liked words and books and theories because they didn't change, they remained unmoving on the page when all around him, Katherine's mother and her mental illness, Katherine and her pain and anger, Beth and her jealousy and spite had been -and still were - a constant evolving mess. He sighed again and went into the sitting room.

"Katherine, I think that..." He stopped just inside the room. It was empty and the French windows to the garden were open.

"Katherine?" He walked out and checked the patio, round the side of the house. She wasn't there. "Katherine?" He went to the front door and looked out of the glass panel. She wasn't there either. Back in the sitting room he looked for her bag, any sign of her. On the sofa he noticed a card and what looked like his own handwriting. He crossed the room and picked it up.

"For last year's words belong to last year's language
And next year's words await another voice.
And to make an end is to make a beginning."
T.S. Eliot

The words had been crossed out in black pen.

Richard went out into the garden again and hurried down to the fence that bordered the fields along the lane. He put his hand up to his eyes and saw, far into the distance, the solitary figure of his daughter. Her head was bent as she ran and, watching her retreating figure, he knew with an overwhelming sense of helplessness, that the decision he'd made - the only decision Beth had allowed him - was the wrong one.

KATHERINE WAS MAKING her way down St David's Hill toward Exeter station when the car pulled up beside her. It was dark, it had begun to rain so she had the hood of her parka over her head, and she carried her holdall in one hand, a carrier bag of food balanced in the other. She had packed up and left the student flat in less than half an hour when she had finally got there. It had taken an hour, waiting at the bus stop, longing, the whole time she sat in the darkening cold, for her father to come after her, to convince her that he'd made a mistake agreeing with Beth. She'd heard it all, every painful word.

It was an empty yearning; he didn't show.

At the flat, she threw her stuff into her bag, packing up the food items into a carrier. She'd need food - she had to start eating properly now – then she tidied the place so that it looked as if she'd never been there and left. Now, hurrying for the train back to London, which she would have to fare-dodge, she heard Mark press the window down and she kept on walking.

"Katherine? Where are you going?"

She ignored him.

"Katherine please, stop and talk to me! Let me give you a lift!"

Katherine glanced sidelong at him from under her hood. "What, to London?"

Mark, crawling along the kerb with his hazard lights on

called out; "Yes! To London! Christ, just get in the car, will you?"

Katherine stopped. She pushed back her hood and said, "Mark, you don't understand. I'm bad fucking news..." her voice fragmented, and she caught a sob in the back of her throat. "Just leave me alone..." Tears welled up. "Fuck," she whispered. That was all she needed, to blub like... like some pathetic... They spilled down her cheeks; she couldn't control them.

Mark stopped the car and jumped out. "Katherine, please? Get in the car. Please?" He looked quickly up the road both ways. "I'm a police officer – I can't keep breaking traffic regulations like this!"

Katherine snorted a half laugh through her tears, then wiped her face with the sleeve of her coat. She handed her holdall to Mark, who flung it onto the back seat, then she came round the passenger side and climbed in, holding her bag of groceries defensively on her lap.

"Where to in London?" Mark asked.

Katherine looked at him. "Did you mean it?"

"Yes! Where to?"

"London. SE11. I'll give you directions once we get nearer."

Mark switched off his hazard lights, indicated and pulled off. In silence they headed out towards the ring road and the M5 to London

THE FOLLOWING morning Mark was up when Katherine returned to the flat. He'd changed the bed and made a start on clearing up, ferrying empty bottles and glasses into the kitchen from all over the flat, washing up. The mess wasn't a

problem – he'd seen worse – and he was quite happy to clear up. It made him useful, and he had a feeling that being useful was as much as she would let him offer.

He heard the front door and walked into the hallway, drying his hands on a tea towel.

"Are you OK?"

She nodded. She was drawn and pale and she looked so fragile that he wondered how she was ever going survive on her own.

"Shall I put the kettle on?"

She shook her head. "We should talk," she said quietly, "I've got something to tell you."

Mark stood where he was. There was nothing heroic about being dumped, he thought, might as well get it over and done with. "Go on."

Katherine took a breath. "I'm pregnant," she said.

For one fleeting moment a flame of hope rose, flickered and then just as quickly, as sense kicked in, it died.

"It's not mine," he said. It couldn't possibly be.

She shook her head. "I'm about six weeks, I think. I've been to the chemist, done a test this morning, in the toilets in Starbucks."

"Right."

Mark looked at her. Her face was pinched, and she was clasping her hands together, almost wringing them. He liked Katherine, he liked her a lot. He recognised something in her; loneliness, the edge of disappointment; the same edge he'd lived with for the past ten years. His Dad had buggered off when he was three; his mum had remarried; nice bloke, if you liked drinkers who regularly tell you to fuck off. Mark had fucked off at sixteen.

He said, "Are you with the father?"

Again, she shook her head. There was probably only

one person it could have been, and she couldn't even remember his name. A one-night stand with a boy she'd met at a party, another student. A hopeless situation.

Mark took a step towards her. "Katherine," he said, "I can look after you. I don't care who the father is, a baby's a baby. We could be a family; I could transfer to the Met, work here and look after you." He glanced behind him at the mound of rubbish and washing up. "Christ knows you could do with a bit of looking after." He smiled. "We could…"

"Mark, don't." She held her hands out helplessly. "We hardly know each other… come on… be realistic."

"Katherine, you can barely look after yourself, let alone a baby. Is that realistic enough for you?"

Katherine flinched, but her face was closed.

"Oh, I see. You're going to get rid of it."

Suddenly she raised her head and looked at him. "As I said, we hardly know each other…" She stood a little straighter and for the first time he thought he saw real strength in her eyes. She said, "If we did, you'd know that after years of feeling desperate and alone, a baby is probably the only thing that will save me."

CI Lewin sat at his desk and stared at the Abbey Salter file on his desk. He had no suspect, no body, nothing. They had to go back to square one and he was too tired and too burdened to be able to even think about it; thank God he didn't have to. He looked up as DS Crowley came into the room.

"It's all yours Bill," he said, nodding at the file. "I am on compassionate leave as from…" He glanced at his watch, "half an hour ago. And until the new CO gets here, you are in charge."

"Thank you, Sir. I'll do my best."

"You'll have to do more than that, Bill," Lewin said. "This is a bastard of a case."

Lewin stood and packed a couple of things into his box; his photos, his pen. He hoped that Debbie was OK at home with Barbara; she'd called twice to find out when he'd be back.

He held out his had to DS Crowley and they shook.

"Good luck."

"Thanks."

Lewin walked to the door and stopped as DS Crowley said, "Sir, do you think Katherine Ross was right? When she came to see us the other day?" He'd already made up his mind to reinstate a massive door-to-door and coastal search.

Lewin shrugged. "I don't know..." He sighed. "But I wish to God I'd listened." He sighed again and rubbed his chest as the old familiar pain started up. "I'll hazard a guess that what happened here in the last twenty-four hours - what I never even saw coming - will ruin far more lives than just the one."

He felt another sharp ache between his ribs and hoisted the box up under his arm. Pain went with the territory, he thought, and now, so did guilt.

24

P RESENT DAY – *Devon and London*
   Tuesday p.m.

IT WAS JUST before midday when Richard Ross unlocked his office in the history department at Exeter University and went inside, dumping his bag on the desk and switching on his PC. He should have been on Christmas vacation, but he liked being at work; it was easier than being at home.

Cracking open the window, he let in some air. He didn't really have any work to do - coming in was just an excuse to escape - so he stood for a while and looked out at the campus, almost unrecognisable from the one he'd known when he'd first started there. Twenty years he'd been a Professor of Modern History, as long as his undergraduate class had been alive, longer than some of them. The place was deserted for the holidays, only a few postgrads hanging around, and the campus seemed forlorn, like a seaside town in winter. It seemed forlorn and empty, and he knew the feeling.

Richard unpacked his bag, noticing the photo of Beth and the twins on his desk, the photo he always placed on the shelf, face down, but that he always found – after the cleaner had been in – replaced on his desk, upright, looking at him. He'd never liked it and now, as he stared at it, he thought again about Beth's eyes. They were 'mad eyes', that's what Katherine used to say, 'mad eyes for a mad cow'. He picked up the picture and looked at Beth's face. She'd been a postgrad student; he was her tutor and classically foolish. A middle-aged man, a wife who was never well, a younger woman and sex, lots of it. He sighed. It was so stereotypically crass that even thinking about it now embarrassed him. Just six weeks into their affair there was the pregnancy – twins – and Beth started making plans. His life, as he knew it, and Katherine's for that matter, was over.

He'd tried hard over the past fourteen years and failed to forgive Beth her attitude towards Katherine and now he'd given up, knowing that resentment was the slow death of a marriage. He'd stayed with Beth and somehow, they scraped along; they had the twins to think about and if one divorce was understandable, two was poor judgement. He had called Katherine, all those years ago, when things had calmed down, but of course she'd changed her number. He wrote to her, but his letters were always returned; read, re-sealed, but returned, nevertheless. On the last one she had written, 'PLEASE DO NOT CONTACT ME AGAIN'. He knew nothing about her, except that she still lived in the flat that her mother had owned. Sometimes, in the past decade, he'd thought about just getting in the car on the spur of the moment and driving up to London, waiting for her outside the flat and ambushing her, but then reason would kick in and he would realise that she wouldn't speak to him, and that it would be a futile and painful experience.

Richard stood, collected up the picture and took it back it to the shelf where it belonged. He placed it face down. It was too late; he knew that, to make amends. He'd missed his chance. It happens; people fuck up, but that didn't make his sorrow any the less painful.

"Got it!" Jenni called out; she jumped up and hurried into DS Dennis's office. "Kerina Hirsch hired the van from Wembley Vans. I've got the registration."

DS Dennis came out into the incident room. "Right, Rob, start checking the APNR data. Good work, Jen. Can you alert all traffic patrols on the routes we've mapped and as soon as we know where she's heading, I want you to let me know. I'm going for police helicopter cover. No-one is to intercept. OK? Make that clear. Track but don't intervene."

DS Dennis went back into her office. She made a call first to her DI for clearance for the air cover and then got on the line to organise it. She sat at the computer, forwarded the email that the DI had just sent her and looked out at the incident room.

"M4!" Rob called. "I've got the van leaving the M4 at junction 7 and heading up the Bath Road towards Maidenhead."

DS Dennis appeared. "Time?"

"Ten forty-three."

DS Dennis looked at her phone. "Keep tracking. That was less than two hours ago, but it's a convoluted route. Why didn't she just stay on the M4 to get to Maidenhead? That seems pretty odd to me. She must know we're tracking her –

if she's as smart as Dr Hardman said. Have you got anything else?"

"Yup A404... She was through Maidenhead and onto the A404 at 11.45. We've got her here at the junction turning on the A404."

"Fucking brilliant." DS Dennis got on the radio to the NAPS. "White Ford minivan, vehicle registration WL67EKX, heading up the A404 north. Yes please, as soon as you have visual contact." DS Dennis put the radio down and shouted across the office. "Mo? Get Nella on the phone. I want to know why Kerrie's headed towards the M40 and the north."

THE FLAT WAS NOW EMPTY, and Kate sat on her mother's old sofa, fretting at the frayed arm of it, worrying a small hole in the cloth. She'd wanted to replace the sofa for years and now she was glad that she hadn't. Every small stain, chocolate, milk, tea, every pull in the cloth and worn patch reminded her that this was her life with Annie. It gave her some small comfort. Standing, she walked to the window and looked out then she turned, walked back to the sofa, picked up the paper, glanced at it and threw it down again.

"It's not right," she said. "I don't think they've got it right. I don't think Kerrie is heading north."

She looked at Nick who sat on a battered old wing chair opposite her.

"Why not? Dr Hardman said she'd got family there."

Kate shook her head. "No, that's not a reason she'd go north." She stared at him; she didn't know why he was still here, but miraculously he was and, reluctantly, she'd admitted to herself that she was glad of it.

"There's something else to it, Nick... something sharper,

something planned..." Kate crossed to the shelf unit and pulled a black box file from it. She tipped a load of photographs out of it onto the carpet. "There must be another reason she's headed north," Kate said. She began rifling through them and Nick crouched down beside her. There was a mix of old snaps, some of Kate as a baby, some of Annie. It was as much as Nick could do not to pick one of Annie up and put it in his pocket. Suddenly Kate seized upon a picture and held it up. It was of an estuary, green hills, pale azure skies, small white yachts moored on a blue river. She handed it to him.

"Kingstanton," she said. "She's not going north..." Kate jumped up and went to the table. She flipped open her MacBook and brought up Google maps. "She's going to turn round," she said, "At some point..." She looked at Nick. "And she's going to head home on the M4, then the M5, to Devon."

Nick came over to the laptop and looked at the map. "But didn't Mark say they've tracked her heading up towards the M40, towards Oxford?"

Kate began to wring her hands. "I have to get to Devon," she said. It was as if she hadn't even heard him, "I know she has Annie in that van and I have to go down there..."

Nick placed his hands gently on her arms. "Kate? Think it through. Are you sure this is right?" But she shrugged him off and hurried into the kitchen. She opened the bin and bent, rummaging in it.

"Kate?"

She began to throw the rubbish onto the floor. "The postcard..." she muttered, "She left me a postcard..."

Nick followed her into the galley kitchen and began to pile the rubbish into an old carrier bag he found on the table. "Kate?!"

She straightened. In her hand she held a small, torn square of blue sky. "The night we..." She took a breath. "The night you were here, after you left, after we'd been filmed, I found a postcard, on my laptop. It was this one. I ripped it up – I thought it was you – It said welcome to Kingstanton. No-one I knew had any idea of what happened to me except Kerrie – not that I knew that. She'd got into the flat – I know she was quite capable of that now, she got into the flat and she left me a message. That's where she's gone Nick, she's gone to Kingstanton."

Nick sighed; he had no idea anymore if Kate was even making sense. "What are you saying Kate? What do you want to do?" he asked.

She opened Google and started looking at train timetables. "I told you," she kept clicking as she spoke. "I'm going to Devon..."

"Whoa, hang on! You can't do that Kate! You can't go chasing after some sociopathic murderer. You've got to stay here, leave it to the police. What if you're wrong and she's not headed there?"

"She's going to Devon, Nick, I know it."

"Kate stop! Think! What if you do follow her to Devon, what then?"

Suddenly Kate stopped and looked at him. There was a silence. "I'm going to call my father..."

"Your father?!"

Kate chewed her lip, staring at the screen. "Yes."

There was another silence. Nick was completely thrown. Good sense told him to leave well alone, to call the police, but emotion crowded any reason – he couldn't think straight.

"Why are you going to call your father, Kate? I thought that was...-"

"... It was, but..." She was trembling and wrung her hands together for a few moments to steady them. "Nick, he tried, lots of times, to get in touch, asking me for another chance, but I kept him away..." She went back to the screen and opened her emails. "I'm going to ask my father to pick me up in Exeter and take me to Kingstanton." She began typing. "If he was serious about wanting a second chance then he'll do it."

She looked up at him and he knew in that moment that whatever she wanted to do he would let her - and he would follow her.

"Will you come?"

DS DENNIS STRAPPED herself into the passenger seat of the squad car as it pulled away. They'd had positive ID on the van; it was parked in a side road off Bullocks Farm Lane, near Wheeler End Common off the M40. The helicopter was over the area already and an armed response unit and a search team had been called. If Annie wasn't in the van they would be scouring the common for her.

"Blues and twos," DS Dennis said. She looked at her phone. "Let's get there as quick as we can." She pulled the ceiling handle down and held onto it as the car swerved violently to the right. A voice came over the radio.

"Zulu Oscar seven, armed response unit on the ground. Approaching the vehicle now."

"Lima Delta two, do you have visuals of the victim or the driver?"

"Zulu Oscar seven, we've got two teams there and it looks like the van is empty."

They heard a scuffle, voices. "The van's empty. No sign of the driver or the victim."

"Christ!" DS Dennis shook her head disbelievingly.

"Zulu Oscar seven, we're on the common now with the dog handlers." There was a pause. "It looks like another vehicle's been parked here DS Dennis." There was another pause, more voices. It looks like she might have switched cars."

RICHARD ROSS SIGHED as Beth told him for the third time where he needed to be at what hour. He was due to pick the twins up from the Exeter Services on the M5 as they'd got a lift from Manchester with one of their university mates. He had switched off as she rambled on and was idly flicking through his emails when he saw one come in from Kate Ross.

Kate. Katherine. His daughter.

He put his mobile down on the desk and clicked on the mail to open it. He read,

Call me.

There was a mobile number, but nothing else. He picked up his phone and cut Beth off mid-sentence, dialling the number on the email.

"Katherine?" He heard her voice and the years fell away. She sounded the same – almost – her voice had deepened, but there was an edge to it. He listened, made a couple of notes on a scrap of paper on his desk then he said, "I'll be there. I promise."

He heard her voice waver as she replied.

"It'll be all right, Katherine..." He didn't know if it would be, but he needed to say the things she wanted to hear. "I won't let you down." And he knew he wouldn't, not this time; he'd waited far too long for a chance like this.

He pressed 'end' and his phone rang immediately.

"Beth."

She was upset that he'd hung up; it was rude... inconsiderate... made her feel de-valued... Richard cut her off.

"Beth, Look, something's come up and I can't collect the boys from the service station...Yes, it *is* very important." He spoke slowly, in the passive aggressive voice that he saved for Beth. He listened to her response then his tone changed.

"My daughter," he said curtly, "my daughter is what is more important than collecting the twins at the service station on the motorway. She's rung me, after all these years, and she needs me, Beth, she needs me and I'm going to make sure that I'm there for her in a way I should have been before..." He waited for a few moments, not really listening to her response then he said; "I really don't care what you think Beth, I haven't done for a long time now, so..." he took a breath and the words she'd said to him all those years ago about Katherine popped straight back into his head. "Just remind yourself how the twins got to university Beth?... That's right, on their own, so I think they can manage to get back on their own, don't you? They're big boys – they'll figure it out."

He pressed 'end' and stood up. He needed petrol; he needed to check the best route to Kingstanton, but most of all he needed to make amends.

NELLA PACED the meeting room in the police headquarters in Middlemoor, Exeter.

"You were right, she's clever," she said to Jane Hardman, "And she's planned this..."

Jane sat and looked at the Abbey Salter case files neatly stacked into piles on the big oval table in the meeting room. She no longer had clearance to look at them and it was too long ago, she couldn't remember the details, but something was niggling her; something she had missed.

"She's changed cars – she's got Annie, or at least we think she's got Annie, so where is she going?" Nella stopped and turned to stare out of the window.

Jane said, "With my patients, I often find that at some point we have to go back to the beginning."

"Was Kate one of your patients?"

Jane shrugged. "I'm not at liberty to say, I'm afraid." But she thought back to the hundreds of sessions that she'd had with Kate – set up by Mark – no payment involved as long as she could use the material for her book.

"Why don't you go back to the beginning," she said to Nella. "I'll go and get myself a coffee and you can start again on these files."

Nella sighed at the prospect. She felt useless stuck down here in Devon, but the DS wanted her close to DI Heddon with the case files on hand, in case they needed any information.

"If I can think of anything I'll let you know," Jane said. She stood. "Start at Kate's involvement in the case, go back over what happened, step by step." She moved towards the door. "I'm going to grab a coffee. Let me know if you need me." She left the room and Nella began looking for the pile with Kate's statement in. She found it and sat down to read.

∽

RICHARD DIDN'T KNOW what to expect, waiting at the entrance to Exeter St Davids station for his daughter to arrive and, when he saw her with the same wild hair, the same, thin, small frame and her face pinched with anxiety, he could have stepped back fourteen years. She was with a tall, dishevelled man who wore jumper and suit trousers with what looked like a waterproof that Richard used to own. They approached, Richard wondered about holding his arms out, but thought better of it. Kate stopped in front of him, a polite distance between them.

"Thanks," she said, "For coming. We need to get straight to Kingstanton."

He nodded. "The car's out the front."

Nick held his hand out. "Nick Farleigh," he said.

Richard shook his hand, but he didn't ask what the relationship was. He saw, however, that Kate stayed close to Nick, walked alongside him and looked at him frequently. They walked out of the station to the car and Richard noticed that it had begun to get dark. Unlocking the car, he said; "We'd better get a move on. Where in Kingstanton do you want to go?"

"I don't know exactly where it is, but Nick's got a map on his phone," Kate replied. She glanced behind her at Nick. "D'you want to sit in the front with Richard?"

Richard didn't hear his response; he was 'Richard', and the distance pained him. He shifted into gear and pulled off. She was here, he told himself, and she'd asked him for help; what did he expect? It had taken him years to destroy their relationship and it was going to take an awful lot longer to rebuild it.

~

Nella opened her MacBook and began her Google search. She found what she was looking for quickly and rang the number on the council website. The phone rang for some time, and she drummed her fingers anxiously on the desk as she waited. Finally, it was answered.

"Good afternoon," she said, "My name is Detective Constable Nella Walsh from the Metropolitan CID. I'm trying to get some information about one of your plots. Do you have a plot there in the name of Hirsch?"

She waited. "Yes, Kerina Hirsch, she has? When was that? Did you say the past few days? Right, that's great, thank you." She pressed 'end', then she stood and paced the room, working it all through out loud.

Suddenly she grabbed her coat and bag and within minutes DC Walsh had left the building, found her car in the carpark and programmed the address of the allotments into the satnav. She'd radio in if she found anything, she thought, and, as impetuous and self-reliant as she was, drove off without telling anyone where she was going.

Richard followed Nick's directions once at Kingstanton and, as they drove along the lane, bordered either side by fields; they saw a dark blue estate car parked on the verge. It was empty.

"Can you reverse so that the car isn't seen?" Kate asked.

Richard glanced over his shoulder and reversed up the lane to a passing spot, just before the bend. He pulled into it, making sure the car was out of sight.

"We need to call the police," Nick said.

Kate shook her head. "No." She climbed out of the car and Nick followed her. "She's got Annie..." She looked up ahead at the allotment. "And she wants me. That's what this is all about..."

"Kate, you're not going to approach this woman on your own. She's dangerous and the place might be wired in some way. Kate, please, not on your own..."

Richard had climbed out of the car. "He's right, Katherine, you can't..."

Kate looked at Richard square in the eye and she said, "I *can,* and I *would* do anything for my daughter. Anything at all if it meant that she was safe." She held his stare for a few moments then she looked towards the allotments.

"Kate, let me come with you?" Nick started towards her, but she glanced back and shook her head.

"Nick, Mark isn't Annie's dad, you should know that. He put his name on her birth certificate so that she had someone, and he wanted to be, tried to be for a while, but it didn't work. I don't know for sure, but I think Annie is your daughter..." She broke off and waited until she had collected her voice. "I feel that she's yours..."

Then she turned and walked down the lane into the darkness.

NICK ARRIVED at the back entrance to the allotments, his chest heaving. He'd sprinted across the fields as soon as Kate left them, keeping as low to the ground as he could manage so as not to be seen, using the torch on his phone and the compass dial to keep track, and now he stood, bent double, the blood roaring in his ears. He took several deep breaths and straightened. Through the gate he could see Kate approaching a shed. She had her phone torch on. He put his hand on the gate to open it and suddenly, out of the dark, another hand closed over his.

"Fuck?!"

He tried to turn, but Nella put her other hand over his mouth from behind and dragged him down under the cover of the hedge.

"It's DC Walsh," she hissed in his ear. "What the fuck are *you* doing?"

Nick struggled to turn, but she kept him in a hold. "Quieten down."

He stopped struggling and she released him. He turned.

Nella was dressed in black waterproofs and wore pulsar night-vision goggles strapped to her head. Nick stared at her.

"Military standard," she said in a low voice, touching the goggles. She crouched down and brought a piece of paper and a camera out of her pocket. "She's in there and so is Annie. Here, have a look." She handed him a thermal imaging camera. He turned it over in his hands. Jesus, this woman was some kind of techno nerd.

"At least I think it's them. The shed is flimsy, and I've detected two main spots of heat which I'm assuming are bodies in there. They're both still alive otherwise I wouldn't be picking up so much heat." She spoke quietly, close to his ear.

Nick looked through the camera at the shed.

Nella went on. "She's rigged something up, something inside the shed and she's put pressure pads around the back and sides, loads of them, I'm picking up the heat from them. There's one by the door too, so they obviously release something, not sure what. Might be explosives."

"Fuck."

Urgently, Nella said; "We don't have much time. I

thought I could do it on my own, but I'm glad you're here. I've made a note of the pads – here."

She held out the paper and Nick glanced at the drawing. He couldn't see much in the dark.

"That's the problem," Nella whispered. "We need to go in together and I'll read and guide you. You up for that?"

Nick nodded.

"Right," she said. "The shed has a back opening, double doors for bigger equipment. We'll head for that." She moved towards the gate, keeping low. "Come on."

As Kate walked towards the shed, she could see that the door was open and that the inside was eerily lit by the blue light of a phone screen. She stopped, eight metres back and called out.

"Kerrie? Annie?"

There was no reply. She tried again.

"I'm on my own, Kerrie, that's what you want isn't it? Me, here, on my own?"

Still no reply. Kate moved closer.

"Don't come any closer," Kerrie said. She had come to the door of the shed.

"Have you got Annie?"

"Yes."

Involuntarily, Kate went to move forward.

"Stop!" Kerrie called. "Don't come any closer."

Kate looked down. She could see places where the grass had been moved.

"What's going on?" Her voice had risen in panic. "Where's Annie? Can I see Annie?"

Kerrie stepped to the right and shone a torch inside the

shed. Annie was stood on a block, just half a metre high, her hands tied behind her back and a piece of tape over her mouth. Her ankles were taped together, and Kate could see a thin wire in a noose around her neck.

Covering her mouth, Kate stifled a sob. She began to tremble. Again, she started forward and Kerrie cried out, "Don't!"

Kate stopped, frozen to the spot. Her hands shaking, she held her phone torch up towards the shed, and with the beam of electronic light saw that Kerrie too had a thin piece of wire in a noose round her neck.

"Kerrie, please... don't hurt Annie... please...You want me, I'm here. Let Annie go and I'll do anything you want. I promise you – just let Annie go? Please? Take me instead..." Kate wiped the tears from her face. "Kerrie? Please..."

"There's nothing you can do to save her," Kerrie said, "it's hopeless Kate. It's hopeless and it will kill you, eventually; the rage and the despair, because you'll always know that there was nothing you could do."

"There is something I can do, Kerrie, you can take me... do whatever you like to me..." She moved forward a small step. "It's easy, you *can* do something about the pain, and you can make it go away... Just let Annie go... Please...?"

"No. It's no good Kate, I told you. It's hopeless."

Kate shone the torch onto Annie and could just about see her face, wide-eyed with terror. She took another small step forward.

"You can try and run towards me Kate, but you'll tread on one of the dozens of pressure pads that I've put down and the block will be yanked away, and Annie will hang. When that happens, you can try and get to Annie before the razor wire cuts into her jugular, but you won't be able to, it's too sharp."

Kerrie stepped back into the shed. "Everything was fine until you came along, Kate. I had it under control, I had shut her up - little Abbey - stopped her from telling everyone about my father, but then you found Lydia and you had to interfere. You wrote that piece in the paper and after that there was nothing I could do. It unravelled, all of it, into one giant fucking mess and I lost him. I lost the only person who knew me, who loved me..."

Kerrie took another step back and Kate shone her torch down to Kerrie's feet. She was stepping back towards a black hole in the floor of the shed.

"When you hang," she said, "if you're lucky your neck breaks, if not, you suffer from brain ischemia; your brain is starved of oxygen; your ceratoid arteries are cut off; your capillaries burst in your brain, your face and eyes; your heart stops and you suffocate. It's slow and painful. That's how my father died."

She took another step back.

"Annie?!" Kate cried. "Annie shut your eyes and keep them shut! Shut your eyes tightly Annie? Please? Do it for me sweetheart..."

Kerrie took another step. "That's not for me, that death. This wire will slit my throat...and Annie's... as soon as anyone comes near, steps on the pressure pads. So, Annie can watch me die and you can watch her die." Kerrie shook her head and smiled. "Nice and neat."

She raised her head and looked directly at Kate. "There is nothing you can do. You are as helpless as I was."

Kate shone the beam onto Annie's face and saw that Annie had squeezed her eyes tightly shut.

"MAKE A NOISE ANNIE!" Kate shouted, "ANY NOISE...!"

Kerrie stepped backwards and suddenly her body

dropped half a metre. There was a loud snapping sound as seconds later the wire went tight. Kate cried out...

Nick took a massive leap forward and smashed into the double doors. They flew open and with his height he towered over Annie, scooping her whole body up towards the ceiling of the shed to take pressure off the wire as the block fell away.

"I've got you," he kept shouting, clinging onto her, keeping her raised aloft so that the wire couldn't pull taut. "I've got you, Annie... it's OK, stay still... I've got you... I'm here."

P RESENT DAY - *Kingstanton, Devon*

KATE SAT with Annie in the back of the ambulance, cradling her daughter in her arms; Annie's neck had been cut and they were waiting to go to hospital. All around them the noise and frenetic energy of investigation throbbed, and the whole place was lit like a circus.

Nick stood a few steps away with Richard Ross, wearing DC Walsh's waterproof jacket to keep him warm, his suit trousers drenched in blood. They were talking, but Kate could see his gaze flicker back and forth relentlessly from her father's face to Annie, and every now and then he caught her eye and held her stare for just a few moments. He was looking at them both, she realised, with a loving fierceness that she recognised; it was Annie's look. Nick was in their life; they were no longer alone and, stroking Annie's hair, she knew that she was glad of it.

DC WALSH STOOD by her car and looked just to the right of DI Heddon's shoulder. He was talking, but as usual, she wasn't really listening.

"I know that I'm not your commanding officer, DC Walsh, and therefore being disciplined will not be up to me, but I do have to tell you that what you did was foolish in the extreme and as a result we have a dead body, and..."

"And a live one..." Nella interrupted. "Sir."

Mark glanced behind him at the ambulance. To be honest, he didn't have the stomach for this; she was right and as irresponsible, stupid, lacking in correct procedure as it was, Annie was alive and she wouldn't have been without DC Walsh.

"Yes, of course, exactly." Mark coughed. "I'm not bemoaning your heroism and clear-thinking DC Walsh..."

"Good, thank you Sir."

"It's just that..."

"Yes Sir," Nella said. "I know."

Mark nodded and decided enough said. She wasn't his problem; let the Met deal with her. She'd saved Annie and bloody good on her. She moved away and went to follow up with the SOCO team.

MARK WATCHED Richard Ross and Nick. It didn't take a genius to see the likeness between Annie and her father or indeed her grandfather. He felt a momentary sadness, knowing that his role, albeit merely an official one, was over. He had no doubt, watching Nick and seeing the way he looked at Kate and Annie, that he wanted to be part of their lives. He hoped that Kate would let him be. He turned to go back to his officers, but as he did so, he saw Nick and Richard cross to the ambulance, and catching sight of the way that Kate smiled at Nick, he knew that she would.

NELLA MADE her way across to the small family gathering at back of the hospital wagon. She could see that there was a fragile intimacy there and that she was probably interrupting, but she edged into the circle nevertheless and looked at Annie.

"Are you guys OK?"

Kate nodded and Annie looked up. She smiled at Nella. "Thanks," she said, "Nick told me what you did, guided him and stuff."

Nella grinned. "With the right technology you can do most things." She dug her hands in the pockets of her waterproof trousers and shifted position uneasily. Nella wasn't good at talking, at choosing the right phrase, but she needed to say something; it was important. She took a deep breath. "You know Annie, what Kerrie said back there, to your Mum? She wasn't right; you know that don't you?"

Annie stared at Nella and wove her fingers tightly between Kate's. Nella glanced at Nick, then at Kate and Annie again.

"Sometimes, life is... well, it's not what you want it to be, things happen, outside your control."

She shrugged. "But Kerrie wasn't right. In fact, she was way off track." Nella paused and grappled for the right words.

"We are never completely helpless, Annie, that's what

makes us human," she said, "there is always, always something we can do."

And with that raw pearl of wisdom, she turned and
walked away.

ALSO BY MARIA BARRETT

Still Voices

The Dream Catcher

Dishonoured

STILL VOICES

Dive into a riveting tale of secrets, betrayal, and the unbreakable bond of love in Still Voices.

Charles Meredith, a young and dedicated history professor, immerses himself in the world of a Victorian crime of passion for his latest book. But little does he know that the passion he craves is missing from his own life.

Lotte Graham, a devoted wife and mother, has always put her children first. However, her world shatters when she uncovers the heart-wrenching truth of her husband's deceit. Meanwhile, Claire Thompson, a solitary student with a vivid imagination, seeks solace in her own fantasies.

A fateful night takes an unexpected turn when Claire vanishes after boasting about a dinner invitation from Professor Charles Meredith. As the police launch an intense search for the missing student, Charles desperately needs to prove his innocence.

In the midst of her own chaos, Lotte fights for her independence, determined to rise above the betrayal that shattered her world.

And amongst all this turmoil, an ethereal presence emerges — a silent voice from beyond the grave.

Sill Voices is a masterfully woven suspense thriller that will keep you on the edge of your seat. Join Charles, Lotte, and Claire on their harrowing journey, where past and present collide, and ghostly secrets, long buried, come to light.

'A skilful and foreboding tale.'

Daily Mirror.

THE DREAMCATCHER

A tale of Friendship, Dreams, and Dangerous Ambitions

Step into the world of high-stakes suspense and thrilling intrigue with The Dreamcatcher, where three close friends set up an investment club and find themselves entangled in a web of dreams, secrets, and danger.

Sarah, Roz, and Janie are ordinary women with everyday challenges, but beneath the surface, they share a burning desire for something more. Sarah faces the struggle of raising her partially deaf son alone, Roz has the daunting task of keeping her farm afloat, while Janie grapples with an unexplainable emptiness in her life.

Everything changes when Janie's brother, Marcus, intro- duces them to Alex, a savvy stockbroker with an enticing idea. Together, they establish an investment group, pooling their resources and diving into the unpredictable world of the stock market. As their luck, instincts, and research lead to substantial profits, their dreams appear within reach.

But as the stakes grow higher, so do the risks. When a seemingly foolproof opportunity arises, the club hesitates before taking the leap. Unbeknownst to them, hidden agendas and dark secrets lurk, threatening to turn their dreams into nightmares. Insider trading becomes a dangerous game, and the women find themselves entangled in a criminal world they never imagined.

The Dreamcatcher is a roller-coaster of suspense that will keep you riveted to the final, thrilling twist. Join Sarah, Roz, and Janie as they navigate a treacherous path where ambition and greed collide.

DISHONOURED

Embark on a gripping journey through time and continents.

In Imperial India, an English colonel's life is forever shattered when a bloodthirsty mob takes his beloved wife from him. Consumed by grief and rage, he seeks a terrible vengeance against those he deems responsible.

Enter Jagat Rai, whose father falls victim to the colonel's revenge. Fuelled by an unyielding desire for justice, he swears an oath that echoes through generations, vowing to make the colonel's kin pay for the sins of their ancestor.

Fast forward to the vibrant streets of 1960s London, where Major Phillips Mills, the great-great grandson of the colonel, dismisses the oath as a mere family anecdote. However, fate has other plans as he and his new bride find themselves drawn back to India, where the ghosts of the past stir once more.

The embers of revenge blaze anew in the heart of Shiva Rai, the latest bearer of his family's unfulfilled oath. Amid the alluring allure of jasmine-scented nights, Shiva's unwavering determination for retribution is challenged by a force more potent than hatred—a forbidden love that defies the boundaries of history.

In a tale that spans over a hundred years, forbidden desires intertwine with a thirst for vengeance, and destinies entangle in an intricate dance of fate.

Dishonoured is a thriller, an historical saga of love, betrayal, and the enduring power of an ancient oath. Delve into a world where the past and present collide, and the price of love and vengeance is paid in ways no one could anticipate.

Printed in Great Britain
by Amazon

46304359R00205